RHAPSODY

NIGHTMUSIC TRILOGY, BOOK 3

HEATHER MCKENZIE

THE NIGHTMUSIC TRILOGY

Book 1: SERENADE

Book 2: NOCTURNE

Book 3: RHAPSODY

Title: Rhapsody / Heather McKenzie
Copyright ©2019 Heather McKenzie
All rights reserved.
Third Edition 2023

ISBN: 978-1-7381530-4-6 (Print)
ISBN: 978-1-7381530-5-3 (Ebook)

House of Hebyzie Publishing, Canada
www.houseofhebyzie.com

Young Adult Fiction / Romance / Contemporary
Young Adult Fiction / Mystery & Detective Stories
Young Adult Fiction / Thrillers & Suspense

Summary: Kaya has minutes to save the man she loves... Luke's life is hanging by a thread, and Kaya must do the unthinkable—go back to her father. It's a worthy way to die, giving your life for the one you love. But not everyone feels that way—Thomas in particular. He'll do whatever it takes to keep her with him, even if it means stealing her precious time. But there's more at stake than just Kaya's life…

Cover Design by: Marya Heiman & House of Hebyzie
Typography by: House of Hebyzie
Editing by: Emily Bueckert and Kelly Risser
Interior: Damian Jackson

Cover Art Credits
© orhideia / Fotolia / © Extezy / Fotolia
© Betelgejze / Fotolia / © yod77 / Fotolia/© MarQue
Visual/© Q from Laxy/©Vector Tatu/© Nawasanga/© Elena
Nasarova/© Leonid

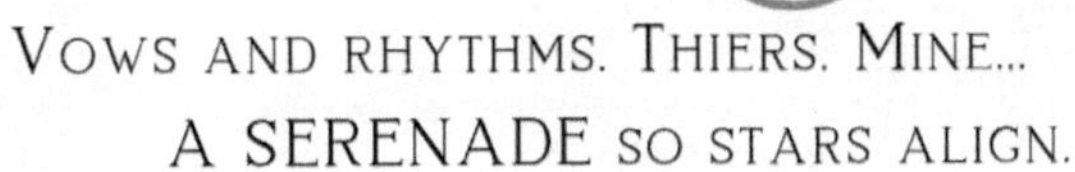

Vows and rhythms. Thiers. Mine...
A SERENADE so stars align.

Promises. melodies. Drifting. Dark...
A NOCTURNE born of breaking hearts.

Prose and passion. Truth. Lies...
A RHAPSODY when love defies.

Words and music. Beginning. End...
The NIGHTMUSIC of foe and friend.

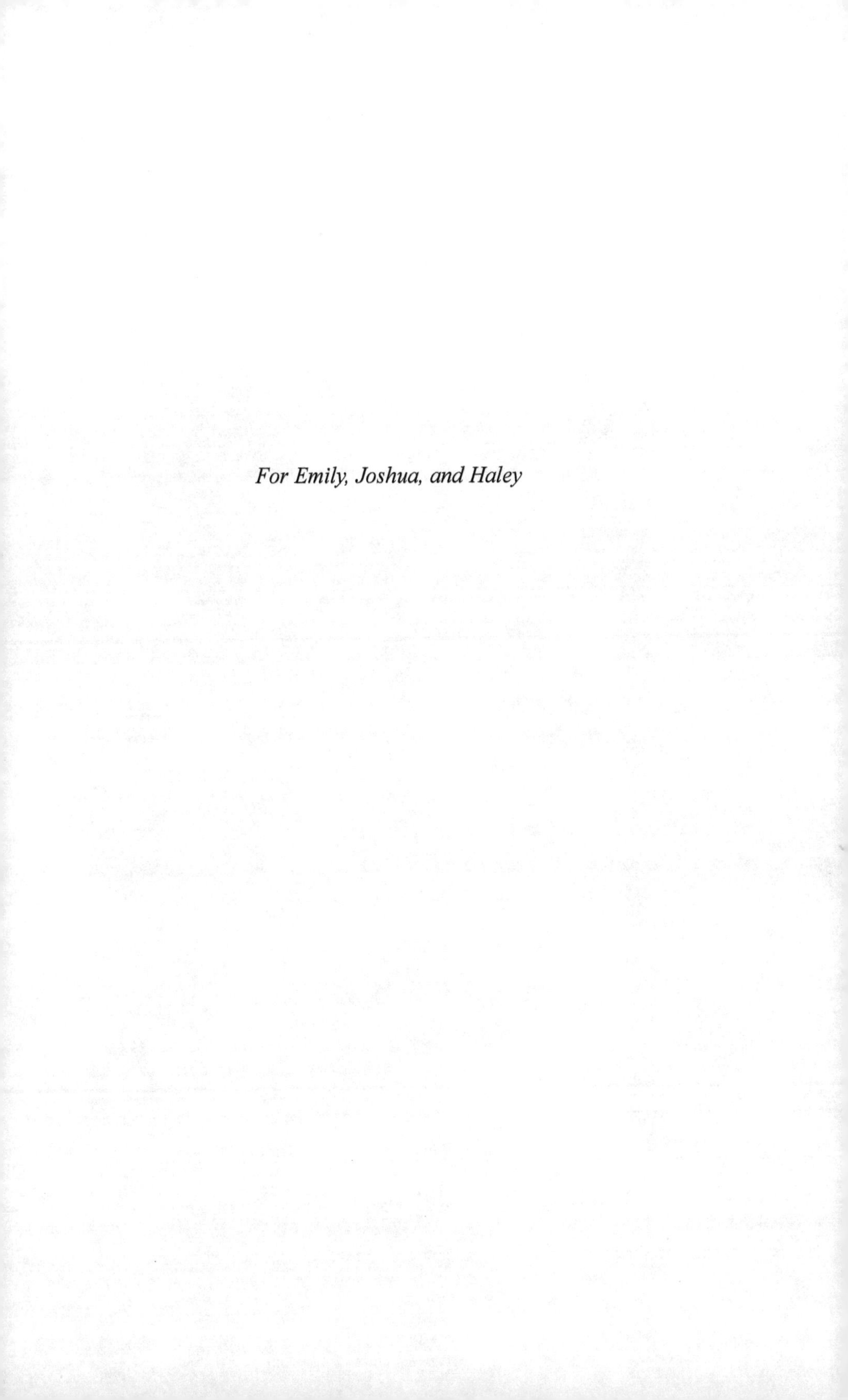

For Emily, Joshua, and Haley

RHAPSODY

He was screaming in terror.

The flames licking at his leather shoes were about to turn his body into a candle in the night.

I should have felt something, I guess. At one point he'd been family. He'd raised me… maybe even loved me once…

But as I watched him burn, begging for my forgiveness, I felt nothing.

You should save him, Kaya.

Why?

There was nothing about Henry Lowen worth saving. He intended to murder me, his own daughter. He shot Thomas in cold blood. Manipulated Oliver. Took Luke from me.

No. I would not save him. Or forgive him.

The only thing I would do for my father is get a little closer and fan the flames.

STEPHAN

1

SAY SOMETHING DON'T SAY ANYTHING

Her laugh was wicked. Bone-chilling. It crawled through the dark and squirmed into my ears. But at least it wasn't my skin that the girl was honing her skills on this time. A man held in a cell not far from mine was being asked the same questions I'd been asked, and was now bearing the brunt of the girl's whip. He moaned but, amazingly, he never cried out.

I was fed and cleaned up, unchained, and given a bed primped with fresh linens. I even put in dinner orders; macaroni with asparagus and creamed spinach on bagels, hoping that William in the kitchen would notice the unusual requests. If I could somehow signal to him that I was still alive, maybe he could find a way to get me out of here.

Get *us* out of here.

Davis was still alive, too. After he told the girl everything he knew about Luke, he was put in the cell with the others. I couldn't count the days he'd been in there, but it had been long enough to break him. When they put him back in the cell with me, I tried to get him to speak. I *begged* him to speak. But he just retreated into the shadows, lips not parting except to eat. He remained quiet even when I overheard one of the guards whisper, *"We're working on a plan... hang tight."* Even that shred of hope didn't prompt him to talk; he'd given up.

My stomach lurched as the girl continued questioning her victim. She was injecting him with that liquid fire, the stuff that made your mouth betray you and offer up your most coveted secrets. There was no fighting

"

it. The truth would be spilled no matter how strong you were. Add a little pain into the mix and getting information was as easy as making a baby cry.

The whip cracked relentlessly. Sharp, dizzying, leather meeting flesh… until a new sound shook the brick walls; Sindra.

She was raging mad. Barking orders and giving commands. Mean as a lion with a toothache and as devastating as a hurricane. I breathed a heavy sigh of relief at the sound of her voice. She'd obviously come to rescue us. Even though we'd had our differences, I knew she wouldn't let me rot down here.

I swung my infected legs off the edge of the bed and wobbled upright. The burns on the soles of my feet had started to heal, but walking was still painful. I got closer to the commotion in the stairwell, the huff of exertion and the thud of bodies bouncing against walls, and I smiled; Sindra was really pissed off.

"Let go of me!" she yelled. "Remove these cuffs at once, that's an order!"

There was panic in her tone. She was not in control.

The stairwell door swung open and crashed into the wall behind it. I called out to Sindra, gripping the bars to keep from falling, Davis stood next to me as six Lowen security guards struggled to get Sindra into the hall. She fought like a wild cat even with her arms tied behind her back and her ankles in chains. She writhed and twisted as they fought to contain her. That dark hair of hers, usually polished and braided, was wild and flowing. She was in her pajamas—a sheer black negligee that was inappropriate even for bed—and although I was shocked to see her 'undone,' what was more unsettling was the obvious terror in her eyes.

"I'm not a traitor. Let me go right now!" she yelled. "I'll have your heads. Each one. *Let me go at once.*"

The guards ignored her threats. Davis and I watched in horror as she was dragged toward the room where the girl with the purple hair liked to do her 'work'.

Davis crumpled and finally spoke. "No…"

The security men left. Quiet filled the space until that laugh rang out again, rattling along the walls and crawling back toward us. Davis went back to his bed and got under his blanket. I stood where I was, unable to move. What was going on? Sindra ruled this place. She was Henry's right hand. What could she have done to land her down here with us?

The girl's voice soared through the dungeon.

"Well, well. Sindra. Isn't this interesting," she said, accent thick. "Who would have thought I'd have the enjoyment of playing twenty questions with you?"

There were muffled sounds, and since Sindra wasn't yelling anymore I assumed she'd been gagged. The clang of metal against metal indicated she was being chained to the ceiling. I could picture it perfectly as it played out—*been there, done that.*

"So, Miss Mighty Sindra," the girl said with sick enthusiasm. "Let me introduce you to this gorgeous hunk-of-a-man over here. His name is Luke Ravelle. Oh wait. Apparently, you two have met before. At a motel where you knew Oliver was staying. Right? Remember Oliver? You were supposed to bring him back. You knew where he was, and instead of doing your job, you warned him so he could get away. That's suicide, Sindra. Henry doesn't like it when people don't do their jobs." There was a pause. A rattle. A whimper. "Now, Luke here is a traitor, too, so you should get along fine. Exciting, isn't it? I get to have my way with both of you, and I know you're looking forward to seeing just how much I've learned. Not that it's cool to brag, but my skills are—shall we say—at expert level now. Then again, I did learn from the master."

Any shred of hope I had of being rescued by Sindra did a one-eighty and headed for the exit. Not only was my chance at freedom about to be tortured, but in the room next to her was exactly what Henry needed to lure my baby girl right into his lair—Luke.

KAYA

FAIRIES WEAR BOOTS

I stalled, not wanting to make the call, and instead stared out the truck window at the trees whizzing by. I let my mind drift and found myself pondering the question; if I had three wishes, what would they be?

I guess if the wishing rules were lax, first I would wish for countless more wishes, although there would probably be some sort of restriction on that. So, if faced with only three, my first would be to have Luke, here by my side, healthy and well and still loving me even though I'd made such horrible mistakes. I would explain the note I left him. Beg for his forgiveness for leaving and for saying such horrible things that I didn't mean in a backfiring effort to protect him. Yes, my first wish would be *him*. And my second? I'd wish for a normal family; a father that didn't want to use my reproductive organs for financial gain and a mother that wasn't a psychokiller now dead and buried in an unmarked grave, and a grandfather I didn't have to hide from. This second wish would give the genie a run for his money because my dream of holidays spent playing card games at family reunions with endless amounts of love and forgiveness, was certainly the most farfetched wish of all.

But my third? Impossible. This wish would be to undo what could not be undone. I killed a man at the Carlson's ranch. It was in self-defense, but I had blood on my hands now, just like my father. And if the genie granted me a fourth wish, I would ask to never be anything like Henry Lowen.

With Oliver at the wheel and Thomas moping in the backseat, the town of Banff neared. The feeling of being home should have lifted my spirits. It's surrounding mountains, snow-covered and crystal white, reached gloriously into the sky. The winding highway, lined with flat towering rock on one side and thick trees and turquoise streams on the other, hugged such stunning cliffs—all so breathtakingly beautiful. But that wasn't why I couldn't get any air; it was time. No more stalling.

The phone in my hand shook.

Oliver turned off the radio and did up the windows. Thomas fidgeted. I held my breath as my finger hovered over the keypad.

"You're sure about this?" Oliver asked, worry pulling his mouth into a thin line.

I was sure that I had to get Luke away from Henry or he'd end up dead. "Yes," I said, hoping I sounded braver than I felt. Going back to the estate and being locked up again certainly wasn't on my to-do list. But if that's what it took to save Luke…

Thomas was on the edge of his seat. "What are we going to tell Seth?" he asked, rubbing his forehead.

Oliver patted my leg then returned his hand to the steering wheel. "We aren't going to tell him anything."

Seth and Lisa were ahead of us, leading the way to our rendezvous point in Banff. They were under the impression that once we were all gathered there, we would mastermind some way of breaking into the estate and rescuing Luke together. This plan was a compromise between all of us. If Seth had his way, I'd have been shipped off to some remote place and hidden in a metal box covered in *fragile* stickers. Convincing him that I was coming along and that I would be part of the rescue party had almost resulted in blows. If he knew that I had made my own plan, one that excluded him and involved exchanging me for Luke, he would have gone ballistic.

Just like Thomas had.

The cell phone was becoming hot as blazes in my hand. The number just sitting there, waiting for me to hit send and dial up the most heinous human being this side of the equator.

"Wait," Thomas said, grasping my shoulder and leaning forward.

He smelled of mint gum and cheap soap. I twisted around to face him.

"Tell me again why you are calling Henry?" he said. "Remind me why you think he'll exchange Luke for you, and not harm you afterward?"

Thomas was rattled. The worry in his eyes made his brown irises almost black. I pretended his concern didn't bother me and that I was completely in control, willing my hand to stop shaking so it wouldn't give me away. "Henry needs me. That means keeping me alive."

"No. He needs an *heir*. So, once he realizes that you *aren't* pregnant—cause after a few months or so that will be pretty obvious—what then?"

"By then, Luke will be safe and all I have to do is wait it out until I turn twenty-one." It wasn't quite as simple as that, but I'd spare Thomas the sordid details. "Then I'll be free."

"Or just plain old dead."

I laughed, trying to ease his mind even though we shared the same thought.

"Jeezus, Kaya. You don't turn twenty-one for two and a half years." Panic wavered Thomas's voice. "That gives Henry lots of time to figure out how to get an heir from you. Doesn't he have a fertility lab? Isn't that sort of thing his specialty?"

"Technically he needs an heir from me and *Oliver*. And he won't have Oliver."

Oliver gulped so loud I found myself eyeing his throat.

"Besides, I'm not weak anymore," I added. "I can handle myself."

Thomas tugged anxiously at the neck of his shirt. "Ah heck, no one thinks you're weak. You're the toughest chick I know. I mean, look at what you've survived. It's incredible. But once Henry has you, you'll be at his mercy. And it terrifies me to think of what he'll do."

I reached to cover his hand with mine.

"I'm sorry, this is just a really bad idea," he said.

Oliver nodded. "Thomas is right."

There was nowhere to go but straight ahead, and no other choice but the one I'd made. "You both know I have to do this." I took in a deep breath, steadying my fluttering chest. "Henry was taking a risk that I would even see that cold medicine commercial he staged and seemingly promoted. It was meant as a message to me and that means Luke's life is literally hanging by a thread. Henry doesn't make idle threats. If I don't go back, *Luke will die*." That thought stopped the flutter and replaced it with steadfast determination. "Besides, I know it won't take too long for you and Oliver to find a way to get me out."

"And if we can't?"

"Then the both of you can move on. Forget about me and live your lives."

Oliver shuddered, and the truck swerved. Thomas made a low grumbling sound. The tension between us increased significantly.

"You two need to relax," I said, hoping I sounded calm and collected. "I'll be fine. Really."

No response.

"Anyway, I'm doing this, and you both promised you were with me. There's no going back now."

Thomas and Oliver exchanged a glance in the rear-view mirror that was alarming, but they made no objections. Breathing a sigh of relief, I put the phone on speaker for all to hear. Then I pushed the dial button.

It rang once.

Twice.

Then a voice so cold my body lurched with bone-jarring shivers cut through the silence.

"Apparently you watched my latest commercial," Henry said, too superior for niceties. "I wrote it and directed it myself. What do you think?"

"I think you're sick."

"Oh, my darling daughter, you say the darndest things. Are you on your way back home?"

Home. Hilarious. My hand had stopped shaking. My heart rate was even. "I'm not sure yet. I could be… if you make me a deal."

Henry chuckled. "A deal? I have what you want. So, in exchange for Luke, unharmed and released from his current situation, you will come home. And you will bring Mr. Oliver Bennet—my loyal, adopted *son*—with you."

I didn't skip a beat. "I don't have any idea where Oliver is."

"Oh, don't try to pull one on me. He's right beside you, as *always*."

I glanced at Oliver, whose teeth were clenched and eyes glued to the road. No way would I give him up. Offering myself was one thing… but Oliver? Never.

"I truly don't know," I lied, keeping my cool because Henry could smell fear from miles away.

The arrogant prick laughed. "Well then stop moving," he said smugly. "Wherever you are he won't be far behind."

"No, really. He left me, for good. We had a fight and he's out of the picture. Permanently."

"Is that so?"

"Yes. So, I will only come back if you make me a deal."

There was a pause. "Nah," Henry said after a while, adding a dramatic sigh. "You know, I have the feeling you aren't taking this seriously enough, Kaya. You might need some incentive."

I held my breath when I heard the unmistakable sound of a man moaning in pain—of Luke moaning in pain. *"Tell your darling Kaya to come home, will ya, Luke?"* Henry ordered, and a sharp crack was followed by another moan. *"Say it!"*

"Luke!"

Tears sprang from my eyes as his voice, breaking with pain, tried to soothe me.

"I'm fine. Run, Kaya." Voice like butter… vivid blue eyes… "Get as far away from your monstrous father as you can."

The world around me disappeared in a dizzy haze. I fought to breath. The cracking noise came again and Henry spoke in a tone that buzzed around my head like a swarm of hornets.

"Enough time wasting," he said. "Be at the gates in twenty minutes or Luke dies. After that, I'll kill someone else every hour you are late, starting with Stephan."

Stephan.

"I'll be there," I said.

Henry's voice oozed with triumph. "Ah, that's a good girl."

"Don't hurt him," I begged, no longer calm, or in control.

"Just don't keep me waiting. I'll take one finger for every minute you're late. Oh, and Kaya… I can't wait to see you."

Click.

I stared at the phone, clinging to the silence like it might bring Luke back. "And I—can't wait to kill you."

3

CRY ME A RIVER

The truck came to a screeching halt on the side of the highway. Oliver got out and marched around the vehicle to the passenger side. My door was yanked open, I was pulled out by my sleeve, and now I stood face to face with my ex-fiancé/ex-bodyguard, confused by the turmoil in his eyes.

He yelled over the roar of the rushing river as a semi-truck whizzed by. "I can't do this." He was vibrating. "I can't hand you over to your father. I'm sorry, I know I said I would help you get Luke back and I will. But not this way!"

I had fifteen minutes to get to the gates or Luke would be dead. *Fifteen.*

"Listen, calm down Oliver. I'll go on my own. You don't have to have anything to do with Henry. I'll be perfectly fine. You just take me there and walk away. Like we planned."

"*No.*" He was pacing. "I'm not *ever* walking away again."

Thomas was out of the truck too, standing between us, eyes shifting from the empty road, to me, then back to Oliver. A feeling of dread came over me as the sky let loose thick flakes of snow.

"What exactly are you saying, Oliver?" I asked, the wind biting at my cheeks.

He rubbed his hand over his hair, shirt straining around his biceps. "I'm saying that I am *not* taking you back to the estate. Back to your father."

13

"But I have to go. You know this."

Oliver had that look on his face that meant all the arguing in the world wouldn't sway him. "No."

Panic twisted my stomach into knots. "Back me up, Thomas," I said, turning to face him, wondering why he hadn't moved or said a word. "You know this is what I have to do. Get in the truck and drive me, please. *We have to hurry.*"

Thomas just stared at his feet.

"Thomas?"

His gaze lifted to meet Oliver's in a wordless exchange, and I backed away, sensing mutiny.

"You promised you'd help me," I said, barely able to get the words out.

Thomas shook his head. "I know. And I'm sorry."

My breath caught. "Sorry?"

Thomas checked his watch. "Oliver, you go. See if you can get Luke out on your own or at least buy him some time. If you're not back at our rendezvous point in twenty-four hours, I'll hide Kaya."

This wasn't happening. "No, Thomas, you can't be serious."

Ignoring me, Thomas spoke directly to Oliver. "Trust me. I'll protect her with my life. You have my word."

Feeling my world breaking into a million pieces and drifting through my hands, I clutched my chest as I glared at Thomas. "Your word? You gave me your word, too, you know. Both of you promised you would take me to Henry. If I don't go, *Luke will die!*"

A car rushing by kicked up a whoosh of air that had us shielding our eyes, and when I took my hand away, I was staring into the truck at the keys still in the ignition. Inching around the hood toward the driver's door, adrenaline flooded my veins as I dove into the truck, only to have Oliver follow and shove me over to the passenger side. I snatched the keys, got out, and did the only thing I could think of; I ran. I knew they would follow me, but eventually I could circle back and get to the truck before they caught up. I was fast. I could do it… I could do it—

I didn't get far. Slammed to the ground with bone-jarring force, my body collided with the asphalt and my arm was pulled back behind me. When I realized it was Thomas pinning me down, my pain was forgotten and replaced with fury.

"*Get off me,*" I yelled, writhing beneath him, face connecting with the road.

"I'm sorry," he said. His belt was off, and he was using it to secure my hands behind my back.

"I'll kill you! Let me go or I swear *I will kill you.*"

Thomas didn't falter. He pulled me upright, tossed Oliver the keys, and began dragging me toward the ditch. When Oliver sped past us in the truck, terror escalated as my chances of saving Luke began dwindling by the second.

I fought with everything I had.

"Stop. I'm trying to protect you. This is for your own good," Thomas begged, frantically heading down into the ditch and onto the river bank.

"I should have shot you when I had the chance!"

It was a horrible thing to say. Tears rolled down his cheeks as I fought him. He was heading for a stand of trees—the best place to hide a screaming girl from oncoming traffic—and there was no way I was going willingly. He picked me up and slung me over his shoulder.

Time was ticking…

Thomas didn't falter. He was a man on a mission, marching over the slick, snow covered rocks, stumbling but not stopping. Then it hit me; his wound. The neat and tidy little hole from a bullet that magically missed all his vital organs was almost in proximity to my knee. And since it was still healing and very tender…

I calmed myself down, willing my body to be still.

Then I struck.

As he doubled over, I took advantage of the motion to fling myself backward and off his shoulder. For a moment I had the upper hand, finally free as I fell… only to keep falling into darkness when my head hit the ground.

LISA

4

HELL HATH NO FURY

I thought I would never see that look on Seth's face again, but there it was, pulling his features into an ugliness that matched the evil lurking in his heart. I was an idiot to assume that I'd cleansed his soul, or changed him into a better man, because all at once, in the blink of an eye, it became painfully obvious that I hadn't.

Thomas came in the door carrying Kaya, unconscious in his arms, and Seth's eyes never left her face. His expression was dark, unsettling, cutting through the stale air in the dismal house like laser beams through fog. The way he clenched his jaw, wrung his hands, and cracked his neck set me completely on edge.

Thomas was too wrapped up in his own torment to notice anything amiss. Covered in scratches, his stitches torn, a bite mark on his arm and what was sure to be a black eye forming rapidly, he carried Kaya into the dilapidated house and gently placed her on a ratty sofa.

"She's going to hate me forever. I didn't know what else to do," Thomas moaned.

The paper-thin walls of our rendezvous point shook almost as much as the cowboy's angst-ridden voice. He was beside himself, wincing with discomfort as he dropped down onto a wobbly kitchen chair. Attractive, with dark, soulful eyes, pouty lips, jaw line sharp as a knife and a body lean and tight from hard work, he was so easy to get lost staring at that I almost didn't notice Seth drugging Kaya.

Almost.

And I really hoped I was just seeing things.

The glass of water he'd put to her lips when she started to come around looked innocent enough, but Seth had added a clear drop of liquid taken from a vial in his coat pocket, and I'd been in enough seedy bars to know what that was about.

I felt sick.

"Is she going to hate me?" Thomas asked.

Seth was pacing back and forth alongside the couch, eyes not leaving Kaya even for a second. I pushed my questions into the corner of my mind and reached across the kitchen table to pat Thomas's arm.

"She'll get over it," I lied. "Right Seth?"

There was a detached tone to Seth's voice when he replied. "Of course," he paused to press his fingertips to Kaya's distressingly pale neck. "She'll forgive you when she realizes you were just doing what you thought was best for her."

Is that what Seth thought he was doing? What was best for her? Maybe I was misinterpreting what I was seeing and the vial was full of vitamin D.

Doubtful.

Thomas slammed his fists down on the table, and I nearly jumped out of my skin. "We need to take her to a doctor." When he stood abruptly, the chair behind him wobbled. "I mean, she hit her head, but not *that* hard. How long has she been unconscious, a couple of hours? She was starting to come around and now she's out cold again. We need help."

I watched Seth's reaction, waiting for him to admit to drugging Kaya, *hoping* he would clue us in to what was on his mind—but he said nothing.

And this set off every warning bell in my head.

"I'm taking her to a hospital." Thomas snatched the truck keys off the table.

Seth's whole body jerked into action. He put his hands up. "A hospital is out of the question, Thomas. You know that. She'll suffer far worse than a concussion if Henry gets a hold of her, and he has this entire town under watch. Besides, all her vitals are fine. She's going to be all right."

Thomas gave this some thought, then folded onto the kitchen chair and held his head in his hands.

"She's a tough girl," I reminded him. "When she's awake, we can get her to her father like she wanted and get Luke back. That's the plan still, right, Seth?"

Seth's eyes met mine briefly and what I saw in them made my skin prickle.

"Sure," he said.

I felt my entire world fall away. Right there and then. The life I'd dreamed of with Seth—of kids and dogs and Christmases in the mountains—all gone. It seemed the instant he got the call from Thomas saying Kaya was unconscious on the side of the highway and the plan had changed, *he* had changed. We shared everything—a home, our desires, a bed—but apparently, he hadn't shared his intentions concerning Kaya.

I was in love with a total stranger.

Thomas could not sit still. He marched over to the couch. "She's so pale… Oh, God…"

He lifted Kaya's hand, and her lack of response completely rattled him. Breath catching in his throat, he marched off into the kitchen so we wouldn't see the tears in his eyes. I held my tongue, assessing the situation as Seth barricaded the front door—whether from intrusion or escape, I couldn't tell.

"Think that will stop Henry from breaking in?" I asked, motioning with a shaky hand to the chair he'd wedged under the doorknob.

"Uh, no. But you never know who else might know the code to this dump."

Oliver had suggested this house as our rendezvous point. Apparently, bands from the local nightclub were put up here on weekends and it was empty during the week. It was right in the heart of Banff. Within walking distance to the Bow Springs Estate…where Luke was being held…

"Let's get some rest. At ten o'clock tonight we'll git goin' whether she's awake or not," Seth said, checking Kaya's pulse again.

"Where are we going?"

Seth cleared his throat. "Not sure." He was lying.

"Why at ten?" I asked, my girl senses going into overdrive, warning bells screeching.

"There will be less traffic."

"What about Luke?"

"We'll figure something out," Seth said brusquely, and then to my horror, began tying Kaya's hands together.

"And…why the ropes?" I asked, heart pounding.

"In case she fights us."

Thomas bolted into the room, eyes widening at the knots Seth was securing. "What the heck are you doing?"

Seth didn't glance up. He was completely focused on his task. "She's not thinking straight. We gotta keep her safe and get her out of here. If she wakes up screaming, I'd hate to have to—" Seth stumbled over his words. "Uh, try and calm her down if she's unreasonable. It's just a safety precaution."

"It's not right." Thomas shook his head. "Untie her Seth. When she wakes up, we'll ask her what *she* wants to do."

Seth laughed. "First of all, did you not use your own belt to restrain her back there on that highway? You figure it's okay if *you* do it, but not me? I mean, c'mon, Thomas. You know what she wants to do—give herself to save Luke. Which is pure idiocy. Letting her do what she wants will be her death sentence. I thought you and I were finally on the same page about this."

Thomas struggled to agree with this logic. "Seth," he said calmly. "I've changed my mind. You have to untie her. I'm not going against her wishes ever again."

"Oh really? Even if that means she ends up dead? Because that is most certainly what will happen if we let her have her way."

Thomas shifted uneasily, conflicted. "I just want what's best for her," he said softly.

"We all want that." Seth agreed.

I bit my lip because I couldn't bite my tongue. "And what if I don't agree?"

Seth's eyes levelled on mine. There was no warmth in them. Nothing familiar. "I'm sure I can make you see it my way."

Kaya started to moan. Seth jumped to his feet and Thomas dove to her side.

"Where am I?" she asked, eyes fluttering open.

"We're in Banff, Kaya," Thomas said sweetly, kneeling next to her and affectionately caressing her cheek.

Kaya scanned the room, then realized her hands were tied. "Why am I —" she paused, then jolted upright. "Luke! Oh my God. How could you, Thomas? *I have to go to him*."

Thomas was muttering apologies as Kaya struggled against the ropes. "Please, Kaya, calm down," he begged. "This is for your own good."

Kaya fought harder, squirming away from him, pulling at her restraints.

"Settle down now and just stay where you are, girlie," Seth ordered. He had a glass of water in his hands and stepped in beside Thomas. "Drink this. You hit your head pretty hard and—"

"Shut up!" she screamed, throwing her forehead at the glass and sending it to the floor. "Shut the hell up, *both of you.* Untie me now. I have to go to Luke… don't you understand? I'm running out of time. I have to go *now!"*

Seth grasped her shoulders. "You're not going anywhere." His tone was menacing. "Besides, you're over four hours late. There will be nothing left of him now."

I went numb and Kaya went into a complete rage. I watched two grown men wrestle her to the couch, Thomas with tears in his eyes pleading with her to calm down and Seth manhandling her with a detachment that gave me shivers.

"I hate you! I hate you so much!" she screamed at Thomas.

At those cutting words, Thomas backed away like he'd been shoved by a bulldozer. Kaya continued to scream. Seth—not wanting to alert the neighbors—slammed her down and pressed a knee to her chest. When he flattened his hand over her mouth, I'd had enough.

"Stop it, Seth."

Kaya's arms were flailing. I was worried he was cutting off her air.

"Let her go." I began to reach for the gun at my ankle, about to point it at his head because I didn't know what else to do to stop him.

But Thomas finally snapped back to his senses. He grabbed Seth by the collar and violently yanked him off of Kaya. The coffee table broke under Seth's weight and an ancient television fell to the floor. "Don't you touch her. *Don't even look at her,"* Thomas warned. "Or I swear to God I'll rip your fucking arms off."

Sweating and shaking, he stood between Kaya, who was gasping for air, and Seth, who was menacingly rising to his feet. As the two men stared each other down, I dove to Kaya and pulled her into my arms. I whispered that I was on her side as I frantically worked at the knots around her wrists.

"Don't you dare untie her, Lisa," Seth warned.

I ignored him, until a familiar click stopped me cold; it was the click that meant whatever we had between us was most certainly *over*.

Seth inhaled deeply then spat at the floor. "Thomas, put your hands up and move aside, or I'll blow Lisa's pretty little blonde head to bits."

Seth had perfect aim. I looked up to see the barrel of the gun in line with my forehead.

Thomas put his hands up.

"Good boy. Now, go sit in that chair."

Thomas obeyed, the shock on his face turning to rage.

My blood turned to ice in my veins. "Seth, what are you doing?"

Seth tossed me the power cord from his cell phone, his face unreadable. "Tie Thomas's hands to the back of the chair."

"What? No! Stop acting ridiculous, Seth. We're in this together, remember? You're not thinking clearly."

"Do it!" he roared, lowering the gun so it was aimed at my heart. "Do it Lisa. Tie Thomas up or I'll shoot you and then do it myself."

As if in a dream, I did as I was told.

"Now get on the floor behind him," Seth said.

I didn't move. Fuck him.

He cocked the trigger and pushed the barrel of the gun against my temple. Those hands that had made love to me, were now about to take my life.

"Just listen to him, Lisa," Kaya said. "Please."

My hands were secured to Thomas' and I remained frozen in stunned silence as the weight of reality began multiplying. When Seth was satisfied Thomas and I were secure, he focused on Kaya again, who all the while had remained perfectly still. It was obvious that she didn't want to put our lives in jeopardy even after what Thomas did to her. Even though I agreed that she should trade her life for Luke's.

"Why are you doing this?" she said to Seth as he checked the knots around her wrists.

"I can't let you leave again," Seth replied, voice monotone. "I'll never get you back if I do."

Kaya studied him a moment, then spoke softly. "But why do you even care?"

"Care?" Seth said, pulling back with exasperation. "You think that I just... *care*? It's more than that. Dammit, I risked everything for you. I don't *care*, Rayna, I... *love* you. Always have and always will."

Dead silence. Astonished silence. *Disturbing* silence.

"Rayna?" Kaya said carefully. "Uh, Seth, I'm Kaya. *Not* Rayna."

Confusion swirled in Seth's eyes and he shook his head irritably. "Yes. I know who you are, *Kaya Lowen*. I'm not an idiot!"

He was flustered. Embarrassed. He didn't notice me give Kaya a subtle nod in the direction of my ankle.

"Tell me," Seth said, clearing his throat loudly then checking his watch. "How is your head, *Kaya Lowen*?"

She didn't answer, but her eyes met mine briefly enough to convey that she understood where my handgun was.

"Your head?" Seth asked her again.

Kaya tested her neck, tilting her chin side to side, and winced with a gasp. "It hurts."

The innocent, syrupy-sweet tone of her voice made Thomas's breath catch and Seth fold like a taco.

"Maybe you could get me a glass of water?" she said, brilliant green-eyes shining, long lashes fluttering. "You look like you could use some too, Seth. It's been a long day for both of us."

Completely disarmed, Seth's gruff exterior melted away and he strode into the kitchen. When the water tap came on, Kaya furiously gnawed at the ropes around her wrists with her teeth. When it went off, she straightened up and put on a sweet smile.

"Thanks," she said.

Seth kneeled before her, tipping the glass to her mouth, and I prayed that he wasn't drugging her again. I felt Thomas's fingers working at my restraints while Kaya licked water from her lips, slowly, mesmerizing Seth with her every move and knowing that's exactly what she was doing.

"So, what's next?" she asked, keeping him focused, distracted.

Seth gulped. "I'll know soon enough."

Kaya batted her eyes innocently. "What are you going to do with me?"

Forehead wrinkling in concentration, Seth rubbed his temple then pulled at his shirt collar as if the room had grown unbearably hot. He had his face a little too close to Kaya's when he answered. "Listen, you'll be fine." He pushed her hair back over her shoulder. Narrowed his eyes on Kaya's mouth—he was seeing her as Rayna again.

"Seth," I said, barely able to speak. "What are you doing?"

He flinched like he'd woken from a dream, then he stood and backed away.

"Have you lost your mind?" The words were like knives in my throat. "What about... *us*? We were a thing, remember that? Like, about four hours ago? What happened? What's going on?"

His tone was cold as ice. "I'm sorry I involved you in this, Lisa. I didn't think things would go this way. I wish I could trust you but your loyalty to Luke outweighs your common sense. And you, too, Thomas. Even though you try to do what's right, I have a feeling you will do whatever Kaya wants, and I have to protect her no matter what."

I felt pure panic. The scars on Seth's cheek from Kaya's fingernails seemed to darken as a reminder of exactly what he was capable of. "And why is that?" I asked. "I would like to know. Dear Lord, if anything, you owe me a reason why."

Seth stood, the gun hanging idly by his side as he resumed pacing. "She's worth a billion dollars, Lisa. Giving her up is like winning the lottery and then tearing up the check. *A billion dollars...*" His eyes drifted to Kaya, and he eyed her possessively. "Because of her, I can have everything I've always wanted."

I gulped so hard it hurt; money wasn't his only motive. "What have you always wanted?"

"You ask too many questions," Seth snarled.

Kaya spoke softly. "If you let me go, I'll give you all the money you want. You know I can do that, Seth."

He glanced at his watch. "No. If I let you go, you'll get yourself killed and I'll have nothing."

Thomas was working at the knots again. I could feel them loosening and the circulation coming back into my fingers. The timing would have to be exactly right for me to get the gun from my ankle before Seth could take aim. But then what? If I had to, could I shoot him?

Kaya wiggled to the edge of the couch. Her feet were on the floor, her hands in her lap, and she appeared unfazed by Seth's madness. "Lisa loves you," she said softly, lowering her voice and leaning forward as if she were just a friend concerned about his relationship. "You shouldn't just throw that away. You were good together."

"I do love her," he said.

That hefty word-punch to the head sent me into a free-fall of regret at having thoughts of shooting him.

"But she's not Rayna," he continued. "And I've come to realize that the only way I can fill the loss of losing the love of my life, is with her daughter. Alive or otherwise."

Regrets and guilt be damned.

At my back I could feel Thomas tense — he'd gotten my hands free. Time slowed when Kaya asked for another sip of water, then came to a terrifyingly clear halt when she picked up her feet and slammed them into Seth's knees. The glass fell from his hands as she launched herself at him, and my pant leg fought me as I retrieved the gun. Finger on the trigger, I hesitated long enough for Seth to shove Kaya off of him, and then I aimed.

But I couldn't do it. I couldn't shoot him.

Seth swung his gun in my direction, and I could see by the way his jaw was set in determination that I might not have a choice. A siren outside blocked out Kaya yelling as she pounded her fists at his back, momentarily throwing off his balance and a clear shot at me. But he recovered quickly, and there was no doubt when he refocused that he was intent on ending my life.

So, I ended his first.

LUKE

5

MAN IN THE BOX

I kept my eyes shut. I didn't want to look at the metal instruments laid out on the silver tray—mere feet from my chained ankles—or the whips that the girl liked to flick across my bare skin…or Sindra, quiet and limp, chained and hanging from the ceiling, probably dead.

At least I'd lost all feeling in my hands. The raw skin and bruised bones under the shackles around my wrists were only a dull ache now, and my consciousness was fleeting. I would fall in between being awake and being asleep, the strange drugs flowing through my veins confusing each state. "Be a good boy and I'll bring you something from your past to play with," the purple-haired girl had said. "I'll show you that I'm not all that bad."

Did I dream it? I wasn't sure.

Sometimes I heard other voices. One I didn't recognize—deep, husky, and definitely male—kept calling my name and telling me to stay strong. But it could have been the girl playing one of her tricks, so I ignored it.

The creak of rusty hinges as a door opened caused a shiver to roll up my spine and the welts on my back to burn madly. I tried to keep my legs straight so I wasn't hanging from my wrists, but the strength to stand just wasn't in me anymore. I was giving in to the pain that surged through my shoulders, my neck, and every part of me that the girl had toyed with. I was close to breaking, so I did the only thing that kept me sane—I thought of Kaya. Her beautiful smile. The way her face lit up and made me feel like I was ten feet off the ground. The way she'd bite at her lower lip when she was nervous. How her hair felt in my hands, her skin beneath my fingertips, the shine in her eyes when I said her name… *Kaya.* God, I loved her. I would give anything, *anything,* just to tell her that.

"Luke?"

Her voice…my every thought clung to it. I squeezed my eyes shut even tighter, not wanting to let go of whatever dream I was falling into, picturing her face so vividly in my mind.

"Luke, can you hear me?"

She was so stunningly beautiful that all I could do was stare. Her midnight hair flowed down past her shoulders and milky white skin glowed against the deep emerald color of her dress. It was the same dress she'd been wearing when we first met in the garden, the long slit in the side revealing a hint of a toned thigh. Bathed in a soft light that made her shimmer, the love of my life was reaching for me…

"What did they do to you?" she asked.

I wanted to answer, but I had no words. It was as if my mind was disconnected from my body. Her breath was hot on my skin as her hand brushed my cheek, like an angel hovering around me, the warmth of her, the sound of the air rushing in and out of her lungs, was pure bliss. I allowed myself the thought that maybe I wasn't dreaming. Maybe this was real, and she was truly saving me…

But no. That was impossible.

"I'm going to get you out of here. Don't worry," she said, and wrapped her arms around me.

For the first time in ages, I was warm. When I felt the shackles loosen from my ankles, I tried to thank her and tell her how much I loved her. Then my arms dropped to my sides and I was unable to do anything but fall to my knees, hands free and limp in my lap. She gripped my shoulders, holding me up.

"Kaya…" I said, finally finding my voice, but the sound of it in the room made the vision of her disappear.

"C'mon, wake up, Luke," said someone who *wasn't* Kaya, and who was lightly slapping my cheeks.

I knew I'd imagined her, but the shackles were gone from my wrists and ankles, I was on my knees, and there was someone next to me…

"For God's sake, Luke, wake up."

No. Couldn't be.

Forcing my eyelids apart, I was shocked to see dark irises, dark skin… A face I'd become all too familiar with. I blinked in shock as the circulation started to come back into my hands — and along with it, pain. Pain everywhere, head to toe. Gasping, I fought to breathe.

"Luke. It's me, Oliver. Can you see me now? C'mon man, say something."

"I… uh…" My throat was so dry I couldn't get a word out.

He had a glass in his hands and a panicked look on his face. "Drink," he ordered.

I gulped down water, then promptly threw it up. While Oliver patiently made me drink more, it was then that I noticed a body on the floor behind him; a Labcoat flat on his stomach and head twisted to the side. Oliver was sweating, beads of it rolling off his forehead and there was a cut on his cheekbone. He was breathing heavy, like he'd been running—or fighting.

All at once reality snapped into place.

"Oliver?" I said, making sure it was really him and I wasn't hallucinating again.

He smiled. "Ah. There you are." Relief momentarily washed over him. "Can you stand?"

He'd put a blanket around my shoulders. I clutched it tightly, pulling it across my chest and wincing at every fiber that rubbed at my raw skin. With Oliver's help, I got to my feet, but had a tough time staying upright.

"How did you find me?" I asked, wishing I could see straight. Wishing my muscles would wake up and fully co-operate. My heart rate was too fast. My vision too blurry.

"Let's just say I spent a while down here myself. Unfortunately."

The desperation to escape was overwhelming.

"Listen, Luke, I had a bit of help getting down here, but now I'm on my own. We've got about five minutes before every alarm in the building goes off, so we gotta act fast, all right? You have to do as I say."

I glanced at the silver tray with the scary tubes and injection needles, and then at Sindra's lifeless body just hanging there. I motioned toward her, but Oliver just shook his head and started dragging me across the room. I stumbled along beside him, my arm over his shoulder, leaning on him to stay upright. We stepped over another Labcoat face down on the ground, and I'd hoped to see a flash of purple hair or the cactus tattoo, but it wasn't the girl.

Once we were through the doorway, the stench of human odor hit like a wall. The door to the stairs seemed forever away as we passed by rows of metal bars…with people behind them.

"Wait," I said, pulling back. There are others down here."

Oliver stopped, and an alarm sounded from somewhere over our heads, increasing the panic in his eyes. "Ah crap," he muttered, letting go of me. At the bars, he peered into the dark. "Who's in there? How many of you are there? How can I get you out?"

No one replied. Or moved. Dark human-shapes remained unnervingly still.

"Hello?" Oliver said urgently.

The male voice that had been calling out to me, the one I thought was a trick, came from an opposite cell.

"Just leave them and go," he said.

Oliver spun around. "Stephan?"

The thin hands of an older man wrapped around the cell bars. A kind face with a thick brown beard and glistening eyes pushed forward. Sores grazed his cheeks and his fingertips were missing fingernails—probably handiwork of the girl.

Oliver gasped and lunged for the bars.

Stephan spoke in a quiet but rushed tone. "Relax, Oliver. I'm okay. Me and Davis are fine for now, I promise. Besides, you'll never get this door open without a key and any minute now security will know you're here. Please… just go."

Oliver desperately shook the bars. "Davis? You're in there too?"

Davis didn't move from his cot. He just stared blankly at the floor.

"The guards take the keys with them," Stephan said as Oliver began searching about frantically. "And anyway, Davis is fine. He's not injured. You must *go*…"

I knew who Stephan was from Kaya's glowing description of him. And Davis—I'd met him on the mountain. He was full of humor and wit. Lighthearted, loud, and boisterous… This place, these *people,* had broken him.

Eager to help Oliver, I tried to stand, but my legs failed me and I collapsed, only capable of trying to catch my breath.

"I can't leave you, Stephan," Oliver said, shaking the bars violently.

Level-headed and calm, Stephan reached out to clutch Oliver's shoulders. "If you don't get out, we are doomed down here, and so is Kaya. She will come back for him." He glanced in my direction.

Oliver had tears in his eyes when he finally turned away, devastated by having to leave his friends behind. When he hauled me to my feet, Davis's meek voice rose over the sound of the alarm.

"Don't leave me down here, Oliver. I'm sorry. I'm sorry I left you before at the ranch. It won't happen again… don't leave me…"

The desperation in Davis's voice brought Oliver to a standstill.

"There's no time," Stephan hissed. "*You have to go.*"

"The tray…" I said to Oliver. "Get them the tray."

He knew exactly what I meant. Running back to the room where I'd been whipped, tortured, and pumped full of God-knows-what, he proceeded to put everything resembling a weapon onto the silver tray next to the tubes and needles, then slipped it under the cell bars and into Stephan's waiting hands.

"I'll come back for you," he promised.

"I know," Stephan replied.

Davis was off his cot, rattling the bars between him and his freedom, no longer subdued. "Don't leave me down here, Oliver. *Don't leave me…*"

He kept calling out, but Oliver was dragging me relentlessly up the stairs and did not slow down even for a second. Not even when I came to my senses and told him we had to go back, at least for Sindra.

"She can rot in hell," he said.

6

DIRTY LAUNDRY

Winding through a maze of dark hallways, up a few flights of stairs, and then into one corner of an elaborate ballroom and out the other, the noise of screeching alarms eventually faded. Oliver kept us moving, sticking to the shadows, knowing which doors to hide behind and where the floor would squeak beneath his boots and my bare feet. My body was so weak all I could do was gasp for air and blink away the dark spots in my vision. When we came to a stop, I slumped against a wall and sunk to the floor while Oliver pried open a door that read 'staff only'. Dragging me through a locker room, down a steep flight of stairs and then entering some sort of cavernous storage area, I felt my body fading.

Oliver's beefy hand slapped my cheek. "I don't want to have to carry you, Luke. Stay with me a few more minutes."

I blinked the world back into focus and found myself in a cavernous room amidst lifejackets, pool noodles, broken lounge chairs and shelves full of chemicals for the pools. I was stumbling over my feet and knocking into things, even with Oliver's arm in a death grip around my waist.

"This area isn't used anymore," he said breathlessly. "It was for the janitors when the pool was open to the public. There are no cameras in here…"

Legs trembling and stars flashing before my eyes, the pain in all my limbs, even in my fingers, was just too much. Oliver was a tower of strength, determinedly supporting me, weaving us around stacks of aban-

37

doned furniture and piles of umbrellas in a room the size of a high school gym.

"C'mon. Keep moving, Luke," he huffed, arm tightening. "We're almost there."

Where 'almost there' was, I didn't care. I just wanted to lay flat on the floor. He persisted, though, his strength defying logic. He was dragging and maneuvered my failing body to the back of the room through mounds of seemingly endless rubbish. When he doubled over to catch his breath, I fell to my knees.

"We're backed into a corner. Nowhere to go." It took all my energy to talk.

Oliver seemed confused. "It's here. I know it's here," he muttered, straightening up and making his way over to a desk that was pushed up against the wall. Chairs piled up around it went crashing into other chairs when he gave it a shove, and then he seemed pleased to have uncovered a large hole in the wall.

"Jackpot," Oliver said, reaching for me. "You go first."

"Go where?"

"It's a laundry chute. You'll be fine. I promise," Oliver said. "There will be a hundred old towels at the bottom to break your fall. And if there isn't, well… that will suck. Now hurry up. I have to go last so I can try and pull this desk back against the wall."

This seemed like a bad idea. I just wanted to lie down and disappear into the darkness trying to steal my vision.

"Luke, it's either take your chances here, or die back in that room," Oliver said.

Right.

I took his outstretched hand and he pulled me to my feet. When I stuck my head into the hole, I was staring into the darkness of a metal tube, which wasn't comforting in the least.

An alarm started ringing, this one louder than the others and suddenly joined by the unmistakable roar of police sirens and firetrucks. Oliver wasn't having any of my hesitation. "Listen, it held me up as a kid, so it will hold you too," he said, then he grabbed me by the back of the pants and shoved me in.

I was falling, then sliding. My arms and legs pushing against the sides did nothing to slow my descent as I sped forward on my stomach, and I'll be damned if I didn't stifle a yelp. When a pin dot of light came into view, I was mercilessly launched toward it and onto a mountain of towels—I'd landed and broken neither bone nor fear of dark tunnels.

My heart was beating too fast, though. Lungs choking on a cloud of dust that my landing had created. I counted my lucky stars, then I heard it; the rattling of the metal chute as Oliver barreled toward me at breakneck speed. I rolled out of the way and narrowly missed his feet colliding with my face.

"Ha!" he said, bouncing back upward. "What a rush! You all right?"

I was still fighting to breathe, coughing again, and hurting more than ever. I managed a nod but remained on the towels, suddenly not caring about anything except for not moving.

"Thank goodness they didn't disconnect the motion sensor lights, or we'd be in the dark and—" Oliver's elation came to a grinding halt. He was looking at my back. "Oh man. Luke. I'm so sorry they did that to you."

I tried to get up, but I was so cold, shaking as if I'd dove into a glacier-fed lake. "Ah, it's not so bad," I said, collapsing back onto my face.

"Just stay there. Rest right where you are, okay?" Oliver said. "The entrances to this laundry room were sealed off long ago. There's no way in but the way we just came. You're safe for now. I promise."

Beneath my battered body, I imagined the mildewed towels had become the most expensive feather bed. When did I last sleep? When was the last time I had laid down? I noticed a spider scurry out from under a yellowed corner, and I didn't even care.

"Just rest," Oliver said, voice fading in and out of my ears. "I got this."

KAYA

7

WATCHA GOT COOKIN'?

Lisa kicked the walls, tugged on her hair, then pounded her fists against her forehead as if that would change anything. She said the word 'no' over and over with varying degrees of anger, which then gave way to a sadness that cut so deep it bled out onto the rug beside Seth's body. Slumping down to the floor next to him, her chest heaved in a heart-wrenching shudder as I tried to comfort her.

"Lisa, I'm so—"

She put her hand up to cut me off, not wanting to hear me, preferring instead to hide her face against her knees and rock back and forth. We sat in silence for the longest time. Emergency vehicles rushed past the house, oblivious to our nightmare as their sirens wailed, then faded off into the distance. A car door slammed. A kid yelled at another kid from across the street and a stereo boomed. There was so much action outside. But inside? The whir of the furnace was the only sound now. There certainly was nothing coming from Seth—because he was dead.

As a doorknob.

From a bullet to his neck.

There had been a brief struggle for air before he collapsed, limp and lifeless to the floor. His eyes were now wide and blank, just like Ben's had been when he died. And it was all I could do not to scream and scream and scream…

His blood spreading out across the carpet was shaped like a butterfly, wings reaching out to Lisa and nipping at my toes. I pulled my feet up off the floor just as a motorcycle next door fired up. Another siren blared, a dog greeted his owner with an excited bark. Thomas spoke and startled me out of my skin.

"Untie me," he said.

The butterfly was reaching for him, too.

"Kaya—"

Head pounding, nerves rattled and raw, I felt so betrayed and hurt by him that I preferred to get lost in Lisa's sadness instead of feeling my name on his tongue split me right down the middle.

"I'm sorry, Kaya, so deeply sorry. Please... I'm on your side I promise. Untie me. We can't just leave Seth there on the floor. If someone comes—"

Now I gave Thomas my full attention. "I can't believe you did that to me, Thomas," I said, absently rubbing the back of my head where the rock took a go at it.

Thomas flinched. "I couldn't just let you go off and... and—"

"And what?" The combination of fluttering and crushing in my chest was unbearable, and so was the unmoving, stunned, and horrified expression now settling over Lisa's face.

Thomas shuddered. "Risk never seeing you again. Risk you dying."

"You had no right," I raged. "If Luke is dead because of this—because of *me*—I'll never forgive you. If you're going to try to control me, tell me what to do, or force me to comply with your wishes, I don't want anything to do with you!"

His dark eyes settled on mine with a ferocious passion. "What would you have done, Kaya, huh?" His cheeks flamed red. "If Luke decided he was going to walk off the edge of a cliff and see what happened, would you let him? Would you take a risk with his life? No. No, I don't think you would. Now, I'm sorry for what I did—I went about things the wrong way that's for sure—but I don't regret it at all. I love you. There... I said it. Dead bodies, crazy messed-up family, and no hope in hell of ever winning your heart, *I love you*. So, if you can't deal with that—if you can't deal with a friend that just wants to keep you alive—then leave me tied up and start running because I won't stand back and watch you throw your damn life away."

His voice rattled the tiny house and shook me right to my toes. He was staring intently, with a dare on his lips and a prayer in his eyes.

"Leave me," he roared, tears threatening to spill as he motioned to the door. "Now!"

I didn't know what to say. With every fiber of my very being, I didn't want to go. I was still raging mad, but... something about Thomas pulled and held tight. I wanted him in my life, and my inability to leave along with the tears now rolling down my cheeks, clearly told him that.

"Please, Kaya, *untie me,*" he begged, voice softening, swallowing hard.

Kneeling beside him, I worked at the knots around his wrists while avoiding his gaze. When free, he dropped to his knees before me.

"Look at me," he said.

I was too angry, hurt, and confused, worried for Luke, as well as incredibly sad for Lisa.

"*Please.*" Thomas's breath caught. His hand cupped my chin and he tilted my face up to his. I could tell he wanted to pull me close, and I hoped the glare I was forcing forward was a warning not to. "I'm sorry," he said sincerely. "Truly I am."

I wanted to scream at him, slap him and scratch his eyes out—and melt into him and cry against his chest with his arms tight around me. So, instead I inched away and tried to focus on only one thing; Seth's staggering betrayal.

"Lisa?" I reached out to touch her arm. She was fixated on the gun discarded on the floor next to her.

"I'm okay," she said, suddenly leaping to her feet and clearing her throat. Tossing a grungy blanket over Seth's body, she wiped angrily at her eyes. "What are we going to do with him?"

I had to be strong. For her.

"Go see if there's a freezer in the basement," I said to Thomas.

He was eager to comply. "On it."

Lisa put her hands on her hips. "And, what about the rug?"

I held back the urge to throw up. "Pretty sure there's no cleaning it. See if you can find a knife and a garbage bag. We can cut out the stained parts at least."

Lisa turned to head for the kitchen, then stopped abruptly. "I'm not a very good friend," she said, her back to me, her tiny shoulders bearing too much weight. "I wanted you to have your way, but only because I wanted Luke back. I put your life above his, Kaya. He would hate me for that.

And Seth—" she could barely say his name. "I had a feeling. I saw... *things*. But I ignored them."

"You did what you thought was best. I won't hold it against you."

"So, now what?" she said with a gulp.

I felt wicked saying it: "We clean up this mess and dispose of the evidence."

Lisa nodded. "And *then* what?" she asked, hand over her heart as Thomas began dragging Seth's body across the room and down to the basement freezer.

"We get Luke back. Whatever it takes."

After cutting the stains out of the rug, we sat down to a mound of TV dinners Thomas had heated in the microwave, the food turning to acid in my mouth when I realized they'd been removed from the freezer to make way for Seth's body. Silence crackled with tension, and swallowing became impossible when Seth's phone, on the table between me and Lisa, began to ring.

"How well do you know Regan?" I asked, certain that's who was calling.

"About as well as I knew Seth," she said dismally. "Which apparently was not well enough."

"Maybe you shouldn't answer it..."

Shaking her head, she put the phone to her ear. "Hello Regan." Leaning against the stove, she wearily pushed food containers out of the way. "No. Seth's out for a walk, checking the perimeter as he always does. I have Kaya with me and we are working on a—what? No. Oliver went on his own and... Don't yell at me, Regan! We are—" Lisa was fighting tears. "Stop it, Regan. We are working on it and—"

There was no resistance when I took the phone from Lisa's hand. I braced myself, putting it to my ear with a deep breath. "Regan, calm down or I'll hang up on you," I said.

A heavy intake of air. A long, forced sigh. "What is going on, Kaya?" he asked, tone cutting.

I pictured his anxious face and those freckles dotting his tanned cheeks. His hand—minus a few fingers, courtesy of Rayna—was probably pressed against his temple or fidgeting with his thick red hair. If Seth had answered the phone, he would have addressed Regan as 'Dr. Death,' which was a term that brought back a not-so-good memory of having my heart restarted after an overdose of sedatives.

"We've had some complications," I said, realizing I had that same metallic taste in my mouth that I had when I'd woken up slung over Seth's shoulder in the forest. Had I been drugged again? "Lisa is just a bit… upset."

Regan's temper was barely restrained. "As am I. Yesterday Seth said he had a plan, but he wouldn't tell me what it was. Now I hear that Luke still isn't free. What are you guys doing about it?"

The food in my stomach wasn't sitting well. "I'm not sure yet," I said honestly.

"Seth doesn't have a plan, does he? He's just saying that to keep me quiet. Tell me Kaya."

"How is Louisa?" I asked, changing the subject.

This threw him. All anger left his voice. "Huh? Oh. She's perfectly fine. Whining for Lisa constantly but that`s to be expected. She has a rash on her arm, but it's healing. I'm keeping an eye on it."

"Good. And you?"

Regan paused. "Me? Uh… I'm fine, too, I guess. Still can't move with this bloody cast on my leg. My fingers that aren't there are throbbing all the time and I'm worried sick about my best friend but other than that, I'm all right. Wait, you're distracting me, Kaya. What's going on? Is it Luke? What aren't you telling me?"

I cut him off. Barely able to speak. "I don't know how Luke is. Oliver went off on his own to try and get him out, but now… I don't know about him either."

Regan sighed dramatically. "Oliver won't get caught, he's too smart for that. And Luke… well, Henry won't kill him," he said, trying to appease both of us. "He's too valuable. Henry knows he's the one thing he can use to get to you and it wouldn't be a smart move to kill him. Not yet, anyway. I honestly believe that, given those factors, we have a small window of time, Kaya."

I held on to Regan's words. "Thank you," I said, closing my eyes and praying feverishly it was true. "Regan…" I started, then paused.

"What?" he asked.

"How well do you know Seth?"

Lisa and Thomas froze.

"Why would you ask me that?"

"Well, sometimes I'm just not sure if he's, um, on the same side as us. I wonder if I can trust him."

"Oh." Regan seemed to give it some thought. "He's got some issues, but then, don't we all?"

I couldn't look away from the shredded carpet. "Yeah."

"What aren't you telling me, Kaya?" he asked intuitively.

"Well, he kept—uh, *keeps* checking his watch."

"Why?"

"No idea."

"So, Seth is acting a bit more strange than usual? Is that what you're saying?"

I coughed nervously. "Yeah. You could say that."

"Huh. I mean, I like the guy, but between you and me, I've had my reservations about him since day one. Just a feeling, ya know? I've never had an actual reason not to trust him. I mean, he saved my life when he fished my dumb ass out of those falls, and he went back to that mountain to save you and Luke, so I think he has your best interest at heart. Besides, doing anything to jeopardize getting Luke free would really tick off Lisa and he's fallen madly for—"

"He tried to shoot her," I interjected.

Silence. Regan struggled to regain his ability to speak. "Please tell me she is okay."

"Yes. Physically."

I could sense Regan's relief, and then his rage. "Whatever the hell his reason was, I'm going to kill him for that. Lisa is… well… dammit, you tell that bastard to phone me the second he gets back."

My throat went dry. "I can't. He's *out for a walk*."

Silence. "I see. One of those walks you sometimes get *lost* on?"

I had no reply. But it was reply enough. We both knew only so much could be said through a cell phone connection.

"I don't know what to do," I admitted.

I could hear Regan thinking. His brilliant mind clicking in time with the clock on the stove. "You must bring him here to me. Understand? I'll *deal* with him and set things straight. And I'll make sure that his friends in frightening places don't get involved. This must be handled carefully, or a hornet's nest of epic proportions will hit the proverbial fan. Okay?"

I felt a massive surge of relief knowing Regan would help us. "Yes."

"And tell Lisa I'm sorry. She deserves better. And that there is a child here that loves her with all her heart and needs her to come back soon."

I didn't have to tell Lisa that. She could hear Regan's soaring voice plain as day in the quiet house. Her posture crumpled at his words.

"All right," I said, close to tears.

"So, for now, what can I do for you on my end?" Regan asked, and I could hear Louisa talking to Brutus in the background.

I let the sound of the child's voice sit in my ears a moment before answering, "pray."

8

HEY MAN, NICE GOIN'

candle flickering on the table smelled like jasmine and didn't mix well with the turkey and cranberry sauce leftovers in the garbage can, or the bleach lingering in the living room. My fluttering stomach threatened to get the best of me, but I couldn't allow it. I had people to take care of. A monster to deal with.

When I picked up the phone to dial Henry, Thomas lunged for my wrist.

"Wait," he pleaded.

The look in his eyes tripped my breath; he was torn between letting me make my own choices and pinning my hands behind my back. I needed Lisa for support, but she was curled into the corner of the couch, lost in emotional chaos.

"No, Thomas. It's time."

He lowered his voice. "I'll do whatever you want. I promise. But—"

"You have to quit making promises you can't keep."

He nodded and gently took the phone from my hand and put it on the table. "Just hear me out."

I waited for him to speak, but he just stared, so deeply I had to blink and remember to breathe. I didn't resist when his hands grabbed mine and he pulled me up off the kitchen chair to face him. There wasn't much space between us and the heat in the room rapidly increased. Gold from the candlelight danced in his irises and played in his black hair, and it brought me back to our night under the tree; dancing, being free and

51

happy...and dammit if it didn't feel right—perfectly, right. We were chest to chest, and although I was still angry at him, I couldn't say no when he pressed his mouth to mine. It was sweet. Soft. The kind of kiss that moved mountains and lit stars—and made the hole I was falling into that much deeper.

Days ago, I thought Thomas might be my future. But then again, days ago I thought I would never see Luke. I had done the math, jotted down on pen and paper the reasons why Thomas was perfectly right for me, and the pros wildly outweighed the cons. He was someone I could spend a safe, happy, love-filled life with. He was a lighthouse in a dangerously dark world. He was a choice.

But.

Whatever love I felt for Thomas wasn't even close to the all-consuming, soul-binding love I had for Luke. Not. Even. Close.

I watched Thomas's pulse race at the base of his throat. "I meant what I said before." His cheeks flushed. "Kaya, I love you."

I put my head down, focusing on his hands still firmly latched onto mine. "Thomas... I—"

"I know," he said, letting go, arms dropping to his sides. "I just wanted to remind you that you could walk away right now and forget all this. Forget *Luke*."

Now Lisa glanced up, and if looks could kill, Thomas would be insta-dead.

I put my hand on his chest, his heart crashing furiously beneath all his toned muscle, and I cursed my defiant fingers for staying there too long. How I wanted to put my head against him, feel his hands in my hair and linger in the shelter of his arms. Could he sense that? He caught my hand in his and pressed it back over his heart, holding me to him, making my head confusingly dizzy with anger and longing and everything in between.

"Let me take you away from all this," he said, barely whispering. "I'll give you everything. My heart, my soul... *everything*. You would have the most beautiful life with me, Kaya. I can support you, give you a family, keep you safe and protected, be everything you need. I would do anything to make you happy. Just say the word."

I had to remind myself to breathe. I wanted that life with Thomas. But not as much as I wanted *any* kind of a life with Luke.

"I have to call Henry," I said.

Slumping back down dejectedly into the rackety kitchen chair, Thomas's eyes grew watery, his face so pained I was drowning in a sea of guilt. I had to swallow back the words that would make him feel better because, although true, telling him that I loved him too would make me a betrayer.

I picked up the phone.

Dialed Henry while Thomas tensed.

But Henry didn't pick up, and Henry always picked up—weird.

I dialed again. Nothing. The candle flame flickered. Thomas stared at his hands. Lisa remained glued to the couch. Time seemed suspended in uncertainty.

Then a sharp knock at the front door made us all jump.

"Oh crap," Thomas said, bolting upright.

Lisa stood, too. Her face dark as she scooped the gun up off the floor, snarling and alarmingly unstable. "I'll handle this," she said.

I blocked her. "It's probably nothing. Put the gun down."

The knock came again, this time louder.

Thomas peeked around the sheet draped over the living room window. "There's no cop car. I have to answer it."

Lisa and I stood close but kept to the shadows while Thomas gathered a breath then casually unlocked the deadbolt. There, wavering like a breeze would blow him over, was a wafer-thin man in waist-length dreadlocks and a white shirt covered in stains. The distinct smell of weed floated off him and into the house. Thomas recoiled slightly from the stench.

"Can I help you?"

"Oh, hey man, ya. I had a feeling you guys were here already since the windows were covered up and all. Wasn't thinkin' you'd be rolling in this early, but hey, that's cool. Everythang all right?" The man confirmed he was high with long, drawn-out vowels.

Thomas coughed. "Uh, yeah. Of course. Who are you?"

The thin man hovered in the doorway, smoke from a cigarette curling around him. "You're in the band playing at Jack's this weekend, right?"

Thomas nodded.

The man seemed relieved. "I'm Moe. I look after the house. I'm the guy ya call if anything goes wrong, or if ya need to get some weed or somethin'."

"Oh, I see." Thomas extended his hand. "Hi Moe. I'm… *Johnny*."

Moe took a drag of his cigarette, then extended a tattooed palm. "Oh, as in Johnny Cash? I get it. Heard we was having a country band. I don't usually dig that vibe, but heeeeey, whatever floats your boat. Got chicks in the band?"

Thomas's back muscles tensed. "Nope. Just four other dudes. And they're all sleeping right now."

"Ah, hence the candle light. Good on ya for saving power. Environmental awareness is pretty rad."

Thomas didn't move aside to let Moe enter. "Anyway…"

"Right." Moe blew a half curious plume of smoke into the house. "Well, as I'm sure you noticed, my number is on the fridge if you need anything. The complimentary meals are in the basement deep freeze and fresh towels are in the tub. Pretty sure I washed 'em. Or, maybe not. Don't remember. With all the craziness going on around here I thought I'd better check in and make sure there was no one hiding out or somethin'. Ya know? With all the freaky stuff going down."

Thomas pulled the door open a little wider and peered behind Moe's mountain of dreadlocks at the busy street. "Whadya mean? What's going on?"

"Haven't ya heard the sirens?"

Thomas nodded. "Yeah."

"There's action at the Bow Springs Estate. Ya know the old hotel that looks like a castle? Some lunatic went all terrorist and blew up the gates. Trees are on fire and half the roads are blocked off. I think every cop in the province is there. It's nuuuuts. They haven't found the guy that did it yet, either."

The cell phone I'd left on the kitchen table started to ring. An ear-piercing, soul-jarring sound cut off Moe's words and made my heart race. Thomas didn't budge.

"Uh, you gonna get that dude?" Moe asked.

Thomas shook his head as if waking from a dream. "Uh, yeah. I guess I better. Hey thanks for checking in on us, Moe. Make sure you catch our sets on Friday, I'll buy the first round of drinks."

The offer of free booze lit up Moe's eyes as the door was slammed in his face.

Thomas spun around to either grab the phone, or grab me, but I was pressing the talk button before he could do either, and the man who raised me, held me in his arms as a child, locked me in my room and manipulated me, crawled his way through the phone to gnaw on my eardrum.

"How dare you do this!" Henry raged.

He was fuming. I'd heard him angry before—yelling at staff, threatening guards—but this was pure and utter fury. He was *livid.* I was intrigued.

I used my sweetest voice. "Hello, Henry."

"We had a deal, and this is how you treat me? Your own flesh and blood? Did you really think that little diversion of yours would solve things? Huh? Was setting half the mountain on fire worth it? Now the cops are involved, and John Marchessa is probably sniffing around here, too. I know you're near. I know you are in town somewhere and I have every single road and trail in and out of this place on lockdown. If you know what's good for you, you best come back here on your own or—or—"

He faltered. The mighty, Henry Lowen, *faltered.*

"Or what?"

"Or I'll find some more of your friends to take my anger out on," Henry spat.

Why wasn't he threatening me with Luke's safety? Or Oliver's?

Because he didn't have them!

I stood a little taller. "I don't have any friends. You made sure of that."

A pause. "How about Stephan then? I'll—shred him to pieces."

There it was again. A hesitation. *A lie.* Things had spun out of Henry's control. I could feel it. He didn't have anyone I loved to barter with.

I let a smile creep into the corners of my mouth and went out on a limb. "We both know that Stephan is dead," I said, testing the water, dipping my toes in to see how deep it was.

"Then I'll find Oliver and your pal, Luke. Mark my words, Kaya Lowen—they won't make it off this estate alive unless you come back here."

Bingo. Henry was so rattled he'd slipped up and pretty much told me everything I needed to know; he had no one that I loved to barter with.

For one spectacular moment, I held the keys to the crazy bus.

"Ya know, I was going to come back," I said, grinning. "I thought it might be nice to spend some time with you. But—"

He was barely breathing. "But what?"

"Meh. I changed my mind. You're boring. And kinda predictable."

A sharp inhale. "If you don't come back here, right now, I'll—"

I cut him off. Mostly because I'd started to giggle. And the giggle turned into a laugh that almost had me doubled over. I stopped myself long enough to end the conversation with what I knew would shake him out of his hundred-dollar socks.

"I'll see you when I'm twenty-one, asshole."

Then I hung up. And while Thomas and Lisa watched me with unreadable expressions, I took the phone to the kitchen counter and whacked at it maniacally with a butcher knife.

Then I finished my TV dinner.

LUKE

9

SALT IN THE WOUND

I woke face down in the musty towels with my skin on fire, but it wasn't the pain or the awkward position that brought me fully around—it was the smell. Oliver was kneeling beside me opening a bottle of antiseptic, and it took me right back to that mountain, gazing at Kaya while she dressed my wounds and stitched me up. Once again, I was painfully aware of her absence.

"Sorry to wake you," Oliver said. His voice was loud in the cavernous room, bouncing off the cement walls. "But I'm kinda worried about infection."

I winced when he started dabbing at the wounds on my back. "I appreciate the doctoring," I said through clenched teeth.

"Yeah, well let's just hope this ancient stuff works. It's as old as the hills but should be better than nothing. You look pretty bad."

I reminded myself to breathe as the pain escalated. "Pretty sure that crap is… doing something."

"Hurts, eh?"

Stinging. Throbbing. Aching… heart aching. "Where's Kaya?" I asked.

Oliver sighed. "I had to leave her with the cowboy."

My chest now hurt more than my back. "You met the man in the video that Sindra showed us?"

"Yes. His name is Thomas. He'll take good care of her."

I had no doubt of that.

A jealous rage coursed through me that I couldn't suppress. I wanted to kill that man.

"Oh relax, Golden Boy. Kaya's not dumping you for Thomas if that's what you're worried about."

He pressed the antiseptic-soaked cotton to a throbbing spot between my shoulder blades and as much as I tried, I couldn't stifle a moan.

"Yeesh. This one is deep," he muttered.

"Promise me... she's all right," I said, feeling my stomach in my throat.

"Kaya? Uh huh." Oliver was distracted with his task. "Perfectly fine. Thomas, uh, well he looks at her like... you do. And as much as that makes me want to pound his face in, I know she's in good hands." He paused. I could feel his eyes studying my back. "This is unreal. I can't believe they did this to you."

I gulped; 'they' was actually one very sadistic girl. But I would keep that to myself.

"*They* wanted to know where Kaya is and I... I couldn't help it. I told them everything I knew. The miscarriage, Sindra coming to our motel room—I couldn't hold back. They injected me with something, and as much as I tried to keep quiet, I just couldn't."

"Hey." Oliver sat back on his heels. "It's all right. I know what it's like to have control of your mind taken away from you. I've been in the same boat you were, at the hands of someone sadistic and power-hungry, too. There's nothing you could have done so don't beat yourself up about it. That's what *I'm* here for."

My skin felt like it was on fire. "Sindra, right? Is that how she got into your head? How she controls you?"

Oliver flinched. "*Controlled.* But yeah. I've since kicked her out."

I thought of the beautiful dark-skinned woman not making a sound while the girl performed some of her 'greatest work'. It was worse to watch it than to feel it myself. "Well, if it makes you feel any better, Sindra got what she deserved." I swallowed back an acidic taste. "And probably a little more."

Oliver forced a weak laugh. "Good. When I first came here, I was just a kid, Luke, and I trusted her. I spent months out of every year for as long as I can remember down in that dungeon. *Months.* The memories have been coming back to me in waves now, and I wished they wouldn't.

Things I thought were strange dreams, or nightmares, were real. Sometimes I even relive the pain, too." He coughed, and his lungs sounded wheezy. "Sindra always handed the whip to someone else or gave instructions on exactly how she wanted certain 'exercises' to be played out—never getting her own hands dirty of course—but she was the one in control. She wormed her way into my head so she could use me as her puppet. So, I don't care what happens to her. I just hope she feels as much pain as I did."

"Oliver, I had no idea." I tried to roll over, but he pressed his hand to my shoulder.

"Just stay put."

He twisted the cap off a silver tube and began applying a sticky substance to my skin. The stinging subsided somewhat, and I could breathe again.

"It wasn't long ago I wanted to kill you," he said, gently working on the wound.

"Yeah." I choked on liquid pooling in my mouth. "And now we're practically dating."

"Ha," he snorted. "You wish dickhead."

I stayed where I was, letting Oliver doctor me and not wanting to admit to myself that the kindness in his touch was almost euphoric after suffering at the hands of the girl. When he was done with my back, he dressed and wrapped my wrists. Managing to get onto my side, it was then that I got a solid look at him; he had a gash over his eyebrow that had left streaks of dried blood on his cheek, a swollen and cut lip, knuckles that resembled hamburger meat, and he seemed to be favoring his left arm.

"Whoa. You better apply some of that sticky crap to yourself," I said.

Oliver shrugged off my suggestion and offered me his hand.

"How did you break into the estate, by the way?" I asked, embarrassed to need his help maneuvering off the mountain of towels with quivering legs.

Grinning, Oliver latched on to my elbow, keeping me upright while my head adjusted to the change of position. "I shoved a rag halfway into the gas tank of the truck, then taped a jerrycan to the tailgate so petrol would trickle out in a nice, even trail. After, I jammed the gas pedal with a rock, set it in drive, and let it head toward the estate gates. As luck would have it, I just happened to have a pack of matches—"

"Holy shit!"

Oliver was proud of himself. "Yup. I dropped a flame from a safe distance, and… *kaboom!*"

I had to laugh. But then I clued in. "Wait a sec… you blew up *my* truck?"

"Yup." His eyes shone deviously.

"I thought I'd heard an explosion, but I didn't trust my mind. The girl was just about to inject me with something. She had a needle in her hand and that look in her eye, and…" A chill rolled up my spine. "Thanks for saving me from that, Oliver."

"Well, I kinda owe you one for not letting me drop off the side of that cliff. And for not leaving me during my, um, *rehab*. I would be dead and rotting somewhere if it wasn't for you." His arm was around my waist now, coaxing my feet to shuffle over to a stool where I could sit and catch my breath. Clearing his throat, he straightened his shoulders. "Anyway, you ain't saved yet, Golden Boy. They know we're here somewhere, and it's only a matter of time before—"

An explosive cough stole his words and he struggled for air, doubling over. When the coughing quit, he spat a slick red line on the dusty floor.

"Uh oh," I said.

Oliver quickly reined in whatever fear briefly shone in his eyes.

"How long has this been going on?" I asked.

"It never quit," he admitted after a moment.

I felt something stab at my heart; worry. Worry for this big lug that had once tried to kill me. "We need to get you to a doctor."

He laughed, but there was absolutely nothing funny. "I'm fine. Chillax, Luke" he said.

But he wasn't, and now we both knew it.

At the end of a hall lined with dozens of washing machines, drying racks, shelves of dusty towels and bottles of soap, we came to a brightly painted, windowless room with staff schedules on the walls and tattered newspapers on the table. I was glad the lights still worked or we'd be in a pit of darkness, and with the number of cobwebs and other things lurking in the corners, I would not be cool with that.

Oliver wrestled open an ancient vending machine and we greedily guzzled back warm Coke's and stale nacho chips. I could feel the food giving my cells energy and clearing my mind, bringing to light the sound of sirens and the stomping of feet over our heads as mice scurried across the floor; I pulled my feet up onto the chair when one as big as a cat got a little too close, and made a note to avoid the abandoned shoe it dove into.

"Why does this place seem like it was left in a hurry?" I asked, hoping the stale food and syrupy drinks would settle down in my stomach.

Oliver was digging through a locker. "Because it was. This is one of four laundry rooms in the estate. It was blocked off even before Henry took over. Four women died within hours of each other and Radon gas was thought to be the cause, so every entrance was sealed off until someone could figure out how to fix the problem. Turns out the women that died were involved in some sort of cult and Radon had nothing to do with it. But by the time that was discovered, years had gone by and nobody bothered to open it up down here. It wasn't needed anyway."

"Lucky for us."

"There used to be six entrances to this room, and now they are all sealed and plastered over. If you were walking through the halls upstairs, you wouldn't realize that behind seamless wallpaper and old armoires are boarded up doors. I think anyone who would have known about this place is long gone."

Oliver tossed me a pair of size twelve boots and a beige canvas shirt with a name tag that said 'Lou'. The boots fit. The shirt however was too tight and the fabric against my back was like sandpaper. I left the buttons open. "How do you know about it then?" I asked.

"When some of my memories came back, I recalled a cook telling me about this place. I had spent months creeping around, trying to find a way in because I thought it might come in handy when Sindra wanted to get back to 'training'. One night when I was desperate to get away from her, I found that hole in the wall. I spent a few nights down here until I got hungry, then crawled my way back up."

"How old were you?"

"Ten, twelve? I don't know. But I got the ass-whoopin' of a lifetime when Sindra finally found me."

"These people are sick," I said, stating the obvious.

"Yeah. And it took me way too long to figure that out."

My heart broke for Oliver. He didn't deserve to be treated that way. Hell, nobody deserved to be treated that way. "Well, don't beat yourself up over it. That's what I'm here for."

He laughed. "Hilarious. You couldn't punch your way out of a paper bag right now if your life depended on it."

And then it came at him again, this time lasting longer; the cough was increasing, leaving him breathless after, his hands red with blood.

"Not a word, Luke," he warned.

I nodded—there weren't any, anyway. Sindra had told me in that motel room that if his lungs didn't heal on their own, he had no hope of survival. Would Oliver soon be another victim of Eronel Pharmaceutical? Like my mother?

"Listen, Luke, you have to rest, get your strength back, and then we have to get out of here," he said, wiping his hand on a crispy, used napkin. "Then we find Kaya and get her far away from this madness. All right?"

I nodded again, feeling a tightness in my chest at the mention of her name.

"You gotta keep yourself together," Oliver said perceptively. "She came back here, *for you.* She intended to trade her life for your freedom, but the cowboy stopped her. She will still try to find a way to do that again if we don't get out of here and get to her first."

I had no idea. Maybe I didn't hate the cowboy so much—

Nah.

"You can't let her down," Oliver continued. "I'm going to help you get out of here and—Lord Almighty—help you *get the girl.*" He choked a bit on those last words. "But you gotta promise me that when you get her back, you'll keep her… far away from Henry."

Never mind promises or vows, or rights and wrongs—or threats even —it would take an army the size of Jupiter to stop me from getting her back. And keeping her away from her family? That was at the very top of my priority list.

My reply was unnecessary, but I had to be polite. "Of course."

KAYA

10

REVELATIONS

Twenty-seven hours crawled by. I tried to sleep—my body desperately needed the rest—but my mind was in overdrive and not allowing it. Morning came and went. The afternoon dangled over pins and needles, and when the sun left the sky and brought the chill of evening, there was no sign of Oliver or Luke.

It took a lot of convincing to get Thomas to agree, but I had to go to the estate and see for myself what was going on. Maybe there was a way in now. Maybe by some stroke of luck, I'd find Luke among the crowd. I had to do something besides just sit and wait. At the very least, I had to get out of the death-filled house.

The night air took my breath away. It was full of that icy promise of snow. None of us had proper clothes except Lisa and she was bundled up in everything she owned. Seth's backpack had been tossed into the freezer with him and it just seemed all sorts of wrong to dig it out, so Thomas tried to disguise me as best he could with what he had, which left him bare-armed in a t-shirt and jeans.

"We need warm jackets and food, then we'll see how close we can get to the estate," he said, linking his arm through mine when we hit the street.

I must have been invisible swimming in his jean jacket and hat, because two women almost fell off the curb to twist around and check him out. One, blatantly ogling him, even spilled coffee on her coat. I glared hard at a thirty-something blonde with caterpillar brows who unabashedly winked. If Thomas noticed, though, he didn't care. He was purely focused on getting us to 'Gary's Mountain Wear Boutique' a block away.

Except for my short chocolate bar excursion in Radium, I'd never really been shopping before. This was a simple clothing store with serious-faced clerks and shelves of brightly-colored clothes, shoes for running, hiking, walking, and biking, which made my head spin in an oddly enjoyable way.

Thomas had directed me to keep my chin down and focus on my toes with my shoulders slumped forward, but so many things were catching my eye. And so were the people. This is what normal folks did. They worked. They went on holidays. They laughed and held hands. They complained about price tags and picked out their own clothes and their own *things*. Everything I'd ever bought for myself had been ordered online with Stephan breathing over my shoulder. Here I could feel the fabric, smell the perfume and leather belts, and admire a shiny case of sunglasses and Swiss army knives guarded by a massive stuffed grizzly bear.

"This is amazing," I muttered.

"Oh geez, it's just a ski shop Kaya," Lisa said, irritated, miserable, and rightly so. "All the cool designer stuff is on Main Street. It's stuffy in here. I'm going outside to keep watch. Hurry up."

Thomas was sifting through a rack of ladies' shirts. Next to him was a display case of sparkly rings, and hanging on the wall behind that, snowboards decorated like beautiful works of art. Of all the incredible sights to take in, though, Thomas was what fully captured my attention. He examined labels, shook his head at whatever didn't appeal to him, and then nodded to himself when a garment seemed right. He was so assured. So comfortable. Like he belonged here, even though it was a brand-new place to him. I was mesmerized watching him pick out clothes for me. And I felt special. I felt… loved.

"Found you these, *hun*," he said with a wink. "Do you have a color preference?"

He was holding up two sweaters—one blue, one black. I just shook my head. Truly, I was so overwhelmed I couldn't even pick out a pair of socks.

With a grin that covered some of the worry on his face, he tapped on the brim of his cowboy hat so it came down over my forehead. My head wobbled, the hair piled underneath the hat making it way too heavy.

"Keep your chin down," Thomas reminded me, casually glancing around the store. *"And slouch. Henry's men could be anywhere."*

I'd been so caught up in the moment that I forgot the severity of our situation. Right. Head down. Slouch. Examine a pair of wool mittens and not Thomas' arms still covered in goose bumps from our walk outside. Be discreet. Fade into the background. Stay close to him... *close to him.*

"These sales are final," the girl behind the counter said.

Thomas nodded. "All right."

She licked her lips. "You know, we do have a dressing room. I could help you try on the men's items before you buy them."

"No thanks," Thomas said, pushing the items he'd picked out toward her.

A machine beeped. Our things were being folded and stuffed into plastic bags.

"It's nice that you're buying clothes for your, um... friend," the clerk said, digging for info with a flirtatious shovel.

My eyes met hers. For a moment, I was dirt she'd picked out from underneath her pointy fingernails. I felt small, miniscule, and inconsequential in the path of her purple contact-lensed gaze—as was her intention—and I thanked Henry for not sending me to high school.

The clerk's eyelids fluttered so much I thought she might fly away. "We had some of those 'ripped and wrinkled' t-shirts come in last week," she purred to Thomas. "They're all the rage now. I could show you some... they might suit your friend better."

Wow. This chick was a bitch. Out of the corner of my eye I saw Thomas grin, then he reached for my hand and brought it to his lips. A feather-light kiss, warm like a summer breeze, brushed the back of my hand. It took my breath away.

The clerk's, too.

"No thanks," he said. "My wife doesn't really follow trends. Besides, her clothes will end up crumpled on the floor of our bedroom once I get them off her anyway. I can always add my own rips in the process."

My cheeks burst into flames. The clerk gasped like she'd been slapped.

A thousand dollars later, Thomas was wearing a black wool coat out of the store and held bags full of warm clothes for us both.

"You clean up nice," I said, admiring the fabric that stretched across his broad shoulders and how the color complemented his tanned cheeks and hair.

He handed me the wool mittens I'd been examining in the store, eyes glittering like black diamonds. "Is that a compliment, *wife*?"

Lisa groaned. I'd forgotten she was behind us.

"Maybe," I said, feeling my cheeks get even hotter.

Thomas genuinely began beaming. His smile stretched wide, but instantly faded when two men crossed the street and started heading in our direction. Walking too fast to be shoppers and too slow to be locals, the emotionless robots were certainly Lowen Security; we were caught. Running from them would give us away. So, Thomas grabbed my hand and put the smile back on his face.

"Let's get some lattes, my love," he said enthusiastically in some sort of Texan accent that was loud enough for anyone in a mile's range to hear. "It's bloody cold in this country. I can't believe people live here." He turned to Lisa. "How bout you, sis? Coffee? Or should we just hit up the liquor store, so you can drink yourself into your usual stupor?"

Lisa played along. "Do you always have to be such a jerk? I shouldn't have to defend myself when we're on holidays." She lightly punched my shoulder. "Why don't you stick up for me occasionally, *Alicia*? Tell your stupid husband to back off. There's nothing wrong with having a glass of wine in the evening."

The men approached, cast a brief glance at Thomas, then thoroughly checked out Lisa—who was a better disguise than my cowboy hat and jean jacket with her Barbie figure and flowing blonde hair—and paid me no mind. The Lowen robots didn't even notice me.

And that came in handy the closer we got to Main Street.

There were so many people. Of every size, shape, and color. It was incredible. I'd lived on the edge of town all my life, only seeing it through bulletproof car windows. Being here on the street amongst the organized chaos, felt surreal. Magical. I was absorbed into it, becoming a part of the moving masses. Restaurant doors were open, warm, and inviting, and all sorts of food smells wafted through the air. At a candy store lined up twenty deep, a man strummed his guitar and sang something beautiful while people dropped change in the case at his feet. Endless streams of cars slowly ambled by, stopping for people crossing the streets who were as wide-eyed as I was. I sidestepped a sleepy dog tied to a post and ducked out of the way of a pair of skis slipping from their new owner's hands. Excitement crackled the air, and not just because of the red and blue cop cars with lights blinking on every corner, but also the music pouring out of the nightclubs and the partiers eagerly awaiting entrance.

The Royal Canadian Mounted Police trotted by on their beautifully groomed horses, and I was about to reach out and touch one but I was pulled into a coffee shop with Thomas' hand tight around mine. Log-cabin-style walls bathed in yellow light surrounded people sipping and talking and studying on their laptops. The fragrant air made my mouth water.

"I'll get the coffee and muffins," Lisa said, moving in line behind a couple of girls giggling madly at something on a cell phone. "What do you want, *Alicia*?"

It took a moment to respond to my phony name because I was so entranced by the warm and inviting atmosphere of the place. A group of girls were seated at a corner table. Figuring they were about my age, I wondered what it would be like to be them. Hanging out with friends… being 'normal'.

"Alicia?"

"Oh, right. Coffee. Uh, I'll have whatever you're having," I answered, mostly because the menu choices were baffling—there were so many different names for coffee and steamed milk.

"All right then." Lisa was digging out her wallet. "You go fix yourself up. I'm buying today."

She pointed down a hallway toward a ladies' washroom, and Thomas was dragging me there before I even knew my feet were moving.

"Whoa is it busy in this town," he said, ducking into the washroom with me and locking the door. He had a black parka out of a bag and was ripping off the tags. "I know I said hiding in plain sight would be best, but even in my hat and jacket you're stunning. Getting too many looks."

He was full of crap.

The cowboy hat was stuffed in a garbage can and my tangled mess of curls fell to my waist. "We need scissors," I said, catching my reflection in the mirror.

Thomas smiled. "Nope. We have *this*."

In his hands was a furry yellow toque with knitted cat ears, strings for whiskers and little button eyes. He pulled it down over my head, then to add to my 'style,' he positioned a pair of yellow tinted sunglasses over my nose.

I looked insane. "You're not serious."

"Yeah. Animal hats are all the rage. You literally look like everyone else here. Just add this scarf and—"

"I am pretending to be your wife. No one would believe that a man who looks like you would be wandering around the most romantic place in Canada with a girl in cat ears and ski goggles."

His eyebrow lifted. "A man who looks like me?"

"Oh, come on now. Girls are drooling all over you. They think you're hot and you know it."

I could feel his gaze on me deepen while I removed the hat. After taking the green scarf from his hands, I draped it over my head, wrapping the ends around my neck before securing them with a knot. I'd walked past a few ladies outside who were dressed this way. The scarf concealed my hair and most of my face. The new parka came next. Soon I was swimming in a luxurious cloud of goose down that came down to my knees. The warmth and comfort of it made me sigh.

"Thank you, Thomas," I said, hugging myself. "I'm instantly warm."

He wasn't listening. "And what about you? Do you think I'm hot?" he asked.

I gulped down a massive yes. A *screaming to be released from the pit of my stomach* yes.

"You're all right," I said instead.

He reached for a lock of hair that had escaped the scarf. His face came close to mine. Too close. His thumb stroked my cheek, and butterflies danced in my stomach as his gaze lowered to my mouth.

"Green suites you," he said.

I pulled back, but there was minimal space in the bathroom and I bumped into the hand dryer, turning it on. "I'm still mad at you."

I was. But clearly not enough to push him away when he reached inside the parka to grab hold of my waist. And certainly not angry enough to say no when his hands settled on my lower back, pulling me tight to him. It was a bold move. One he should have been slapped for. It brought our hips impossibly close together and trapped the air in my lungs— making my chest heavy with guilt. Although 'technically' I wasn't in a relationship with Luke anymore, this was wrong. I had to tell Thomas to back off and stop touching me, even though…

"I'm fine with you being mad," Thomas said. "I won't let it ruin our date."

That caught me off guard. "Date?"

"The weirdest date ever, but yeah. You and me, are on a date. "

I fought back the urge to let my hands wander over him and forced my best irritated voice. "Let me go, Thomas. We don't have time for whatever is going on in your head. This isn't a date. We're planning a rescue mission."

He laughed. "You're so beautiful when you're trying to be angry at me."

"Oh, stop it. You are incorrigible and—"

He stole the words off my tongue with his pressing mouth, and I'll be darned if after the first shock, I didn't eagerly respond. My body defied me as his fingers slipped under the back of my shirt, making me feel crazed with the heat. Heart racing, common sense flushing down the toilet, my hands were clutching the back of his head, getting wrapped up in the moment and pulling his face to mine. I let my mind drift to a safe place where nobody was searching for me. Nobody was dead in a freezer. Nobody I loved was hiding and fighting to stay alive. There was only Thomas, me, and that promise he made to me at the house sparking madly between us. "Remember our night together?" he murmured, loosening the scarf to nibble at my neck.

His breath, hot against my skin, was a vivid reminder—not that I would ever forget.

"Imagine what that would be like now that you're in love with me," he said. "Imagine how I could make you feel."

Oh. My. God. "I… I am not in l-love with you," I stammered.

He leaned back to peer into my eyes. Smiled. Then reached down to roam two shiver-inducing hands down my thighs. Before I knew it, I was lifted and wrapping my legs around his waist.

"Yeah, you are," he said, breathing hard, pushing himself against me, turning on the hand dryer again. "You're just too scared to admit it."

I was a fly stuck in a glue trap, stuck in the realization that he was right… and stuck in the ladies' bathroom in a coffee shop with a gorgeous man who I wanted to touch every inch of and get to know in every way possible which was wrong… so wrong…

"You're wrong," I said.

"Am I?

His mouth moved over mine desperately, eager to show me what he knew to be true. I was so overcome with physical desire for him my control was slipping. I had to remind myself that if there was one thing I had learned in my short teenage life so far, it was that *lust was not love.*

"Kaya…" Thomas breathed, "You know you want me, the same way I want you. It's okay to admit it. You're not cheating on anyone. You're not betraying… him."

"We have a friendship agreement, remember? You're crossing the line and making it increasingly impossible for me to resist. And I need to resist."

"I can give you more than friendship," he said eagerly.

Lust was not love. Lust was not love. But was this lust, or love?

My heart skipped, flipped, pounded in my throat.

"I'm so sorry," I said, unwinding myself from him and adjusting the scarf across my red cheeks. "I can't give you what you want."

He turned away, cursing the dryer when it came on again. "We better get going then. Someone keeps knocking on the door."

I hadn't heard a thing, but I turned to leave anyway, desperate to escape.

"Oh, but wait…" He reached for my arm and held it, turning me to face him. The turmoil on his face made my chest hurt. "Gimme the glasses," he said, choking slightly on the words, and after popping out the yellow lenses, he handed me back empty, thick black frames. "Here. Now they look like regular glasses."

They did. I was unrecognizable now. The parka completely hid my shape, the scarf fully concealed my hair and my heated cheeks, and the glasses obscured my eyes.

"Oh, and hey…if we're pretending that you're my wife you should probably have some bling."

He dug around in one of the bags until he found what he was searching for—a huge diamond ring with stones all around the band.

"It's fake—obviously—but I think it's kind of pretty," he said.

"Oh. Thanks."

I tried to keep my face emotionless as he made a show of ever so slowly slipping the ring onto my finger, and barely registering an actual knock at the door while everything about him consumed my senses. I held back tears when he raised the back of my hand to his mouth, just like he did in the store. But this kiss was different. It was a kiss that said I could have him for eternity if I wanted.

But I was Luke's, and Luke was mine. And Thomas… Thomas was…

"I'm sorry I said I hated you." I had to fill the air between us.

His breath caught. "It's okay. I deserved it."

"And I understand why you did what you did. I'm not angry anymore."

He bit his lip. "Thank you."

The knock at the door grew louder. Urgent.

"You know," he said, staring at the ring on my hand glittering madly in the bathroom lights. "I'm going to do this for real someday."

"Do what?"

He smiled. "Marry you."

We immersed ourselves back onto the crowded streets, holding hands like we were a regular couple, sipping coffee neither of us wanted. Lisa followed, impatiently hissing at us to hurry up, while Thomas hissed back at her that it would cause attention. I felt as if in a dream playing the role of a tourist, buying chocolate marshmallows and posing for a picture next to a life-sized plastic moose, all while my heart was in my throat with worry and guilt and mounds of confusion.

At a souvenir shop about to close, Thomas ducked in and bought me a little jade bear on a chain. *For good luck* he said when he hooked the clasp behind my neck. To the onlooker, and hopefully two of Henry's men heading our way, he was a doting husband and we were a vacationing couple madly in love. No one knew that our entwined hands and plastic smiles were covering up increasing fear as we headed toward the last place in the world I should be. I was risking my life getting close to my former home. And so was Thomas.

Lisa was doing this for Luke. I was doing this for Luke. But Thomas? He was doing this for me, and that realization hit like a tornado.

"Maybe we'll get lucky and the perfect plan will unfold before our very eyes," he said quietly. "I'm thinking the estate can't be so heavily guarded with all these goons on the street."

"It's worse than you think. I promise."

"Geez. More prison than castle, eh?"

"Yup," I nodded. "Inside, every hallway is gated and has guards posted, and there are men at each entrance, not to mention the training quarters where at the very least there are hundreds more. Henry's minions are beyond loyal and will shoot on command without second thought. They'll follow orders no matter what they entail."

Suddenly, my feet stopped dead in their tracks; how was I possibly so selfish that I allowed Thomas to come with me? To be out here in the line of fire? What was I doing? I had to turn back.

But... Luke.

The scale was balancing in the most gut-wrenching way, tearing me clean down the middle, perfectly in half.

A crazy question popped into my mind.

"What is it?" Thomas asked, noticing my cheeks pale.

I shoved the question away, but it came back and smacked me full on in the face. I removed my hand from Thomas' and stared up at him, ignoring the steady stream of people having to go around us. I patted the jade bear, feeling it on my chest next to the maple leaf and the cougar tooth from Luke. Now the question was unavoidable; *was it possible to be in love with two people?*

"Kaya, you look like you've seen a ghost." Thomas's dark eyes flooded with concern.

Was I in love with two people? The thought of living out the rest of my days without Luke, *or Thomas*, made the future seem impossibly bleak and unbearable. My stomach twisted up around my spine.

"Kaya... what's wrong?"

My mind was reeling. I had to focus on something else. Anything else.

From over Thomas's shoulder, there was a familiar sign across the street. "That's the Derrick Bar."

Thomas followed my gaze, confused, and pulled me out of the crowd.

"I made a really good friend there once," I said.

His smile didn't meet his eyes. "That's nice, hun. Let's keep walking, shall we?"

I stayed glued to the sidewalk, still split down the middle with whether to run away from the estate, or to the estate. "She was a waitress there, her name was Angela," I said to Thomas. "She was amazing. Bold and strong. Colorful too, like one of those snowboards in that store."

Lisa had stopped a safe distance behind us and was pretending to check her cell phone. I heard her loudly clear her throat—a signal to get moving. We were being watched by two men across the street standing just outside the doors of the Derrick. Thomas faked a smile and pretended not to notice. He latched on to my hand again just as a young man in a ski jacket walked past and very blatantly took a picture of Lisa with his phone.

"Creep!" she yelled, giving her unwanted photographer the finger, then she began shouting off every threat she could think of to divert attention away from us.

Ski jacket man bolted. Thomas motioned to go after him, but I had hold of his coat, digging my fingers in as I knew the picture of Lisa was being sent to Henry—we didn't need Thomas's picture taken, too.

"She disappeared," I said.

"What? Who disappeared?" Thomas's eyes darted between me and the man running through the crowd.

"Angela. My friend," I continued, holding Thomas firmly, pretending to only notice him and no one else. People rushed by and the men across the street were focused on us now, peering through the crowd of swinging arms and varying strides. "The last time I saw Angela was in *that* bar."

Thomas, confused, led us off the main street, around a corner, and into a shadowy store doorway. A small 'closed' sign in the window glowed gently.

"Those men across the street… they're watching us." Thomas said.

I nodded and pulled the scarf down a bit lower over my forehead. "That could happen to you, you know. You could disappear, too."

Now I had his full attention. It started to snow. "What are you getting at, Kaya?"

"You shouldn't be around me."

Thomas shook his head, clueing in to what I was getting at. "Uh, uh. No way are you doing to me what you did to Luke. I get it. You're worried about those you, er, *care* about. But I'm a big boy. I can handle myself. And if you leave me just to keep me safe, I swear, Kaya Lowen, that I will turn myself over to your father and offer up my body in the name of whatever messed up science he's into."

He was too close. Too close in every way. The question remained… and I had to get out of the shadows and be in the crowd again. That was the only way I could think, and I needed to think.

But two steps out of the doorway, I realized the men weren't across the street anymore—they were approaching us. Thomas must have noticed too because he pulled me back toward him with such force it knocked the air out of my lungs. Then his lips were on mine. His hand was at the back of my head, encouraging me to kiss him back. *"Don't look at them…"* he whispered against my jaw. *"Just make it look real."*

I didn't have to fake it. I let Thomas hungrily press his mouth against mine—his body, too—and I responded in kind. We were breathlessly wound up in each other as the men strolled past and wandered out of sight. Then we just stood there after. Unsure what to do. What to say. Stuck in our little cocoon of each other. Thomas had his hands on my cheeks as if he might never let go, his nose inches from mine. I could feel his heartbeat in his palms.

"Tell me that you don't love me," he said, the glow from the closed sign in the window making obvious his flushed cheeks, lighting his dark eyes.

"I don't love you."

He jutted out his chin and dropped his hands. "You are one heck of an actress."

And then we were walking again—or were we floating?—toward the edge of town, hand in hand, quiet and confused. We became part of the crowd making our way toward the place I'd spent almost my entire life wanting to get away from. When we came to the bridge and could see the towering spires of the estate looming in the distance, I recalled standing on a fifth-floor balcony, watching the river that separated the estate from the town, and wondering what it felt like to go across the bridge on my own. Now that I was doing just that, I still didn't know how it felt—I was too wrapped up in whatever was going on in my heart to truly acknowledge where my feet were.

But when the bridge was behind us, the flashing lights of fire trucks and police cars brought back reality with a slap. Gone were the metal structures meant to keep out armies, and twisted remains of the gates lay scattered about. Reaching up the mountainside was a swath of black where only ash covered the ground. Police had taped off the area, keeping people safely behind the lines, but reporters were lurking amongst them taking pictures of a truck—or what was left of one—and interviewing staff.

"What the heck did Oliver do?" Thomas muttered.

We stayed hidden within the crowd. Security was everywhere. Police were everywhere.

"This is pretty nuts, eh?" said a man next to Thomas. He was one of many surveying the disaster, dressed in a brand-new parka—price tag dangling from his sleeve—and head covered with a hat that might have been roadkill.

Thomas cleared his throat. "Uh, yeah. What happened? My wife and I came to take pictures. We weren't expecting *this*."

"Well, they think whoever drove that truck into the gates was a terrorist."

"Oh my gosh," I said, trying out a British accent.

"That's bloody awful," Thomas said, mimicking me and giving my hand a squeeze. "Did the guy get caught?"

The man was pleased to have our attention. A drip of water clung to the end of his nose. It was mesmerizing.

"Nope. Police ain't saying much." He crossed his arms over his chest. "But my buddy was coming back from a hike and saw the whole thing. He says the guy was certainly trying to blow the place up. He was carrying a bomb or something when he ran off. Cops still haven't found him. I bet he's probably scoping out some restaurant in town. Terrorists like the crowds."

An older woman next to me was eavesdropping and couldn't hold her tongue. "This wasn't the work of a terrorist. We're in Banff. That's ridiculous!"

The man leaned across us to address the woman, the drip still dangling. "I heard it first-hand, lady," he said defensively.

Thomas and I backed up a bit, giving them room to argue, and the woman—wide as a refrigerator—stepped in front of me. "Well, I heard it's the work of the Right Choice Group. They've been protesting Henry Lowen for years. Can you imagine? What sickos. Can't they see the good he does in this town?"

"No way. This was terrorists," Nose Drip countered.

Then the arguing broke out. Team terrorist against team Right Choice Group. When someone else chimed in, Thomas and I moved through the crowd to get a better view of the carnage and hear other stories brewing amongst people. We avoided the eyes of Lowen security that were in full force at the ruined gates. For a moment I thought I'd been noticed when a guard stepped toward us, gaze centered on me, and I could tell Thomas thought the same by his sharp inhale. But the guard retreated, blank gaze returning to his face and focus drifting off over our heads.

"Do they even know what you look like?" Thomas asked close to my ear.

"A few might. I was kept in my room under lock and key. There are no pictures of me anywhere. Henry didn't allow them."

Thomas sighed. "Your princess life was certainly no fairy tale, was it?"

I shook my head.

"I saw the guy who did it..." I heard a girl say from a few feet away.

At first, I thought she was talking to me, but realized another girl was getting the info I was desperate to hear. I sized her up out of the corner of my eye. Short blond hair, and the worst teeth I'd ever seen, obvious even in the low light. Her friend had a spiky blue hairdo that was quite unflattering, was taller and probably quite shapely under her puffy coat.

"Yeah. He came out of the trees after that truck blew up and ran toward the estate. I know he got inside. And... *I know who it was,*" the blonde said.

"Are you going to tell the cops?" asked the girl with blue hair.

"I did. I told them everything and nobody cared. I tried to talk to one of those security guys too but was completely ignored. So, to hell with them. My dad used to work for the Lowens. They fired him, so I don't give a crap what happens to that place."

I was gawking at the blonde now because she was oddly familiar. Then I realized it wasn't because of the way she spoke, or her strangely curved nose—it was the sapphire earrings dangling from her ears that I'd given to her father years ago. Driver Dan—the gambling addict with all the kids who smuggled pizza in for me and snuck me out of the estate to meet Angela—had given them to this girl.

"...and the guy who did it? He's freaking *gorgeous,*" she continued. "Like, movie-star gorgeous. Absolutely dreamy. Once when Dad snuck me into the estate, we ran into him and I almost couldn't breathe."

Well, that confirmed they were talking about Oliver—the description was extremely accurate.

"I got fired, too," I offered.

The blonde was taken aback, obviously offended that I had been eavesdropping. "Uh, excuse me?"

"Oh, sorry. I overheard you talking about your dad. I know him."

The girl didn't give a crap who I knew. "All right then," was all she said and rolled her eyes at her friend.

"I hate that place too," I said casually. "They fired me because I tripped and dropped a plate of mashed potatoes in Henry Lowen's lap."

Now the girls giggled, either at my story or my pathetic desire to share it with them.

"Where is your dad?" I asked. "Still in town?"

Now I was getting the 'she be crazy' look. "Yep."

"I'd like to visit him. Where is he exactly?"

Driver Dan's daughter was having none of me. Her hands went to her hips. "Same place as always."

I hid my frustration. "And can you tell me where that is?"

Dan had taught his kid some street smarts. "Listen, I'm not giving someone I don't know my home address."

I put my hands up in defense—and the ring on my finger caught her eye so I changed tactics. "Oh, of course! Sorry. It's just that I got a huge promotion and sold my house. I have tons of clothes I don't want anymore, so I thought I might bring them by before I head off to London."

I had Dan's address and phone number two seconds later.

"What are you going to do with that?" Thomas asked, eyeing the piece of paper in my hands.

"I'm not sure yet. Dan could be an ally, though. He might come in handy if we need him."

"Well, in the meantime, you're attracting attention," Lisa warned from behind us. I'd forgotten—again—that she was even there.

Indeed, two Lowen Security men were ducking under the tape and coming our way, and this time, we recognized each other. We moved through the crowd, and they followed. We sped up—they sped up. We swerved—they swerved. So Thomas and I started shoving our way through people, going the only way we could—back to the bridge. Lisa was already halfway across it when a police car angle parked to block the exit.

We were caught.

And then someone shouted *there she is... don't let her get away...*

I did the only thing I could think of; with Thomas's hand in mine, I yanked him off to the side of the mouth to the bridge, where the ground gave way to a sharp, downward slope to the river, and I dove.

11

GIMME SHELTER

I heard Thomas grunt in pain when we both came tumbling to a stop, but there was no time to ask if he was okay. Leaving our shopping bags on the shore, we crouched alongside the moon-lit river toward the underbelly of the bridge. Scurrying onto the concrete footing where it met the water, we climbed the steep slope until we were nestled up against the inside edge.

Thomas was breathing heavy. "You okay?" he asked.

I knew I had a few scratches on my knee and my injured arm was throbbing madly, but nothing was broken. I was more worried about him.

"I'm fine," I said, catching my breath. "Where are you hurt?"

"My stitches have torn open. I think. Can't see it, but it feels a bit… uh… *oozy.*"

In the faint light I could make out his hand pressed to his stomach. "Dammit. I'm sorry Thomas. Sorry I dragged you here. I knew the risk but—"

"Hey. It's all right. We're fine. I'm fine. Besides, now we know that Oliver got away. So that means we can assume that he's with Luke and they're hanging out together, happy as clams, two peas in a pod, bromancing. You know, buddylicious—"

"Yeah. I get it." He was distracting me from his injury, so I knew it was bad. "We can rest here for a second, then we are going to have to crawl back up to the road and make a run for it. Can you do that?"

A cough that wasn't from either of us made us jump. Thomas gripped my hand so tight I winced.

"Hello?" he said into the dark.

"Why don't you just head across the river from up here?" said a male voice up over our heads.

"Uh, who's there?" Thomas asked.

Someone who sounded educated, groomed, and quite articulate replied. "Christopher George Smith. But my pal's call me Ed."

"Are you by yourself, Ed?"

A heavy sigh. "Always."

A lighter flame lit Ed's eyes. He was perched up in the long expanse of steel stretching out underneath the bridge. From what I could see, Ed came here a lot. Blankets, jars, boxes of cookies, pop cans and an old radio were arranged around him.

Ed touched the flame to what might have been a cigarette, but probably wasn't. "You can get to the other side easy. You just crawl along the beams. They're wide as my momma's ass. You just can't stand up or you'll hit your head."

The bridge shook as a car drove across. "What do you think?" I asked Thomas, his grip on my hand making it numb.

"Seems like a really bad idea."

"Good first date memories, though."

"We can reflect on it someday and laugh."

"Tell our grandchildren," I said without thinking.

Time came to a crashing, head through the windshield, ass over tea kettle, stop.

"What did you say?" Thomas said, barely a whisper.

"I—uh, nothing. Nada." I was glad I couldn't see his eyes all that well. "Thomas, really, it was just a slip of the tongue. Please… don't read into it. Okay?"

He exhaled heavily and let go of my hand.

Ed coughed out a plume of smoke. "I hate to interrupt what seems like a heartfelt moment and all, but the cops are out in full force tonight. I see some flashlights coming this way."

"Thank you, Ed," I said, reaching for Thomas, who had grown quiet. I got a hold of his coat sleeve, urging him ahead, and Ed fired up his lighter to guide us toward him. The closer we got, the more obvious Ed's face and

the sores covering it became. I pretended it didn't bother me and that I
didn't care, but I had to ask.

"Why are you here, Ed?"

His lighter went out. "My family doesn't approve of me getting high.
They think I can just flip a switch in my head and turn off the addiction,
but it doesn't work like that. When I'm up here, I can't see the disappoint-
ment on their faces."

The air chilled another ten degrees. Flashlight beams narrowly missed
us. "I'll help you," I said, not completely sure how, but really wanting to.
"Someday."

"Ha." Ed laughed. "That's a kind thing to say, darling, but I don't want
any help. This is the life I chose. When I decide it's over, all I have to do is
jump. Now... get going. No sense being caught for whatever it is you
did."

With Ed's back to us, on a two-foot-wide beam that felt like only an
inch wide, we crawled above the rushing river.

"Are we nuts to trust a drug addict?" I said to Thomas's backside.

He quietly kept moving ahead.

"This is turning out to be a very strange date," I offered.

He said nothing.

Metal shaking overhead. Slime squished between my fingers. "Please
tell me this isn't pigeon poop..."

Thomas paused, seemed to sway, then carried on.

He worried me. Not because of the immediate danger of falling to his
death into the river below, but his silence. It felt like a warm blanket had
been pulled from my shoulders. Like I hadn't eaten all day. Like something familiar and comforting that had always been there, suddenly wasn't.
I was hurting him more than his wounded stomach was, and I didn't know
how to fix that.

When at one point he stopped and hung his head, I barked orders at
him to keep moving and received only a detached 'uh huh'. I wondered if
some of the slime—the bits that were warm, anyway—was his blood.

With a rush of relief at the end, we carefully made our way
down the steep concrete and onto the riverbed, both plunging our
hands into the icy water to scrub them clean. There were footpaths
snaking off left and right up the bank, so we picked one and headed
up and into a stand of trees. Twice Thomas had to stop and catch

his breath, but eventually we found ourselves in someone's backyard.

Across a lush, landscaped patch of grass dusted with a fine layer of pure white snow, we could see into the windows of a beautiful home and the family gathered within. They were centered around a fireplace. Maybe fifteen or so adults appeared to be completely captivated by a dancing child. Twirling and tapping his toes, was a small boy putting on a show for his audience. The scene was so warm. So cozy. So… everything I wanted.

Thomas wordlessly reached for my hand and for the longest time we just watched. Thomas familiar with that kind of life—missing it I assumed—and me in awe of it, dreaming of what it would be like.

A barking dog got us moving again.

We walked hand in hand and got back onto Main Street, but we were desperate to get off it. My hands were covered in scratches and small cuts, and Thomas was slightly hunched, unable to hide his pain. We didn't blend in anymore. It took all our resolve to put on neutral faces when we crossed the street toward a corner block of restaurants that were letting out the last of their customers. With great effort, we smiled and straightened up as we passed a police officer who—thankfully—paid us no mind. We were halfway to the end of the block when out of the corner of my eye, something stole my breath.

I couldn't help but stop and stare. Pink flamingos decorated a rundown brick building, and a nightmare I'd had about it for years came back to me in a rush. A tremor shot up my spine and wrapped its bony hands around my throat. I choked, unable to peel my eyes away from the place that looked the same as it had the day I almost died—except for the plywood nailed across the entrance and windows.

"What is it?" Thomas asked. He was so pale.

"Nothing," I said, forcing my feet to get moving, leading him away and miraculously keeping my head together. This was not the time to have a meltdown. I had to take care of him and get us away from all these people.

Through alleys and parking lots we stumbled until we were finally on the street that led back to the band house.

"What happened? Back there, at that place with the pink birds?" he asked.

"Flamingos," I corrected.

"Yes. There. What happened?"

The streetlights blinked. Two cats hissed at each other. "I had my sixteenth birthday party there," I said.

"Oh. Let me guess; you didn't get a pony?"

I wish I could have laughed. "If only."

"I need something to keep me walking," Thomas said, pain catching his words. "So spill it."

I had never talked about that night. Not to Oliver. Not to Anne. And certainly not to the therapists that Henry had hired. Dredging up the past didn't seem helpful. I mean, what was done, was done. You can't go back and change anything so analyzing the crap out of it certainly didn't seem like it would do me any good.

But it was just a story now. Just a story.

I took a deep breath and let the words tumble. "I was really sick of Oliver one day, so I took off across the marble floor in one of the banquet rooms to get away from him and slipped and fell. Oliver took me to the emergency because by the way I was crying he thought that I'd broken my ankle. I knew it was fine, but I suddenly realized I had an opportunity to get him fired. You see, taking me off estate grounds was completely against the rules, and I knew firsthand what happened to guards who broke the rules. Especially ones who endangered my safety."

"Oooh, how evil of you," Thomas said, wincing as we stepped over a curb.

"Of course, after x-rays and lots of attention from nurses, I was diagnosed with a sprain and sent home with a tensor bandage and crutches. On the way back to the estate, we drove past that restaurant. I'd never actually been into Banff or seen the shops or the people or…anything, and the pink-painted brick building with the dancing flamingos was so intriguing. *I wish to go there someday* I'd said mostly to myself. But Oliver heard me. He went to Henry and begged him to allow me to have my sixteenth birthday there. Amazingly, instead of firing Oliver, Henry agreed."

We were at a park where two swings hovered over a little patch of snow-covered sand and a teeter totter waited for sunshine and kids. Thomas sat on a bench pulling his coat tight around him, and I sat next to him.

"You gonna make it?" I asked.

He smiled at me in the moonlight. A stunning smile. "I'm fine. I just want to hear the rest of this story, and my ears work better sitting down."

I made circles in the snow with my shoes. "The amount of planning and security that went into getting me off the estate was so tremendous you'd think I was the queen of England. Oliver regretted suggesting it, and I was still mad he hadn't been fired. He was so nervous when the day came that he had to change his shirt three times before we left, and there were so many weapons tucked in around his three-piece suit he set off alarms. By the time we got to the restaurant, we probably sweat off ten pounds. I thought once we got inside, I could relax and have fun, be a part of the real world for a few hours. But it was then I realized my elaborate birthday party was an elaborate business meeting that involved cake. The restaurant had been closed to the public and the guest list was the who's who of town, none invited by me.

"When a massive chocolate and vanilla cake was carried to the table, I didn't want to be there. Flamingos shmallingos. It was worse than sitting in my room alone with smuggled-in pizza and just as lonely. Stephan was halfway through a bottle of scotch, Henry was talking on his phone, Sindra was texting, and I remember Oliver reaching over and giving me a pat on the leg and thinking that of all the people here, he was the only one paying attention to me. The candles on the cake were lit and melting, and through the wavering heat of the flames I couldn't ignore the smile on his face as he waited eagerly for me to make a wish. I suddenly felt bad for running from him, for being such a brat, and for wanting him to get fired. In his eyes I could see he genuinely cared for me, and that was the moment things changed between us."

I took hold of Thomas's hand, leading him away from the bench and back onto the sidewalk. The color had come back into his cheeks, and he stood a little straighter. I kept talking, unable to stop the story now.

"I made a wish that Henry would put aside his phone and watch me blow out the candles. That's all I wanted. Just to feel important to him if even for a second. But that wish never happened. I did, however, get his full attention when one of the waiters pulled the knife I was about to cut the cake with from my hand… and held it to my throat."

"Oh… Oh, Kaya. How awful," Thomas said, eyeing the scarf that covered the scar on my neck.

"Before I even realized what was happening, a man outside dressed as a traffic cop blew apart the restaurant window and I was dragged back from the table. Everyone was screaming—except Oliver. He had a gun pointed at the waiter's head—at both our heads actually—and had crouched down to completely ignore everything around him but me. The traffic cop had a gun pointed at me too, and he'd yelled *shoot at me and my buddy will slice her open. Shoot at him and I'll put a bullet through each of your heads,* and just to prove he was serious, he shot the guard behind Henry."

Thomas stumbled. "Whoa."

"Seven died that night."

"How did you, uh… not? Die that is."

"Oliver. He'd been teaching me self-defense and drilling into my head what to do in those kinds of situations. So, I kept my eyes on his, like he'd told me to, and waited for his signal—even when the waiter dragged the knife through my skin. We both knew they didn't want me dead, or I would be."

I took in a breath, recalling that moment all too vividly.

"Even though I felt my life draining out of me, I held onto Oliver's gaze. When he gave me the nod, I picked up my feet, using all my weight to pull the waiter forward, then stood as fast as I could, slamming my head into the underside of his chin. His head snapped back, and Oliver shot him between the eyes."

We were at the backyard of the house. I couldn't believe I'd talked about this nightmare and was still standing. "I remember lying on the floor as Oliver's body covered mine, bullets ripping through the air around us. All those pink flamingos, hand painted so painstakingly, were splattered with blood, and Oliver's hands were covered in it, too. He had them tight around my throat, trying not to choke me, but desperate to save me. Without him—"

Without him I'd be dead.

Thomas was speechless. We'd stopped at the gate to the yard, and his hand was resting on the latch. He regarded me with such sadness in his eyes.

"Oliver was shot twice before Stephan took out the traffic cop, but he wasn't fast enough to save the chief of police, two politicians, an important judge, and two other guards. It's amazing that I'm alive."

"So, was this an attempted kidnapping?"

"Yes. One of many."

Thomas untied the green scarf around my neck and traced his finger down my scar. His warm hands made every nerve stand on edge. "I'm glad you're still alive," he said. "Good thing Oliver is, uh, incredibly committed."

Oliver.

So much had happened to create that bond between us. I felt a sting of tears at the thought of all he'd done for me above and beyond the call of duty. He'd offered up his life for mine so many times. I always felt like I owed him, and it took a lot to realize that owing him didn't mean marrying him.

"I need to get him back, too," I said to Thomas.

Thomas nodded, his fingers grazing my neck, thumb running over my jaw. "Both. We'll get them both back. I promise."

He reached for the latch on the gate, then stopped. Turning to face me, he lingered a moment, extending our first date under the stars. Arms around me, hot breath on my forehead, Thomas placed a feather-light kiss on my temple.

"I wish you loved me half as much as you love that other guy," he said.

Thomas took a bullet for me too. Risked his life for mine just as Oliver had. My first true friend also saved me from Ben and a breaking heart. I did love him. Most certainly. But was it partly because I felt like I owed him too?

"Thomas, I'm—" What was I? In love with him? Not in love with him? "I'm tired," I said, because anything else to come out of my mouth would have been the harmful truth or a hurtful lie.

MARLENE

12

NOT A BARBIE GIRL IN A BARBIE WORLD

I f the lady at the beauty counter told me I had great bone structure one more time, I would have ripped her spine out through her throat. She dabbed. Plucked. Dabbed some more. Applied crap out of one jar, covered that crap with more crap from another jar, and then spackled over the whole mess of crap until the birthmark covering half my face 'magically' disappeared.

I hated her.

Not because she had perfect skin, expensive clothes, and hair that could be a weapon in a zombie apocalypse, but because she was intent on making me into something I wasn't. Yes, the goal was to cover up my face to appear to look normal, but *only* for today. Only because I'd made my way into Banff and didn't want anyone to take notice of the tall girl with the western clothes and purple face. If this were a normal day, I'd stroll through these miserably busy streets and cast my best intimidating glare at anyone who looked at me, then scowl at their discomfort as they embarrassingly shrank away.

My birthmark was my superpower.

Kaya was the only person I'd met who hadn't initially been intimidated by me. Back at Mom and Dad's with a shovel in my hand in the garden, I had given her my best 'go to hell' glare. Heck, I think I might have even bared my teeth. But she barely flinched. She just stood before me, unfazed, while I stared hard enough to turn Medusa to stone. She stayed put. Stared back at me. And for some reason, I felt like she was looking at *me*—not at some poor, adopted farm girl with a birthmark covering half her face that everyone felt sorry for.

That kind of person was hard to find.

So today, for Kaya, I put a smile on my face and allowed the plastic Fembot at the makeup counter to coat me in chemicals. I even paid for her services and bought the jars of the crap. Now I just needed a living Ken doll and a pink corvette.

The disguise must have been good, too, because Kaya and Thomas didn't even recognize me.

I'd spotted him first. Thomas—impossible to miss—strikingly handsome and wearing a black wool coat that suited him, stood confidently amongst the chaos of people gawking at the Bow Springs Estate. Kaya, however, was fidgety, restless, and clearly nervous. She was slouching to make herself shorter and had a green scarf wrapped around her head to hide her hair, but I knew it was her. And that was confirmed when I got a glimpse of her hand tightly woven into Thomas'.

I was happy to see her, but I could have kicked her ass at the same time. Why on earth had she gone to the estate? So close to her nutso daddy? She had been attracting the attention of the guards as she chatted up some blonde broad with buck teeth, and when they started following her, I was forced to create a diversion. I had to summon up my deepest voice—the one I used to call the horses with—and yelled, "There she is, don't let her get away!"

Then I ran. Toward the estate, in the opposite direction of the bridge and Kaya and Thomas. I crawled under the tape, stumbled a few times for show so the out of shape cops could catch up, and barreled over ash covered ground and through a patch of brush to the towering building that looked like a castle. I got onto the driveway, laughing to myself at the absurdity of one lone girl outrunning cops and security guards, until the lights came on over my head in a blinding glare. I knew, but could not see, that there were twenty or so guns pointed at my head. So, I put my hands up.

When they realized I wasn't Kaya and assumed I was just a shoplifter scared of getting caught with a pockets full of makeup, I was tossed aside like a bikini on a nude beach. No one gave me a second thought or glanced at me and my spackled face as I sauntered back down the road, got under the police tape, and edged back into the crowd.

Except for one girl—the one with bad teeth and gaudy earrings that Kaya had been talking to. "Are you a reporter?" she'd asked, fluffing up her hair.

I was covered in soot, had twigs in my hair and was positive my jeans had shredded knees. By no means did I look like one of those polished pixies you saw on television. But I had gone *under the tape* and nobody cared. So, I straightened my back and faked a smile.

"Sure am," I said to the stupid girl and her stupid friend. "ZTLA News, Los Angeles. And you are?"

She talked. And talked. And talked. And I listened—that's what news reporters do—and that's what friends do who want to look after their stupid friends who are being hunted down because their family is messed up, and they are out stupidly wandering around in plain sight. When I had the name and number of the girl's father—someone named Dan—and was told that he was a person 'the weird scarf lady moving to London'—also known as Kaya Lowen—might contact, I breathed a sigh of relief; I had a way to find my friend, so I could kick her stupid ass.

LISA

SCRAMBLED AND FRIED

I crept downstairs to the basement, empty except for the freezer in the corner. I'd been in and out of sleep, trying to wrap my head around what had happened, and I needed to remind myself that it was true; Seth was dead.

Kicking aside boxes of thawing TV dinners, my stomach lurched. I knew what a dead body looked like. I'd been around a few—my mom, both grandparents, my dad, and my stepdad—but never someone who I had loved.

I would have given Seth everything.

And he tried to kill me.

What did that say about me? My judgement? How many men had I trusted with my heart *and* my body, only to have them both broken and beaten? I thought Seth was different. I thought he genuinely loved me, but apparently whatever Kaya was worth meant more to him than I did.

I hated to admit to myself that I'd momentarily hated her for it. Despised her. I wanted to put her pretty little head in a blender. The cowboy's, too, for fawning all over her with what was undoubtedly true love bursting from every single one of his perfect pores. Why couldn't I have someone like that? What was it about me that attracted the absolute worst men? What was it about Kaya that attracted the absolute best?

Maybe I was so desperate for love I overlooked a few things.

I put my hand on the freezer. The plastic was cold. Should I look at

Seth's face and risk the nightmares that would follow? Would I find any answers? Probably not, but I was steadying myself and lifting the lid…

He was on his side, chunks of the upstairs carpet draped over him, skin a greyish green, ice on his lashes, lips bloodless, and cheeks puffy. Unmistakably, most certainly, *dead*.

My legs threatened to give out. The room got real dark for a moment, but a tear rolling down my cheek stopped me from falling. I was so angry that all at once the floodgates opened. I hadn't cried in… well, *years*… but now I was bawling my eyes out. I cursed him, cursed the tears, cursed the entire world.

"How could you?" I said, wanting to shake him.

Of course, he didn't answer.

My past hit with brutal force: The times I'd been beaten and berated by my stepdad while my mom stood by, not caring if I lived or died. The streets, intent on sending me six feet under but still better than the abuse I got at home. The nights in jail that were safe places away from the boyfriends who were no better than my father.

But there was also Luke. Always there to pick up the pieces and glue me back together. A true friend whom I wished loved me the way I loved him—Seth had been the one to make me forget that wish.

I cried harder. For my past and for the future I would never have. My tears hit Seth's frozen cheek. On impulse, I reached to brush them away, shocked by the rock-hard feeling of his skin.

"Bastard," I spat, gagging, and reached to shut the lid.

But something caught my eye. Amidst the torn carpet pieces and stuck to a frozen splatter of blood, was a slip of paper. Seth's handwriting was distinct—the way he curled his letter 's' and hooked the bottom of his letter 't's—I would have recognized it anywhere. Peeling it away from the carpet, I slammed the lid closed and examined it closer; *2130 Georgia Street, Vancouver. Noon.*

An address and time that meant nothing to me, but I suspected meant something to Seth by the way he'd been checking his watch. I shoved the slip of paper into my pocket and headed back up the creaky stairs, careful not to wake Kaya and Thomas who were sound asleep on the couch with their coats and shoes still on. The sun was starting to come up, so I sat at the kitchen table, hoping I'd be out of tears by morning.

Kaya woke up first. After a quick glance at my puffy eyes, she pulled up a kitchen chair next to me, leaned in, and gathered me in her arms. I didn't want to be comforted, or coddled, or shown any sort of sympathy, but her embrace melted away the wall I couldn't hold up any longer. There were no lies behind her affection for me. No ulterior motives. Nothing but the simple desire to make me feel better.

I hadn't realized I'd needed that so badly.

She rubbed my back while Thomas rose, checked the bandage on his stomach, then went about clanging around in the kitchen. I was so numb and emotionally drained, all I could do was let Kaya continue to hold me.

"I'm sorry," I said against her hair.

That made her arms loosen in order for her to lean back and study my face. My eyes were so swollen I could barely see her, and my head pounded. Now I remembered why I refused to cry all these years. It made a person feel like crap.

"Sorry for what?" she asked.

I took in a breath, hoping my voice wasn't as raw as my agony. "I'm sorry for being a part of the Right Choice Group. For working with Seth, Regan—and Luke—to kidnap you. I know it was wrong, Kaya. I really do. I hope one day you'll forgive me."

She reached for a lock of my hair, toying with it for a moment, then looped it behind my ear. "We all do things sometimes that we're not proud of. I do appreciate your apology, Lisa, and I think, given the circumstances, I would have done the same." Her arms wound around me again, her hand soothing and warming my spine. "Thing is," she said quietly. "I wouldn't change anything that happened for the world. Kidnapping me saved my life. I'd still be locked up in my room right now, and I never would have met Luke. I'd go through it all again for even just one more minute with him."

Whatever Thomas was doing in the kitchen came to a crashing halt. With his shoes and coat still on, he marched out the door.

I stared after him. So did Kaya, the expression on her face unreadable. For a long while we just held each other's hands, concentrating only on breathing in and out. Then Kaya rose and went to the sink, soaked a cloth in cold water, and returned to dab it at my eyes—just like I'd done for her once.

"I'm sorry too," she said.

"For what?" I asked.

"For noticing weird things about Seth and not saying anything."

My chest. Hurt. "It wouldn't have made a difference."

Kaya nodded. "Still though… I can't believe… I—I'm just so sorry this happened to you."

The clock on the wall ticked. The sun grew brighter.

"Kaya," I dug out of my pocket the slip of paper I'd found and put it in her hand. "I found this on Seth. In the, uh… well… *downstairs*."

She shivered as her fingers brushed over the stained letters, then placed it back in my waiting hand.

"It's Seth's handwriting," I added. "I think it has something to do with you and why he kept looking at his watch. I'm going to go there and see what I can find out."

Kaya shook her head. "I don't think that's a good idea, Lisa. I have a feeling that whatever is there, can't be good. What if it just makes you feel worse?"

"I just need some sort of explanation. Anything. And really, I couldn't feel any worse."

Silence fell between us as we both eyed the bare patches of the living room rug. I felt a catch of breath in my lungs and that sting of wetness building behind my eyes again. I had to change the topic. "Ya know, Kaya, you and I are a lot alike," I said, embarrassingly sniffing and rubbing at my swollen eyes.

Her face lit up, as if it were a good thing to have some likeness to me. "In what way?"

"We both have the worst parents ever."

She tried to smile. "Oh, right."

I had the feeling she was hoping I would have said something else. "And we're both strong women," I added.

That was what she wanted. "I'm trying to be," she said, squeezing my hand.

I squeezed back. "I have realized today that tears don't make us weak. They make us human."

"Well then I'm as human as they come," she said with a smile.

I laughed. It felt strange. "Apparently, I am, too."

She threw her arms around me. She was so strange, this incredibly trusting, loyal, and stubborn girl.

"You know, you've grown, Kaya," I said after a while, realizing she was being comforting. "I can feel a change in you. Whatever went on at that ranch gave you strength. What was it? What happened there?"

Her breath caught. I could feel her body tense. "Thomas. Thomas happened there."

"Oh?" Her heart speeding up meant I'd hit a sensitive button. "Did you, uh… you know…"

Kaya's cheeks turned pink. "Technically no."

"But now you have yourself a bit of a predicament, I assume?"

Tears filled her eyes, and she nodded her head.

"So, what are you going to do?" I asked.

She slumped back in the chair, hair loose and falling around her shoulders. There was a quiver to her lower lip.

"Kaya?" I urged, reaching for her hands, holding them in mine.

"I'm in love with Luke," she said, almost defensively.

"I know. That's obvious. But… what about Thomas?"

She shivered and pulled the puffy coat tight around her chest. "I definitely feel something for Thomas too," she admitted. "It's just not as intense as the feeling I have for Luke. Oh hell, Lisa. I don't know."

"That poor cowboy is going to have his heart broken, isn't he?"

"I'm stringing him along. I know… I mean, *I know*… I will never feel for Thomas what I feel for Luke. But there is something there for sure. Something deep that I crave more of. I've been trying to deny it. Pass it off as friendship. Make excuses why I would be feeling this way. But last night when he put this ring on my finger…" She paused, holding up a glittering, fake, diamond monstrosity. "I realized that Thomas is exactly right for me. He is the perfect man offering the perfect life. He really is the one I should be with. He wasn't forced upon me. He was my *choice*. And I can't pass off what I feel for him as something it isn't any longer. This feeling that keeps wrapping itself around me that I can't break free of… At first, I thought it was just lust. I mean, he's so incredibly beautiful."

I agreed wholeheartedly with that.

"And then I compared him to Oliver." She continued. "I owed Oliver and that blurred the lines for me. I see that now. And I thought maybe I was doing the same with Thomas. But waking up next to him on the couch and letting my mind shut up and my heart just speak for itself, I know that it's love. I can't deny it, Lisa. I'm in love with him. And if it wasn't for Luke, I would run off into the sunset with Thomas and never look back."

A sharp inhale came from the kitchen and startled us both. Thomas had returned and was standing in the doorway with a carton of eggs and a loaf of bread, his eyes wide as plates. We hadn't heard him come in, but we knew by the look on his face that he'd heard our conversation.

Kaya stood, cheeks red as a tomato, and now she was the one to bolt out the door. As it slammed behind her, Thomas just stared at me in stunned silence. I could see his hands start to shake, the eggs trembling before he dropped them to the counter. I rose from the table and grabbed him by the sleeve when he motioned to go off after her.

"I know what you heard, but it doesn't change anything," I said.

He was having trouble catching his breath. "Oh, it sure does."

I dug my fingers into his coat. "If you do anything to jeopardize us getting Luke back—"

He shrugged his sleeve free of my grasp. "Never. I would never do that. I made a promise I would help her, and I won't break a promise to her ever again. You can be certain I am going to get Luke back for her even if it kills me."

My respect for the cowboy multiplied. He was a good man. If I was to be very selfish, I would want Kaya to pick him, just so Luke might consider me once again. But I wasn't going to be *that* girl, so I gave Thomas a fair warning. "In the end she will pick Luke. You know this."

His eyes were filled with determination when they centered confidently on mine. "We'll see about that."

KAYA

HALF A DOZEN OF ONE, SIX OF THE OTHER

Thomas came charging up behind me, out of breath. "Wait. Kaya, stop. Please."

There was no point running from him, where would I go? I hoped my cheeks weren't as red as the sign I'd stopped under, and I hoped he hadn't overheard everything I'd said to Lisa.

"I heard everything you said to Lisa."

I could feel the heat rise even more in my cheeks. "Great," I muttered.

"And..." Grabbing me by the shoulders, he spun me around to face him. "I'm going to make us some breakfast."

He had that sparkle in his eyes that lit up his whole face. I was suddenly very confused. "You ran after me to tell me that?"

"Well, that and you shouldn't be out in broad daylight where someone might see you. *And* the thought of you walking down the aisle toward me in a flowing white dress with a real diamond on your hand and spending the rest of my days with you and our children and our grandchildren, makes me want to pick you up and start running and never turn back. But..."

Be still my pounding heart.

The smile left his face. "But we're going to get Luke back first."

"What?" I searched his eyes to see if he was joking or teasing, but no. He was standing here, speaking the truth. "You're still going to help me? Even after knowing... knowing that—"

"Knowing that if Old Lukey Boy was out of the picture, you'd be all mine? Yes."

"Why?" I felt the tears come, choking my throat.

"Because I want you fair and square. I want you to be with me with no regrets. No what-ifs. I want you to have the opportunity to choose between me and him."

"You know who it—"

"It will be me," he said quickly.

"Thomas. No."

He lunged forward and planted his mouth firmly over mine, cutting off my protest. I had to tell him I would choose Luke. I tried to tell him. But his tongue was parting my lips and urgently seeking mine, his kiss more passionate than it had been last night. I thought I heard someone yell '*get a room*' when my hands wove into his hair. Now that I had admitted to myself how I felt for Thomas, I couldn't stop my body from responding. My mouth moved in sync with his. He was so warm, so soft, so…

NO.

Oh Lord, it was a massive effort to pull away.

"You've got to give me a chance," he said breathlessly. "That's all I want. You have my heart, Kaya, forever and always."

I was going to break his heart. "Listen, this stops now. All right?" There was a flutter in my chest. "Nothing you can do or say will change what I feel for Luke. *Nothing*. You're just catching me in moments of weakness. You must know when I'm kissing you, I'm thinking of him. When I'm lying next to you, I'm thinking of him. I'm sorry. You and I will never be anything more than, this."

I motioned to the distance between us, feeling a stab of guilt at the hurt on his face. He clenched his hands, took in a deep breath, and just when I thought he might storm away, bridged the gap between us instead and just smiled. It was that same cocky grin that I'd first encountered on his face that morning in the kitchen when I dropped the bag of flour. It completely unhinged me, knocked me off balance—and made me want to slap him at the same time. His hands were reaching for my face, and I just stood there, caught in his pearly white trajectory as his fingers trailed along my jaw and down my neck. He was setting me on fire. Rendering me helpless with his touch. The jerk knew exactly what he was doing.

"You're lying," he said, as if the words '*I want you*' were written on my forehead with a Sharpie. "That might have been the case early on, but not anymore. But you go ahead and tell yourself that if it makes you feel better."

"What would make me feel better is if you stopped hitting on me. *I'm taken.*"

He grinned madly, the desire increasing in his eyes. "Not yet you're not."

Ugh. I wanted to scream. He was exasperating. Cocky. So self-assured I felt like kicking him right in the ba—"

"So, scrambled or fried?" he asked.

I gave my head a shake. "Huh?"

"Breakfast. How would you like your eggs?"

I put my hands on my hips and warned them to stay there. "I want an omelet. Tomato and mushroom." I sounded bitchy—good.

"Your wish is my command, Princess."

"With cheese," I added.

A dog was barking from somewhere and a kid was laughing. The mountains, snow-capped and shimmering, were revealing all their glory in the clear, morning light. The air was cold and clean, and shops opening their doors sent aromas of coffee and fresh baked bread into the breeze.

"I'll make you breakfast today, and every morning for the rest of your life," Thomas said.

I gazed up at him, pretending to be exhausted with the topic, while I imagined him doing just that. Laughing with me. Going grey… kids… dogs… white picket fence… the same thing I wanted with Luke. The same thing I would *have* with Luke.

"Thomas. I am not going to choose you."

His breath caught, but only for a second. Steely determination and confidence shone in his eyes. "Yeah. You are," he said with a wink.

I had a mouthful of the most incredible omelet I'd ever eaten, either because I was starving or because watching Thomas cook made me eager for whatever his hands were working on.

"We can't stay here any longer," he said, stirring sugar into his coffee.

I still had Driver Dan's phone number in my pocket. "I might have a place to stay. That man whose daughter we met is easily bribed." I said, rubbing the fake diamond ring on my finger and wondering why I hadn't taken it off.

"And what are we going to do about Luke?" Lisa asked, barely touching her food. "It's obvious we can't just waltz in the front door and take him. Did you two figure out anything on your 'walk' last night?"

Thomas shook his head. I did the same. Somewhat embarrassed that we'd gone through all that and had come up with nothing.

"Great." Lisa couldn't hide her annoyance. "Then what about… *Seth*? We can't leave him here."

The food caught in my throat for a second. "We have to take his body to Regan… Thomas, can we fit the freezer in the back of Seth's truck?"

Thomas nodded.

Lisa pushed her plate away and headed upstairs, phone in hand. "I'll call Regan and let him know he'll be getting a delivery. Maybe he'll have some idea of what we can do about getting Luke back, since we're coming up with nothing."

She slammed a bedroom door behind her, but I was okay with her taking her frustrations out on us. What she had gone through was unimaginable. I was surprised she wasn't a puddle of muck.

Thomas stirred his coffee idly, something very heavy on his mind.

"And the house?" he asked. "What are we going to do about this place? Our prints are everywhere."

Easy answer. "We have to torch it."

Thomas gave me a nod of approval. "You're one tough cookie, aren't ya?"

I felt sick at the thought of destroying someone's property. "Burning this place down doesn't make me tough. It makes me an arsonist."

Lisa's voice, slightly muted but higher in pitch, could be heard from upstairs, and I could tell she was talking to Louisa. She was telling the child that she would come home right away and that she loved her. I was so grateful Luke's little sister had Lisa and was genuinely loved.

Thomas lifted his eyes to mine and inhaled. "You know, this could be a fresh start for you, Kaya. Think of it; all the stuff that's happened could be gone and forgotten forever. Put behind you. You burn this house down and walk away, leave Banff, leave everything, and just start over. You could come away with me and just be happy. You could choose me, and all your problems would disappear."

I stayed my temper. "Luke is *not* a *problem.*"

"Choose me, Kaya."

As if he hadn't even spoken, I lit the horrid smelling jasmine candle on the table. The newspapers scattered all over the house would ignite easily. The flames would catch curtains. Walls. I knew what I had to do, and it wasn't what Thomas so desperately wanted.

I steadied myself.

"This is what's going to happen, Thomas; Lisa will look after Seth's body and go back to Louisa and Regan. I will figure out Luke and Oliver. And you… Thomas… you will look after yourself. This will be your new beginning, not mine. You can be free of me and all this craziness, because I am officially telling you that you don't have a chance. Whatever we have beyond friendship is going to burn to the ground along with this house."

The hope in his eyes disappeared. He opened his mouth to protest, then changed his mind.

"Yep. You really are tough. Tougher than I ever imagined."

That wasn't the reaction I was expecting. "How's that?"

"I mean, hey, look at me. I've done everything right. Even took a bullet for you, and you're still choosing the other guy. You're turning down *this*…" He made a sweeping gesture down his body. "No woman has ever been able to resist me."

"Well, I must admit, it's, uh, not easy."

He gave me a smile that could have melted an iceberg. "Well, you're passing up some quality goods here, so this Luke guy must be something pretty special."

I gulped so hard it hurt. Luke was *everything.* But Thomas was everything, too.

From a safe distance we watched the fire. It started slowly, smoke snaking out from the little house, grey fingers crawling into the blue sky. When it became thick, wide plumes of black, that's when the roof burst into flames. Fire trucks arrived. Neighbors pointed and watched from across the street. Very quickly the little house was swallowed up and turned to black bones.

And I was officially a criminal.

With the freezer strapped down in the back of the truck, we parked behind a motel to say our goodbyes.

"It wasn't supposed to go this way," Lisa said, hands gripping the steering wheel, still conflicted over saving Luke or going back to Louisa. "But she was crying for me, Kaya. Sobbing. Regan couldn't do anything to get her to stop. She needs me. But Luke needs me, too. Oh God…"

I put my hand on hers. "I know. But if Luke were here, he would tell you to go to her. Above and beyond everything, he would want his little sister safe and happy *with you*. Besides, I've got this. I promise you, Lisa, no matter what, I will get Luke, and we will all be together again. In the meantime, just look after that little girl. And look after, uh, Seth. Don't leave any loose ends. We don't need his cop or biker friends sniffing around."

"Regan and I are on it. No one will ever know what happened here besides us."

"Good." I reached for the door.

Her hand caught my jacket. "If you need me—"

"I know where to find you."

We held each other's gaze for a moment. I didn't want to cry and neither did Lisa, so with a mutual nod, we parted ways.

The truck ambled off, and then it was just me and Thomas, alone in the parking lot, watching Lisa heading for the highway. I adjusted the scarf around my head, making sure it covered as much of my face as possible, hoping to hide my gut-wrenching anxiety of now having to say goodbye to Thomas.

"So, I guess this is the part where we go our separate ways," Thomas said, hands in his pockets, collar flipped up against the cold.

"Yes," I squeaked out, feeling sick. I twisted the ring off my finger and dropped it into his palm. "You are free, Thomas. You deserve to be happy. I want the best life for you." The words were like knives in my throat. I meant them, but they hurt to say.

He poked a finger at my chest, then flattened his palm against it. "You really don't think I, uh, stand a chance of winning your heart, do you?"

Those big brown eyes…I had to inch away. Dig deep. "No."

His hand fell away and the sadness that overtook him almost brought me to my knees. He swayed, then leaned in and kissed my forehead. Mouth lingering. Our hearts met and crashed together madly for one last time.

"Then this is goodbye."

All I could do was nod.

He waited. I felt the heat of his gaze but stood firm. He so desperately wanted me to stop him from leaving, but I couldn't. I had to let him go.

The weight of the world stomped on my heart.

"I love you," he whispered.

Then he turned and walked away.

Thomas… walked away.

I loved him. My heart was crumbling into pieces. I was doing the right thing…I knew I was. But it hurt. Hurt. So. Bad.

Come back, I yelled at him in my head, denying the temptation to run and throw myself into his arms. Beg him to never leave me… Because now I was alone. More alone than I'd ever been in my entire life.

The tears threatened to drown me. My feet got moving, wandering across the parking lot, to where? I had no idea. And suddenly I couldn't see through the heartache and longing for the man I had just turned away. The sobs came on uncontrollably, bringing my numb limbs to a dead stop. I tried deep breaths, but the air was too thin.

I had come to the lowest of my low.

This was agony. Sadness. Loneliness serving a most bitter bite. I was denying what was true in my heart, thinking I could just turn it off. But there was no switch for that. No easy out. I wanted Thomas in my life. As a friend. As an absolute best friend. And that feeling of loss was as crushing as if he had died.

I contemplated going and hanging out with Ed under the bridge.

A hand clamped down on my shoulder. Thomas's voice, full and deep and breathless, stroked my ears.

"I can't leave you. Not yet…" he said.

He was crying, too. His trembling hands reached for mine. Through tears, he was putting the fake ring back on my finger. "Even if I can't have you the way that I want, I need your friendship. I need you in my life. So, if it's cool with you, I'm going to stick around for a while. I'm not ready to say goodbye."

I nodded eagerly, wanting desperately to make us work somehow.

"And besides, I made a promise to you, remember?" his voice broke. "This time I am going to keep it."

I collapsed against his lean body, feeling his heart thumping in his chest. Nothing could have loosened the grip I had on him; I wasn't ready to say goodbye, either.

"Oh, Kaya," he said, holding me as tightly as I was holding him. "You don't know what you've done to me."

"I wasn't thinking of someone else," I said, unable to stop this bit of truth from bursting out.

I felt his body tense. "What?"

"At the coffee shop. In the store doorway. This morning on the couch, and then on the street corner… I wasn't imagining you were someone else. I just wanted you to know that."

He pulled in a lungful of air, touched his nose to mine, and held my gaze. "I know. That's why I'm standing here."

Stephan

LAST OF NINE

This was the eighth time I'd cheated death. Was there a number nine in my dog-eared deck of cards? Probably not. Even though my strength was back and the ointment the Labcoats had applied to my burns sped up the healing immensely, I was half the man I used to be. I felt vulnerable, even with the makeshift weapon in my hand.

"Remember what I told you?" I asked Davis.

He nodded, having been silent since Oliver left. Not even when I handed him a syringe with a foot-long needle and instructed him where to jab it to kill someone, did he speak. He just sat on the edge of his cot staring at the iron bars, chewing his fingernails. I hoped that when the time came, he would spring to life.

The cell walls were damp and oozing with the ghostly voices of past occupants, but the others were silent. Sindra was silent, too. We waited for the purple-haired girl, while hoping for anyone other than the purple-haired girl.

But hours drifted off into the abyss, and no one came. The usual check-in time passed, and passed again, and then so did the next. It seemed like once the guards had discovered Luke was missing, we'd been completely forgotten.

I kept dozing off, and the scalpel behind my back kept falling out of my hand. The ghosts were sleeping now too, and Davis was snoring—until the sound of footsteps in the stairwell jolted us all upright.

"Remember," I said to Davis, words coming out in a tangled rush.

"Don't kill the guards unless you have to. The Labcoats, though, are fair game."

Davis tensed like a cat about to pounce. The door knob turned. I readied the blade behind my back.

Into the hallway came a maid, and I recognized her at once; Ella. Young and meek, shoulders rounded, and a very childlike face that matched her petite body. Dammit. What was she doing down here? Where were the Labcoats? A guard followed her in, beefy and intimidating with an unreadable expression. He stopped a few feet behind her, eyes darting once at the others on his right, and then to me and Davis on his left. He was young. Maybe only twenty. The adrenalin surging through my blood stopped and curdled into a sick sludge; there was no way I could hurt the maid or this young guard. Davis eyed me, sharing the same dilemma.

Ella set down the dinner tray she was carrying and slipped it under the bars, nudging it gently toward us with her foot. When her eyes met mine, she shuddered. I couldn't imagine what I looked like, but now I knew that it wasn't good.

"I would bring your dinner in for you, but I was not given a key. I hope you enjoy your meal," she said nervously. "It's compliments of the chef."

She turned to leave. Was there no food for the others?

"Wait…" I was about to say her name, but thought better of it. "What's going on with—"

She spun around to face me, eyes darting up and to the left only for a second, but I understood; a camera had been placed in the hall. There was nothing more she could say.

"What's going on with the, uh, bread?" I said, feigning anger. "I said no butter on it!"

"*Oh.* Sorry," she said sweetly. "I'll tell the chef to be more careful next time."

The guard faced me, and I was shocked when his gaze held. "They won't get away with it again," he said, voice rippling with rage.

My heart skipped a beat; he was referring to Henry. To the torturing. To the inhumane treatment of the people stuck down here in the cells. Disgust was all over this guard's face until he reined it in, and his subtle nod at my understanding almost made my knees buckle in relief. Not all Lowen security guards were brainwashed or easily bought. Some still had morals. He was one of the good ones.

Ella and the guard headed for the stairs, past the quietly suffering group of souls locked up in the cell across from us. When they were gone, I practically lunged for the supper tray. *Compliments of the chef* was not lost on me. I'd been putting in strange food orders, hoping to signal William somehow that I wasn't killed in the security room fire. Every meal was exactly what I'd asked for, so I was fairly sure it was William cooking because nobody made risotto the way he did. If tonight's dinner was three poached eggs with tomato relish and creamed spinach—what I'd requested—then my message wasn't getting through because I *hated* spinach. In fact, if the purple-haired girl really wanted to torture me, she could have done away with the whip and pliers and force fed me some of that dirt-tasting, Popeye-touting garbage.

I lifted the plastic dome off the plate. There before me, were three poached eggs with tomato relish, and mashed potatoes with mushroom gravy. No. Flippin. Spinach.

William knew I was here.

And to confirm it, there was a note, wrapped neatly in plastic and placed under one of the eggs. I almost fainted at the sight of his beautiful hand writing.

> *I know where you are. Working on a plan. If you get out before I can rescue you, get to the south kitchen. Refrigeration room seven is disabled and in it is everything you need. You'll be safe there, I promise.*
>
> *Be careful, my love—W*

A key for the refrigeration room was at the bottom of the mashed potatoes, and the best meal I'd ever eaten was nourishing, tasty, and full of hope.

For hours we rested. Davis remained on the edge of his bed with the massive needle in his hands. The scalpel I'd planned to use had never left mine. When the stairwell creaked again, we were ready.

Two Labcoats were followed by the young guard that had accompanied Ella. They had come to check my burns and administer injections for healing. I recognized the first Labcoat by his smell; cheap, spicy cologne mixed with unmanageable body odor and chronic garlic breath. And I remembered him laughing when The Girl pulled off my fingernails—he thought it was rather funny—and I had gagged on his odor in between screams. The second Labcoat was more robot than man. His eyes were soulless, blank discs, and he never uttered a word or flinched no matter what horrors unfolded around him.

It was all I could do to remain calm, heart beating out of my chest. When the key finally made its way into the lock and the bars slid to the side, I could barely breathe. The guard entered first, stun gun in his hands—with the power off. His eyes met mine, and we exchanged a subtle nod.

The Labcoats followed, and before I could even give Davis the cue, he was springing from his bed at them. Acting for the cameras, I lunged at the guard and hit him as realistically as I could, grateful when he stumbled backward and pretended to fall unconscious. Although fake, it undoubtedly was a boost to my masculinity.

"*Stay down,*" I whispered to him, then turned to help Davis.

But my help wasn't needed.

At all.

Davis was unleashing a fury on the two Labcoats that left me with no choice but to get out of his way. Rage and revenge exploded from him as he violently stabbed and slashed at both men, backing them into a corner. Blood splattered as they tried to defend themselves, both dropping to the floor as Davis dropped the needle and reached for a pair of needle nose pliers.

"Stop it, Davis," I said firmly, horrified by what he was doing.

His arm pummeled up and down in a brutal rage. The Labcoats weren't squirming anymore. Their gurgling had stopped. But Davis kept stabbing.

"Stop it, Davis," I repeated.

He was manic. Tears spilled silently down his cheeks.

"Davis… they're dead."

Chest heaving, he finally dropped the pliers, and a grim shade of satisfaction came over his face. He stepped back, every vein in his arms and neck bulging, chest heaving, and for a moment I feared for my own safety.

"Let's get out of here now, all right?" I said softly.

Davis took in a deep breath, not displaying any regret over what he had done, and I suspected if I wasn't here, he would continue. The white T-shirt stretched over him was soaked with sweat and the Labcoat's blood.

His feet were bare, but he didn't flinch when he stepped on a shard of broken glass. The instability in his eyes was absolutely frightening, and I warily watched him pick up the ring of keys that had fallen to the ground.

"Ready?" I asked, stepping into the hall.

"Sindra," was all he said, and he was charging toward the room we'd heard her screaming from, frantically trying keys in the lock until one clicked.

When the door opened, it brought me to my knees; there she was. Chained to the wall. Beaten and bloody and covered in cuts and welts from the whip. Her hair had been shaved off and she was dressed only in black and blue bruises that covered her thighs and torso. Her eyes were open, but they were distant and unfocused. The glorious and revered Sindra had been broken, and I wondered by the mess of her if she even had any hours left in her life. She barely registered it when Davis removed her shackles and she fell into his arms. I grabbed a coat from a hook and together we maneuvered her into the sleeves while she moaned in pain.

"Davis?" she croaked, eyelids fluttering as she drifted in and out of consciousness.

He scooped her up into his arms. "It will be all right," he said, voice tight. "I'm getting you out of here. You're safe now."

In moments, whoever was in the security room would see us on camera and there would be no escaping. Davis stood still, staring down at Sindra in his arms as if he'd forgotten what we were doing.

"Davis, we have to hurry," I urged.

He shook his head then bolted from the room. We passed the others in the hallway as we made our way back to the stairwell. I tossed them the keys and the scalpel that was still in my shaking hand.

"You shouldn't have done that," Davis said darkly as we headed up the stairs. "They don't *want* out. They want to die."

I was about to ask why but changed my mind when I could hear muffled screams followed by the thud of bodies falling to the floor.

No amount of scotch was going to make me forget this day.

LUKE

16

OUT OF THE CELLAR

Oliver was certain that this time we'd have a way out of the laundry room, and I had to admit, I admired his positivity.

We were on the last of six stairwells that led up to various sections and floors of the estate, all barricaded and boarded up at the bottom and the top. Our hands were bloodied and swollen from prying away boards and bricks, and legs tired from climbing God knows how many flights of stairs. At the top of each, we'd been met with a wall of solid concrete. This stairwell was our last hope.

The vending machine was almost out of food, the remaining pop was warm and making nasty sweaters on our teeth, and neither of us had slept at all. Whether it was day or night or one day or the next, it was impossible to tell. Exhaustion was getting the better of me. Oliver too, obvious by the increasing hunch in his broad shoulders and the short answers to my questions.

"Why so many entrances?" I asked, willing one foot in front of the other and drawing in a lungful of damp, musty air. *One step, two steps… fifty steps…*

"Big building," he said breathlessly.

"The laundry chute… I don't think it will hold our weight if we have to climb it."

Oliver was struggling. "It won't."

"So, if this stairwell ends with another concrete wall, we're screwed."

"Thanks for pointing that out, Captain Obvious."

We must have been somewhere around the third or fourth floor, and I felt a burst of energy when I could see a sheet of plywood covering the exit at the top and not a cement wall. There was the faint echo of footsteps behind it too, and voices, muffled but encouraging.

Oliver collapsed behind me while I wondered what was on the other side; a hallway? One of many ballrooms? A guest suite? Henry Lowen's office? I was filled with even more energy at the thought of running into *him*. Getting my hands around his neck would be so satisfying.

Painstakingly stabbing at the plywood with a butter knife I'd found in the break room, I worked at trying to make a hole big enough to see through. I felt crazed wondering where Kaya was, worrying about her so intensely that I didn't notice the floor shake with approaching footsteps.

"Be quiet, Luke," Oliver warned.

I held still. Many guards marched past. I even heard the swish of their swinging arms.

"They're patrolling," Oliver wheezed.

I sat back on my heels, the tiny hole in the plywood staring at me like the light at the end of the tunnel. When it was quiet, I got back to work, ignoring stinging blisters and the uncontrollable shaking of my arms. Either the lack of food and sleep or the lingering pain of my healing wounds had made me weak. When the knife slipped from my grasp, Oliver snatched it up without second thought.

More footsteps. We waited. We remained quiet. And when there was only the sound of our heavy breathing, he took over, shaving and slicing off hunks of plywood while sweat dripped into his eyes. When he faltered, I took the knife, putting my shoulders and back into it, using my body weight as leverage because the strength in my hands was failing. When we finally had a hole a few inches across, I wrenched my fingertips in and pulled off a foot-wide strip—only to find a wall of stone.

Oliver sighed so heavily I thought he'd never catch another breath.

"This is fine, Oliver," I said, taking on the positive role now. "At least it's not cement. We can get through this."

"Yah," he muttered bitterly.

"Really, if we can get a few pieces loose, we can at least see what we're dealing with."

"I just… I know where this wall is, Luke. And we couldn't be breaking through in a worse spot."

He drew in a long breath, but it seemed to be an effort for him. His dark skin seemed grey, like it did in that hotel room when he was going through withdrawal.

"You don't look so good," I said.

"Tired," he muttered.

I pulled away some more plywood then started picking at the mortar. The dull knife was frustrating and slow going, and I had to stop when I heard another rush of footsteps.

"This is going to take forever," I said, my hair soaked against my cheeks. "We need better tools."

Oliver's reply was a cough. He covered his mouth and his eyes began to water madly as his chest heaved violently. More footsteps were approaching.

"Dammit, they'll hear you," I said, dropping the knife and reaching for him. "Quick, get downstairs."

He clung to the railing as I followed him back down to the laundry room, cough growing louder and more aggressive. I was half worried he might hack up a lung and half worried he might take the fast way to the bottom if his feet gave out, so I kept a grip on him. Guided him through the long hallway of spider web-covered laundry machines and shelves of linens. I was relieved to get him to the break room and onto the makeshift bed.

"I'm fine," he said, closing his eyes.

He wasn't. "I know," I said, patting his shoulder. "You just need to rest."

He didn't object.

I wrestled open a pop and held it out to him, my hands shaking harder and leaving my own trail of blood from broken blisters all over the place. I stumbled and realized I needed rest, too.

"We have to have our wits about us once we get through that wall," I said, falling into a creaky chair.

Oliver was already asleep.

I finished some flat root beer, scarfed back some stale chips, and stretched out next to him on my stomach, letting the wounds on my back breathe. I closed my eyes. I thought of Kaya, dreamed of her. On a beach. Her pink painted toes. Stretched out on the sand next to me with sunlight dancing in her eyes... Then I dreamed of all the ways I could make Henry

Lowen suffer for what he'd done.

Persistence and luck helped coax away enough stone to reveal the backside of a piece of furniture. Oliver and I made a hole big enough to fit through, then pushed an armoire, massive and ancient, out of the way. It screeched across the marble floor, thankfully not toppling over, and we crawled out from behind it into a dark hall.

The air was much better here. Cool. Clean. *Rich*. I breathed deep as I took in my surroundings; it seemed I had stepped back in time. Medieval and dim, a cavernous hallway was lined with flat stone and gold framed portraits lit by the orange glow of gas burning lamps. There were no windows. No doors. Only stairs at each end—one set winding up, the other twisting down.

"Which way?" My voice sounded too loud.

Oliver shoved the armoire back against the hole while I kept watch. "Left."

I followed him and almost collided with his backside when he spun around and headed in the opposite direction. "Nope, right."

"Ya sure?" I asked.

He sighed. "Nope."

"Ah, that's comforting. I thought you knew this place."

"So did I. Now stop yammering and let me think, Golden Boy."

"I hate that nickname," I muttered, following him down the stairs and into a room of antiques covered in thick layers of dust. Worn, blood-red carpet led us from there into another hall, this one lined with many doors and silvery grey brick walls. At the approach of chattering maids, we slipped into a dark alcove that covered a now boarded-up public wash-room. There, we waited. Held our breath as four vacant-eyed guards marched by, then a man with a cart, then four more guards… and it seemed like we would be waiting for hours when another stream of people rushed past. So when the coast was clear, we bolted, only to slow and creep along a dimly-lit wall until it opened and overlooked one of the many ballrooms. Below was a vast and opulent space with what was either the sunrise, or the sunset, sneaking in around thick velvet drapes. Oliver seemed flustered, his hand running over his cropped hair, eyes darting about nervously as he peered between the rungs of the railing we'd hunched in front of.

"This is *not* a good place to be," he said.

As if on cue, the unmistakable stride of a man below us moving with purpose echoed and shook the room, the heels of his shoes striking the marble floor and black glossy hair matching their shine. I blinked, crouched lower next to Oliver, and felt my pulse race; there, hands sparkling with diamonds and wearing an immaculate three-piece suit, was Henry.

Every part of me was consumed instantly with rage and hatred. The desire to leap over the balcony and crush him with my bare hands was so intense I saw red. I was standing again.

And then I wasn't.

"If you move one more inch, I'll kill you myself," Oliver hissed.

He'd gotten a hold of the back of my pants and yanked me to the floor.

"That's his office," Oliver whispered.

Henry was heading toward a doorway where a guard in the standard issue camo garb stood waiting, semi-automatic assault rifle slung over his shoulder.

"You've got one more hour, and one hour only!" Henry roared at him.

The guard, stocky and wide, stood his ground, not flinching.

"Have all the guest rooms been checked?" Henry asked.

"Yes, sir. Twice. Every room in this building and the North Section has been thoroughly searched. All boarded-up spaces as well. Every nook and cranny, inside and out—kitchens, pool area—no rock has been left unturned. There is no sign of them anywhere."

"Well, we know they're still here!" Henry was yelling now. "Oliver got *in. So, where the hell is he?"*

The guard kept his composure. Oliver, however, couldn't hide the slight smile pulling at the corners of his mouth; apparently, seeing Henry upset pleased him, too.

"We will find them," the guard replied.

Henry paced a moment, eyes cast downward, pinching the bridge of his nose. "When you do, Oliver gets returned to me alive and unharmed. Understand?"

The guard must have nodded because there was no audible reply, just the sound of the wind whipping around outside, hammering against the windows with a fury that matched Henry's.

"But kill the rest. Sindra, Davis, Stephan—when you find them, get rid of them. And Mr. Luke Ravelle—save me some recognizable pieces to send my daughter."

Oliver tapped my shoulder and pointed up; a camera aimed on the ballroom was now swiveling in our direction. We crept off the balcony and back into the safety of yet another long hall, stopping at a gate that blocked us from going any farther.

"Let's hope they haven't changed the codes," Oliver muttered.

I half expected sirens and red flashing lights to alert everyone in the estate where we were when he entered a series of numbers on a keypad— but the gate swung open easily and we passed through. Then we were ducking behind ornate pillars of marble, grateful for the shoddy lighting, moving up more stairs, hearts beating and sweating bullets.

"Why are all the windows painted black?" I asked, feeling desperate somehow for any clue to the time of day.

"I dunno. This is new."

Dodging cameras and hugging the walls, every door we passed was locked, every window completely sealed and covered. When we came to yet another gate—beyond it a corridor with a thick worn carpet leading to a leather couch—I knew exactly where we were.

"Kaya's room?" I said.

Oliver nodded. "No key required. It's the only room with a digital code like the gates."

"Are you sure this is a good idea? I mean, isn't this the first place they'll search?"

Oliver was through the gate and locking it back in place. "You heard that guard, they've already checked everywhere. It should be fine."

I wasn't sure if Oliver was thinking straight. I had the feeling that he was so used to being here it was giving him a false sense of security. With all the technology Henry had—gates in the halls, cameras, digital codes— you'd think he would have some sort of trap laid. I mean, wouldn't they expect Oliver to use the codes? Wouldn't they have changed them?

"You've got a guy in security on your side," I said.

"I think so," Oliver replied, distracted, heading toward Kaya's room.

He's done this a thousand times, I thought as I watched him quickly punch in a set of numbers and push open the door. He strode into the room and all at once his shoulders folded, breath catching with a gasp. A handful of shells and pretty stones had caught his eye, and he picked them up off a bench where they had been set down next to a pink jacket. He closed his eyes.

"They were, are… hers?" I asked.

My voice seemed to startle him. "Yeah. Every time we went for a run, she had to fill her pockets. I gave her heck the last time. Told her it was unnecessary. But she saw beauty in things that I never did." Oliver set the shells and stones down, carefully, and a rush of turmoil overtook his features. He strolled into the middle of the room where the faintest scent of men's cologne lingered and a half-full bottle of scotch was parked in front of a fireplace.

It was easy to forget that Oliver loved Kaya as much as I did. Easy to forget that he was suffering from heart ache. You don't fall out of love with someone because they don't want you anymore, you just find a way to deal with it—I wasn't sure if Oliver had dealt with it.

"We need to find Stephan," I said, hoping to keep him focused. "It doesn't sound like he's on Henry's Christmas card list. Me neither since he's requested I be chopped into pieces. But, bonus for you, at least you're wanted alive."

"Yeah. Well, we both know why that is," Oliver grumbled. "He wants to use me to manipulate Kaya again. He still thinks he has control over my mind. He still needs me to get her—"

He didn't say the word pregnant because it caught in his throat and held there. We'd gotten to know each other, Oliver and I, but that was one thing that was not discussed. Ever. The thought of his hands on her, exploring the most private details of her body, knowing her the way I so desperately wanted to… made me completely crazy.

I had to stay calm. Breathe. "You're in control of your mind now, Oliver. We're going to get out of here, get Kaya somewhere safe, then do whatever we can to stop Henry Lowen from ever hurting another person."

Oliver wasn't listening. He was bee-lining to the scotch with blinders on, not wanting to look around the room at the countless memories I could tell were being awakened in him. He put the bottle to his lips and drank heartily.

I went on, mostly talking to keep myself together. "We need to find clothes so we can blend in. Get some of those camo getups the guards are wearing. You must have a stash of stuff in here, Oliver. And there must be some food somewhere."

I let my voice trail off. Oliver was staring at the thick drapes covering the window. "This place really is a fucking prison," he said dismally.

I crossed the room, gently taking the bottle from his hands.

"Yes. It is," I agreed.

"Why didn't I see that?" he said, his tone thick with guilt and sadness. "Why did I think this was okay? Hell Luke, I wanted to marry her, to keep her here. I took advantage of a young girl who depended on me for her safety, and I thought it was okay because I *loved* her. What on earth was wrong with me? What have I done?"

I took a swig of the scotch, silently agreeing with his every word.

"I went along with it," Oliver continued. "With everything. Good Lord, I didn't give her one second of freedom. Not even in her own bed."

His gaze travelled to the door nestled beside the bookcase. It was there Kaya had slept. I gulped down a queasy feeling—and it wasn't from the scotch. Oliver was shaking now, his chest rising and falling, hands balled into fists. His eyes met mine for a moment, and they were about to spill over.

"This whole time, she wasn't safe… *from me*," he choked out. "I was just as bad as her father. I should have… I should have known better."

The big lug fell to the floor with a thud. Down on his knees he went, body slumped forward as he cradled his head in his hands. Was he crying? Oh, dear Lord, please no. I could handle angry Oliver, jealous Oliver, sick and vomiting Oliver, but not this.

Man. I really wished I hated him.

Oliver sniffed, rubbing irritably at his nose. "I should have taken her away, like she wanted. She begged me to take her away, but I was too loyal to Henry. If I would have listened to her, opened my eyes to what was going on, we wouldn't be in this mess. We wouldn't be… she would —Oh my God."

I took another swig. "Oh, shut up," I said. "No more 'coulda, shoulda, woulda' from you. What's done, is done. It's blatantly obvious that you realize your mistakes and have learned from them. So, time to forgive yourself, all right? I mean listen, we've both screwed up. Done stupid things. Heck, Oliver, after my mother committed suicide, I ended up selling drugs and moving in with a child abuser, which resulted in having my little sister hurt and taken from me. Then I kidnapped a girl. Do you hear me, knucklehead? *Kidnapped a girl.* So, we're both guilty of doing wrong. But I know Kaya understands why we did the things we did. I have to believe that in my heart or I might as well just lie down on the floor next to your pitiful face and drown myself in scotch."

With an eyebrow arched and a stunned expression, Oliver's pity party ended instantly. He nodded toward the bottle in my hands.

"Didn't you used to have a drinking problem?" he asked.

The sip I was about to take never made it to my lips. Instead I thrust out my hand to pull Oliver to his feet and handed him back the scotch. My mouth and racing mind were watering for more of the liquid fire that turned my insides out and numbed my emotions. But I needed my wits about me and booze wouldn't help. It sure hadn't in the past anyway.

"Thanks," he said shaking off his meltdown and capping the bottle.

"That's what friends are for."

Oliver cleared his throat. "Apparently you are. One. Err, friend. I guess."

I had to laugh. "So, what now, *bestie*?"

Oliver huffed. "I tell you what. I won't call you Golden Boy, and you don't call me Bestie. Ever again. Never. Ever."

I had to laugh. "Got it."

Now we were both staring at the curtains.

"Day or night?" Oliver asked.

There wasn't the slightest suggestion of either, and I feverishly hoped these windows weren't painted over, too. "Are we putting money on it?"

"I have none," he said.

"Have you ever had any?"

"Nope."

"Have you even had any other girlfriend besides Kaya?" I asked.

He seemed uncomfortable. "Uh, no."

"Any other job?"

Oliver shook his head. "What does this have to do with the time of day?"

I shrugged. "Just makes me understand you a little better."

Oliver cleared his throat. "You don't gotta understand nothing but this; if it's day, you shower first. If it's night, I shower first *and* get first dibs on the stash of granola bars in the mini fridge, and you don't judge me when I get to the bottom of that scotch afterward. And—"

"Oh c'mon, Oliver."

"—and I get the couch. You get the bed."

The thought of sleep buckled my knees. The thought of sleeping in Kaya's bed made my mouth go dry. "Fine."

Oliver reached for the heavy velvet drapes, pulling them aside just a bit, enough to see the glare from the light inside the room hitting the window—and the shadow of the heavy iron bars behind them. We both gulped; it really was a prison.

"All dark," Oliver said, uncapping the scotch. "No sun. No stars either."

KAYA

17

SWEET ESCAPE

We'd interrupted Dan binge-watching *Game of Thrones,* so he was already irritated when he answered the door, then completely horrified when he recognized my face.

"Good Lord, child," he said, anxiously scanning the towering trees and the long stretch of empty road behind us. "It's after midnight. What are ya doin' here?"

He didn't invite me and Thomas in, or bother with formalities. He just stared at me—his ex-boss's very wanted daughter—like I was the one on television killing a dragon.

"I need your help," I said, snow falling on my shoulders, shivering, feet soaking wet from walking all day. Dan's log house on the outskirts of town hadn't been easy to find or get to. Perched on a steep incline with a backyard stretching up the side of a mountain, his home was remote and nicer than I'd expected. When he finally did invite us in, the warmth and coziness of it began to soothe my frayed nerves.

"Anyone see you come here?" Dan asked, rubbing his bald head, slipping a dead bolt in place behind us.

"No. I swear."

"The police have been here, and your dad's men, and your dad himself. All was askin' about you. Digging through my house and turning over everythin'. Whatcha gone and done, Miss Lowen? Got yerself in a whole mess of trouble, have ya?"

I could see a couch in his quaint living room, thick and inviting, with popcorn on the table next to it. It was all I could do to continue standing in the threshold of his home and not make a beeline for it. I felt oddly hot and cold and a deep shiver kept rolling up and down my spine.

"Miss Lowen?"

"The only thing I'm guilty of is not wanting to go back to my cage," I said, badly needing to sit down.

Thomas's hand pressed against the small of my back, steadying me as he spoke. "We mostly just need a place to rest for a while. It's been a long day. We would be so incredibly grateful for your help."

I could hear the fatigue in Thomas' words, but I leaned into him anyway, sighing with relief when his arm stretched across my back and pulled me tight. He was holding me up.

Dan sucked on his teeth and adjusted the waistband of his flannel pajamas. Making the decision to let us in was hard for him. "You know, I always thought it ain't no way for a kid to live. Cooped up like that. Like you is. You got no public schoolin', or friends, or nothing that kids should have. It ain't done ya much good now, has it?"

"No." I agreed.

He ushered us into his home, and I could have fallen over with relief. My socks made wet prints across the floor to his kitchen table. He asked us to sit while he started a pot of coffee. Then, he locked every door and covered every window. When he joined us, so did a box of Oreos that tasted so good I thought I'd died and gone to cookie heaven.

"So, why is yer daddy so hell bent on rippin' the town apart to find ya?" Dan asked, stirring his coffee... and stirring and stirring... "How on earth did you find me?"

My head spun with every turn of his spoon; I was mesmerized by the movement.

"Kaya," Thomas prompted, watching me with concern before gesturing at the fourth cookie I'd taken but only mangled into a crumbling mess and forgotten to eat. "Dan asked you something."

"Oh. Sorry. Yeah, Georgia," I said, meeting Dan's curious stare. "Your daughter. I recognized the earrings she was wearing. The ones I gave you the night you snuck me out to the Derrick bar. And as for my dad, he's just an asshole. It's all about money. Always has been. You know that, Dan."

"Hmmm. But he's got a real bee in his bonnet. Something's under his skin, and it's more than a couple of bucks."

"Yeah. Because I'm worth a billion of those bucks," I said flatly.

Dan turned white, then pink, then red, then shoved an entire cookie in his mouth.

"I need you to hide me. Please. I have nowhere to go," I said.

Dan munched and took a very long time to swallow. Then he shook his bald head. "Can't do that. Sorry, Miss Lowen."

Thomas wearily put down his coffee. "Every hotel and motel in town is under watch. We have nowhere to go."

The glasses Dan was wearing made his eyes bigger. Like a fish. Bulging. Like a fish squirming on a hook, caught and dangling… spinning… squirming… I had to look away, at anything else.

"Do you know what would happen to me if I got caught hiding her?" Dan said, jutting his chin in my direction. "I gots three kids to care fer, and all I know how to do is drive for a livin'. I went from being a well-paid limo driver to pizza delivery man. Henry ruined me the last time I helped her, and heaven knows he don't give second chances. So I'm sorry, but you folks is on yer own."

"I can pay you." My words flopped all over the table, lighting up Dan's fish-bulging eyeballs. "My jewelry bought you this house. Imagine what my cold hard cash could do."

Dan pushed his glasses farther up his nose. "Keep talkin'."

"When I turn twenty-one, I will inherit—"

"Whoa there," he put up his hands to cut me off and was shaking his head again. "That's a long way away."

I struggled to remain calm and upright. "Not really."

"Uh, I'm sorry, Miss Kaya. I can't risk it. Now, finish up yer coffee, and I'll make ya a couple of sandwiches for the road. Ya best be on yer way. It could be worse than losing my job if yer daddy finds you here. The only reason I'm still livin' after that Derrick incident is because I have history with him."

My heart sank. Thomas reached over and put his hand on mine, but I had to pull away—his affection and understanding would only encourage the tears behind my eyes. Also, his hands were so cold. Like ice. It didn't mix well with the strange unsteadiness and odd thickness in my head. Cloudy vision was making my temples throb. It made me question what I was seeing when a figure appeared in the kitchen doorway and pointed in my direction.

"You're that girl I gave Dad's address to."

I blinked hard—floral pajamas, messy blonde curls, piercing brown eyes puffy with sleep, and bad teeth.

"Hi, Georgia," I said, struggling with my tongue.

Crossing her arms over her chest, she glared. "You tricked me. You're not here to give away squat."

No point lying. We couldn't stay here anyway. "Yes. And I'm sorry. I'm desperately in need of some help, and your father was the only person I could think to ask."

Dan sat back and crossed his arms over his chest, too. "Uh Georgia, this is Kaya Lowen," he said.

Georgia rolled her eyes. "Yeah, Dad, I kinda figured that out from listening to the entire conversation through these paper-thin walls. Thought she'd look different, though." My ratty appearance was assessed and then Thomas received the once over, too. "And who are you?"

Thomas absently dragged a hand through his hair. "The name is Thomas. I'm Kaya's uh, friend."

Georgia's piercing gaze returned to me. "So, you're the one they say is locked up all the time at the estate and never allowed out?"

"*They* are correct—whoever they are."

"You have bodyguards?"

"*Had*," I corrected.

"And one of them was Oliver, right?" There was a shift in her eyes at the mention of his name.

"Yes."

"And you're runnin' away?"

I couldn't help but sigh. "I'm trying to."

"Huh," Georgia said. Her eyes stayed fixed on my face. "I'm eighteen. Same age as you... You know, some people around here think you don't really exist, but I knew you did because Dad told me about you. Are you running away because you've got it bad there?"

I took in the cozy house with family pictures everywhere, drawings and notes pasted to the cupboards, counter laden with cookies and fruits, and I imagined that Georgia had a fairly good upbringing with her single dad.

"There's a bit more to it than that," I said, swallowing back the sudden desire to tell her everything—that my mother was a monster and now dead, that I killed a man, that Ben died because of me and that the refriger-ator in this kitchen seemed too loud… and didn't Gwen Stefani have a song about a refrigerator? *Sweet Escape*? "Let's just say that if I get taken back to the estate, I will have to kill myself before I turn twenty-one."

Dan cleared his throat. Thomas choked on his coffee. Georgia just stared, eyes laser focused as if peering into my mind. "Why is that?"

"Money. Power. Both falling into the hands of those who will abuse it and use it to hurt people."

Thomas gulped hard.

Dan regained his composure and rolled his shoulders. "Sorry you're in this predicament, Miss Lowen, but I can't help you."

Georgia turned on her father. "What? That's all you have to say, Dad? Did you not hear what she just told you?"

"Shush now, Georgia," Dan said. "They're leavin'. We don't want no trouble from Henry."

To my shock, Georgia shook her head of curls, rounded the table, and came to stand behind me. Her lemon-scented hand clamped down on my shoulder.

"No, Dad. My bedtime stories used to be about this girl's life and how she was treated like some piece of property. She's no different than me, ya know. Remember how you always used to say that you'd like to bring her home 'cause you felt sorry for her?"

Dan shifted nervously in his chair. "That was years ago."

"Well, the only thing that's changed over the years around here is money, and from what I recall, she's the reason we have this house and why Jeremy and Leah were able to go off to college. It hasn't changed who we are. We have to help her."

Georgia remained behind me, hand not budging from my shoulder, staring her father down, and although it was clear Dan didn't agree with her, his face was beaming with pride when she spoke.

"We are going to do the right thing," Georgia said. "She can have Leah's bedroom for as long as she wants. It's the least we can do."

Dan sighed heavily, but eventually he nodded his head in agreement.

Georgia victoriously clapped her hands like we were about to have a slumber party and braid each other's hair.

"Thank you, so much," I said, wondering why my throat felt like I'd swallowed shards of glass, and why Georgia's blonde curls were swirling now too, winding and dangling from her head like little staircases leading to her scalp… the spoon in the coffee… the refrigerator singing…

Thomas stood from the table. He thrust his hand out to Georgia, took it firmly and sandwiched her petite palm between his. "Thank you so much," he said.

Georgia melted. Her pink lips struggled to stay over her bad teeth. She started talking about sandwiches… what kind would Thomas like? She thought he looked hungry. I heard her ask me something, but the loud refrigerator had turned everything to mud in my ears. I was fading, resisting the urge to put my head down on the table and nod off. It was now one-thirty in the morning according to the clock above the stove. I stared at the second hand, imagining the noise it was making… tick… tick… tick… like a horse's gait. Hooves in the snow. Ben… Ben had died. I'd shot a man in the barn. I'd let Luke believe I didn't love him. I'd taken solace in Thomas's arms for my own selfish needs. I was…

"Kaya?"

Thomas's hand over mine was so cold it hurt, but it anchored me to the table while my body seemed to slide off the chair. I heard him mumble something about needing rest, and I didn't resist when his arms moved under me. I felt strange. Hot and cold at the same time. Stomach queasy now too and swallowing really hurt.

"Good Lord, she's burning up," I heard Georgia say with a rushed and urgent tone. Was her hand on my forehead?

Voices. Swirling blonde curls. Cookies… the fridge yelling now… and I was in Thomas' arms, moving past school portraits of Georgia and her siblings on the walls when Thomas released me onto a soft bed. "Was there something in that coffee?" I heard myself ask. "I feel weird."

And then, nothing made sense.

18

SAY MY NAME

I couldn't tell if I was dreaming or awake.

There was a storm in my head, icy gusts of semi-consciousness making my heart jump out of my chest. I was dragging my feet, trying to outrun it, only to dig a trench with my toes and move deep into an odd darkness. I seemed to stay there a long while, until Thomas lifted me up and into a room cast in golden light. His voice, soothing and kind, melted the ice clinging to my skin and brought lavender painted walls into focus. He was putting wet cloths on my forehead and bitter liquids in my mouth. I watched him, needing to keep my eyes open because the moment I shut them, I saw the past; the musicians at the motel… what were their names? *Thomas, what were their names? I can't remember. I need to know their names…*

Ice. On my forehead. My cheeks. The back of my neck. *It was too cold.*

Oh. Right. Dustin and Marie, and Rusty. That's who they were. The musicians. All shot. All dead because they just happened to be where I was. *Did I tell you that, Thomas? See why you shouldn't be anywhere near me? People die. I don't want you to die. I love you, Thomas.*

My eyelids were so heavy it was an effort to pry them apart. When I did, the most beautiful face stared back at me. Why was Thomas crying? His eyes, dark pools of glistening shadows, were spilling over the blackness beneath them.

"Thomas," I said, crushed glass lining my esophagus. "I think you need to sleep."

The bed creaked. Whose bed was I in? I guess it didn't matter. Thomas was here, lying down next to me.

And then he wasn't. What happened to him? Was he sick? Hurt? Did he leave?

Panic racked my mind. Visions of him dying and me not being able to do anything about it circled in an echoing nightmare. Where was he? *Where was he?*

"Thomas!"

I called for him. Or maybe I screamed, I couldn't tell. And when his hands were on my cheeks, his voice soothing in my ears, I could breathe again.

"Relax, Kaya," he said softly. "I'm right here. I'm not leaving you."

Then, eventually, the storm raging in my mind and body, stopped.

My teeth hurt.

I opened my eyes to see Thomas, and the anguish on his face had me bolting upright.

"What's going on?" I asked, my throat no longer feeling like I'd swallowed barbed wire. "Are you okay?" I reached for his cheek, half expecting him to disappear, but the cheekbone and strong jawline beneath my fingers were real. He smiled, and relief washed over me like a tidal wave.

"Shh, it's all right." He took my hand away from his face and pushed me back onto the pillow. "Your fever finally broke. Jeezus, Kaya, you had me worried sick."

I shook my head in confusion and saw stars for a moment. "Fever?"

"We couldn't call a doctor, so Georgia gave you her leftover antibiotics and—"

His voice broke. He gulped hard, and his thumb rubbed against my cheek. It brought moments back; Georgia dragging me into a cold tub while I fought with her. Thomas dressing me in a pair of pajamas and sleeping next to me. Dan hovering his moon-shaped face over mine and asking me questions I couldn't answer. Day turning to night. Night turning to day.

"Oh my God. How long have I been—?" I didn't have enough strength to finish the sentence.

"Three days," Thomas answered.

"Luke!" I swung my feet over the edge of the bed and stood for a few seconds before collapsing into Thomas's arms. "What the heck is wrong with me?" I asked dismally as he tucked me back into bed, my mouth way too full of saliva.

"You caught something nasty," Thomas said, adjusting the blankets. "Probably when we were under that bridge. Who knows what we touched." He rose and reached for a glass of water, handing it to me with a look that said *drink.*

The water felt good going down, but it flipped around once it hit bottom.

"Georgia doctored you. Fed you crushed cloves of garlic and covered you in all kinds of medicinal oils. I don't know what I would have done without her."

It was then that I realized I reeked. Absolutely, totally*, reeked.*

Thomas grinned at my crinkled nose. "Yeah, you could use a bath. Or two." He stretched out beside me, folding his hands under his head. "Maybe in the morning though, all right? It's late. We need to sleep."

I didn't know if I could bear the smell coming off my skin. Worse yet was whatever was plastered to my chest had turned hard and crusty. It was some sort of yellow paste covered with… leaves?

"It's a mustard plaster," Thomas said, reading my mind. "Georgia figured that would help draw out whatever was making you sick. Reeks worse than the garlic, though."

All at once I was too tired to care about anything but the wellbeing of the man who had stayed by my side. "Are you sick?" I asked.

"Nope. I don't get sick," he said with a sleepy exhale.

My eyelids were so heavy I couldn't prop them up. My arms useless stumps. "Thank you, Thomas," I said. "If you weren't here, I don't know what I would have done. "

"Shh," he said, pulling the covers up to my chin. "I'll always be here."

19

OUT OF THE FOG

It was still dark outside when I got up and showered, almost passing out twice in the process. I practically crawled back to bed because my legs were shaking so violently after. I had no strength at all. Even toweling off my hair seemed an impossible task. Thomas was out cold, and I was grateful for his warmth when I curled up next to him. I counted sheep. Counted Thomas's deep and even breaths. And when sleep just wasn't having anything to do with me, I resolved to be content with the comfort and coziness of the dark and the man beside me.

It was five in the morning. Birds were getting warmed up for their performances. The sun was about to break through the dark. A dog barked, and I was reminded of how Brutus sounded when he was angry, and how the birds had always ceased to chatter when they heard him, like they did now.

Thomas rolled toward me and muttered, "Who let the dogs out? Who? Who?"

I would have laughed, but the barking increased, and then Georgia was bursting into the room with sleep-flattened curls, a thin housecoat belted at her waist and pillow lines on her cheeks.

"Thomas. Thomas, get up. You must go to the other room. Jeremy's room. Hurry!"

Thomas sat up but was still asleep. "Wha—"

"*They're here,*" Georgia said, and tugged a half-asleep Thomas from the bed and shoved him out into the hall. She came back to me, yanked my damp hair into a ponytail at the back of my neck, then shoved my head onto the pillow. "Lay down and pretend to sleep," she ordered, then turned off the light. "Don't let them see your hand, or your eyes. Remember our plan."

I had no idea what plan she was talking about, but I didn't get to ask when a knock at the front door of the house rattled the windows. I searched my mind for instructions that I must have been given in a feverish fog while footfalls overtook the kitchen. All at once, I had no doubt who was looking for me.

What was I doing putting this family in danger? Putting Thomas in danger? Stupid... had I not learned from the past? What now? Should I go out the window?

I sat up, head spinning so hard I didn't sit up too long. No. I wasn't going out the window. I wasn't getting out of this bed either. Georgia had told me to pretend to sleep, so I would. I was too pathetically weak to do anything else anyway.

Pulling the covers up, I closed my eyes. Georgia's voice, high pitched and irritated, reached me loud and clear through the thin walls and heavy blanket.

"Seriously?" she was saying to whoever was at the door. "This is the fourth time you guys have been here. This is getting annoying. You're not the police, you have no right."

Dan quieted Georgia. And then I heard my name—multiple times. Shivers worse than when I had the fever stole through me. There was a thud just outside my door, then Thomas' angry voice.

"Who the hell are you?" he asked.

Someone I didn't like the sound of returned the question. "Since I'm the one with the gun, why don't you tell me who the hell you are?"

"I'm Jeremy. Dan's son," Thomas said. "I live here. You can't just barge in like—"

My door was thrown open and the light switched on. I did my best 'startled awake' face, blinking at four boot covered feet, careful to keep my eyes lowered. I clutched a pillow, making sure it covered up my hand.

"You idiots!" Georgia yelled. "You woke up my sister. Do you know how long it took us to get her to sleep? Jeremy brought her home from college because she's wasn't feeling well, and she's been puking all night.

Coming out both ends of her something fierce. She was just finally starting to get some rest."

I knew the shadowy cast that would be on the men's faces without even looking at them. Their soulless, vacant gazes were part of the outfit, and necessary for those trained to kill on demand. Since there were two of them here, that meant there would be many more outside, so if they wanted to drag me from this bed and take me kicking and screaming to the estate—they could. And considering Henry had the police under his control, no one would stop them.

"What's your name?"

I was being asked by a guard with pants too short. His ankles were visible above his boots and his socks mismatched. I found this terribly funny. It really wasn't, but I couldn't help it, I snickered. Then I giggled.

"Uh… she must still have a fever," Georgia said in my defense.

Unfazed, one pulled out his phone to take a picture of me, so I lurched forward, hung my head over the side of the bed as if I was about to throw up, and started retching.

"Oh no… Leah…" Georgia said, breezing into the room then stopping as if I was a fatally contagious, malaria-infected mosquito-zombie. "Are you going to puke again? Do you need the bucket?"

She created just enough of a stir in the air to let loose the most unpleasant smell of garlic, mustard plaster, and whatever other stench was lingering on my clothes. I didn't have to continue fake gagging when I caught a whiff. When Georgia placed a trash can a few inches from my nose, then recoiled from me, for some reason the guards completely forgot about taking my picture and made for the door.

"If you see Kaya Lowen, you contact us right away," one of them said when the other was already long gone.

We all waited for the front door to shut. For a car to disappear back down the drive. For the dogs to stop barking. And then we all breathed a sigh of relief.

"How did you know they wouldn't recognize her?" Thomas asked.

Georgia was gingerly picking up my reeking clothes. "They have no idea what Kaya looks like. I figured that out when they came here the first time and thought *I* was Kaya. So, I figured it was worth a shot."

"Good call, kiddo," Dan said, hugging his daughter, then he rubbed his hands together and grinned at me. "Well, *Leah*," he said fondly. "It seems like you're feeling better. I'll make you your favorite bacon and eggs for breakfast, and you can tell me all about your courses in marine biology."

Dan laughed all the way to the kitchen. Georgia took my clothes to the washing machine. Thomas took his first breath in minutes, and I wondered if I might need that bucket back.

Warmed by the fireplace, we were centered around a coffee table covered in all sorts of sandwiches and cookies. Two golden dogs snored lazily at Dan's feet, Georgia picked at her fingernails, Thomas stared distantly at the fire, and I watched the afternoon drift away. I was feeling horrible, not with sickness but with worry, and the tea Georgia brewed only made it worse. It had an earthy scent, reminding me of autumn, of the mountains, of the river... and Luke. I could barely swallow it.

"Throat sore again?" Georgia asked.

I hadn't realized she'd been watching me so closely. "No."

My reply brought a collective sigh of relief.

"You know," Georgia said. "I think part of your illness was caused by emotional trauma." She eyed me from across the living room, legs folded under her and a pillow clutched to her chest. Her blonde hair was pulled up high on her head and a few strands had escaped around her temple. "Right now, I'm reading a book on how your mind affects your health. It's a big part of holistic medicine. I think you've gone through so much in the last few months that your brain had to shut down for a while. Makes sense to me. I can't even imagine what you've been going through. It makes me feel sick just to *hear* about it."

Thomas had obviously told her much more of my story than I thought he had, and this was confirmed by his sheepish expression and sudden interest in his hands. I was okay with it, though. Georgia was insightful and intelligent. Had I simply judged her based on our first meeting outside the estate, I would have thought her a flighty, simple-minded teen. Not so. Medicine was her passion, specifically homeopathy—the traditional sort that treated the mind, body, and spirit. My respect for her increased by the hour, and her opinion became one I realized I valued.

"So, Luke and Oliver have been in the estate for seven days," she said, thinking out loud. "How can I help?"

Thomas was about to speak, but Dan beat him to it, leaping to his feet and dropping a half-eaten sandwich, instantly snatched up by a waiting dog.

"No way, Georgia. It's one thing to let Kaya stay here, but past that, I'm drawing the line. I am not going to allow you to get involved in any of this."

Georgia bounced to her feet, too. "That will be the day you tell me what to do. You might be my father, but I am eighteen and if I want to help someone, I will."

Whoa. I couldn't imagine talking to Henry like that. Dan was spineless, and speechless, and under his daughter's challenging glare, he stumbled for a reply, only to give up and plunk back down dejectedly.

Georgia eased back onto the couch, clutching the pillow. "I will help you," she said to me, "but you need one more day of rest to get back on your feet before we do anything. Coming down with a fever again isn't going to help matters much."

I nodded. Thomas smiled and gave her a wink that made me slightly uncomfortable.

Georgia eyed her father's sullen face. "So, we need to find a way to break in to the estate, get Luke and Oliver out, then get you all someplace safe."

Logs snapped and crackled in the fire. "Basically, yes," I said dismally.

"It can be done, Kaya," Georgia said.

"It just seems… impossible."

"Not at all. We just have to brainstorm. Where there's a will, there's a way. My momma always used to say that."

Dan blanched, and his rocking-recliner came to a stop. "Yeah, and it didn't work out so well for her, did it, Georgia?"

Georgia dug her nails into the pillow, heat rising in her cheeks. "It wasn't her fault she was sick, Dad," she said defensively.

Thomas boldly asked, "What happened to her? To your mom."

Dan's gaze fell to his lap, clearly uncomfortable, but Georgia cleared her throat. "Well, since Kaya opened up to us, I guess we can share, too. Right, Dad?"

"Georgia—" Dan started.

"Dad, just because you can't talk about it, doesn't mean I can't." Straightening up on the couch, she smoothed back the hair at her temples.

"My mom took her own life. She got sick when I was seven. I tried every-thing to make her better—soups and teas, prayers… whatever my child's mind could come up with. But nothing worked. She drank a cup of rat poison and vodka on purpose one night after we all went to bed."

Georgia paused. It was obvious this wasn't a fully healed wound. The room grew still. Even the fire flames seemed to freeze mid-lick.

"She took her own life?" I asked carefully.

"Yes. We have that same connection, Kaya. I know your mom committed suicide, too."

"Is that why you are so interested in medicine?" *And helping me*? I thought.

The dogs were both snoring. "I'm sure it has something to do with it."

"What was your mom sick with? Before she, uh, took her own life."

Georgia shook her head. "She was just really depressed. Then she became increasingly violent. No one knows why. Dad took her to doctors, but they could never find the cause. They think maybe it was something genetic and the psychosis was brought on by stress."

"Genetic," I muttered, feeling a nudge of worry for my new friend. "Could you have this too?"

Georgia sighed. "No. Me and my brother and sister were adopted. Mom couldn't have kids. But we were a happy family, and that didn't seem to bother her. It was only the last two months of her life that she seemed to go crazy."

Dan perked up. "Don't use that word, Georgia. She wasn't crazy."

Something about the familiarity of the conversation set my nerves tingling. I had heard this story before. Heck, I had 'lived' it.

"She *was* crazy," Georgia said. "Why else would anyone attack their husband with a butcher knife? Or drown the dog? Or take her own life? For cryin' out loud, Dad, she put on her Halloween costume and swal-lowed rat poison, *on purpose*. That is crazy, there is no other word for it."

As to be expected, Dan didn't say anything.

"Did she try to have children of her own?" I asked, feeling a knot in my stomach.

Georgia shrugged her shoulders.

"Dan?" I was on the edge of the couch, not feeling so good. "Did she seek medical intervention to try and conceive?"

"Uh, that's rather personal," he snipped at me.

"I know. But please, tell me."

He eyed his daughter briefly because she was waiting for the answer, too. "Yes. Merrill couldn't have children of her own, and we weren't allowed to adopt more than three. After Georgia came along, we just wanted a little sister or brother for her, so we got medical help. But nothin' worked."

I leapt to my feet. "What sort of medical help?" I asked, tossing the question at Dan like a dagger.

His eyes widened in confusion. "Uh… I dunno. Some drugs recommended by Ms. Sindra. Your dad specializes in fertility, and she said it was the best thing on the market."

I gasped and flattened my hand over my mouth, then ran for the bathroom to hurl up everything I'd eaten.

"Kaya, what is it?" Georgia's hand was on my back until the retching stopped.

Taking in a deep breath, I sat back on my heels to peer up into the face of yet another child whose mother had been taken by Cecalitrin. Taken… by Henry.

"We have more in common than you think. I know what made your mother sick. I know why she died."

Back on the couch with the dog now at her feet, Georgia inspected the bite mark on my hand.

"Cecalitrin made your mother do that, to her own *baby*?"

I couldn't help but notice Thomas flinch. His hands had curled into fists and his jaw tensed like he might hit something.

"Yes," I said.

"I want to kill him," Georgia said. "I don't mean 'psycho killer with a machine gun' or anything like that. But I am going to find a way to give Henry Lowen a taste of his own medicine. Of that, I can promise you."

She got up, took two cookies, and left the room, leaving Dan to stare off after her in awe.

"Well, she's gonna have to get in line," Thomas said, rising to stand before the fire. He was shaking with fury. "I've got first dibs. What I wouldn't do to get my hands around Henry's neck."

I moved next to him. "Thomas, no more talk about killing, okay? My heart can't handle it."

There was a soft knock at the door, but Thomas didn't seem to hear it. As Dan padded down the hall, Thomas turned to face me, his hands reaching for my shoulders.

"The more I learn about your life, the more I want to drag you away from here and force you to leave it all behind. Leave *them* behind. It's all I can do to sit idly by."

He was staring so hard I had to turn away. Dan was muttering to whoever was at the front door. I turned my head in that direction, but Thomas grabbed my chin.

"Look at me, Kaya," he said firmly.

He wasn't giving me any other choice.

"Let me take you away from here."

Dan was yelling for Georgia. *"It's that reporter chick again to see you. You might as well come and talk to her."*

Thomas was so focused it might as well have been only me and him on the planet. Zombies could have been at the front door, and I doubted he would notice.

"What do you think has changed in the last few days?" I asked.

He gulped hard. The front door was opening, hinges squeaking. "Everything. When you were sick, do you remember any of it?" he asked.

"Well of course I do."

"Who did you call out for?" his eyes eagerly searched mine. "Whose name did you say when you were so sick all you could do was lay there? Who was it you wanted next to you so badly that you practically screamed his name?"

"I was feverish, I don't r-remember."

"Yeah, you do," he said, his tone making me want to pull away and run.

Whoever had come in the front door was standing not far from us now and clearing their throat. It was so strangely familiar that Thomas finally took notice. His hands dropped to his sides when a woman, polished and stunning with auburn hair piled up on her head and tall body draped in a pant suit, shook her head at us in annoyance.

"Kaya," she said, hands on her hips. "Does no one working for your maniac father know what you look like?"

I couldn't believe who I was seeing. Breaking away from Thomas, I practically fell on my face stumbling forward at a million miles an hour. I threw myself into strong farm-girl arms that tightened around me affectionately, and I couldn't hold back the tears. She was here. And real. And I was unable to let go of my friend. My beautiful, heavily-covered-in-makeup, friend.

"*Marlene,*" I breathed.

I could feel her smile. "Ya. I missed you too, dumbass."

LISA

20

MAYBE EVEN FOREVER

The last half hour of the drive back to Louisa took forever. The truck was low on gas, but I didn't dare stop in town where the cops were fueling up, too. I was on fumes, coasting downhill and feeling relieved when the familiar valley opened around me. With the sun going down in my rear-view mirror and sleep tugging at my eyes, I kept driving, motivated by holding that little girl in my arms.

Through the snow, Louisa barreled out the front door toward me with Brutus close behind, her little blue princess dress covered in dog hair. Scooping her up and holding her tiny body next to mine released our tears. For a long while, I kneeled in the front yard of Seth's home, not caring about the snow melting beneath my knees, doing nothing but listening to Louisa breathe.

"Please don't leave me again," she said after a long while.

I made a vow I hoped to keep. "I promise, I'll never leave you again."

While Regan and Ellis took care of Seth's body—the details of which I did not want to know—I read books to Louisa. Crawling into bed next to her, surrounded by plush toys and a very out-of-sorts Brutus, my mind drifted to Luke. I couldn't do anything for him but read story after story to his little sister and care for her the way he'd want me to. When I turned the page in a book of dinosaurs, Louisa stopped my hand and asked about him, and I told her he and Kaya were on holidays. Then she asked about Seth, and I told her he had gone away for a very long time. Maybe even for forever. She grew quiet, her tiny fingers tracing a picture of a baby triceratops when she finally said to me, "I'll look after Brutus for him. I'll be the bestest mommy, just like you are to me, Lisa. I'll never leave him either."

I knew now without a doubt what I had to do.

I put the address I'd found on Seth's body out of my mind and absolved all thoughts of responsibility to Luke. I was a mom now, and that had to be my priority. Me, Louisa, and Brutus the dog, were a family.

LUKE

21

FOOD FOR THOUGHT

"We've been holed up in here for eight days," Oliver said, fingers digging in to the arms of an overstuffed recliner. "If I have to eat another granola bar or stare at your sorry face for a minute longer, I think I'll explode."

"There are no more granola bars," I said dismally.

We were reeling from yet another botched attempt to leave the room. The first time we had made it back to the gate, but Oliver's code didn't work to unlock it so we had to come rushing back. Today's attempt at prying the locked gate open was foiled when the floor thundered with approaching boots. Now, our nerves were fried, our stomachs were sticking to our spines, and our positive pep talk policy had expired.

"I guess we're scaling the walls. Might as well start gathering up the sheets to tie into knots."

Oliver's chin pressed into his neck. "Have you looked outside… looked *down*? I mean—"

"I'm kidding, Oliver."

He relaxed. "Oh. Sorry. Just need some real food," he mumbled.

I thought I heard him say something else, but realized the keypad on the door was beeping. Someone was coming into the room, and we still hadn't barricaded the door.

Oliver bolted upright and we both headed for Kaya's room, but had to stop and crouch behind Stephan's bookcase instead when it was clear we wouldn't make it. I got on my hands and knees and Oliver pressed himself flat against the many spines of Stephen King novels. Holding our breath, we waited for the onslaught of guards—fully expecting confrontation and to be no match against them with our weapons made from sharpened toothbrushes and spoons.

But there were no guards. Just the rattle of a cleaning cart and the slim outline of one person, and she was singing. Oliver arched an eyebrow in question.

"It's a maid," I mouthed to him.

A feather duster was swiped over the coffee table, hearth, and the top of the piano by a young girl. She made her way to the counter that housed the small fridge and sink, and when she noticed all the empty food wrappers, her singing stopped—but only for a second. Her actions then became rushed. She was collecting the garbage, and her song grew louder; *lie low, lie low, you've nowhere to go... just wait, just wait, we'll tell you when it's safe...*

Was it a warning? Or a Disney song?

From under a stack of linens on her cart, the maid pulled out a silver tray and placed it in the fridge. Her song repeated as she began fumbling with small paper boxes. Getting on her hands and knees, she placed them along the baseboards beneath the counter, and then unexpectedly, her eyes met mine. She saw me, plain as day, but just got back to her feet and pushed the cart toward the door.

"Guard. I'm all done in here. Let me out," she said.

The door squeaked open. The cart went out with the maid. The lock beeped.

"Why was she in here?" I asked when enough time had passed before we both tentatively moved back into the middle of the room.

"Mice," Oliver said.

I was at the door, pressing my ear up against it and hearing nothing. "Mice?"

"Yup. The whole building is crawling with them. They keep putting these glue boxes in the rooms to catch them."

He was holding one the maid had put on the floor, and I involuntarily shivered. I hated mice just as much as I hated spiders and millipedes. "Did you hear the song she was singing? She saw me plain as day. Looked me right in the eyes as if she was fully expecting to see someone—"

"Holy shit!"

My heart practically stopped at Oliver's outburst. I turned to see him by the fridge holding the silver tray left there by the maid, and I was fairly sure there were tears in his eyes.

"Pancakes. Luke, it's pancakes! Two big plates of 'em with maple syrup, scrambled eggs, and hash browns!"

I rushed to Oliver, half expecting him to fall to his knees and praise the Lord Almighty for his favorite foods. I patted him on the shoulder, knowing his joy wasn't just because of pancakes, it was the relief of knowing there was someone in the estate on our side; we weren't in this alone.

"It must be someone in the security office. That's the only reason we haven't been caught on camera and there haven't been guards searching this room daily," Oliver said as he peeked out between the curtains at the dark sky.

"Lucky us." I patted my stomach, now blissfully full.

"So what now then, Luke? Do we sit and wait for instructions? Hope that maid comes back with more food? It just doesn't seem right to do nothing."

"We're trapped anyway, so I might as well beat your ass at cards for a couple of days. If there's no change after that, then yeah, we're scaling the walls."

"Not in a million years will I hang over the edge of this balcony. I'd rather eat dust and die in a pool of my own self-pity and stubbornness."

"Well, you'll be doing that alone."

Oliver sighed and let the curtain fall back into place. "I knew you weren't kidding. You're crazy enough to do that, aren't ya?"

Being high up didn't bother me, and I liked the rush of going down. "That's how I got out of here the first time. Through that door in the garden."

"You jumped?"

Hunger had shrunk a few of Oliver's brain cells.

"No," I said, stifling a laugh. "I had gear on the other side."

Oliver settled back into his favorite chair. "When was that?" he asked.

Hadn't I told him about the night I snuck in? "Kaya's eighteenth birthday. I posed as a waiter. Wandered through the whole place until I found this room."

"Oh right," he said absently, picking at his fingernails.

"I thought I'd been caught when you came after Kaya in the garden."

Oliver's forehead creased, puzzled. "You were in the garden? The night of her eighteenth?"

"Uh, yeah. I just told you, that's how I got out."

Something seemed to click in place in Oliver's head. "She was different after that night. I could feel it. But the whole time I thought it was because of… me. "

"Oh?" I was intrigued. "Yeah, that was the first time I met her. Although at the time I didn't know who she was, I just knew that she—"

I stopped.

"Go on," Oliver said.

"Uh, this is still kinda weird talking to you about her."

He nodded. "Yeah, no kidding. But whatever. Keep talking. You knew that *what*?"

I swallowed hard, remembering how the green gown matched her eyes, how it fit her body, how she smiled at me the very first time and what she said.

"I knew that—" A lump grew in my throat. "She was the person I wanted to give the world to. What I wanted to fight for."

"You knew that right away?" Oliver's face twisted with disbelief.

"Without a doubt."

"Huh." Oliver pondered this a moment. "So, it was love at first sight. That's essentially what you're saying."

"I hadn't really thought of it that way. But yeah. I guess so."

He laughed and slapped his leg. "That's ridiculous."

I was completely taken aback. "What?"

"Yeah. Ridiculous. Totally. You can't fall in love with someone you've known for minutes."

"And why not? Are there rules? If so, no one told me about them."

Oliver sounded like a hundred-year-old man. "Because love has to mature. It takes time. It's not instant."

Now I was the one to laugh; how would he know how I felt? "Then what would you call it?" I said, staring him down. "And how would you know if you've never experienced it? I am living proof that love at first sight is a thing. Now, I don't really care if you believe it or not but let me tell you that it's the most real thing that has ever happened to me. Without any doubt, without any reservations or hesitations, I knew when I saw her that I loved her."

Oliver wasn't having it. "That is as unbelievable and corny as one of those chick romance novels. I mean, I'm not doubting an attraction, but insta-love? That just doesn't happen, Luke."

"You know, just because you haven't experienced it doesn't mean it's not real. You can't see the air we breathe, but it's there. Dig where I'm coming from?"

Oliver cleared his throat, the smile disappeared from his face, and he wrung his hands. "Or how 'bout this: maybe it's just easier to tell yourself that it's not possible, than to realize you had it in your hands and let it slip away."

He was talking about himself and what he had with Kaya. I considered putting my hands over my ears when he continued.

"I might have thick skin, but my heart laid bare before you is vulnerable. Tread lightly or not at all," he said.

I stifled a laugh. "What did those pancakes have in them? Whose poetry are you reciting?"

He shrugged his shoulders as his mood plummeted. "I dunno. Poe? Joyce? No one? Who cares."

Sad brown eyes met mine from across the room, and if I could have sunk into the couch and disappeared, I would have. It was like looking at a wounded puppy.

"What are you going to do when this is over?" I asked, needing to get his mind onto something other than Kaya and thus re-instating the positivity policy. "When we get out of here—and notice how I said *when*—what's on the agenda?"

Oliver shook his head and seemed to clear away the thoughts that had been clouding up his eyes. "I haven't given it any thought, really. This is all I've known since my parents… well, you know, died."

I did know, and I wished I didn't. Oliver reliving that nightmare when he was sick would haunt me forever. "I thought you'd probably be off hunting down the guy that did it," I said offhandedly, wishing I could light the fireplace—the room was so cold.

"Well, I would love to do that, but I have no idea who it was," Oliver said, putting his feet up on the coffee table.

I was confused. "Yeah, ya do."

"What do you mean?"

"Uh, you told me who did it back in that motel room."

Oliver leapt to his feet, wild-eyed. "I did *what*?"

"You told me," I repeated, unsure why he suddenly seemed like he might yank my thoughts out through my ears.

"What did I say? I know I saw the whole thing, but I've blocked it out. I spent my childhood erasing every single moment of that evening from my mind, and as an adult, I can't get it back. Luke, *what did I tell you?*"

That name, spoken in the dead of night in Oliver's feverish little-boy voice, was permanently etched into my eardrums. I could hear it now and picture the torment in his eyes when he told the man to stop stabbing his mama.

"Anderson Manning," I said. "You told me that Anderson Manning killed your family."

I didn't realize a black man could become so pale, and then fill back up with a color that could only be described as *rage.*

"I'm guessing that now you have an agenda once we're outta here?" I asked, very carefully.

He gave his neck a crack to one side, then the other. "Put it this way, if we don't have a way out of here real soon, *I'll* start tying the sheets together."

MARLENE

2 2

BITE ME

Nonsensical yapping was eating up the precious silence. Somehow, we were at the top of Mount Ridiculous and diving at breakneck speed into Lake Stupid. Everyone was throwing ideas around on how to get Luke and Oliver out of the estate; *climb the walls and break in... overtake the guards... fly in overhead and drop down onto the roof...and* I couldn't take it any longer.

"We aren't in a James Bond movie for God's sake!"

That shut them up. Good. To heck with Thomas and his machismo, Kaya and her complete lack of regard for her personal safety, Dan with nothing but insanity in his every word, and Georgia, so smart yet so dumb with the worst ideas of all.

"What do you suggest then, Marlene?" she said. "Got anything? Or are you just gonna sit there and judge."

I had the strangest feeling this girl was jealous of me, which was satisfyingly weird. I'd left on the makeup covering my birthmark, so she still hadn't seen my purple face. Maybe I would uncover it and glare at her. Make her squirm a little.

Kaya shot me a look that said, 'play nice.'

I put on my thinking cap, tugging it down hard over my ears. "All I know is that we can't fight an inferno with a watering can. We have no firepower—" I nodded in Kaya's direction, "—only bargaining power."

Georgia fluffed up her curls. "Well, I think poisoning them is the easi-

171

est." She crossed her arms over her chest, adamant that this was the solution.

I couldn't get over her stupidity, or her neon-green fish scale leggings and purple sweatshirt emblazoned with the words 'bass ass chick'. "Yeah. Poisoning. Cool, Georgia. 'Cause everyone in that dismal place deserves to die? C'mon, Blondie, be smarter than that. We don't want to murder innocent people—Henry already has that covered."

Georgia shivered and pulled her knees to her chest, the firelight glinted off the leggings making them look even more… well, *wrong*. Worse yet, for some reason I wanted lime Jell-O, and that was super disturbing.

"I mean, c'mon people," I continued, "we aren't going to get Luke and Oliver out of there by dressing up like Batman or—" I dared a glance at Georgia's pants. "Aqua girl? Nor are we going to suddenly develop mad helicopter driving skills. All we truly have is our smarts. Can't we use them for a second?"

"I'm up for that," Thomas said, oddly agreeing with me.

"Good. Well, all I know is this—when I had problems with the gophers, I shot 'em. When I had problems with the rats in the barn, I trapped and caught 'em. In this case, I think Henry is so far underground there's no chance of shooting him, so he's more of the rat type. Now, what do you use to lure a rat? What sort of dangling carrot would be irresistible? Butter covered? Steamed? Fresh outta the dirt? Made into cake with frosting?"

Man, I really needed to eat something.

"Dripping in gold and diamonds," Kaya said. Her eyes, shadowed with bruises from lack of sleep and worry, sparkled with an idea. "We could create an even bigger distraction than Oliver did, without blowing things up. We can put Henry in a situation where he must be on his best behavior, while we sneak in under the cover of a huge event. Like Luke did on my eighteenth birthday."

Thomas's teeth clenched at the mention of his nemesis. I detected a tinge of green in his cheeks, too.

"Maybe I'll throw a party and invite the whole town," Kaya said, face lighting up.

Georgia shook her head. "Oh, no. There's not much room here, and we don't have many dishes."

"No, Georgia, not *here*," Kaya said softly. "The estate. *My house.*"

Blonde curls and a whirl of green bounced upward, startling the dog. "Oh, a Christmas party! I love Christmas! Candy canes and Bing Crosby. Presents and Santa—"

"No!" Kaya and I both shrieked in unison.

Georgia deflated like a popped balloon. "Well, it's too soon for Easter, and Valentine's day is kinda lame. So….?"

"A winter masquerade ball," Kaya said. "We can blanket the town with invitations and make sure all the 'important' people get one. When half the town descends upon the estate in disguises, we can easily slip in amongst them."

"Sounds good, but assuming we find Luke and Oliver, we won't be able to waltz them out the front door. Henry will have some sort of system, arm bands or stamps like they do in bars. Two unmarked men leaving would be obvious. So, how would we sneak them out?"

"On my eighteenth, Luke got out through a door in the stone wall at the edge of the terrace garden, which is right outside the biggest ballroom. If we can get gear up there, once they are through the door, they can rappel down. I just have to have someone in the security room turn off the alarm."

"I have an insider who might do it," Dan said. "Arnold owes me a huge favor and a few thousand bucks. He also cheats on his wife, so if he ain't cooperative, blackmail will work."

"And I have dresses," Georgia said eagerly. "We can do our hair and—"

I had to cut her off. "You really think Henry would go along with this?" I asked Kaya.

She smiled. It was the first one I'd seen on her face yet. "He will if he knows I'll be there."

I raised my cup of hot cocoa to her. "You, my dear, are the carrot he cannot resist. Let's just make sure we dangle you well out of his reach."

Thomas didn't raise his glass. "This isn't a good idea." He was wringing his hands nervously. "It's not safe to let Kaya anywhere near there. Besides, how will Luke and Oliver know what to do? We don't even know if they are alive."

Kaya gasped, and her eyes grew wide as open barn doors. She drew in a few long, deep breaths to steady herself. "Somebody on the inside is helping them. It would be impossible to hide for this long without assistance. If they were dead Henry would be flaunting that in my face. Besides, Stephan is still in there, too. If I can contact him, he will help me. I have to believe that this will work, Thomas. I have to… or I… I don't know what… I-I…"

She was on the verge of tears. Thomas quickly changed his tune.

"Yes. You're right. Of course this will work," he said, affection oozing from his voice, hand covering hers. "We'll find… uh, *them*."

Dan piped up. "At least what we gots on our side is the fact that not everybody likes your daddy. I think once we get the ball rollin', we'll have more help than we need."

Everyone nodded. Then there was silence for the first time in hours. It was blissful. Until Georgia ruined it with her whiny voice.

"Tell me, Kaya, why is Henry the way he is? What made him so evil?"

Kaya was caught off guard. "Money? I guess. I dunno."

Dan spoke from the kitchen with a mouthful of chips. "Henry was always a jerk. Even in high school. He was just born that way."

Kaya straightened up. "You knew my—er, *Henry*, in high school?"

Dan poured the crumbs from the bottom of the bag into his mouth. "Well, before that actually. For two years we went to the same grade school. He was scrawny and poor lookin' and got teased all the time until he hit a growth spurt and packed on height and muscle. His favorite thing to say was '*I'll own this town someday. Hell, I'll own you, too*'. I dunno how many times he said that to me. In grade nine, he was the biggest kid in class, and nobody messed with him no more. What I remember most about Henry back then were his eyes. Not so much 'cause of that crazy green color like yours, Miss Kaya, or the dark circles underneath 'em from working every odd job he could find, but the darkness in 'em. They were clouded with… oh, I dunno… hate? The classroom would always go silent when he entered—which was exactly sixty seconds after the bell. He put people on edge. Made 'em nervous. Even teachers. I remember Mrs. Stewart running out in tears after he 'schooled' her on something of some sort. He became a real bully in high school after that. Not the 'beat you up' kind, but the 'mess with your head' kind. The heads and jocks worked for him, selling cigarettes and weed because Henry was the kind of guy who could bribe you into doing things ya didn't want to do by getting your brains so twisted up you thought you was happy to be doin' it."

Whoa. I didn't think Dan was capable of stringing more than two sentences together, but there it was. He grew quiet for a moment, no doubt remembering something he did for Henry that was unsavory judging by his scrunched eyebrows and twitching lip.

"We were in the same math class for a semester," he continued, pushing his glasses up higher on his nose. "He knew numbers and calculatin' better than anyone and could make even the fiercest teacher cry by wit alone. I asked him for help once, but figured out that it wasn't a good idea to ask Henry for anything. You'd pay for it ten times over. Heck, if ya even peeked at him outta the corner of yer eye, he'd throw a book at yer head and charge ya ten bucks for lookin'. And if ya noticed Lenore... oh boy."

Kaya was on the edge of the couch now. "My... uh... *Lenore*? The woman who raised me?"

"Yep. Pretty little red head. When her family came to live here and took over the estate, Henry was like a dog on a bone the moment he saw her. I don't think she ever really wanted anything to do with him to be honest; he was poor, had no family. Lenore's daddy certainly didn't approve of him. He was in an uproar when they started datin'. Oh boy, I remember that well. Lenore's daddy coming to the school and withdrawing her, making her get home schoolin' instead. She was mad as a toothless beaver, screaming for the whole town to hear how she'd make her daddy pay for 'ruining her life'."

Kaya was blinking hard, taking it all in. "So she got engaged?"

Dan seemed incredibly pleased that he had information worth sharing. "Yup, probably for spite. I was workin' at the estate when the news hit. I don't know how Lenore managed to get her daddy to finally agree, but lo and behold, the mighty John Marchessa caved and put on the wedding event of the year. I ain't never seen so many people in one place. I think all three estate ballrooms were full. I was in charge of driving Henry and Lenore to the falls outside of town for wedding photos, and it's funny 'cause neither of them even knew my name, even after all those years in school we'd spent together. I guess when you get yerself a bank account as big as yer head, the 'little people' become unrecognizable."

"That still doesn't explain why Henry is a psychopath," Georgia said challengingly.

Kaya flinched. "Does it have to?"

I stepped in, needing to shut Georgia up for Kaya's sake. "Maybe

Henry is just the way he is, just *'cause*. Ya know? Some people are just bad. No rhyme or reason to it. No fault of anyone's and no fixing them either. I mean, does it really matter why the dude sucks? Nah. Onward and upward. It is what it is, and exactly what that *is* don't matter."

With that Kaya stood, a strange expression on her face. 'Thank you' she mouthed to me as Dan started going on about high school football because apparently now that he'd decided to talk, he didn't want to shut up.

Lost in thought, Kaya made for the front door and Thomas went to follow her. I tugged on his sleeve, encouraging him to leave her alone, and she walked silently out into the night with her coat in her hands. Thomas crumpled to the couch and wouldn't meet my eyes. I was going to have to have a sit-down with him, see what I could do to help the boy out. In the past when he had girl problems, his heartache—if that's even what it was—only ever lasted a few hours. He would move on, get another girlfriend, and that was that. But this was different. Thomas had fallen for someone, and despite his charming and stunning self, he was not going to get the girl.

"So. Invitations," Georgia said, gleefully clapping her hands together and looking at me like I'd just been elected head of the party planning committee. "Gold or black? I think black. Maybe just a *touch* of red because it is close to Christmas and all. Crisp white font… it's super classy. Ooh, and masks! We can make some matching ones, I have feathers. And I told you I have dresses, right? What's your size? We can fix them up, add some sparkle and sequins…"

I put my hands over my ears. *Shoot me now.*

YOU ARE INVITED TO:
THE FIRST ANNUAL BOW SPRINGS ESTATE
Black and White
MASQUERADE
BALL

FRIDAY NOVEMBER 3RD at 6PM
Hosted by: Henry Lowen (no RSVP required)
COCKTAILS
LIVE MUSIC
DANCING
FORMAL ATTIRE AND FULL MASK
ARE MANDATORY FOR ENTRANCE.
LADIES WEAR WHITE, GENTLEMEN
WEAR BLACK

OLIVER

CLOSE TO YOU

The maid arrived earlier than normal, not only leaving breakfast in the fridge, but two neatly folded black suits with shoes, masks, and an invitation to a masquerade ball. Inside was a handwritten note:

> *Go where two were brought together by fate,*
> *At exactly tea time don't be late,*
> *To get there, rock and roll the gates.*
> *P.S. And most importantly, don't drink all my scotch, buttheads.*

"Stephan." I felt a rush of relief that he was alive.

Luke was reading over my shoulder. "*Where two were brought together by fate…* I would assume that means in the garden where I met Kaya. That door hidden in the stone wall is how I got out before."

It annoyed me to no end that he was probably right.

"She has to be the one behind this event. Using it as a cover. Stephan obviously figured out how I escaped. Maybe *she* told him," he added.

We both contemplated that for a moment. Kaya was planning to rescue us; a chill rushed through me.

Luke paled. "I hope she doesn't do something—"

"Stupid." I finished for him.

Luke gulped hard. "Ya."

Silence.

He re-read the note. "So, what would tea time be?"

"Seven minutes after seven. For months, Kaya made tea at exactly that time. It became a joke." My thoughts drifted back to one of those evenings. The fire burning, the warmth in the room a big blanket of comfort as Kaya sat curled up in her favorite chair.

"Calling Oliver, come back to earth there, buddy," Luke said, giving my shoulders a shake.

I suppressed a cough that was tickling my voice, and swallowed back a metallic taste on my tongue. "Rock and roll at the gates. What could that mean? Oh, of course."

Luke tipped his head expectantly. "Care to share?"

"I'm to use Davis's code, taken from his favorite song—*The Number of the Beast*."

"Ah. Iron Maiden. The boy has good taste." Luke was fumbling through the cup of pens on the piano, smiling to himself. "I guess we will be rappelling our way to freedom after all. It's pretty steep on the other side of that door, think you can handle it?"

I couldn't tell if the sudden tightness in my chest was from my lungs acting up or this new fear of heights that had come at me from out of nowhere. I ignored the concern on Luke's face. "I'm cool with it," I lied. "Really."

His blue eyes met mine and held. There was something that made them impossible to stare at, yet impossible to look away from.

"Oliver, of this I can promise you," he said, intensely serious. "*I won't let you fall.*"

He meant it. The words let go of the air in my chest because I knew this man, that I could now call friend, had my back. Quite ridiculously, it kinda choked me up. "Thanks, Golden Boy," I sputtered.

Luke had a pair of scissors in his hand and was heading for the bathroom. "You won't be calling me that much longer," he said.

"And why is that?"

I could hear the scissors, metal against metal, furiously snapping back and forth. When Luke emerged from the bathroom, his hair resembled that of a Muppet caught in a blender, and I laughed so hard I couldn't breathe.

"Whadya think?" he asked, grinning.

Tears rolled from my eyes. He'd just chopped his hair off in chunks and strands of it stuck up all over the place. "Well, you're right, I can't call you Golden Boy anymore," I said when I regained control. "Nor can I call you skilled with scissors, either. I hate to say it, but you even took it past being 'artsy'. Did you even look in the mirror?"

He shook his head and honey-hued hairs drifted off him. "I figured I'd blend in better like this."

"Blend in? More like stand out like a sore thumb." Even more than he already did just by being… *him*. "I'll get Stephan's clippers and try to fix that mess."

I didn't want to shave Luke's head to the scalp, so I put on a number three clip and got it nice and short all over without leaving him bald. A jealous part of me half hoped his good looks would fall to the floor with his hair, but nope. The angles of his face were more prominent, and the blue of his eyes more startling. He simply appeared more rugged. More mature. And I really wanted to hate him for it.

He rubbed his head. "Feels weird. But I like it. Thanks, man."

I laughed and coughed at the same time, getting a mouthful of that hard-to-swallow taste.

"Ah crap, Oliver. You're not getting better, are ya?" Luke asked.

I had to be on my game tonight. So did Luke. So I continued with the lie I'd been feeding him. "I'm fine. Like I told ya, it's getting better every day." I fought an insane tickle as I said it.

Luke's hand came down on my shoulder. "We're getting out of here," he said reassuringly. "We're going to find you a doctor and get you all fixed up. All right?"

I nodded, reeling slightly from the cough, but mostly from the depth of this friendship. "You really mean it, don't ya? You won't let me fall."

His gaze held mine, and I was staring at the sun. "Nope."

I put out my hand, shaking his firmly. "Back atcha."

We crept out into the carpeted hall.

Davis' code worked at the first gate and the second, and once we were through the third, we started to hear the hum of many voices. We moved into the belly of the beast and met unexpected groups of guests. Some were just lost, but most were sneaking around, eager to check out the famed Bow Springs Estate. We donned our masks and wandered with them, moving past the guards hovering in every corner. We ogled the art on the walls, took a moment in the observatory hall, then breezed along behind a group of giggling girls until we were in the main lobby. It was easy. Too easy.

Streams of people were coming in through the main entrance, milling about, waving their invitations like they'd been handed a golden ticket on American Idol. The only people unmasked were the guards, which made the guests a mass of black and white faces, one completely indiscernible from the next.

The Empress Ballroom was buzzing. Hundreds of voices rose in pitch over melodies plucked by violinists. Gleaming in the low light of the chandeliers, white and black flowers strung together with gold threads hung from the ceiling, draped the walls and adorned the pillars and windows. Henry had outdone himself on the décor. Amidst the guests were countless tables overflowing with food, making my mouth water madly. I didn't have to fake my sudden interest in getting to the closest one.

"Cake," I said, moving deeper into the room with Luke following. I was trying not to cough or let my eyes dash around madly; Kaya was here somewhere. I could feel it. And acting casual was almost impossible.

"Hey," Luke grabbed me by the forearm, pulling me aside to let people behind us pass. "What if we get separated?" he whispered.

One of the guards, a man I most certainly recognized, glanced our way, but only briefly. "Then we meet at the chocolate fountain."

Luke shook his head. "No, seriously. If something happens, if things go… *wrong.*"

I considered this. We had no phones. No addresses. No… nothing. "There's a place I went once when I was young. It's always in my dreams, but in a good way." I remember the faces of my family in this dream. It was the last holiday we took together. "Vancouver, at the end of Davie Street, go to the shores of English Bay and watch the ships on the horizon at twilight. We will find each other there eventually—I hope—and one of us better not be empty handed, if you know what I mean."

Luke nodded. "If she still wants me."

I sighed. I couldn't help it. "Still? After all my pep talks, you still think she might dump you for someone else? I mean look around Luke. She did this *for you.*"

Luke went to rub his hair, remembered it wasn't there, and dropped his hand. "I guess if she's still with the cowboy, that's my answer right there."

"I'll beat him senseless for ya if that's the case, all right? Problem solved."

That got his smile back, and he discreetly gave my hand a squeeze. "Thanks."

The room kept filling up, and it was uncomfortably chaotic. The exit to the garden at the far end seemed like a million miles away. Above us, the second-floor balcony that bordered the room was packed full as well. Laughter, flirting, drinking, white gowns circling over our heads—and a guard every five feet keeping watch.

"We need girls," I said under my breath.

Luke had a cube of cheese in his hand and was trying to figure out how to eat it without tipping up his mask. "Maybe *you* do," he muttered, forcing a smile and putting the cheese in his pocket as his eyes darted around the room. He could feel Kaya's presence, too.

"Seriously, we need to mix in better. Two men don't go to a masquerade ball together."

"We could hold hands, Oliver. If that's what you're suggesting."

Ignoring him, I headed to the bar.

"Was it something I said?" he teased, close behind.

"Drinks," was my reply, mostly because I felt that tickle in my throat and was worried about tempting it into a full-blown cough.

"I like drinks," Luke said intuitively. "I'll go get them. You get the girls."

Music blared, and other instruments joined the violins. In the middle of the room, people had started to dance. As ladies' skirts drifted and floated amongst the legs of black-suited men, I felt a small hand seize my arm.

"Care to dance?" said a female, face covered with a jeweled mask outlined with tall feathers. They swished when she spoke. "It's a good song."

I inched back slightly. I realized I'd said we'd needed girls, but there was something about this one that set me on edge. I had to remind myself that she would help me blend in.

"*Can* you dance?" she asked.

The skin of her neck was aged like she was in her seventies, and stiff white hair streaked with purple was pulled up into an intricate bird's nest atop her head. I found her repulsive.

"Dancing isn't really my thing," I said, hoping for just idle chit chat until I had to leave.

"Come now," she said, not taking no for an answer. "We're at a ball, darling. That's what people do—they dance. Are you going to deny an *old* woman?"

Luke had his back to me. I casually noted the time; we had fifteen minutes. From over his shoulder, I realized I had the full attention of a guard, so I nodded at the lady while beads of sweat began rolling down my back. Looping her arm through mine, I led her to the dance floor.

"I'm Isabelle," she said, and her voice didn't match the rest of her. Not only that, it was strangely familiar. Had she been one of Kaya's teachers? She had a strange accent I couldn't place that stirred a distant memory. I twirled her away from me, mostly because I hadn't thought of a name for myself yet. When I pulled her back, the palm of her hand came flat against my chest.

"I'm, uh… Samson," I said, then instantly regretted it.

"You're a wonderful dancer, *Samson*," she said, eyes studying mine. "I knew you would be."

"Oh? How's that?" I asked.

Masks and shoulders whizzed past, my own mask obscuring my vision. When it seemed to slip, I quickly adjusted it. It was then that I noticed a couple, hand in hand and eyes on me, turn away and drift off into the crowd. My pulse quickened. Even disguised, with her back to me, long white dress flowing out behind her instead of sweat pants and hair pulled up into intricate waves, I would know Kaya Lowen anywhere.

Keep it together, Oliver. Keep it together.

I spun Isabelle away, checking my watch again as I did, then twirled her back toward me. The motion hitched my breath and a cough nearly doubled me over. It left the tell-tale signs of my illness on my hands, which I tried to discreetly wipe off on my sleeve; good thing blood blended well into black.

Isabelle wasn't deterred. "Oooh, that cough sounds nasty," she said, remaining too close, face inches from my chest and peering up from behind her mask. "You should probably see someone about that."

I politely tried to remove myself. She caught my arm.

"One more," she insisted.

I noticed Luke moving through the crowd, a drink in each hand, and his eyes caught mine. He made a subtle chin nod to the garden doors, and I nodded back, wondering if he had seen Kaya too.

"I must go," I said. "My friend is waiting for me. Perhaps I'll make my way back to you later—"

A cough racked my lungs again, thankfully only lasting seconds this time. Isabelle did not blink or shy away. She just waited till I was done, then leaned in again.

"I have just what you need for that cough," she said, rising on her tip toes to get close to my ear.

I got a better view of the makeup packed on her skin. Were the wrinkles *drawn* on? And the dark patch beneath her ear… was that a covered-up tattoo?

"Ya know, there is medicine you can take for that," she said. "If you come with me, I might be able to help reverse the damage done by those little blue pills."

I froze mid-step, mind reeling. "I have no idea what you're talking about."

Her hand tightened on my arm. "Oh yes, you do. Come now, dance with me, *Oliver*. Or with one motion of my hand, your friend Luke over there—so obviously heading for the garden—will be dead in seconds."

A ballad swelled, a singer joined in, lyrics swirled with the noise of the room. The beads of sweat on my back multiplied and were rolling between my shoulder blades. I felt my forehead dampen, the mask sticking to my skin. But I moved my feet in time with the music. Hand in hers.

"Ah. Good idea, Oliver. As much as I would like to have Luke back to play with, you could be quite a lot of fun, too."

"You're the girl...the one who… tortured him." I could barely breathe with anger. "I could kill you in a split second. Snap your spine—" I put one hand at the back of her neck, the other at the small of her back, holding her like a lover would, but threatening her with the pressure of my hands; it would be so easy. So satisfying.

Her eyes dug into mine. "I found the guard in the control room that was supposed to open the gate at… oh, what was it? Seven minutes after seven? And that little maid that liked to bring supper to you in Kaya's room—Ella, I think her name is—I have her, too. Chained up in the basement where I believe you spent quite a lot of time in your youth."

I could no longer pretend to dance. "If you hurt them, I'll—"

"You'll *nothing*. I know Kaya is here. She is the one who planned this little soiree. The silly girl thought it would be a clever way of sneaking you and Luke out under the cover of all these people. But there is one of her and hundreds of us. So, play your cards right."

I lowered my hand, placing it on her arm. "Have we met before?" I asked through gritted teeth.

"Oh yes," she hissed, her accent thicker now. "But I won't hold it against you for not remembering me. I had pink hair back then, and I wasn't wearing stage makeup to look like an old woman. You almost choked the life out of my friend Barry at the Derrick bar. Remember him? I bet you'd like to do the same to me right now, wouldn't ya, darlin?"

The waitress. The one who Kaya snuck out to go and see the night we…

"Angela?" I breathed. Stunned.

There was no way this was the pretty girl covered in tattoos who Kaya had thought of as a friend. After that night at the bar, Davis searched for her, but she had gone missing…but it was clear by the madness in her eyes where she'd ended up.

"What the hell happened to you?" I asked as my stomach churned.

She smiled. "I was offered a taste of the good life. And now you're going to do exactly as I say so I can have the full meal deal."

KAYA

THE STARS FELL ON MY HEAD

I stood in the ballroom just as I had so many times as a kid, only this time my nerves were wildly on edge. Not because Henry was looking for me or maybe even *at* me right now, or that Oliver had recognized me while he was dancing with an older lady, or the intense hum of the crowd, the armed guards circling the entire room, and the fact that the knife I'd strapped to my leg had to be left behind because there were metal detectors at the front doors... No, it was because of Luke. *He* was here. And when I saw him, I didn't know what I would apologize for first.

Maybe the fact that I was holding Thomas' hand.

Thomas' fingers tightened over the makeup covering my scar and the freshly inked stamp courtesy of the guards at the entrance; Marlene had been right. There was no way Luke and Oliver were just wandering out the front doors to their freedom. The exit was separate and manned as heavily as a US border crossing.

As we weaved through the room, Marlene and Georgia stayed close. Our dresses and masks were identical, hair all done up the same, turning us into a trio of anonymous guests. I gripped Thomas' hand even tighter, fearing that if I let go, I might not be able to find him in the sea of matching people. Plus, I was so nervous I could barely get my feet moving. He led the way, a fake smile plastered to his face, black hair curling at the back of his neck. When we made it far enough into the room to feel a rush of night air through the open garden doors, he suddenly stopped.

"Dance with me," he said.

"Thomas, there isn't time for that. We only have minutes to get outside."

"Thanks, love." He ignored my protests and immersed us into the mass of people moving in time to a lilting ballad.

"Seriously," I hissed. "What is wrong with you?"

Thomas' eyes were dark stars behind the mask. There was a pleading look to them as he moved one hand to my hip, urging me closer, and with the other removed my champagne glass and placed it on a waiter's tray. The feathers of my mask brushed his neck when he leaned in.

"First of all, we're being watched—two guards beside the column—so we have to pretend we're enjoying ourselves," he murmured against my ear. "And, I just need a moment. One more moment with you, before you see… him."

Any moment now Luke and I could be face to face, and suddenly I was unable to find my voice anywhere. I think it fell to my feet and was swallowed up by my floor-length skirt. I tilted my head back to look up at Thomas, and, noticing the two guards, moved in close enough to blend my body heat with his. We were certainly being watched, but upon contact, chest to chest with Thomas, my senses dulled to only him.

"Kaya," he said, as the crazy thing between us increased and wouldn't let up. "I just want to remind you that you can still pick me."

Where was my voice now? Probably six feet under.

"And I love you," he added.

I unraveled like a ball of yarn and fell into the pit with my voice. It took a good long while to climb up and shake off the dirt.

"Thomas, this is our last dance," I said, meaning it fully and completely, even though I was as mad for saying it as I was mad for him.

His feet started moving to the music again, guiding me along, drifting calmly to the rhythm. "We'll see about that," he said. "The night ain't over, princess."

Princess. That word was a shove back into reality.

The room around Thomas came back into view. Marlene and Georgia had disappeared, and the guard straight ahead by the garden door was looking in our direction now. The music had changed to a waltz, and Thomas was oblivious to it all.

"I think we should get some air," I said to him. "It's kind of hot in here."

He was staring at my mouth, and his gaze lowered to the swell of my dress. I could sense the effect my bare skin had on him.

"You are, uh… stunning in that dress," he breathed, cheeks slightly flushed.

"Air?" I repeated.

His eyes met mine. "Uh, yes. Air. Air is good," he said, clearing his throat.

We linked arms and took our plastic smiles to the garden doors. We were two lovers seeking a place to be alone, escaping the crowd. The guard let us pass and go out into the chilly night air while we maintained our act—that also wasn't an act.

"I am grateful for you," I whispered to Thomas once we were outside.

He'd grown tense, muscles in his arms rigid. "Yes, I am a good distraction."

His tone was odd and face unreadable behind the stupid mask. Was he implying something? Or was he reaffirming the fact that *we* were a distraction, out here to cause a scene if we had to, so Luke and Oliver could escape unseen. That was the plan. That's why Georgia and Marlene were out here too, flirting with a guard standing at the pathway entrance. Dan—smoking a cigar with a few other men next to a blazing fire pit—was laughing extra loud at absolutely everything. At least there weren't many guests marveling at the ornamental trees and shrubs sparkling with snow. It was too cold.

Stars twinkled, the moon was full, and I tried to remain calm while Thomas kept the pace at a stroll no matter how much I pulled against him. We eventually found ourselves at the end of the garden, alone beneath the old Mayday tree empty of all its beautiful flowers and leaves.

Thomas took off his jacket. "Here," he said. "You're going to freeze to death."

I hadn't felt the cold at all. The white gown, although thin up top and not covering my shoulders, had so many layers from the hips down that it held in the heat. Besides, my heart thrumming madly was keeping my blood warm. "I'm all right," I said. "Really, I'm fine."

I handed his jacket back and noticed a shadow approaching on the path.

"A guard is coming," Thomas said, then with a sly smile added, "Kiss me."

Clouds drifted over the moon. The only light came from two golden lanterns hanging in the tree. Thomas reached for my hands.

"No," I said firmly. "That was our last dance, Thomas. I wasn't kidding."

This could be the premise for the scene we were to cause; a lovers' spat.

I put my hand on Thomas's chest and stepped back from him. I'd forgotten about the shadow of the man coming toward us, until the clouds overhead drifted off and the moonlight took over, lighting up his black suit and mask. My hand dropped. Thomas tensed.

Luke.

I knew it was him. No one else could capture my mind that swiftly even with his face disguised. No one else made my chest flutter like this and cause massive surges of warmth and elation to steal through me with that complete and utter rippling madness of love. *It was him.*

Luke. Luke. Luke. Luke...

The breath left my lungs. The shape of his broad shoulders, the way he tipped his head to the side, his newly shorn hair—darker—and moonlight reflecting in his eyes...

Breathe.

I made to run to him, but Thomas latched on to my wrist with a death grip. He said nothing as Luke came closer, and only by sheer will was I still upright.

"Let go of her," Luke said.

I wrenched my arm free and backed away, finding the strength to stand on my own two feet in the same place where we'd first met. Where I'd fallen for *him*.

"Luke, I'm sorry—I—" Words caught in my mouth.

His gaze shifted between me and Thomas. Studying us. "It's okay, Kaya. I'm just grateful you came to help us get out of here, and that I get to see the man who stole you away from me."

The stars fell on my head.

"I'll go. You won't have to worry about me anymore," he added.

Every single one of them.

He was moving to the garden door, and I was picking my teeth up out of the dirt and brushing them off so I could speak. "No. Luke, I mean I'm sorry I lied to you back at the beach. And the note—I didn't mean it. I promise. I just said all those horrible things because I thought it was the right thing to do to keep you safe. I'm so sorry for all that."

He untied the satin ribbons of his mask and its black crystals shattered when they hit the ground. He was so heart-achingly beautiful, but the pain and confusion tugging at his perfect features could have felled a forest in one swipe.

"What about him?" Luke said, motioning to Thomas.

Thomas remained still as stone, waiting for my answer, too. The truth was something that would hurt them both, but lying was not an option.

"I d-do love him," I said, feeling a sting of tears behind my eyes.

Thomas gasped, and Luke almost doubled over.

"But," I continued, putting my hands on my chest, hoping Luke would fully realize my honestly. "Not the same way I love you. My heart is yours, Luke, if you'll have it. I want to be with you, and you only."

Luke's eyes lowered and he stumbled slightly, not expecting that answer at all and unsure how to react. He was shaking his head, backing away. "You don't have to spare my feelings, Kaya. I won't hurt him. I'd like to, but I won't."

Oh my God. *He doesn't believe me.*

"Luke, you don't understand—"

I wasn't throwing words at him to protect him this time, and I was so desperate to untangle my lies that I failed to see two men come out of the dark. Before I could warn him, Luke was jumped from behind. But his attackers didn't stand a chance. In a blur of precise movements, Luke connected fists to faces before weapons could even be drawn. When another two rushed at him, Thomas pulled me protectively into the shadows of the tree, and we watched Luke's lethal reflexes in awe. His speed and agility quickly overtook the guards who were now unconscious on the ground.

"Jeezus," Thomas muttered when Luke straightened up, chest heaving and hands still fisted, staring at us across the limp bodies strewn at his feet.

"Only because of her," Luke said, barely winded, "are you still standing."

The guards were coming in full force now. I could hear their feet thundering down the path. "You have to go, Luke," I pleaded.

"What about your father?"

"I have a way out. He can't hurt me. Just go."

Luke shook his head, turmoil in his eyes. "I can't leave Oliver—"

Suddenly everything became a blur of black and white. I was forcibly removed from Thomas's grasp and thick arms circled my chest. When the confusion cleared, there, staring at me with that smug sneer that made me want to rip his eyes out, was Henry. His suit was too tight. His hands covered in too much jewelry. Hair controlled with too much gel. He was shinier than the knife being held to my neck.

Thomas was contained by a man twice his size while Luke fought off two trying to hold him down. As I watched in horror, more guards descended on him in droves. Outnumbered, Luke lashed out and took a hit to the jaw that sent him to his knees. Pulled back up to his feet with his arms held behind his back, he could only stand there while the guards took turns hitting him.

When I screamed, Henry irritably told the guards to stop.

"Impressive," he said to Luke while four cautious men struggled to keep him under control. "You would have been an excellent addition to my team, Mr. Ravelle. There might be a lucrative position for you if you're interested."

Luke spat at Henry's feet.

Henry shrugged his shoulders and turned his attention to Thomas, eyeing him curiously. "Didn't I kill you already?"

Thomas glared but said nothing.

"Ah… I get it," Henry tapped his temple. "You were playing dead on that beach, and Sindra decided to play nice. Lucky for you."

The rat's gaze then fell to me. I didn't shudder. I didn't cower. I showed no fear.

"And Kaya, my sweet daughter," he said. "So nice of you to come home. I've missed you."

The man twisting my arm behind my back laughed and pushed the blade of his knife harder against my throat. A knife, *not* a gun. Weird. That was so not Henry's style.

Something wasn't right.

"Just so you know," Henry said casually to the sweaty man breathing heavily against my ear. "If you hurt my daughter, I will rip you to shreds so slowly even your dead relatives will feel it."

Sharp as a tack, everything came into focus; we were divided. Henry and his armed men with Luke on one side, and me and Thomas and our opposing captors on the other side.

"Tell ya what," a familiar voice said. "I won't kill your precious daughter if you make me a deal."

A female in a white gown came marching out of the shadows. It was the older lady that had been dancing with Oliver. She pointed a thin finger at Henry—but it was Luke who flinched. He seemed to shrink back away from her, and I detected a hint of fear in his eyes.

"How ya doin, Kaya?" the female said to me.

Did I know her?

Gin and jewelry… confessions… dancing and laughing… tattoos and pink hair and a mutual love of zombie movies… the Derrick Bar…

"Angela?" The knife pushed harder against my windpipe. Was I dreaming?

"The one and only," she said, giving the man with the knife a nod of approval.

This was not possible. "Why are you… What is—?" I couldn't talk. The blade was cutting off my air.

The girl pulled off her mask and wiped her mouth across her arm, taking off whatever makeup she'd used to cover the lower half of her face with. "Yup, it is really me. Miss me, love?"

Angela. The waitress. *My friend.* The person I'd confessed everything to one night when I snuck out of my room. Her face was one I would never forget…

A million questions flowed all at once, but I didn't have a chance to ask any.

"Yes, yes. That's your pal, Angela," Henry said, bored. "And what a good friend she turned out to be. She was certainly easy to convert—she became one of my best truth seekers since Sindra trained her so well—but apparently, she's become a bit greedy. What a shame."

"No," I said, the world tipping on its side. "You're wrong. She's my friend." The girl I once knew was completely focused on Henry, appearing entirely the same but entirely different. "Angela, you're here to help me, right? Please tell me that's what's going on."

Even as I said it, I knew I was wrong.

Henry snickered.

Angela shook her head. "Sorry, darling." Her Aussie accent thickened, and I was brought back to memories of her serving cold coffee and bad jokes. "I've been waiting a long time for this moment and gone through absolute hell at the hands of your insane father to get it. There's no going back now."

Betrayal, on the deepest level, *hurt*.

Luke tried to shake free of the men holding him, but he was shoved to his knees.

"You're lying," I stammered.

Henry had grown impatient. "Would you like to see what your so called 'friend' is capable of?" He turned to the guards holding Luke. "Make him stand. And take off his jacket."

Luke's jacket was removed and tossed aside, then Henry marched up and pulled his shirt open down the front. Luke's bare skin caught the light and held it as the buttons scattered and made a tinkling noise on the stones. Bare chested, the claw marks of the cat were a reminder of the day I'd saved him, and the tattoo, black on his ribs, a reminder of why he'd kidnapped me. His eyes met mine, locked on, and for a moment, we were back there, just me and him…

Then they turned him around.

And my heart stopped.

His beautiful skin was a mess of deep red lines and gashes. Some still swollen, some raised and healing. Henry poked the widest one, and Luke gasped.

"She did that to him," Henry said, pointing at Angela. "With a whip."

I waited for Angela to deny the accusation, but she just smiled.

"Luke, is it true?" I said, feeling my stomach flip.

He bowed his head with an almost imperceptive nod.

"*You*… did that… *to him*?" The rush of blood to my head was roaring, and the knife held to my neck meant nothing as I stared at Angela.

She licked her lips rather wickedly. "Mmm, yes," she said, gaze lowering hungrily on Luke. "That is my handiwork. He was so deliciously fun to play with."

I saw red. Pure, thick, and so deep it was almost black—RED. "And you let her," I hissed at Henry.

"Ha, no. I am a terribly busy man, Kaya. I don't have time to keep tabs on my employees. She was told to get information from him, not whip him. That was her own doing. I would never condone anything so barbaric."

For the first time in my life, I knew what extreme rage and anger felt like. It coiled up in my guts like a spring ready to release as my blood turned to liquid fire. I recalled all of Oliver's teachings. His lessons in self-defense. His instructions were clear and fueled by rage as I drove my foot as hard as I could into the knee of the man holding me, not caring about the sting of the knife when his leg snapped backward. Then I swung my elbow back, connected with his jaw, and snatched the knife from his twitching hands before he hit the ground. I lashed out at the man next to Angela, cutting through his jacket and instantly seeing a satisfying red line. He backed away, weaponless, exposing the backstabbing conniving bitch that I intended to kill.

I meant my threat. "You are going to pay for every single bit of pain you caused him."

The self-assured look on Angela's face dissolved, and for a moment I thought my threat had put the fear of God in her. Then I realized that her and her men were unarmed, and I was her bargaining power—her leverage and lifeline—and I was *not* under her control.

"Ah." I smiled, feeling rather wicked as the power of rage surged through me. "You figured I'd still be that wimpy, bumbling idiot you first met. That I'd just stand here and cry. Not anymore. Due to the number of knives that have been held to my throat, I'm a fucking expert at this now."

The man whose knee I broke moaned. I kicked him hard in the balls.

Henry clapped his hands together and let out an amused laugh. "All right, nice work, daughter, but this is getting tedious and I have a house full of guests to attend to. So, what was it that you wanted, Angela? You were attempting to blackmail me, so I might as well hear what you have to say."

Angela stuttered, keeping an eye on me as I inched toward her, the man whose jacket I had cut was already off and running. "I want five million," she said to Henry, trying to keep it together. "I know you have it in your office. I will give you Kaya as soon as the money is in my hands."

"But you don't have Kaya, do you? Not physically or mentally. You hurt the man she loves. There's no forgiving that."

The marks on Luke demanded retribution. The knife steady, I felt myself lurching forward, but with one wave of his diamond-covered hand, Henry beat me to it. Silenced guns put holes in Angela. Too many to count. She crumbled to the ground, and the only thing my knife sliced through was the empty air where she once stood.

The man holding Thomas turned and ran too.

"Sorry, Kaya," Henry said. "I didn't want you to have to deal with that. Blood on your hands is a horrible thing to live with. Thought I'd save you the pain and torment."

"Thanks," I said, realizing I meant it as a strange rush of warmth for my father came over me. Remembering sparse childhood moments when I felt what might have been love, stories read to me while I sat on his lap, the comfort of his arms—all these things made me question absolutely everything I was doing. But the second he took a handgun from his jacket pocket and aimed it at Luke, clarity snapped back into focus.

"You've been excellent bait, Mr. Ravelle." Henry's leather shoes crunched one of Luke's fallen buttons. "But I'm afraid you're no use to me now."

"No!" It burst from me with blinding force. "You won't see a single cent of my inheritance if you hurt him!"

Thomas was at my side, and I shoved him away so he wouldn't stop what I knew I had to do. Moonlight glinted off the blade as I pointed it at my own chest, holding it with two hands so I could plunge it into my heart. The air became colder. The mayday tree where Anne and I carved our names shook.

"Kaya, no," Thomas muttered when I warned him to stay back.

I had Henry's full attention now—my sixteenth birthday wish was finally coming true.

"Let him go," I demanded. "Or I'll do it. I'll kill myself. I won't live in this world without *him*."

Luke's eyes met mine, bluer than blue in the soft moonlight—and I had to look away.

Henry laughed nervously. "You won't do it. You don't have it in you."

I pushed the tip of the knife into my chest, feeling the sting of the skin coming apart and the heat of fresh blood travelling down between my breasts. Luke was struggling now, calling my name, pleading with me to stop, but I tuned him out; funny how clear things became when faced with saving someone you love.

Henry ordered his men to stand down. "You'll never get that knife through your ribcage," he said. "But go ahead and try. I've got a medical unit in the north building that can put you back together again."

I wasn't sure if he was right or not, so I moved the knife lower and pointed the tip of it at my stomach. At that place between my hipbones. I remembered Luke's hand there, stretching out flat against my bare skin that night in the tent, and took in a deep breath; I would slice my womb right open. No heir would come from me. "Henry, there are some things you cannot fix."

Luke, stunned and shaking, gasped for breath and shoved the guards closest to him backward.

"Huh. It appears that you really do love Mr. Ravelle," Henry said, clearly shaken. "So, tell you what. I'll let Luke go, and I won't shoot Thomas either. All you have to do is marry Oliver. Tonight. Simple. That way no one gets hurt—including you."

I poked the knife into my stomach, pushing against the fabric, tearing a small bit of the satin Georgia had so diligently sewn glittering crystals onto.

"I promise I'll let them go," Henry said eagerly, his hands up. "On my honor."

"You have no honor," I spat.

Henry lowered his gaze. "I'll remind you that I still have Stephan."

I wasn't sure whether he did or not, but I couldn't read him now. His truth and lies blended into a blur.

"Thomas," I said, eyes never leaving Henry's, "get over there by Luke."

"I'm not going anywhere without—"

"Now!"

Thomas inched away from me, the guns aimed on him following his every move.

"Luke, open the door," I said.

Luke pushed aside frozen vines and pulled. With a screech the metal door gave way and opened to expose the edge of the cliff.

"Can you get down?" I asked, unable to look at the tears in Luke's eyes; I had to stay focused on Henry and the knife in my hand, the point of it so close to breaking my skin.

"Yes." Luke's voice almost shattered my concentration.

Henry cleared his throat. "So, what will it be Kaya? I have a commissioner of oaths here, and I've already informed our guests that there will be a wedding tonight. I wouldn't want to disappoint them. So agree to marry Oliver or I'll kill him, too."

Luke jolted. "Don't you dare."

"Oh, did I forget to mention that?" Henry said smugly. "Yes, Angela found him quite easily in the crowd and now he's waiting for his bride. Without one, he's useless to me. So what will it be, Kaya? I am being exceptionally kind-hearted today by letting everyone you love keep their lives. All you have to do is say 'I do'."

"You're going to make me marry my brother."

"Legalities. I can work around them."

"Then, so be it." I nodded.

Henry grinned like he'd won the lottery, and all the guards retreated on his request. "I'll let you say goodbye to your, uh, friends. The alarm is off, and they can go happily on their way—if they don't fall to their deaths. You've got six minutes to be at the South entrance of the Empress ballroom. Any later and I'll start killing everyone."

Henry was singing to himself as he walked away. Thomas and Luke rushed toward me, and it was then that I dropped the knife.

OLIVER

FOR BETTER OR WORSE

Being stuffed in a closet wasn't on my agenda, so I threw my weight around and broke a few noses, bruised up a few shins—nothing too exhausting—and made them work for it. I knew escape was futile, but I wanted to give Luke enough time to get away.

Now there was no chatter amongst the men who stood guard in the empty guest suite, just a lot of moaning and wincing. I hadn't recognized anyone in this batch of Henry's minions. They all looked… odd. Something about them not quite right. Their eyes just seemed *empty*.

A knock at the door startled me. "Are you decent in there?"

It was Henry. If I had any hair on the back of my neck, it would have bristled.

The closet door opened, and there he stood, smug as a cat who caught a mouse. His black hair was slicked back, eyebrows groomed and waxed, and his suit tight enough to show off the fact that he had a very good team of personal trainers. Was he wearing eyeliner? He was positively comic-book villainous. Slithering next to him was his lawyer in white boots polished to a blinding shine, as well as a thin, pugnacious man with glasses perched on a bird-like nose. These two were unaffectionately known as the snake and the hawk.

"Time to come out of the closet there, Oliver," Henry said, then laughed. He was in a good mood, which meant something bad was about to happen. I noted that the guards were back far enough that they wouldn't be able to stop me from killing my ex-boss with my bare hands.

"Looking good, Henry," I said, eyeing his naked throat.

"What? You're not calling me 'sir' anymore?" he said, feigning being offended. "Ya know, Oliver, that hurts."

"Oh, darn."

He slapped his leg like I'd said something funny then followed it with a chesty laugh. "But tell ya what, since you will be marrying my daughter in, oh, four minutes, why don't you just call me *Dad*."

His words floated through my ears. I was only half listening because whatever scheme he was dreaming up, I would not be part of. I figured I might as well kill him now and face the consequences. It wouldn't take long. In a split second, I could deliver a two-knuckle blow to his windpipe.

He saw it in my eyes. "You're not going to hurt me, Oliver," Henry said, although he backed up a few inches. "That would be a really bad idea."

"Why?" I asked.

"First, because if you don't go along with today's events, I will kill Stephan and Davis. And second, because I am about to give you everything you've ever wanted."

I inched closer. The guards raised their guns in unison. "And what might that be?" I growled.

Henry smiled. "My daughter."

Along with a stack of papers for me to sign, Henry supplied proof of his threat; Stephan, Davis, and Sindra, all bound and gagged. Stephan was the only one whose eyes were clear, even though his face was riddled with burns. Sindra and Davis both stared at the floor, their faces bloodied and beaten.

The pen in my hand snapped in half.

"I had a wonderful assistant for a while," Henry mused while the man with the bird nose rushed to the get the papers away from the spreading ink. "She found these three hiding out in the kitchen. You may have met her. In fact, I believe you danced with her tonight."

I cringed. "Angela. The waitress from the Derrick."

"Yes," Henry said. "You'll be happy to know that Sindra trained her, and in return, she got the same treatment she gave you all those years ago. Sweet justice, isn't it?"

I found myself agreeing to the absurdity of the logic as I glared at Sindra; what she did to me was unforgivable.

"However," Henry said, eyeing Sindra with disgust but for entirely different reasons. "Angela is dead. She was a traitor, just like Sindra is, and she made the mistake of threatening me, which is never a good idea."

Sindra hung her shorn head and leaned against Davis with closed eyes. The deep-cut white gown she was wearing shifted to expose too much of her chest, which was bruised, and I realized that the dark shades under the sheer fabric that hugged her thin body were more bruises. Although I didn't feel sorry for her, I snarled at the snake lawyer who was openly leering.

"So, here's the deal," Henry said. "You, Mr. Oliver Bennet, are going to sign these documents. My lawyer has assured me that it will make the marriage completely legal. And then, the moment you kiss the bride, I'll let Stephan and Davis walk out the door."

"I don't believe you," I said.

Henry seemed truly offended. "On my honor, Oliver. I promised my daughter that I would let her friends go if she married you and she agreed. I have her in another room signing her life away, too."

There was no way Henry was going to let anyone walk out of here alive. Absolutely no way. He could do whatever he wanted with Sindra, I didn't care. But Stephan and Davis? I had to be smart.

"They get to leave, *now*," I said. "And that includes Arnold in security and the maid, Ella." Stephan's eyes were wide, as if he was trying to relay a message to me telepathically. "And William in the kitchen," I added.

Stephan's shoulders relaxed, but Davis tensed. His eyes held mine, unblinking, and it was the first he acknowledged me since he came in the room. When his head tilted toward Sindra, I knew what he wanted.

"Sindra too," I said, cringing. "They all walk out of here right this minute or I'll just take this pen…" the hawk had placed a fresh one in my hand. I stepped back from him and pressed the tip of it against my neck, "and end all of this."

Henry sighed. Shook his head. "What's with everyone wanting to kill themselves today? Geez, it's sickening. So much drama."

Henry might have been joking, but he knew me well enough to realize I was not faking. What he didn't know was that I was dying already and probably would be doing myself a favor by getting it over with faster.

"All right, fine," he said with an exaggerated wave of his hand. "You…" he pointed at a guard with a swollen eye and bloody nose. "Take these three and the others outside. Lead them through the gates and let them go. Record it and send it to me so I have proof for Oliver, and make it fast. We've got a wedding starting soon."

They were ushered to the door.

"Oh, and Sindra," Henry said. She froze. Terrified. "I suggest you disappear rather thoroughly because eventually I will find you so we can discuss your betrayal."

Sindra's eyes lifted to meet mine, and I almost felt sorry for her. *Almost.* She conveyed the words *thank you* to me, as did Stephan, but Davis walked off without a glance back.

The excitement in the ballroom escalated when a long red carpet was rolled straight down the middle. I stood at one end with the hawk, and Henry at the other with a microphone.

His arrogant voice ignited the room. "Good evening, ladies and gentle-men. I'm so honored you are all here. It is a truly special day, because any moment now, my beautiful daughter will marry her long-time love, Mister Oliver Bennet. This is a father's dream come true!"

Cheers and clapping. Someone said 'whoot'. Then the gossip followed. *I thought Kaya Lowen wasn't real... no one has ever seen her. Maybe she's unfortunately ugly. Who is the poor groom?*

I had to tune it out and concentrate on the inky splotch from the pen on the tip of my finger. I wasn't sure what to do or how to feel. I was being manipulated again. Used. And even knowing that Stephan and the others had made it safely across the bridge and hopefully out of town, I stood there like a lump. Doing nothing. Henry's words rattling around in my head.

I'm going to give you everything you've ever wanted... my daughter.

She truly was everything I ever wanted.

But not this way.

I needed to cause a scene. Make a run for it. But Kaya would be walking down the aisle toward me any moment now. I would be expected to hold her hands. Say vows. *Kiss her...* kiss her... kiss her... and what if she kissed me back? What if she changed her mind and now wanted me the way I wanted her?

Ugh. I had to snap out of it. The lines of reality should not be so blurry.

But since I was dying anyway, maybe just for one moment I could pretend that I really was about to have what I always wanted.

The wedding song lilted through the room, light and airy. The women got teary-eyed. The men, impatient. At the far end of the room, Henry beamed as if he'd inherited the world, and then up behind him came my bride-to-be. She latched on to his arm, stood straight as an arrow, squared her shoulders, and held her head high. Henry didn't even so much as glance at her, intent only on leading her down the carpet toward me.

She was the most beautiful bride. Her mask of feathers and glittering jewels did not conceal the upturned corners of her perfect bow-shaped mouth. The dress—a ridiculously blingy thing with a long train and bodice that barely covered her top half—flowed behind her as she walked. She was breathtaking, stunning, self-assured, and without the slightest hint of weakness or fear about her. And she was most definitely *not* Kaya.

The closer she got, the more it became obvious that the dress was meant for someone shorter and thinner. Not that this girl was heavy by any means; she was perfectly curvy with an ample chest, toned bare shoulders and arms and almost as tall as Henry. She owned the room. I was captivated. Everyone was captivated—except Henry. He was so busy watching the reaction of the crowd he didn't even realize the girl on his arm wasn't his daughter.

The girl's eyes gleamed with mischief, twinkling like the devil was dancing in them. When she came to stop mere feet from me, she winked and smiled so brightly I couldn't help but smile back.

Henry had moved off to the side, leaving her to walk up onto the small stage alone. She kept her back to the room as her hands reached for mine. I noted right away the roughness of her skin and the calluses on her fingertips as I held them. Hawk man was saying stuff... words and blah blah... but I was awed by the strength of this girl's hands. I let the feel of them dull the chatter. It was just her and me. Me and her. And I was saying *I do*... and so was she... and we were exchanging rings, and a strange heat expanded and fluttered in my chest in the most inexplicable way.

"You may kiss the bride," the hawk said, adjusting his glasses.

Had the room grown so quiet my heart could be heard? It pounded madly. I was supposed to remove this girl's mask and kiss her… and I found my hands trembling.

"Waiting ain't gonna make me any prettier," my bride said with a grin.

I reached for the ribbon at the back of her head, released the bow, and unveiled the most beautiful face I'd ever seen.

I forgot where I was.

"You may kiss the bride," urged the hawk.

I put my trembling hands on her cheeks. "I'm Oliver," I said.

Her brown eyes levelled on mine. "And I'm Marlene."

Marlene. I kissed her. Never had I kissed anyone other than Kaya, but I kissed this girl. And I didn't want to stop. I felt my hands shake as I held her cheeks, letting them glide across her skin when she finally pulled away. When she turned to face the crowd, they began clapping and cheering—and that's when Henry's face fell.

It took a nose dive.

Crashed.

Hit the dirt.

And it was awesome to see.

Marlene raised our clutched hands and silenced the crowd. "Thank you all so much!" she said loudly, and suddenly a pin dropping would have sounded like a drum set falling over. "It is so wonderful to finally be able to meet so many of you fantastic people and have you here at my wedding!"

Henry still hadn't picked his jaw up off the ground.

Marlene smiled madly. "You know, after being ill for so long, I never thought I'd have the opportunity to marry, but with the love and dedication of my dear father and his medical research, I am healed! It's my dream come true. Healthy and married to the man of my dreams. Thank you from the bottom of my heart, *Daddy.*"

Her excitement seemed so genuine that the kiss she blew to Henry slapped when it hit his cheek.

"I know this is an unusual request," she went on as I watched her in complete awe. "But then again, this is an unusual wedding. I'm hoping that all of you will escort me and my husband," she winked at me deviously and squeezed my hand, "into town to mark the beginning of our new lives together. Walk with us! Let us celebrate with all of you as we head off on the start of our new lives together!"

Brilliant. Absolutely bloody brilliant.

There was more cheering. A surreal level of excitement filled the room as this girl, Marlene, led the way with the air of a queen. The crowd broke in behind us, following obediently as we headed for the doors. No one tried to stop us. Not one guard made a move. We marched out of the ballroom, through the grand lobby, down the marble steps into the cool night, and through the gates.

I felt freedom on so many levels.

But we were exposed now. Anyone could be carrying a weapon, or working for John Marchessa, or taking the rare opportunity to kidnap the billionaire heiress and exact revenge on her father; the threats hadn't changed.

I switched into bodyguard mode, just as desperate to protect this girl holding my hand as if she were Kaya, but a cough stalled me. Tripped up my feet. Marlene tugged me forward not slowing for a second.

"I got you," she said softly. "Just follow my lead, all right, big guy?"

Guests were close behind, some marching along beside us now, cell phones in hand.

"You're a target out here," I said, eyeing the bridge coming up. "John Marchessa—"

"Yeah whatever," she said, cutting me off. "I know all about that weasel pimple. He can kiss it. Just stay close, I'll look after you, Oliver."

I didn't know if my voice would work. "All right," I said, stunned and rather lightheaded.

We made it to the bridge, and I didn't have to glance back to know that Henry and his men were completely unprepared to have hundreds of people escort us into town. They were getting directions on their earpieces, and the command would be to protect the asset. *Me*. I was still valuable, Marlene however, was not, and I had no gun, no backup, no—

"Almost home-free there, hubby," Marlene said as the bridge shook beneath us.

Her skirt was kicking up around her feet, exposing black hiking boots, the toes scuffed and worn. "Who *are* you?" I asked through a fake smile and noise bordering on chaos.

"Kaya is my best friend," she said.

I almost stopped walking. "That's ridiculous. She's—"

"Safe."

Marlene kept smiling as cameras flashed, people called her Kaya, and the crowd pushed us ahead. I wanted to break into a run now that we were across the bridge, but thought it might incite panic. Things were getting out of control.

"We both love zombie movies," Marlene said, or practically yelled, her grip on my hand not letting up. "Hate mayo and would rather eat rocks than cook. She's with Luke by the way."

A sudden weariness gripped me from out of nowhere. I felt myself slow, and Marlene marched faster, practically dragging me down the street.

"Where are we going?" I asked.

"I have a car waiting. Just up ahead."

My body was defying me, but Marlene was having none of it.

"Come on. Keep up, it's not far," she hissed.

But that cough came at me and stopped me dead in my tracks. Marlene stopped too, then turned around abruptly and yelled at the mob.

"Stop!"

She held her bouquet high in the air, and the squeals from the women trying to shove their way to the front of the line were deafening. Marlene was stalling so I could catch my breath, and while she waited until she thought I was okay, time stood still. The wind had scattered her hair around her face, the pins were gone somehow, and there was such determination and strength in her eyes I became as awestruck as the crowd.

"Are you ready, ladies?"

Cheering. Squealing. Marlene had the power and control of everyone behind her with a bunch of stupid flowers—I would never understand girls.

With her back to the crowd again, Marlene swung the flowers over her shoulder and sure enough, panic ensued. You'd think she'd tossed a bucket of diamonds by the way the pushing and shoving escalated. We took the opportunity to run, just as shots rang out.

I didn't bother to look back or even try to figure out who was shooting at whom, all we could do was head for the car. I'd always thought Kaya was fast for a girl, but Marlene was faster. I had a tough time keeping up with her and could barely catch my breath once we got into the backseat.

"You all right there, big guy?" she asked.

I nodded, and with tires squealing and headlights gleaming, in her eyes I caught a glimpse of a life I hadn't known I'd wanted until now.

On the edge of town in a motel parking lot, I was vaguely aware that we were switching vehicles, and with Driver Dan at the wheel of an old truck, we headed out of town under a blanket of stars. I should have had a thousand questions for Dan, but I could only watch Marlene practically shred the dress trying to get it off as if it were suddenly acid. When she caught me watching her out of the corner of my eye, her voice lowered in warning.

"Quit being a perv. You keep your eyes in your head and your hands to yourself or I'll smack the crap outta ya."

"Sorry."

I had no doubt she would. But she was pulling a black T-shirt on over perfect golden skin and a white lacy bra, and then cargo pants over a flat stomach and a knife strapped to her ankle.

"Hey, what did I tell you?" she barked, turning to face me, brown eyes boring into mine.

I fumbled. "I'm sorry, it's just that... I, uh... well..."

She blinked at me, waiting for an answer, and I noticed her cheek had a darkness to it, a bruise maybe? The highway lights only momentarily lit her face. Before I could stop myself, I was reaching for her.

Only to have my hand slapped practically right off my wrist.

"Don't you dare touch me," she said.

"I'm sorry, I thought—"

A cough came and stole my words. Ripped them right from my tongue. The tang of blood filled my mouth, and I hoped in the dark of night, she wouldn't see it on my hands. I was swallowing hard. My mouth dry. I felt incredibly dizzy and my mind was drifting as Marlene's face came in and out of view, the look in her eyes changing from wanting to kill me to concern.

"Ah crap. How many glasses of champagne did you drink, Oliver?"

Her voice fluttered through my ears, and I thought of the hawk, handing me a glass and then another, and in my nervousness, downing two more off a waiter's tray. Or, was it three? They were small glasses.

"Five, maybe," I said. "Not sure."

"Five? Who drinks five glasses of champagne? Especially a dude? Oh well." Marlene was smiling, her fingertips were on my forehead pushing me back gently into the seat. Was she bunching up her discarded dress and putting it behind my head? It smelled nice.

"Georgia spiked the champagne. She may have sedated half the town."

"Who is Georgia?" I asked, although I didn't care.

Marlene snorted. So unladylike. So perfect. "A really annoying blonde chick with too much time on her hands."

The truck ambled along. "Where are we headed?" I asked, but my words were slurred.

"To that place you've always wanted to go. The one that's 'in your dreams'."

Was she mocking me? Oh well. I didn't care. I closed my eyes.

"Well, nighty night there, big guy. Don't worry about a thing. You and most of the town will sleep well this evening."

"Yes. Goodnight, Marlene," I tried to say, but darkness swiftly took over. Marlene. Marlene. Such a beautiful name, Marlene, I didn't want to forget it. Not ever. It was so perfect, so perfect... *Marlene*.

"Yeah, whatever, weirdo," I heard her say.

2 6

SHE'S NOT JUST A GIRL

I woke with the sun in my eyes and the smell of gasoline in my nose. It took a minute to get my bearings; I was in the backseat of a truck —a rusty thing that should be in a junkyard—and Marlene's wedding dress was stuffed underneath and around me, cradling my head and keeping me warm. There was a ring on my finger…

Marlene.

I sat up. The sun was directly overhead, beating down on lush foliage and green weeds surrounding a crumbling gas station. We were just off a highway, and the mountains were only pin pricks in the distance. It was warm. There was no snow. How long had we driven?

I noticed the top of a head of amber hair from someone leaning down beside the truck, and I rolled down the window.

"Mornin, Oliver," Marlene said as I got out of the backseat and stretched. "Flat tire. I hope I didn't bend the rim."

There was dirt on her hands and a dark smudge on her cheek. No one was helping her.

"Where's Dan?" I asked, scanning the area.

"I dropped him off at the last town. He needed to get back to his kids."

The truck was jacked up, and Marlene was pulling off the flat. Some kid in beige coveralls and knockoff Ray Bans was leaning against the gas pump, uselessly watching. I gave my head a shake at the putz.

"You're changing the tire? *By yourself?*"

Marlene's snarl was her only reply.

215

I took off my suit jacket. "I'll do it," I said, motioning toward her.

"What?" she stood slowly and stared me down, tire iron in her hands. "Listen, if you want to help me that's fine, but just so you know, I'm not helpless."

"You can go on and wash up. You got some dirt on your face. Hand over the—"

I was shoved backward so hard I almost landed on my ass. Big brown eyes full of rage levelled on me, and a finger was pointed at my face. The kid bolted for the store.

"Let's get one thing straight, Oliver," Marlene roared. "I'm no damsel in distress. I don't need saving, or protecting, or any sort of looking after. I'm going to fix the tire on my truck, and you're going to get your ass in the passenger seat and do a whole lot of nothing. And if you ever treat me like I am useless, weak, or incompetent with that macho baloney of yours, your man-danglers will be bathed in barbecue sauce and on the dinner special at the next truck stop. Got it?"

I backed away, hands up in self-defense. "Sorry, I—"

"And quit with the 'sorry' bull crap too! What is that, six times now you've apologized to me since we met? How about you just man up already and don't do stuff you need to apologize for in the first place."

Whoa. Who was this woman? A rush of heat pulsed through me with her every word. My feet were moving, my hands opening the passenger door of the truck as my body obeyed and my mind spun. I watched her shake her head, muttering to herself as she wrestled the spare tire on and tightened the lug nuts.

She caught me ogling her in the side mirror. "Honestly, if you didn't mean so much to Kaya, I'd take the next logging road and drop you off at the end with a stale sandwich and no bug spray."

I smiled despite myself. Even though she appeared to hate me, something about her intrigued me so deeply I couldn't conceal the strange giddiness tingling down my spine.

"Speaking of sandwiches, I could get us some," I said, hoping to break the ice and pointing to the gas station. "In there." Then I realized I didn't have any money.

"Already did that," Marlene said. "Look on the seat next to ya."

I was so busy checking her out that I hadn't even noticed the brown paper bag. Ravenous, I tore into a cold, crusty sub layered with mystery meat and plastic cheese. I ate while she finished with the tire.

Poking her head into the open window, she tossed in the tire iron. "We're gonna keep this up front just in case." She eyed the paper bag. "I hope you saved me a couple of those."

A couple? They were foot long sandwiches. "Yes, of course."

"Good. Get down," she said.

"Pardon?"

Marlene smiled and reached in for a ratty ball cap resting on the dash. She made a quick attempt to stuff her hair up underneath it. "Two suits are getting out of a flashy BMW behind us. One is carrying heat. So *get your head down.*"

I leaned over, almost burying my face in the bag of food, and waited for what seemed like forever until I felt the truck lurch as Marlene lowered the jack. She climbed back in and turned the key in the ignition. I was about to tell her to get in the back so I could drive, then remembered that might end up with my private parts salted and deep fried.

"They won't recognize me," she said under her breath, "but you're like a neon sign at midnight."

Why wouldn't they recognize her? She had just walked down the aisle pretending to be Kaya Lowen, her face captured on every recording device.

"Just trust me, okay?" she said as if reading my mind, then tossed her jean jacket over my head.

I didn't answer because she wouldn't have heard me anyway. Cranking the stereo up as loud as it would go so the bass threatened to stop my heart and blast apart the windows, Marlene spun the tires out onto the highway while Led Zeppelin's *Whole Lotta Love* blared through the speakers.

"*You need coolin', baby, I ain't foolin',*" she sang at the top of her lungs.

And right there and then, with my face buried in a bag of submarine sandwiches, everything I thought I knew about women was completely obliterated.

"Marchessa, Lowen—whoever those suits were working for back there —they can *kiss my ass,*" Marlene yelled between song lyrics, and the truck fishtailed obscenely.

Yep, completely obliterated.

27

PRIORITIES

It was an hour before sunset, and through stifling traffic, construction re-routes, big city chaos and masses of people everywhere, Marlene calmly maneuvered the truck to our destination. It sputtered in relief when we parked in a motel lot, the ocean sprawling out before us like a luxurious glittering bed.

As soon as the salt air filled my lungs and my shoes hit the beach, a childhood memory resurfaced. I was six again, holding hands with my little sister and pulling her away from the water. *This is not a safe place to swim,* Mom was saying to both of us, the red scarf tied over her hair billowing out behind her. Maisy, the youngest and bravest of us all, gave Mom no mind. Her little feet were bare. She was off and running into the water, ignoring Mom's warning about the rocks. Maisy was soon ankle deep, tears instantly streaming down her face, and I marched in, shoes and all, and picked her up. Of course she fought me even though she was being rescued. She was stubborn, like my brother, and just as mean; when her tiny hand reached out to hit me, it was caught by Dad.

"Don't hit Oliver," he said.

He'd been passively standing by with one eye on the ships and the other on his watch, but his children had his attention now. "Your brother is just trying to protect you, Maisy," he'd said. "That's what family does; protects each other. Right, Ollie?"

There was pride in Dad's eyes when he towered over me, patting me on the head, but there was sadness in them, too. Worry furrowed his brow.

He held my gaze while Maisy ran off to chase a crab, and what he said next put the weight of the world on my shoulders.

"If something happens to me, you'll protect your family, won't ya, kiddo?"

I crisscrossed my fingers over my six-year-old heart. "Yes, Dad."

"You'll protect them with your life. Right?"

I nodded.

"Promise me!" he said with a ferocity that made me jump.

"I promise," I said.

Dad's eyes glazed over. "Good, 'cause I'm counting on you."

That was the last time I'd heard his voice, and his words stayed with me forever. I'd carried them around until I'd found Kaya, and then I made her the focus of that promise I'd failed to keep.

I talked to the heavens—to my dad. "After all these years, I've finally realized that what happened wasn't my fault. Now, I have a name. I know who took you from me. Also, I know *why,* so, I can let go of the guilt that's been eating away at me all this time. And, get even."

Why was I suddenly able to do this?

Marlene came running up behind me, breathless. "Can you believe it?" Her cell phone was thrust at my face.

Marlene?

She pointed to the phone. "On the news they're saying the gunshots at the estate were the result of one of the guards drinking the 'tainted' champagne and falling on his gun. My Lord, Henry is amazing at covering things up. I watched him just now, not even batting an eye when he was interviewed, blissfully happy about the marriage of his daughter to her bodyguard. You'd think he'd at least falter or break out in a sweat."

Her voice trailed off when she realized my mind was elsewhere and that maybe she'd interrupted a private moment. She cleared her throat and changed the subject. "Um, it's beautiful here," she said softly. "You know, I've never seen the ocean."

"Neither has Kaya." I stared off across English Bay at the oranges and reds lining the horizon.

Marlene stared too, her jaw dropping slightly in awe of the sparkling water and distant ships and barges. "Why are all those boats just sitting there?" she asked.

I turned to admire her. She was shielding her eyes, feet inches from the lick of the waves, back straight as an arrow. I liked how the breeze made her eyes squint and her hair flutter. I liked how her chin jutted out when she was staring hard at something.

"Free parking," I said with a lump in my throat. "They will sit there for hours, sometimes days, waiting until the time is right to go into the harbor."

Here in the heart of Vancouver, hotels and restaurants dotted the shoreline, people ran and cycled the sea wall, and the hustle and bustle of it all ended at the beach. It was peaceful here. Beautiful. And it all disappeared completely when Marlene turned to look at me. Those big brown eyes... oh so badly I wanted to reach out and push the windblown hair from her face and look at them closer, then wipe the new smudge of dirt from her cheek.

She saw me staring and quickly turned away. "Stop looking at me," she snapped.

"No. You're beautiful." It just came out of my mouth.

She spoke into the wind. "I'll beat the living daylights out of you if you ever say anything like that to me again."

I stifled a laugh. "Stop threatening me. All right? Obviously, you're not so good at receiving compliments, but that's no reason to be nasty. Besides, a man should be able to admire his *wife*."

"Wife, eh? Well, *hubby*, if you want to keep your eyeballs and your hands, you best be keeping them to yourself."

I grinned madly at her. I knew I was smiling like an idiot, but I couldn't help it. She brought out this feeling of elation in me. A happiness I'd never experienced. And, I suspected she was trying not to smile, too. When she turned and faced me, her lips pursed as if to give me a tongue lashing for something, but her eyes said otherwise. I wanted to kiss her again, here, on this beach with the sun setting and the ocean serenading. As if in a dream, I inched forward, just slightly, then bridged the gap and reached for her face. Her body tensed in fear—or what might possibly even have been terror.

I stepped back at once. "I'm so sor—"

We both heard it; my name carried on the wind along with the squawk of a bird and a car alarm going off.

"She's here," Marlene said, relieved to be released from the awkward moment, eyes still wide.

She was referring to Kaya, and I should have been anxiously scanning the beach to see her, but I wanted to know why Marlene, a girl who didn't seem scared of anything, was terrified of an affectionate advance. What had I done wrong? I wanted to ask, wanted to know everything about her, but there was a female approaching. Black hair trailing out behind her and tears streaming down her cheeks. I braced myself as Kaya dove into my arms, and then gave myself over to the rush of love that flooded in with the familiarity of her.

My girl.

I buried my cheek in her hair and returned the embrace. She was thinner than she was weeks ago. More delicate. But I held her tight anyway and for much longer than would have been proper if it wasn't us.

"I was so worried," she said after a long while, her head against my chest. I could feel her tremble.

"Back atcha, my girl," I said.

Luke was standing behind her, a relaxed smile on his face and his hands in his pockets. Thomas—eyes shadowed like he hadn't slept in days—was a few feet behind Luke. We exchanged a polite nod.

"I can't believe our plan worked," Kaya said to Marlene when she finally broke away from me. She was tying her hair back from the wind, cheeks flushed and eyes dazzling. "You saved them. You saved me. I'm so grateful for you, Marlene, so very—"

"Ah, quit yer blubbering," Marlene scolded as Kaya forced her into an embrace. "You're all right?"

"I'm fine," Kaya said, pulling back to ponder her friend. "But hey…" she paused and regarded Marlene with a puzzled expression. "Someone could recognize you." She reached for Marlene's cheek to wipe at the dirt that seemed to gravitate to her face. "Why are you still wearing makeup?"

Marlene's eyes darted nervously in my direction. "I'm not wearing any makeup," she said loudly, and reaching for Kaya's hand, led the two of them to a log of driftwood that glowed in the lowering light. There they sat and spoke in hushed voices.

"How did Kaya get out?" I asked Luke, barely able to tear my eyes away from them.

Thomas spoke before Luke could. "Climbed her way down with us."

That got my attention.

"She was so brave," Luke said proudly.

"It was a stupid thing to do," Thomas said icily.

Luke snarled. "Yeah, because staying where she was and being locked up and forced to do things against her will would have been better."

Huh. It seemed that Luke's seemingly endless patience was being tested. How entertaining.

"She could have died."

"Are we going to keep discussing this, Thomas?"

The tension was thick between the two of them, and I realized—quite unexpectedly—that I was just an onlooker now. I wasn't trying to tame the old jealous monster that would have reared its ugly head because the girl I loved also loved these two blokes. Somehow, my chest felt lighter. Easier. And when Marlene's laugh made me turn to look at her again, I knew she was the reason why.

The sun was rapidly slipping away. The air growing colder. My heart skipped a beat when the girls rejoined us, and Marlene stood at my side.

"Well, what now?" Kaya asked, caught in the net of Luke's blue gaze. "All of us but Thomas are homeless and since everyone thinks Marlene is me, she has a huge target on her back. We have to hide her."

"We could keep moving. Not stay in one place too long. Separate if we must," I suggested.

"I think we should stay together," Thomas said, pushing the sand around with his toes and clearing his throat. "You know, strength in numbers."

Luke reached for Kaya, his hand tight around hers as he warily watched Thomas. "Why? You're free now. You can go home. There is no reason for you to stick around."

Kaya seemed to become pale. Thomas stared at her, not caring about the man at her side who could take him out in a second.

"I'm not leaving Marlene," Thomas said. "Not in a million years. She needs me."

We all knew he meant he wasn't leaving Kaya. It was obvious by the way his eyes hovered over her, the way he forced his arms to stay still at his sides when he really wanted to reach out and pull her away from Luke. Tension amongst the three of them was a simmering pot about to boil over.

"I don't need a babysitter, Thomas," Marlene said. "You can go."

Kaya's eyes clouded. There was a storm raging in her heart.

"Actually, you *all* need me," Thomas said. "Money is pretty handy, and I'm the only one who has any—besides you Marlene—but a couple of hundred bucks isn't going to go far. You guys can't even rent a motel or a car without me. What's in your wallet, Luke? Do you even have one? No, don't answer—" Thomas put his hands up, blocking replies. "Besides that, I do truly need to stick around. Marlene's safety is my priority."

Marlene was about to complain, but one look at Kaya's hopeful face changed her mind. "Yeah. You're right. I, uh, need you Thomas," she said.

Luke could barely hide his irritation. "So, it looks like we are all sticking together then."

Relief flooded Kaya's face. I gave Marlene a discreet nod of approval to which she rolled her eyes.

Luke rubbed his head. "Well, as you all know, I have a little sister that could use some extended family and a lot of spoiling. So, how about we spend some of your money, Thomas, and do a little Christmas shopping on the way back to Seth's ranch? Lisa is there and it's safe."

Kaya hated Christmas, but she squealed with delight and threw her arms around Luke. "That's perfect," she said. "Thank you."

Luke all but turned to a puddle. He couldn't help but smile. Actually, none of us could help our smiles. The word *family* had struck a chord amongst us, and Luke, bless his forgiving heart, extended the offer to Thomas graciously.

"For now… truce," he said.

Thomas, blinking with shock and relief, squeezed his hand agreeably.

"My little sister, Louisa, loves bunnies," Luke said to him.

Thomas nodded with a gulp. "All my sisters did too when they were little."

There wasn't going to be a bloodbath on the beach today—oh well.

"Hey, are we invited to the party?" said a familiar voice at my back.

I spun around; two figures, one wide and sturdy, one thin and limping, crept up to our circle. Stephan was leaning heavily on a wide, stocky man. He'd lost so much weight his cheekbones stuck out at a horrifically sharp angle, and his patchy beard barely concealed the many new scars. The twinkle in his eye was still there though, and it beamed as he smiled at us now, holding the hand of the love of his life, Chef William.

"Hi, butter bean," Stephan said to Kaya.

"Stephan!" His name exploded out of her, but she was so shocked to see him she didn't move. She just put her hands over her mouth as tears sprung from her eyes.

"My sweet petunia, I've missed you so much" Stephan said, giving the rest of us a polite nod while he let go of William and moved in front of Kaya, arms spread wide.

Sobs instantly racked Kaya's body and brought her crumbling to Stephan's feet. He kneeled and held her like she was a little girl. Like he always had. I felt a bit choked up and tried to hide it. Luke's eyes were threatening to tear up, too, and he tugged at the shirt tight at his collarbone. Thomas shoved his hands in his pockets and kicked at the sand.

"So, you're Luke Ravelle," Stephan said, holding Kaya tightly and peering up over her head to study the man she would do anything for.

Luke nodded. "You must be Stephan," he said. "Glad to meet you again under better circumstances. I'm sorry about back there, in the cells... I—"

Stephan smiled his approval. "You had no choice but to leave us behind. You did the right thing." He gently released Kaya and pulled her to her feet. "Everybody, this is William," he said proudly of the heavy-set man stoically at his side now. "He is my boyfriend."

"Fiancé," William corrected, completely unimpressed with the lot of us.

"Yes, fiancé. Sorry, it still feels sort of unbelievable to say it."

"Oh Stephan, I'm so happy for you," Kaya said, clinging to him again.

I was also about to congratulate Stephan with a bear hug and a hand shake, but he put his hand up to stop me, gaze drifting over my shoulder.

"Wait, Oliver. I brought two others with me, and I hope you won't be upset, but I didn't know what else to do with them."

I turned around to see Davis, completely expressionless and eyes fixed on the sparkling ocean, and Sindra, perched under his arm, cowering.

I felt heat flooding my cheeks. "What is *she* doing here?" I growled.

I was expecting the old Sindra to get up in my face and threaten me with my life or give me an order to stand down, but this Sindra was completely broken. She flinched from my words and turned her face toward Davis, hiding against him as his arm tightened around her protectively.

"They're homeless too?" Luke asked.

Stephan nodded.

"Well, forgiveness is a good thing," Luke said softly, his hand patting my shoulder, urging me to agree. "We've all done some things we're not proud of. No time like the present to move on from them."

He was right. Of course he was right. And by the wounded shape of Sindra, her payback had been more than even she deserved.

I gave Luke a nod.

"All right," he said, taking control of our group of nine. "Seems like we're having a big ol' family Christmas this year. I don't really dig ham by the way. Or gifts."

"Or carols and Santa and cookies," Marlene said.

I couldn't help myself. "Cookies? Really? C'mon already."

"Ooh. First husband and wife spat," Luke teased.

"Oh, blech!" said Marlene, but there was a little grin lighting up her eyes, and I noticed the ring was still on her finger.

"So, onward and upward," Luke said, reaching for Kaya and putting his arm around her. "I have a little sister to spoil rotten."

They led the way. Thomas reached for Marlene, putting an arm over her shoulders, which she quickly shrank away from and punched him for. Stephan and William linked hands, and Davis and Sindra sheepishly followed, glued together as if the slightest separation would kill them both. We all headed off the beach. I was last, savoring the heady breath of salt air and the waning ray of light skipping across the water, my dad's last words fading to a distant memory.

Marlene had slowed. She was at my side and tugging me forward, not scared of me now. "C'mon, big guy," she said. "You should stick with me. We like the same sandwiches, and I'll let you pick the tunes while I drive."

Her big brown eyes held mine, and I was caught; the past would *remain unsettled for a bit longer because the future had become far more interesting.*

December 25th

KAYA

28
HO, HO, HO

I was dreading the day, which was ridiculous. It was Christmas, and all the people I loved were together under one roof. But this was yet another morning I'd woken up alone, and with every passing hour that Luke avoided me, the harder it was to get out of bed.

Yes, there was the 'agreement' that I had my own room and no one should come near it. This was out of respect for Stephan who loudly exclaimed that if he caught anyone touching his 'baby girl' while he was around, they would wake up missing a few body parts. So Luke waited until everyone was asleep, then snuck into my bed and wrapped me in his arms. It was pure and utter bliss, sleeping and dreaming next to him. He'd disappear at first light then during the day seek me out in every corner of the house. We couldn't bear to be away from each other, not for a second.

Until three days ago.

What had I done?

I sat up and dragged a brush through my hair, listening to the ranch house come to life. The sound of feet in slippers swished up and down the hall, the bathroom taps came on, and squeals of excitement erupted from Louisa when she discovered that Santa paid a visit in the middle of the night. *No presents* I had insisted when Luke and I were still back at the coast and everything was perfect. There was no gift he could give me that could compare to being the center of his gaze. Having his heart beat against mine was all I needed. I had apologized for the note and for lying to him and trying to protect him, and he held me close, trembling when he said he understood. *I just want you for Christmas,* he'd said, and I laughed and told him he was being corny and that I loved it—and that I loved him.

"You can't expect me to just give you nothing," he said after we stopped at a gift shop and bought every bunny-related item we could find, the trunk of the rental car was stuffed.

"I really don't want presents." I meant it fully. "But I would like to give you one. What do you wish for?"

He smiled that glorious smile that made the majestic mountains we were heading for pale in comparison. "I told you. All I want is you. If you can give me that, I would never want for anything else as long as I live."

I probably pinched myself a hundred times. Incredibly, I was awake. I told him I was his until the end of time.

Yet, this morning, I had woken up alone.

And I wasn't sure why.

The only good thing about today was at least there would be no priceless blue boxes that Oliver would have to coax me out of bed to open, and no anger that I would have to suppress toward Henry for not being there to personally deliver them. Stephan was freed from having to try to play the parent role and go out of his way to smother my sadness at not having the one thing I wished for every year; my mom and a father that paid attention to me. And mostly, I didn't have to be that whiny, weak, and miserable little girl either.

I peeled back the blankets, shocked by the frigid air, and pulled on a t-shirt, jeans, extra heavy socks, and a sweater. But instead of heading toward the action, I flopped back down on the bed.

I needed one more minute before facing the day.

Knuckles rapped lightly on the door, and then Thomas was pushing it open.

"Are ya decent?" he asked. "Not that I care if you aren't but…uh, hey? Why are you in bed?" He entered the room and shut the door behind him. "The big fella was here with his reindeer and everybody is up except you. Even Marlene has a smile on her face." He smelled of soap. I tried not to notice he was freshly showered, his hair still damp, and skin glowing. He seemed nervous.

"You better not be coming in here with a gift," I said.

There was something in his hand that he tried to discreetly get into his back pocket. A small envelope?

"Nope. Course not. I was just coming to check on you is all."

I smiled up at him, glad he changed his mind and put whatever he was about to give me away. "Thanks. I'm all right."

"My eldest sister didn't much care for Christmas either," he said.

"Don't you miss them? Don't you wish you were home?"

Thomas was so ruggedly beautiful. Even the way he shrugged his shoulders and brushed off his longing for his family was alluring. "I do. But they love me. They understand that I'm doing what I have to do."

"*Have* to do?"

Thomas sat on the edge of the bed, the pink coverlet sinking around his black jeans. "*Want* to do," he corrected. "Being here, with you, is what I want."

"You mean, so you can watch over Marlene."

"Uh, yeah, of course."

Thomas picked at the blanket and I wondered if he was still contemplating giving me the present he had shoved into his pocket. I really hoped he wouldn't. I had nothing to give back.

"What's wrong, Kaya? I can see there's something you're not telling me."

I sat up. I couldn't talk to him about Luke, but I could discuss the other things on my mind.

"What if I didn't have this inheritance hanging over my head? Would things be different? Would I be a normal girl with a mom and dad who loved her simply because she was *theirs*?"

"Whoa. Deep stuff for Christmas morning. But all right." Thomas considered this. Rubbed his chin. "Probably. But that's not what happened. The past is where it belongs, Kaya, in the past. Move ahead. Don't overthink it or sift through every angle of it because what's done is done. Here, and now..." he took my hand and placed it over his heart, "is what matters."

I could feel the heat rise in my cheeks as his pulse thrummed beneath my fingertips. He hadn't touched me since we'd been here. Not even an accidental brush-by. I had to suppress the urge to crawl up to him, put my head on his chest, and relax against him like I used to. There was something so comforting about Thomas, so soothing. But instead, I sat very still, as if the slightest movement might propel me unstoppably forward.

Thomas kissed the palm of my hand, then carefully placed it back on my lap. "I better go," he said. "Everyone's waiting for us and I shouldn't be breaking the agreement."

He rose, then stopped and stared down at me. "You know I still love you," he said, and there was a slight tremble to his hands when he reached out to tuck a lock of hair behind my ear. "And that love is for all the right reasons. When you want me, you just say the word."

I hung my head and sighed. "Thomas, really? You know that I am—"

He put his hands up. "I know… I know. But you're having reservations, aren't you? I can see that your conscience is having a war with your heart. You won't ever have that battle with me, ya know."

I had to give my head a shake. "What the heck are you talking about?"

Thomas glanced over his shoulder to make sure the door was still closed. "I'm talking about the fact that I'm the right choice and you know it now. Luke is a criminal with unclear intentions and who-knows-what kind of motives."

"What?" I wanted to shove him out the door, anger welling up. "Are you referring to what I said to him when we were at that lake? When I tried to make him hate me and leave so he wouldn't be killed by my insane father? That's slinging mud, Thomas. You know I didn't mean it."

"But you realize now that what you said was true." Thomas' eyes lowered, bracing himself for a fight.

"No. It's *not* true. And you can stop trying to mess with my head. You need to accept that there is nothing between us and move on."

"But you belonged to me for a little while, didn't you?" He stared as if he could see clear into my soul.

I held my ground, trying not to yell. "I don't belong to anyone." I was shaking with anger. "Love doesn't make you someone's *property*."

"Ah. So you have learned something from your relationship with Oliver. And you do love me."

This talking in circles was becoming exhausting. I reeled my temper in. "You know I care about you, Thomas. But that's it. Now, just go."

His dark eyes searched mine, digging. "Why do you think Luke is avoiding you?"

This question rattled me. "He is not avoiding me. He is just, uh, respecting the agreement," I said, reminding myself to breathe. "No other reason."

"No. It's because *he knows*." He drew back.

My breath caught. "Knows what?"

Thomas crossed his arms over his chest. "About us. I told him."

The world spun for a moment. Three days ago, Luke had stormed out of the house and walked off for hours after having a conversation with Thomas. When he came back, his knuckles were bloody and his eyes stormy. He claimed he had 'taken a fall'.

"What exactly did you tell him?" I was glad I was sitting down.

Thomas cleared his throat. Cracked his neck. "I told him about our night together. How you… came to my bed. I told him that you are in love with me as well, and he should back off so you can decide which of us you want."

It was like he'd slapped me. The sting of his words seized painfully as I realized that Luke had been avoiding me because of *that*. "Oh my God, Thomas, how could you?"

He stood straight as an arrow, unapologetic. "I'm not going down without a fight, and since I can't beat him with my fists, I'll use logic."

"I was going to tell him when the time was right. He's going to think I'm… I'm easy. Oh my God. *"*

Thomas laughed. "Easy? *A slut*? C'mon. You had sex with one guy, once, and made out with me. That's it. You're human, Kaya, and you are *supposed to* enjoy the pleasures of being one. Now, I don't like Luke, but I'm pretty sure that's not what he's thinking. How many chicks do you think he went through before he got to you? And do you think badly of him for it?"

That thought almost doubled me over. "Thomas—"

"We didn't do anything wrong, Kaya, and you know that, so you can drop the guilt right this second. At least you know that what I have for you is real love, without any ulterior motives. I proved it to you that night when you crawled into my bed and let me have my way with you. I could have done whatever I wanted, but I respected your heart. I took a bullet for you instead, and I would a thousand times over if I had to. Luke is not the right man for you. I am. And it will only be a matter of time before you see that."

With that he left, shutting the door behind him as Louisa hollered, *"Regan got me a real bunny!"*

The rest of the day was a blur. Toys, bunny poop, dishwashing, getting a Barbie leg dislodged from Brutus's throat—whatever I could do to stay busy, I did. The tree sparkled with ornaments, Christmas carols relentlessly droned from the stereo, and Lisa and Thomas sang along while preparing our feast. He acted like our morning conversation had never happened. Luke acted like I'd broken his heart.

Maybe I did.

By four in the afternoon, the sun was getting ready to go down and I found Louisa curled up and sound asleep on Regan in the living room. Her head was on his chest, her favorite blanket was carefully draped over them both. Regan's cast was covered in her artwork, and I was happy to see his toes weren't purple anymore. He had an easy smile on his face, relaxed and sweet, and it was so strange how this cold and calculated brilliant doctor, hell-bent on avenging his sister's death, was softened completely by the child in his arms.

"Looks good on you," I said, almost stepping on a stray chocolate ball.

Regan rubbed Louisa's back—the stubs of his missing fingers still red and rather frightening to look at. "I can't wait to have kids of my own," he said quietly.

"Someday," I said.

Marlene, sound asleep on a love seat, mumbled something incoherent and turned onto her side, pillows falling to the floor. Her makeup was perfectly done and not one bit of the birthmark could be seen. I sidled past her, and my knees brushed Ellis' where he was perched on the sofa. Nose deep in a book, he didn't even glance up.

"Sorry," I said.

Regan's weird little brother gave no reply.

I sank into a plaid chair. It had been Seth's favorite. The fireplace smoldered, logs crackled and spit, and laughter came rolling out of the kitchen. How could Thomas carry on so effortlessly? And Luke, where was he?

"Are you going to partake in the holiday ham or the turkey?" Regan asked.

I was grateful for the distraction. "Those pigs at Marlene's farm were so cute I can't imagine eating one."

Ellis snorted. "But turkey is ugly enough for ya?"

That was the first time he had said anything to me since he'd given me the fake number and map at the Death Race check-in booth. Was he being mean on purpose or was this a weird sense of humor? I decided to give him the benefit of the doubt.

"If I was starving and had to pick one, then yeah, the ugly turkey. But with the amount of food in this house, I can opt out of both."

Ellis was seeking an argument. "Vegetarians are weird," he said. "Cute and fluffy, feathered and ugly, scaled and slimy... it's an animal all the same."

"Well, if your brother was making paella, I wouldn't turn that down," I said. "Regan's rabbit and rice with, what was it... saffron? Oh so good."

Regan smiled as we both remembered that night by the roaring campfire with the river flowing by and mouth-watering food on our plates. "Ah, yes indeed. I'll make that for you again some time."

"By a river? But without the rabbit this time?"

"Of course," he smiled. "I'll toss in some shrimp."

I laughed. "Ew."

"A crumble of bacon?"

"Ick."

"Then it would just be, uh, *rice*," he said, grinning ear to ear.

"Rice is good."

Ellis snorted again. He pulled the hood of his sweatshirt up over his red hair, the same color as Regan's, and brought the book closer to his nose. Although he did have some resemblance to his brother, it pretty much ended at the pale skin and freckles. Ellis did not get the same startling good looks as Regan, and his face was riddled with teen acne. He was extremely mature for a young man, evident in the way he looked after his brother and Louisa, and took care of the ranch and all the animals, so the childish snorts seemed out of place.

I chose to ignore him.

"Where is everyone else?" I asked.

Regan spoke softly as Louisa stirred against him. "Oliver is in the tub with a few cans of beer and quite possibly a Batman comic. Stephan and William are off for a walk, and the weirdos are hiding in their room, probably barricaded in the closet and fixing suicide packets to their molars."

"Regan," I said quietly, "don't make fun of Davis and Sindra. They've gone through *stuff*."

"Well, that *stuff* made them as cooked as the turkey—which I'm pretty sure Lisa is burning. I dropped a candy cane on the floor, and by the way they jumped, you'd think it was a grenade about to go off."

Ellis shook his head. "You mean, you *threw* a candy cane *at* them."

Regan waved his hand. "Alive or dead? Had to find out."

"Well, we need to be nice," Ellis reminded. "You don't know what happened to them back at that place. I mean, you saw the scars on Luke's back. I'm surprised he's not as messed up as they are."

Regan's fingers on his good hand turned white in a seething grip on the chair. Through a clenched jaw he said, "Lucky for everyone he wasn't."

I gulped at the tone in his voice. "Well, it's over now, and Luke's okay." It still startled me how much Regan cared for Luke. "Where is he, by the way?"

"Who?" said Regan absently.

"Luke."

"Luke? Hmm, I don't know anyone by that name." Regan winked, and the color returned to his hand. "He's probably outside. I saw him taping up his knuckles. He… uh, doesn't seem to be having a good day either."

A punching bag hanging from the rafters in the barn had consumed Luke for hours every day. He worked out religiously, alternating between cardio and weights and the bag. But lately his hands had become swollen as his time outside doubled, then tripled, and his shoulders sagged afterward with exhaustion. It killed me to see him plunge his hands into ice water and hang his head over the sink in agony—and I was fairly sure now I knew why.

Thomas.

"Why don't you go talk to him?" Regan said. "There's time before dinner." He nodded toward the kitchen. "Besides, the cowboy seems busy for the moment."

"Why would that matter?" I asked a bit sheepishly.

"Well, because of your, uh—oh bloody hell, Kaya. Really?"

"Really," I replied.

Ellis piped up from the couch. "Man, everyone's gotta pussyfoot around this chick. Just tell her, bro."

"There isn't anything to tell. Put your nose back in your book," Regan shot back angrily.

Ellis sneered and there was that snort again—I was really starting to get the feeling he didn't like me much. I was also getting the feeling that

Thomas had shared details of our intimate moment with more than just Luke.

"Go. Talk to him," Regan said before I could hurl a hundred questions. Louisa shifted around and pulled the blanket up under her chin. "The holiday ends for us tomorrow, and we will be in full on 'how to make Henry suffer and get revenge' mode. Do it now while the time is right and before damages cannot be undone."

He was right. So I crossed the snow-covered ground and braced myself at the barn door where I could hear the smacking of Luke's hands and sharp exhales as he hit a punching bag. Why had I waited so long to talk to him? I loved him. I wanted to spend the rest of my life with him, but I'd made no effort to find out what was bothering him. Instead, I'd waited for him to come to me.

Ridiculous. Childish. Pathetic. He wasn't a mind reader, and I wasn't a toddler.

Easing the barn door open, I snuck in and closed it silently. My nerves were getting the best of me, and I almost tripped over the space heater that failed to keep winter out of the air. Luke was facing the heavy bag hanging from the ceiling. I watched his back muscles contract, and the sweat drip down his spine to the top of his jeans. His hands lashed out in a flurry, and the bag, twice the weight of me, swung on its chain. It was so violent and so personal, I felt like I was interrupting a private moment, but I could not force my legs to move or my eyes to peel away, mostly from the angry marks covering his bare skin. The reminder of his time in the dungeon at Angela's hands were impossible to ignore. Some were fading, but one, deep and red, must have still hurt when he moved. He had told me a bit about Angela and what she'd done, and I'd woken often to his nightmares.

Luke had so many scars. Because of me.

He stopped, hung his head, then viciously kneed the bag once, twice, before his hands followed again. They were bleeding through the bandages when he stopped.

I couldn't hold my tongue any longer. "I'm sorry," I said.

I expected him to jump at the intrusion, but instead he grew very still. When he didn't turn around, I continued.

"I'm sorry for what happened to you at the estate. Angela... I can't even believe that she… that she did that to you." I scrambled for the right words. "I wouldn't wish that on my worst enemy."

He said nothing and marched over to the hood of a car where he'd placed his shirt. Yanking it over his head, he kept his back to me. I thought I might die if he didn't say something.

"I'm also sorry about Thomas."

He leaned on the car now, the muscles in his arms tensed as if he was about to pummel it, but there was no going back. I kept talking.

"I wanted to tell you, I swear. But there never seemed to be the right time, and you were ignoring me, avoiding me and I didn't know why, and I was waiting for you to come to me when really, I should have just come to you. I didn't realize that you knew about Thomas. That all this time you've been thinking so horribly of me."

I was rambling. Shaking. I couldn't take the cold shoulder from him, not for another second.

"I'll go," I said, and headed for the door, but he was before me in an instant blocking the exit. His red-rimmed eyes filled with confusion and hurt, and every part of me ached to comfort him.

"I haven't been thinking horribly of you, but I certainly want to kill Thomas," he said. "With every fiber of my being, just beat the life out of him purely out of jealousy. But never, not once, did I think badly of *you*."

"Then why have you been avoiding me?"

His chest was still rising and falling quickly, his shirt now damp from his skin. "Well, I must admit, I'm struggling with it. Thomas has, uh… touched more of you than I have. I'm not sure how to deal with that. Among other things."

"I'm so sorry."

"You have nothing to be sorry about," he said. "You can't help who you fall in love with."

What??? "No. Luke, it's not like that. I was just—"

He waited expectantly for the words that had failed me. Then, he spoke instead. "You don't have to explain. I understand. But just so you know, I'm not after you for your money."

The words were a slap. "What? I never once thought that."

His hands unclenched.

"I betrayed you, Luke. Can you forgive me?" I asked.

The angst on his face shifted to something else. "You didn't betray me.

You left me, remember? You were keeping me safe and getting on with your life. I can't hold that against you."

I was confused. "Then what else is going on?"

"Thomas had some other things to say."

"Like what?"

"First, he kindly reminded me that I was a criminal. That I had worked for a drug dealer and kidnapped someone, and that I could lose Louisa very easily if anyone on the right side of the law found out. He threatened to turn me in if I didn't give you some space."

I lost my balance for a moment. "He threatened you? Does he not remember that he helped shove a dead man in a freezer and burn a house down? That every single one of us are criminals now? *What the hell is his problem!*"

"Whoa." Luke put his hands up. "I know that. I humored him by listening, then told him to piss off."

My blood was boiling. "So what did he say that got to you then?"

"He explained to me the reasons why he's the better man for you. Said I should back off so you can make a choice. He told me he loves you, and that you—" Luke paled, as if what he was about to say might make him sick. "Love him, too. Believe me, Kaya, all I want is for you to be happy. I don't ever want to be selfish with you, and I thought by keeping my distance—"

"I want a man who will fight for me, Luke," I interrupted.

He balked. His blue eyes grew wide. "I'll fight for you till the day I die."

"Then why? Why would some comment from Thomas affect you so deeply?"

"Because…it's true. I can see it."

I sputtered, "see what?"

Luke crossed his arms over his chest, and his baby blues narrowed. "That, you *do* love him."

I couldn't deny it, nor could I stand there and lie to his face. So, I did the only thing I could think of; I bolted from the barn.

My focus became finding Thomas and knocking the Christmas cheer right off his arrogant face, but I didn't get far. I was halfway across the yard when Luke latched onto my shoulder and spun me around to face him. His blue eyes blazed like the tips of the hottest flames. The falling snow melted against his bare arms.

"I need to know, Kaya. I agreed to back off so you could decide between the two of us, and I need to know if I'm doing the right thing. Are you in love with him? Do you deny it?"

I needed to lie, but I couldn't.

He gulped. "I don't want to hold you back from the life you want. If you need space to decide which of us can give it to you, I'll let you have that. I will wait, or I'll go. I'll do or be whatever you need no matter if it kills me. Just tell me please, tell me what to do."

He was breaking into pieces around me. I had to pick them up. "What I need is for you to not let anyone get between us again, no matter what they say. I'm crazy in love with you. Can't you see that?"

His eyes searched mine. "Yes, but—"

"There are no 'buts,'" I said, trying to make him understand. "There is no human being on this planet I love more than you. I promise you have my heart, fully and completely. I realized that the moment I met you and not once has that changed. I was tested with someone else, someone who, yes, I *do* love, but I passed with flying colors. Thomas only made me realize that my love for you is deeper than any other, and that no matter what is thrown at it, no matter how much it is tested, it will never lessen. Thomas is someone I want in my life, but you… you are someone I would die without."

His mouth eagerly met mine. So desperate. Urgent. My feet left the ground, and I was standing on a cloud.

"Kaya," he said breathlessly, his lips not far from mine as his hands wound into my hair. His body shook, yet the heat coming off him wrapped around us like a blanket. "I love you so much." He held my face, brushing snowflakes from my cheek. "It has killed me to stay away and not touch you, not wake up with you beside me. You're my entire world."

I couldn't reply because he was kissing me again and I was drunk with the taste and feel of him. I never wanted it to stop. Not ever. I could stand in this yard for the rest of my days and just submit to the euphoria of *him*.

But he pulled away suddenly.

"Marry me," he said.

Shock. "What?"

"*Marry me*," he said again, and I could feel the pounding of his heart against mine. We were so perfectly in time. I was speechless. Of course I wanted to marry him. I wanted nothing else in the world.

But before I could reply, before I could tell him *yes*, the kitchen door was thrown open, crashing against the outer wall.

"Dinner is ready," said a male voice that made my breath hitch.

I separated myself from Luke to face Thomas standing in the doorway, and I made the mistake of noticing the dread all over his face. He was breathless too, his wide eyes suggesting the onset of panic. "And hurry up, it's getting cold," he added, voice barbed and shaky, a blinding glare weaving through the falling snow before disappearing back inside.

The sweat on Luke's skin was steaming. "You're getting cold too," I said.

He shook his head and marched toward the house. "Not by a long shot."

2 9

THE TROOPER

Oliver said grace. Stephan poured the wine. Louisa squirmed in her chair next to Lisa, and Thomas held the baby bunny while avoiding my eyes. Davis encouraged Sindra to eat, while Luke, Regan, and Ellis talked about camping. Marlene kept to herself, whole heartedly digging into her heaping plate, only stopping to breathe and mutter that it was amazing—which it was—and William sang along to Bing Crosby between mouthfuls.

It was actually kind of perfect.

Even though I was gripped with seething anger toward Thomas and an intense desire to have Luke all to myself, the tree twinkled, the snow fell, and the Christmas spirit became something real for me for the first time.

When Louisa could sit still no longer, she crawled onto Regan's lap, and Lisa took the opportunity to make a speech.

"I would like to make a toast," she said, taking a sip of wine for courage to continue. "I haven't had Christmas in an exceptionally long time so today has been incredibly special for me. I know we are not technically 'family,' but this is the closest I've been to feeling like part of one in years. So cheers to that." We raised our glasses. "Also, I have something that I want to share; I've decided that I won't let the shitty things people have done, haunt me anymore. As of now, I forgive my father for what he did to me and my mom, and I forgive the men in my life that tried to hurt me. Most of all, though—as I stand here in *his* house—I forgive Seth. I loved him. And I am grateful that I got to feel that with someone."

We all drank to that.

"Where did he go?" Louisa asked. There was gum stuck in her hair. Barbie makeup on her cheeks.

"Where did *who* go?" Regan replied.

"Seth. Where did he go? When is he coming back?"

Silence.

Regan patted Louisa's head. "Fishing," he said, and lifted his glass. "He is on a boat having a wonderful time and might be for a while. So, here's to family, forgiveness, and fishing."

Glasses clinked.

Oliver cleared his throat. "I would like to say something as well." His huge hands were folded before him, and he didn't stand or pick up his glass. He just stared across the table. "Sindra…"

She recoiled as if his words were the teeth of a rabid dog.

Oliver remained fixated. "I forgive you too," he said after a long while. "You've suffered enough, and I hold no ill will toward you. I hope that you can find the strength to move ahead and be well."

Sindra blinked a few times, clearly not expecting that. It took a while for her to speak. "That means a lot," she said. "And for what it's worth, I am truly sorry. So very, very, sorry, Oliver."

The frailness in her tone, and the way she barely lifted her chin from her chest, tugged at me. She had fallen, and just now I realized how hard. Davis remained silent next to her, expression as cold and unforgiving as it was the day we'd all arrived here. He could not forgive Oliver for leaving him in the cell no matter how many times Oliver apologized.

"What did Sindra do that was so terrible?" Marlene asked, and there was a spark in her eyes close to becoming flames. "Oliver?"

The way Oliver clenched his jaw and examined his hands meant he wasn't answering that question, and Marlene was getting ready to lunge across the table at Sindra for an answer.

Luke spoke up. "She was just a really bad boss, Marlene. You know, making him work late hours, no holiday pay, stuff like that."

Marlene was not falling for the lie. "Uh huh," she said, casting Sindra a glare. "Well, if it was more than that, she and I are going to have a problem."

This was Marlene's way of confirming that she cared about Oliver, as if it wasn't already obvious by the way her face lit up whenever he spoke to her. I kind of wanted to take the fork from her hand so it wouldn't 'accidentally' fly across the table at Sindra's head.

Oliver could not conceal his grin.

"And…I have an announcement as well." William cleared his throat, robust belly knocking the table as he stood. His scarred chef's-hand reached to steady his wine glass, then rested on Stephan's shoulder. "Stephan and I are—"

"Wait," Stephan said urgently. "We agreed that I'd be the one to tell her."

William's smile was flecked with impatience. "But you've had *weeks,* my darling. She needs to know."

"I was waiting for the right time."

Ellis snorted. "Here we are, pussyfooting around the princess again."

Stephan slammed his hand on the table with a ferocity that made us all jump. "What was that, young man?"

Ellis cleared his throat as if he had been waiting for a long time to speak his mind. "The universe doesn't revolve around Kaya Lowen. This rich little princess probably had Disneyland opened only for her on a regular basis. Absolutely everything this girl could want was available to her, yet all I hear is ya worrying about protecting her feelings. Good lord! She's just a chick! *Who apparently just wants to be normal.* Normal? As in broke as heck like the rest of us? Watching loved ones die from shoddy medicine? Christmas at my house was preventing my sister from pulling her hair out while Regan was off trying to find a cure to save her, and never having enough money to even buy a comic book. I even had to be my own Santa. All of us, every single one, are here because of her. Because of *you.*"

Ellis' finger was pointed at me and my completely gob smacked expression.

Stephan snarled like he might jam his turkey leg down Ellis' throat.

Regan jumped in. "Done, little brother?" Regan's eyes flashed furiously. "Do you feel better after your little-boy meltdown? First, I'm happy to be here. Have you forgotten that we are eating and have money now—because of the hell *we* put that girl over there through? You bloody stupid little brat. Do you not remember the Christmases when Mom was alive?

The incredibly good fortune we had to be together as a loving family? Kaya never had that. Not once. Just because someone has a crap load of money doesn't mean they're living a fairy tale life. You at least had the luxury of leaving your bedroom and wandering the streets. That 'poor little rich girl' over there was locked in her room with bodyguards and bars on the windows. And Disneyland? You putz, she didn't even go to school. Or to the store. Or to the library. Or hang out with friends. Ever. You know nothing about her life, and your preconceived judgments are ridiculous."

Every jaw hit the table. I think mine actually made a 'clunk' sound.

Ellis was seething, staring at his brother, shoulders rising and falling with each heavy breath. He jabbed his knife into the table by his plate. "I know that she's going to break your heart!" he roared.

"What?" Regan was looking at his brother incredulously. "Good Lord almighty, Ellis, I bloody well do not have a *thing* for Kaya."

Ellis, shaking head to toe, couldn't hold back. "No… *Luke*. She's going to take Luke away from you, and I hate her for that!"

Luke spat out the wine he was sipping.

Regan, smiling now, understood why his brother was acting out. "Ah," he said, ruffling Ellis's hair with his wounded hand, not making any effort to deny the claim. "You're just looking out for your big brother, aren't ya? It's kind of a stupid way of going about it, though. But hey, you must know that I have no illusions about running off into the sunset with Luke. All right? Yeah, I love the guy, but not that way. I want him to be with whoever makes him happy."

Luke cleared his throat uncomfortably. "Uh, thanks man."

Regan gave him a wink. "No prob."

Ellis stared so hard at his plate I thought it might snap in half. Silence fell over everyone, including Louisa. I felt like I should say something, but I didn't even know where to begin.

Thankfully Lisa changed the subject. "So, who wants desert?" she asked.

And pie, cake, and some sort of pudding with hot caramel sauce, made us all pretty much forget Ellis' outburst. All nerves were soothed with sugar—except mine. Stephan still had something he wanted to tell me, and I had a good idea what that was. Marlene—on her third or fourth piece of dessert—decided to take a breath between bites and speak to me, and I knew she was trying to get my mind off Stephan, and I adored her for it.

"I have been wondering," she said, that spark still flickering in her gaze that didn't stray from Oliver for too long. "What was Christmas really like for you? Did you have to spend the entire day in church? Or two weeks before the *big day* attaching creepy porcelain dolls to a plastic pine tree and icing deer-shaped cookies while wearing a musty Santa hat that smelled like Uncle Frank's underarms? Was there a nativity scene made of plywood in your front yard? And did you ever have to lie in the cradle and pretend to be the baby Jesus because the boy who was supposed to do it ran off screaming after a goat licked him?"

I laughed, picturing it perfectly. "Certainly not."

"Hives, then. How about them? Did you look forward every year to big itchy ones because someone always brought mistletoe or cranberries even though you said you were allergic countless times? Or how about tourtiere—mashed meats disguised as a pie—I mean, c'mon already. Or that God-awful Christmas cake you have to be polite and eat? Ugh. Oh, and aspic, that wiggly tomato gelatin salad—I have nightmares about that stuff."

Marlene shivered. Everyone giggled, even Ellis. Oliver's eyes were like bright moons.

"I don't mind the gelatin stuff," I said.

"What? I don't even think I want to know you anymore. You probably even enjoy *shopping*."

Marlene said the word 'shopping,' but she might as well have said 'stabbing yourself in the face'. Oliver was beaming at her. Teeth blinding. "Kaya never shopped," he said. "Stephan ordered her clothes online with his own money, and sometimes Sindra showed up with an armload of ridiculous things she would never wear. We didn't exchange gifts at Christmas either. Henry didn't allow it."

Marlene looked at Oliver incredulously. "Are you serious? No gifts? How sucky is that. And the bodyguard/nanny/hairdresser bought the clothes, eh? No wonder she has terrible fashion sense. Did you know she wore flip flops to a farm?"

"Well, I had nothing else, and no money," I said in my defense.

"None?" said Ellis, and this time his eyes weren't so filled with hatred.

"None. Unless you count the jewelry I had in a safe in my room that I bartered with if I wanted pizza and stuff. And really, Oliver, I always got gifts, remember? Stephan would knit beautiful scarves, and you would get me candy from the fudge shop and—"

"Iron Maiden," Davis interjected.

We all pretended we weren't shocked to hear him speak. He was trying to be part of the conversation, and I was so happy about that I almost forgot what we were talking about. "Oh, yes. Davis introduced me to some great music. Last Christmas, he got me the complete Iron Maiden box set with a concert tour T-shirt."

Stephan nodded fondly. "That's right. I was rather impressed when I heard the vocal stylings of Mr. Dickinson. And hey, how about that year the new maid brought you a puppy? You had a pet for about three hours…" His words trailed off. He'd forgotten that memory wasn't a fond one for me.

"What do you mean, *three hours*?" Ellis said, intrigued and horrified. "Did it die?"

That puppy had lit up my life, until Sindra came to the door with my present from Henry—those sapphire earrings I'd given driver Dan—and promptly made an exchange. I had cried for the rest of the day and still prickled at the thought. Judging by the way Sindra pressed her lips together it wasn't a good memory for her either.

"No, it didn't die," I said, unable to prevent the slight crack in my voice. "It was taken away."

Ellis' eyes met mine. All hostility gone. "Oh."

Oliver and Stephan remembered that day, too. They were left to console a crying child whose loss was far greater than the forfeited affection of a puppy.

I took in a deep breath. "What's done is done. It would have been a nuisance anyway."

Louisa rounded the table, took her bunny gently from Thomas, and went back to Regan's lap.

"Well," William said, standing again and patting Stephan's hand. "On that note, I think it is time to tell everyone what we're doing."

Stephan became nervous. He folded his napkin and smoothed his already smooth mustache. His eyes leveled on mine. His smile did not hide his sadness. "I guess I might as well just come out and say it; William and I are… um… well, we're leaving."

Oliver dropped his fork.

He continued. "William made me promise him that after Christmas we would head east. So, I'm sorry, Kaya, but I have to go..."

His words caught in his throat, so William spoke for him. "Yes, I'm taking Stephan away to wander the world with me and heal and be as far from Henry Lowen as possible. What he went through almost killed him, and his health has suffered. I cannot let him take part in any plans to get revenge or whatever it is you are all thinking of doing, so I gave him a choice; me or you, Kaya. He chose me."

His words hung heavily in the air.

"You'll be on your own from now on," William continued, holding Stephan's hand tightly. "Stephan will be saying goodbye to all of you, permanently."

I wasn't shocked. Stephan had devoted his life to me, and now it was time for him to look after himself. As he watched for my reaction, waiting on edge, Luke patted my leg, and all at once I lost the urge to cry. I had everything I needed. Everyone I needed. This was right. It was time to let Stephan go.

"When are you leaving?" I asked.

William didn't hesitate. "Tonight," he said. "In about an hour."

I was up and out of my chair before another word was said. So was Stephan. Pulling away from William, he enveloped me in his fuzzy sweater arms—those arms that had always been there for me.

"You deserve to be happy," I said.

His body relaxed in relief. "Thank you, baby girl. It's what I have to do, and now that you are well protected and there are people here that love you as much as I do—"

"I'll be fine," I said, smiling and keeping the tears away even though his were flowing. I was strong now, stronger than I had ever been, and he could see it. "You know, every year I wished for my father to spend Christmas with me," I said into his neck. "I wanted my father, but I didn't realize until now that every year that wish actually came true. You were the daddy every little girl dreams of. My fierce warrior and protector—the first man I genuinely loved."

He squeezed me tighter, his familiarity and unconditional love blocking out everyone else in the room. We held each other for a long time. For the last time.

"We're both going to be okay," I said, staying strong for both of us.

"I'll call you on my wedding day." He was choking up. "And always remember, I'm so very proud of you, and I'll love you forever, Chloe Alexandra."

"I'll love you forever too, Stevie Muffins."

An hour later, he was gone.

30

SEVENTH HEAVEN

The whirlwind of the day finally caught up to me. Marlene, Oliver, and Regan were playing a game of charades and everyone else had gone to bed, Thomas being the first within seconds of finishing dinner. Curled up next to Luke on the ratty couch, music drifted softly in and out of my ears. Occasionally, I peeled my eyelids apart to see the sparkling lights of the tree softening Regan's sharp features and adding even more of a glow to Oliver's smitten face. Marlene was basking in Oliver's attention and laughing at Regan's lewd jokes, and this cozy scene made me relax even more.

I was near dreamland when I felt my body lifted off the couch and into Luke's arms. He headed down the hall, avoiding the squeak in the floorboards right outside where Lisa and Louisa slept, and the proximity of his body against mine brought me fully awake. When he pushed open the door and oh so carefully placed me on the bed, desire for him flooded me ears to toes.

"Goodnight, Kaya," he said, leaning in to kiss my forehead.

"Stephan's gone. You can stay," I said, reaching for him, unable to bear the thought of being apart another night.

He seemed wildly conflicted. "I don't know if that's a good idea. I don't think I have the strength to keep my hands off you."

"You don't have to," I said, searching his eyes only to have him look away.

He cleared his throat. "But we have… I uh… well I—"

I knew what he was hinting at, so I mustered up the courage to inform him. "Lisa gave me her, um, birth control pills. Said she would never need them again. I've been taking them since we got here."

"Oh," Luke breathed, wavering above me, not coming closer, but not leaving either.

I was suddenly shaking, but I didn't feel nervous. Not with him. I reached to pull him closer, but stopped when I noticed something on the bedside table. His gaze fell to it too, and we both awkwardly gawked at an envelope with my name on it.

"It's from Thomas," Luke said.

He stepped back and crossed his arms over his chest, clearly unsure whether to pick it up and tear it to shreds, read it, or storm out of the room.

"It's not important." At least, that's what I hoped. My heart pounded, though. I had been so angry at Thomas, shooting bullets at him over dinner with my eyes, but now I wanted to know if he was okay.

I swallowed hard. "Really, Luke, it can wait."

"Don't you want to know what he has to say?" he asked through gritted teeth.

I couldn't help but smile at the big jealous lug, muscles all tense, jaw gritted, eyes staring at the envelope like he was going to fight it. So I got up, went to the closet, and tossed it in.

"It doesn't matter." I shut the door and turned to face the love of my life.

He still hadn't moved.

"Luke," I put my hands on his cheeks and made him look at me. "It doesn't matter what anyone says or does, I am yours. Forever and always."

That released him from his trance. Before I knew it, I was shoved backward onto the pillows as his mouth hungrily sought mine. His kisses were hurried and untamed, like he couldn't get enough fast enough. His tongue explored, and his lips pressed against mine, then they trailed across my cheek and down my throat as he was careful not to crush me beneath his weight. All my senses were consumed with him; the feverish longing in his eyes, the press of his body, the heat and smell of his skin, and the almost frantic way he had started fumbling with my clothes. Palm hot against the plane of my stomach, his breath hitched when the touch of his hands elicited a moan I could not contain.

"Are you sure about this?" he asked.

I didn't want to stop him. He was everything, everything good and real and loving. My truth. My future. My home. I wanted to know his mind, his heart, *and* his body.

"Yes," I said as my hands fumbled over him, eager to feel and see what was underneath the cotton between us. I was grateful when he took his shirt off and tossed it to the floor.

"Sit up," he ordered.

I did, but I pushed his hands to the bed when he reached for me. I had to have a moment to explore him with my fingertips and my eyes.

"You make me crazy," he murmured as I traced the claw-mark scar on his chest then the heavy black tattoo on his ribs. I was elated to cause him goosebumps and turn them into little shivers when I grazed the taut skin over his powerful arms. His eyes became so filled with desire my entire body began melting from the heat. How could a human being be so beautiful? How could I ever stop touching him?

"Take this off," he said, reaching for my shirt.

It was tossed to the floor next to his, then so was my bra, and it was his turn to explore—and I discovered what paradise felt like. When his mouth returned to mine, his hands wound in my hair, and he pressed his weight against me until I was beneath him. Leaning on his elbow, my sweat pants disappeared before I could grasp the fact that I was naked beneath him.

"If you want me to stop I will," he said, voice like butter, melting all over me.

"Luke…" I wanted him so badly it hurt. "I'm new at this. I'm not sure what to do."

"That's okay. I do."

"You're, um, very experienced." A statement. Not so much a question.

He smiled that glorious, mind-melting, heart-skipping-a-beat, fall-to-the-knees, smile. "I've had girlfriends before, Kaya," he said, slightly breathless. "So, you could say that I am experienced enough to know that when you came along, I realized what I felt was entirely new, completely different and totally life-changing. No other woman could ever compare to you. No one else matters."

He waited a moment for an objection from me.

"I don't want you to stop," I said.

He kissed me, oh so gently, then trailed his hand across my stomach to find the part of me that wanted his touch the most.

"Oh, dear God," he mumbled as I became liquid against his touch. Panting now above me, his eyes fixed on mine, and by the fluttering of his lashes, what he was doing felt as amazing to him as it did to me. I surrendered completely to his desires as they unhinged my own. His hips were bare against mine. He was trembling as his knees moved mine apart. Slowly, carefully, he fit our bodies together. His soul met mine. We became one. Ecstasy didn't even begin to be a word to describe what I was feeling. I thought I'd uncovered paradise before, but now I was running through its fields and rolling down its hills. The joining of our bodies through intimacy took the meaning of love to a whole new level. The world disappeared, and there was only us adrift in the universe.

"Kaya Lowen," Luke breathed, holding me captive beneath him, and suddenly his body became maddeningly still. "Will you marry me?"

I hesitated, only because I was speechless, overwhelmed, and somewhere on cloud nine.

"Of course."

He smiled, and his blue eyes lit the room.

He'd been holding back, because now he moved in so deep I couldn't think around it, couldn't breathe, and gave in to waves of pleasure that rocked my entire body. This fueled his fire even more, and when he began to shudder in release, I memorized every nuance of his face to add it to my 'keep forever' memory book.

I was the luckiest girl in the entire world.

Breathing hard with our hearts still in sync, I trailed my fingers down the sweat on his spine. I loved the feeling of his wet skin and the smell of him—the incredible male smell of him. He didn't move off me, keeping our bodies still perfectly joined together head to toe.

"I could do that every minute for the rest of my life," I said against his neck, tasting the salt of him while he worked to catch his breath. I felt him respond to my touch and the strength of his body instantly had mine back in a frenzy.

He started to move his hips again. "Okay."

The sun peeked in through the curtains.

"Do we tell them we're engaged?" Luke said, rolling over to face me, grinning ear to ear with an impossibly gorgeous sleepy-dreamy look about him.

"Tell them?" I was so blissed-out and relaxed I was part of the bed. "I don't know how we will even get out of this room."

Just as I said it, we both caught the incredible smell of pancakes and Lisa's cinnamon rolls.

"Food might be the only thing to tempt me away from you," Luke said, his chin lifting toward the aroma. "I'm absolutely starved."

"Me, too."

Sitting up, I let the blanket fall away, not shy anymore after the incredibly intimate night and better part of the morning we had together. The fact that my body could get such a reaction from him sent my self-confidence right through the roof. I could feel his eyes on my back and knew if I turned around, there would be no getting out of this bed for a long while.

"Breakfast is probably a good idea," I said as my stomach growled.

"Wait." He caught my shoulder and pulled me back to him, tugging the blanket up around us to keep out the chill. "First, I have to talk to you. About last night."

My heart stopped for one insane second. He'd become so serious it was alarming.

"When I asked you to marry me—"

Oh God, was he taking it back?

"I was, well, I was rather overcome at the moment."

My chest hurt. "You mean, you didn't mean it?"

He pulled away to look at me. "What? Jeezus, no! What I'm failing miserably at trying to say is, that I may have asked you under the wrong circumstances. I didn't really do it the right way."

I breathed a heavy sigh of relief as a ring appeared in his hand from out of nowhere. Polished to a high shine, silver curling edges of a pretty band surrounded etched leaves that sparkled in the morning light. It was a bit rugged and not like the gaudy jewelry Henry bought me. This ring had character and charm, and I absolutely loved it.

"I'll buy you a proper ring as soon as I can. This one," he said as he nudged it onto my finger where it fit perfectly, "was supposed to be a Christmas present. I didn't have a diamond to put in it, but I will someday."

"Wait… what? You *made* it?" I stared at my hand in awe.

He nodded. "There are lots of tools in the barn. I found a bolt and filed and polished it. Seemed right at the time."

I remembered not only his bloody knuckles now, but fingertips, too.

"You *made this*," I repeated. Dumfounded.

"I know you didn't want a Christmas present, but I couldn't resist."

I kissed him fiercely, barely able to stop and pull away, so breathless after I could barely swallow. "This is so perfect. So absolutely completely perfect. I don't want any other ring but this one."

He grinned. "So, you like it then."

"Very much."

There was a flood of pink to his cheeks. It was so charming, so sexy.

"So Kaya Lowen, for the third time, will you—"

I cut him off and put my fingers to his lips, trying not to laugh. He was so eager to do everything right. To make sure he was being a gentleman and treating me the right way. But since he was asking me again after I'd already said yes, I knew there was something he was holding back.

"Luke, what do you really want to say to me? Stop trying so hard and just tell me what's on your mind. I'm not some princess you have to follow the rule book for. This is us."

"Not a princess, eh? Well, you could have fooled me."

I rolled my eyes and moved to get out of bed again, but this time he caught me by the waist and not all that gently pulled me tightly to him. His chest pressed against my back, his breath was hot in my ear.

"I promised you I would never hold you against your will, that every choice you make I will support. And I still feel that way. But I don't know if I can keep that promise if it means losing you."

"I understand," I said simply.

"Marrying me won't mean I will try to control you—don't think that for a second. I love and respect you too much to even dream of doing that. But it does mean that I will do everything in my power to keep you. I will never walk away from you again like I did that day Oliver was intent on taking you home. I was weak because I was determined to keep a promise that could have cost me everything. And Thomas—I won't play nice with him anymore. I won't let anyone come between us no matter how convincing their argument is. Even you, if you lie to me again to keep me safe. Do you understand? I want you to marry me. I want you all to myself, and if you say yes to giving me that, I will fight to the death to keep it."

I couldn't speak.

"Do you understand?" His arms tightened, reaffirming that there was no way I would get out of his embrace if I accepted. I mumbled something incoherent.

"So, that said, will you…" he paused, tipping my head back to meet his eyes. "Marry me?"

"Yes," I said without any hesitation because I had never felt more sure about anything in my entire life.

The sweetest, most tender kiss was mine and would be mine for always.

"It's crazy, isn't it?" he said, beaming ear to ear. "This thing between us. I mean, I'm no poet, but I feel like I could write you the most epic poem and set it to some powerful piece of music and sing my heart out to you. I'm so high on emotion right now I don't think I'll ever come down. Do you feel like this too?"

I nodded eagerly. "I do."

"Then you and I, my love, we are a rhapsody."

If there was the slightest, most miniscule part of me that had yet to be his, it was now. I ran my fingers over the scar on his cheek, and his eyes fluttered. "No big church-thing or over-the-top ridiculous wedding dress though," I said, close to becoming unhinged.

His mouth found the tips of my fingers, his tongue so soft, breath so warm…

"But think of how much fun it will be to take it off after," he purred.

Breakfast was going to have to wait.

MARLENE

HOT GUY SAY WHAT?

I could barely keep down my breakfast sitting across from Kaya and Luke at the table. They were grinning ear to ear, and their energy was so saccharin it felt like cotton candy was sandblasting my cavities.

Thomas on the other hand—dark circles under his eyes and a shake to his hands—looked like he'd been up all night trying to give himself a hangover. None of us had missed the new ring on Kaya's finger, but Thomas couldn't tear his gaze away from it. I'd warned him that this would happen. I'd told him to saddle up and move on, but he claimed that he had to remain here and torture himself to help 'protect me'. Yeah, like I'm the one that needed help. The only one doing any saving and protecting around here would be me. The only other person not completely pre-occupied with someone else and with any sense in 'em was Oliver. And he was sick.

I didn't want to notice his cough getting worse, but twice I saw blood on his hands when he assured Luke that he was 'just fine and getting better'. I'd asked him about it, but only got a gruff reply, which coming from a man like Oliver usually meant it was something more serious than a cold. I had heard him this morning, coughing his guts up, and then gasping for air afterward. I stood outside his door—as I had many times— tempted to knock or burst in and demand that he let me try to help him.

But that would mean admitting that I cared.

Oliver made me feel special. Important. And sometimes even beautiful

—which if I ever said mistakenly out loud, I would cut out my own tongue. He didn't realize there was a hideous birthmark covering half my face, and I intended to keep it that way. For some ridiculous reason, Oliver's opinion of me mattered, and darn it if that didn't keep me up at night.

Never in my life had I cared one stinking bit about what anyone thought. But the way his eyes lit up when he talked to me, the way he stole glances when he thought I wasn't looking, and the way his hand gently brushed mine at every chance, I didn't want that to change because of my birthmark. Not that I thought I had a future with Oliver. But secretly and most annoyingly, I was sure dreaming of it.

I liked his laugh and the way his deep-brown eyes rolled in mock boredom when I said something about farm life. I liked the way he talked, using his hands to accentuate his words, and the way he rubbed the top of his head when he was lost in thought. And every day I noticed something else that I liked, and then I gave myself heck for noticing. I didn't want to get too close. I didn't want to care about someone who would flee the moment he saw my real face.

I also didn't want to care about someone who was dying.

Besides, being in love made you look stupid. Like Kaya did right now with that ridiculously giddy smile dimpling her pink cheeks.

"Sleep well?" Oliver asked her when she took a sip of coffee and some dribbled down her chin.

He had asked me that twice already. Of course, I pretended that his question was irritating and replied in an annoyed tone, "why wouldn't I?" to which he just gave a luminous smile.

Lisa sat back and observed Luke and Kaya. She'd pulled her blonde hair up into a ponytail and hadn't bothered with makeup this morning. She was impossibly pretty, and if she wasn't so bad-ass, she would be a girl I'd love to hate.

"Their room is next to mine," she said, handing Louisa a slice of apple. "By the sounds of it, I don't think the love birds had much sleep at all."

Thomas gasped like he'd been punched. Luke pretended to become even more interested in his food, while Kaya's smile widened and the pink in her cheeks increased.

"Dead puppies," Lisa said with a mischievous grin. "And birds with broken wings."

Kaya looked up at her, confused but still beaming ear to ear.

Lisa went on. "Snakes. Food poisoning."

"What game is this?" Oliver asked.

Lisa giggled. "Oh, it's not a game. I'm just seeing if I can get that smile off Miss Lowen's face."

"Ah," Oliver said, remarkably not jealous given the fact that Kaya was his fiancée not long ago and he still loved her. I wondered if that had anything to do with me…

Dammit if a stupid smile didn't stretch over my face, too.

"Lumpy potatoes," Oliver said. "Gin and crowds."

"Mayonnaise and having to wear anything other than sweatpants," I added.

"Country music," interjected Davis. "Garlic-breath and snowstorms."

Despite our best efforts, Kaya's smile grew even wider.

Oliver shook his head and laughed. "Really, Kaya? *Country music and snowstorms?* Boy, Luke must have given you one helluva Christmas present last night."

It was too much for Thomas. He stood abruptly. His legs straightened out before he'd given much thought to it, and the chair toppled back behind him. His skin, now slightly green like it was that time when he had the flu, made his dark eyes darker. He stared at Luke and vibrated with anger.

Luke remained seated, saying nothing, but staring back like he might explode at any moment, too.

Thomas's breathing sped up, and just when it seemed he was about to start yelling, he pulled his gaze away from Luke to concentrate on Kaya. His hate changed to complete heartbreak as he stared at her. "I think it's time for me to head out now," he said. "I'll go pack."

He turned to leave, and the most desperate sound came from Kaya. "No!"

She became whiter than her normal 'been living in a cave and never seen the sun' kinda white. She gripped the edge of the table like a lifeline, visibly trying to remain calm. "No, Thomas you can't—"

He stopped in the doorway. "I can't *what*?"

Kaya had no reply.

Thomas spun around fully to face her. "Well?" he asked, tone biting.

Luke spoke up. "I think we better have a chat, Thomas."

"A chat, eh?" Thomas's hands curled into fists. "I can think of other things to do besides that."

Lisa gathered Louisa up in her arms, and the child's layers of pink chiffon knocked over an empty cup that broke and rolled to Luke's feet. Davis and Sindra pushed back from the table, and Regan sat back and crossed his arms over his chest, delighted at the prospect of a fight.

"We had an agreement," hissed Thomas.

Luke's jaw tightened, and he moved to the edge of his chair. "You had an agreement that was backed up by threats and ultimatums that do not apply. Nonetheless, I listened to what you had to say. I contemplated every aspect of it, and I gave Kaya time as you requested. But as you can clearly see—" Luke reached for Kaya's hand and enveloped it in his. "She has made her choice."

Thomas was about to either boil over or fall over. "But you and I both know it's not the right choice!"

Desperate, crumbling, clutching at straws, Thomas was trying to appeal to Luke's noble nature, but Luke was having none of it.

"Yes, it *is* the right choice," Luke growled.

Any moment now, the kitchen would be a battleground, and I was going to have to stick up for butthead Thomas.

But instead of rising from the table, Luke turned to Kaya, taking in her downcast eyes and cheeks so pale they were almost translucent, and his anger completely evaporated. She looked like a wolf caught in a trap, unsure whether to howl for help or chew her own arm off.

"I respect a man who fights for what he loves, Thomas," Luke said, reaching for Kaya's hand. "I'm sorry for what you're going through. I just hope you will respect Kaya's decision. Just so you know, she and I…"

"We don't want you to go," Kaya interjected.

Luke's jaw clenched as he reined in his jealousy to show understanding and sympathy for the girl he loved. "Uh, yes," he agreed. "Kaya *and I*, don't want you to go. We need you. And Marlene needs your protection."

I was about to set Luke straight about that, but before I could get a word out, Oliver was patting my leg and shaking his head. He wasn't quick to remove his hand after, and it momentarily made me forget where I was.

"We have to stick together," Oliver said, leaving my skin abnormally cold in the absence of his touch. "Right, Marlene?"

I was being asked my opinion? "Right."

I agreed wholeheartedly now because Thomas on his own, in his state, would be a disaster waiting to happen. At least here I could keep my eye on him.

"Thomas, I need you," I said, even though the word 'need' felt like a bunch of rattlers striking my tongue.

Thomas focused solely on Kaya when he answered, "Well, if Marlene needs me, then I guess I'll have to stay."

"Good," Regan said, bored now with the drama. "Problem solved. I guess. Sort of. You could still fight Luke to the death though if you want. *Your death.* By all means, Thomas, don't let us stop you."

"Maybe later," Thomas said.

Regan directed the conversation away from the Kaya-Luke-Thomas love triangle. "All right, well, let's get down to business then," he said, motioning to clasp his hands together then remembering he was missing a few fingers needed to do that. "We've got plans to make, and people to get revenge on. Fun stuff."

Kaya slumped back in her chair, shoulders sagging in relief when Thomas resumed his place at the table.

I picked up some dirty plates and tugged on her sweater. "Come on, dishes don't wash themselves," I said, leading her to the sink.

She blankly stared at the bubbles while I dropped plates into the hot water.

"Buck up, buttercup," I said quietly while everyone at the table discussed the weather. "I know it hurts doing what you gotta do, but ya still gotta do it. At some point you're going to have to let Thomas go."

"But not yet, Marlene. I can't. Not yet."

I handed her a dishcloth, pointed to the sink. "Okay. But the longer you leave the band-aid on, the harder it is to pull off."

"Maybe it will fall off on its own."

"Or, maybe your skin will grow around it and you'll have to use a knife to dig it out. Don't forget about the damage done to the band-aid, too."

She sighed. "Either way, there's gonna be one helluva scar."

"More to add to your collection," I said with a wink.

I gathered more dishes from the table, giving Thomas a pat on the shoulder as I moved past him. He was closest to the porch door, and icy air blowing in between the cracks made his shirt cold. He was still trembling, but the cold wasn't why. If we were back home, I'd take him for a drive or grab one of Ma's pies and a case of beer and take him to the shack. We would argue and fight, and he'd forget all his troubles—I didn't think that would work this time.

"So, we have a monster to slay, folks," Regan was saying, and from out of thin air, he produced a notebook. "We've all had our holiday break, but reality is back. Time to figure out what we are going to do about Henry Lowen."

"Finally," Ellis said, "we can talk about something interesting."

'Interesting' to Ellis meant strategies on how to make Henry's company fold, and how to hide me and Kaya for a few years, and what to do with this house we were staying in that belonged to a dead man…blech. Washing the dishes was more interesting and actually accomplished something.

"I think you should tell us what you know, Sindra," Regan said. "You've had lots of time to meander around in your own head, it must be somewhat back together and organized by now. Tell us all about your wonderful ex-boss. What are his weaknesses?"

She laughed. "None. Henry has no weaknesses. The suggestion is preposterous."

"No," Regan said impatiently, "what's preposterous is that you're sticking your head in the sand. Enough of the bull crap, lady. We all know what you're capable of and what you can do, and we need you on our side now and not cowering next to Davis like a beaten dog. Get it together or get out."

Ooh boy. I liked Regan a bit more.

Sindra cringed from the venom in his voice, and Davis tried to put an arm around her that was shrugged off. A hint of life had come back to her eyes, and whether Regan's intention or not, his words had her sitting a little taller. I'd heard that Sindra was one of the most feared bitches on the planet—Oliver had told me that one night after he'd had a bit too much to drink, and even said he used to fear her—but at the time, I just couldn't see it. Now I saw a glimpse of bad-assery, the thin, bronze skinned woman with the shaved head and arms covered in scars, wasn't flinching like a timid field mouse anymore.

I angled the stainless-steel toaster just right so I could keep an eye on her.

"Sindra," Oliver prompted. "Regan's right. Maybe if you shed some insight, we can figure out our next move."

"I guess I do owe you one," she said.

"More like a thousand," Oliver muttered—and I suspected he wasn't talking about paychecks.

"He tests on humans," Sindra said flatly.

This statement brought Kaya's dishwashing hands to a halt. I plunked the rest of the plates into the sink and gave her a nudge to keep cleaning.

"And?" said Regan, as if it was no big deal.

Sindra licked her teeth. "He wants to 'design' his own army and his own race of people. He has the capabilities, and he just might do it. You see, not too long ago he acquired—"

"Whoa... whoa!" said Regan enthusiastically. "Hang on. Kaya—" Regan snapped his fingers at her like she was a well-tipped waitress, and if he wasn't injured, I'd have broken his other leg. "Come and sit down. You need to hear all this. *Your* head has been in the sand your whole damn life."

Luke and Thomas both growled at Regan, but Kaya dried her hands and obediently went back to the table, sitting on the edge of her seat while Sindra gathered a breath; what we were about to hear was not going to be pretty.

"I could understand Henry's passion for science, and I overlooked many horrible things because of it. I went along with his insanity because it was my job, and I was loyal." Sindra paused, scratched her throat.

"And because you loved him," Kaya said flatly.

"Yes," Sindra said. "Still do. I love him even though he is completely incapable of loving anyone or anything but power. I experimented, tortured, chained up, manipulated, and used people for him. I was as heinous as he was. But I grew to love another. Someone who was just as much a pawn. Someone I couldn't bear to hurt anymore. And when I realized what Henry was going to do to him and to his own daughter, well, I couldn't continue."

Why did I have the feeling Sindra was talking about Oliver? The way her eyes changed and blinked rapidly in his direction, and the way Oliver's nostrils flared in complete disgust, and the unmistakable scowl of jealousy on Davis's face…

Huh. I'd let her talk. Then I'd kill her.

"What you did to Oliver was unforgiveable in my book," Kaya said. "He might be able to let it go, but I can't."

I couldn't stop myself. "Oliver? What did this broad do to you?"

"Another time," he said softly.

"No. What did she do?" I realized I was holding a knife—a butter knife, but a knife nonetheless—and was close to stabbing Sindra in the face. "What did you do to him, Sindra?"

Having just returned, Lisa whisked Louisa off to the safety of the living room again.

"I took control of his mind," Sindra said softly, "by causing him physical pain for years. He came to me as a child, and I did as I was told. I programmed him to obey. I used him for what I needed and manipulated him right down to his own feelings. I was exceptionally good at my job."

Before I knew it, I was flying at her from across the kitchen, about to show her some home-style farm-girl manipulation. Brutus yelped when I stepped on his paw, and thankfully, Thomas grabbed a hold of me before I could get to Sindra's neck. He had an arm around my waist, the other one doing the chokehold that I had taught him. My intentions of strangling the bronze witch were quickly subdued when my own breathing became restricted. Thomas was freakishly strong—when did that happen? A few years ago, I could have tossed him around like a hay bale.

"Don't use my own moves on me, butthead," I hissed, but he held tight, waiting for my muscles to relax. "I won't hurt her. Scout's honor."

Thomas let go.

Oliver stared at me open mouthed, either impressed that I had jumped to his defense or completely horrified to have his past exposed. I felt like an idiot for losing my cool.

"I've got dishes to wash," I muttered and headed back to the sink.

Feeling Oliver's eyes on my back, I plunged my hands into the dishwater. I could feel his gaze go through me, but at least with my back to him, he couldn't see my embarrassment.

"All right, crisis averted," Regan said. "Continue on, Sindra. Tell us what Henry is conjuring up in that lab of his."

"Genetic testing," she replied. "He's figured out how to 'cut and paste' the DNA of a living creature to his specifications."

"By living creature, you mean a human," said Regan.

Sindra cleared her throat. "Yes. The tool he acquired is precise and efficient and has been labeled a potential 'weapon of mass destruction'. The embryos that are modified are not supposed to be allowed to develop for more than a few days, and they must be incapable of growing into humans. It is highly unethical and extremely controversial to use viable human cells. But Henry doesn't have ethics. Nor does he follow the rules."

"I think I'm going to be sick," Davis said.

Sindra went on. "Henry wants to build an army of men with exceptional muscle mass and speed, but mentally weak so programming them won't take so long. All he needs is one to clone, and then he can create as many as he wants. From there, he will design his own race of people. An ultimately higher intellect, disease-resistant race with a designer army to protect them. Not only does he need Kaya's inheritance to complete this, he needs her... well..."

Sindra stopped talking. I kept washing dishes. Brutus growled again. And Regan couldn't contain his impatience. "He needs her what?" he asked.

"He needs her body. He's been keeping her healthy and ensuring her fertility all this time, not only so he can get an heir from her, but so he can harvest—"

"Enough!" Luke slammed his hand on the table. "Not another word!" He had pulled Kaya to his side as if to shield her from the truth. "Whatever you were about to say next, *you keep it to yourself.*"

Arguing erupted. Regan was desperate to hear the whole sordid tale, and Luke was adamant that the conversation be ended. Thomas, remarkably, was on Luke's side, and it seemed that everyone had something to say except Kaya. She calmly wiggled out of Luke's arms, came to stand beside me at the sink, and picked up a dishtowel.

"Who's on dish duty tonight?" she asked.

I had to laugh. "Ellis and Thomas"

"Let's make sure Lisa uses every bowl in here when she's cooking then."

The arguing behind us rose in volume, the only person not chiming in was Sindra.

"Lisa is a darn good cook, isn't she?" I said, passing Kaya a rinsed plate to dry.

"Yup. Never thought I would like cabbage rolls, but yum." She sniffed, then spoke quietly. "Ya know Marlene, if I wasn't around, none of this would happen."

I could have slapped her, and I'm sure the shock on my face is what stopped her from saying anything more. "Don't you dare," I hissed.

"It's true."

"No, it's not true. Your nutso daddy would find someone else to use. Don't you go running off or doing something stupid. I freakin' mean it, Kaya Lowen. If I have to track you down again, I'll staple your butt to the floor when I find ya."

"I'm not running," she said, putting her hand on my arm. "I promise."

I breathed a sigh of relief. "Good. Because if you leave him, it would literally kill him." Of course I meant Luke, whose hand slammed angrily again on the table while Brutus howled his own point of view. Kaya and I just kept cleaning, our backs to the commotion. We were so wrapped up in ignoring what was happening behind us, we failed to notice a knock at the door until it was too late. Until Louisa, bunny in hand, had the porch door open and a rush of chilly air brought the arguing to a halt.

Two men peered into the kitchen through the screen door. I was about to turn around and go to them, but Kaya held me to the sink. "Remember to hide your face. Just keep washing," she warned.

Right.

"Is Seth around?" said one of the men to Louisa.

She was loud for someone so tiny. "Seth? Well of course not. He's gone…" We all held our breath until she said, "Fishin'."

Lisa flew into the kitchen, skidding to a halt behind Louisa. I could see the scene behind me in the reflection of the toaster. Everyone at the table remained seated and quiet, allowing Lisa to take the lead.

"Can I help you?" she asked, blonde hair now out of the pony tail and down around her shoulders.

"We just brought Seth his usual Christmas present," one of the men said. "He'll be snarly if he doesn't get his whiskey. And you are…?"

"His girlfriend," Lisa replied, all of us hearing her pain in that lie. "Lisa."

"Is he around? Can we come in? It's kinda cold out here."

Lisa hesitated. "Oh yes, of course. Sorry, I forgot my manners there for a moment."

The screen door squeaked, the furnace came on, and heavy footfalls rattled the kitchen floor.

"So, how do you know Seth?" Lisa asked.

"We go way back. I'm Harris, and this is my partner Gabe. We were on the force together. It's tradition for us to swing by on boxing day. Funny, Seth never said nothing about fishing."

"Oh. Well, I sort of insisted he host dinner for my family today," Lisa motioned to everyone at the table, purposely ignoring me and Kaya, "and he… well… he didn't like that very much. Maybe now I know *why?*" Lisa eyed the whiskey with disgust. "You know how it is, ya gotta make sacrifices for family, but he didn't feel like it I guess." Lisa stumbled over her tongue and Louisa, firmly at her side in a hideous pink dress, took over.

"My Mommalisa is pretty upset about it," Louisa said, looking up at the men claiming to be cops. "She cries lots about him. He shouldn't go fishing for so long. I think maybe he fell through the ice."

"Ha," Lisa said, nervously. "Kids say the darndest things." She patted Louisa's head. "He'll back soon, honey. Don't worry, he's fine."

Tension was thick. "Been with him for a while, have ya?" said Officer Harris, rolling his shoulders and taking in the room around him.

"Yes," Lisa said, valiantly keeping her composure. "Since February. Anyway, can I tell him you stopped by?"

It was then that Officer Harris noticed Kaya and me at the sink. His eyes caught mine in the reflection of the toaster, and I clearly noticed the gun in the holster at his waist.

"You folks staying for a while?" he asked.

"Nope. Just today," Regan said, leaning back and patting his stomach. He had dumped his British accent for something that sounded American. "We just finished a great breakfast, and now we're gonna sit around and try to be pleasant to each other until dinner."

The smaller cop placed the whiskey on the table. "Well, maybe this will help," he said with a wink.

My hands were in the sink, but I was out of dishes to wash. Lisa had begun false introductions; cousin Luke, brother Davis and his wife Sabine, and I was wracking my mind with what to say when she got to me and Kaya, but Lisa conveniently skipped over us.

"Well, nice to meet you all," Officer Harris said, but there was a tone of suspicion in his voice. "Too bad we couldn't have had a hang with the old boy, but I guess we can catch up another day. Oh, but before we go…" He reached into his coat pocket. "Have any of you seen this girl?"

And I could tell by the uncomfortable silence that Officer Harris was holding up a picture of me on my 'wedding day'. Was Oliver in the picture too?

"Hmmm," Lisa said, scanning it closely. "Pretty girl you're chasing after. You know, there are websites for that. It would save you the trouble of knocking on doors to find a girlfriend."

Officer Gabe was unimpressed. "She's wanted. For murder."

"Oh." Lisa clutched Louisa protectively. "We will keep our eyes out for her then. That's horrible."

I grabbed a vase off the windowsill and plunked it into the sink, pretending to really give it a good scrub while Kaya dried the same spoon over and over.

"What's your name?" Officer Gabe asked.

I knew he was referring to me, but I stayed mute.

Lisa tried to cover. "Oh, that's my cousin."

"I didn't ask you," came the gruff reply, which was rather rude for a cop stopping by to visit his 'friend' at Christmas time. "You. Girl at the sink. What's your name?"

Kaya turned around. "I'm Kate," she said.

"No… not you… the *other girl*."

Kaya slowly treaded through the kitchen to buy me time, making a show of wiping something off the table before sinking down into a chair next to Luke. My mind raced. If I had to face these policemen, things were going to go south really darn quick, and not 'Sunny Florida' south, but all the way to 'Butthole Antarctica' south.

So, I did the only thing I could think of.

"Ah crap!" I yelled, putting my hands to my face. "I got soap in my eyes, just a second."

I scrubbed my face. Running the water and rinsing like a madman until I was sure every speck of makeup that I'd spent an hour applying had come off. When I turned around, everyone would see the purple birthmark, including Oliver. He would see the real me. He would be completely repulsed like most people were…

But I had no choice.

I dried my face, and when I could no longer prolong the inevitable, I turned around, ignoring the collective gasp amongst the room. Both officers recoiled as if I had a flesh-eating disease.

"I'm Melissa," I said, not having to dig deep at that annoyance I felt when meeting new people. I purposely stomped when I took a few steps closer, using my most intimidating posture. Both cops flinched and failed at trying to cover up their horrified stares, so I gave them the *Marlene*. "What? My face? Yeah. It's a birthmark. Sorry if it makes you uncomfortable. Unfortunately, I can't change it. Is that a problem?"

Officer Gabe muttered, "Oh, no, of course not. Sorry to have bothered you. We just thought you were—"

"Someone else," finished Officer Harris as he reached for the door.

Man, I had a knack for clearing the room. We were almost home-free, until Officer Harris noticed something on the floor.

"Oh hey, it seems you got a broken cup there," he said, bending over to retrieve the mug Louisa's ridiculous dress had knocked over. Kaya was closest to it and she pulled her feet away. "Wouldn't want the child to step on it and—"

His words came to a crashing halt when his eyes fell to Kaya's hands in her lap. He did a double take, then studied her face for a moment. Straightening up and putting the broken mug on the table, he cleared his throat as ten faces stared back at him in utter silence.

They knew. But they were outnumbered.

"Well, it's getting late. We'll be seeing ya," Officer Harris said, his tone hurried and tense. "*Happy holidays.*"

Then they were gone.

"They saw her scar," Luke said the moment they were off the porch and heading to their car. He rubbed his thumb over the bite mark on Kaya's hand. "They know who she is."

He was stating the obvious. But what everyone else was in shock over was my face. For the first time in my life, I actually felt as ugly as I really was.

"We have to leave. Now," Luke said.

The car outside was starting up, taking off down the long drive.

"Hello?" Luke said, but everyone was staring at me.

Regan finally spoke up. "Marlene." I flinched at the sound of my name, horrified to hear what he was going to say. "You shouldn't hide that. It's quite lovely."

What??? That was probably just the doctor in him speaking. Someone who was used to seeing all sorts of weird and gross body stuff. There was a murmur of agreement though, and then the room burst into action. Luke was barking orders. Regan was repeating them. And I could finally flee from the kitchen.

"Regan's right," Oliver said, catching me by the hand, and if I didn't like the bloke so much, I would have torn his arm from his shoulder.

"Is he?" I said with my most intimidating glare, realizing it was having no effect on Oliver. "This is the real me you know. Without makeup. This —" I motioned to my face. "Doesn't wash off."

Then came another first. Tears behind my eyes.

Oliver smiled. It was warm and real, and it made his eyes shine. Everyone was moving around us, collecting truck keys and bunnies and clothing before the cops came back with more cops, but Oliver just smiled. Time stood still around us as organized chaos ensued. He reached to touch my cheek, the dark blue under my eye, the deep purple at my jaw, and wordlessly, I let him. I waited for him to come to his senses and run screaming from the room.

"Marlene," he said, pronouncing my name slowly, dropping his hand only when Thomas knocked into him with an armful of clothes. "I hope you never hide your beautiful face again."

Now Brutus was going crazy, barking his own orders. "We better get moving," I said.

But Oliver stood staring, as if the entire world disappeared and I was the only one left in it. And then, before I could raise a hand to slap him or knee him in the balls, he kissed me. The gorgeous prick just leaned in and freakin' planted one perfectly delicate kiss on my cheek.

"The real you is stunning," he said, and then he turned and walked off.

I think I stood there for a full two minutes, shocked, until Thomas stopped and handed me a bag of dog food. I was expecting some snide remark, or some sort of the usual teasing I got from him, but all he said was, "Oliver is right."

LUKE

3 2

PURGE

With Kaya between Thomas and I in the backseat, and Oliver in the front while Marlene drove, the old green truck sped down the highway taking us farther and farther from the ranch house and civilization. I would have headed to a city to get lost in—there were so many places to hide—but I was outvoted, and I hated that I wasn't in control. I also hated that Thomas' legs were touching Kaya's, and he was breathing the same air as she was. But for her sake—good Lord only for her sake—I would play nice.

I glanced out the rear window, not at all surprised to see Davis and Sindra take an exit off of the highway.

"You're right, Oliver," I said, not feeling bad about possessively draping my arm over Kaya and pulling her close. "Davis took off. Him and Sindra aren't behind us any longer."

"We'll never see them again," Oliver said with a sigh. "Davis couldn't forgive me, and there was no way he'd stick around to help protect Kaya knowing he could be captured again. I'm surprised he didn't take Sindra and vanish in the middle of the night."

I shivered at the thought of that dungeon, not blaming Davis for going off on his own.

"I'm worried sick about Louisa," I said, thinking out loud.

"She's fine with Lisa, I guarantee it, Luke," Oliver said. "Henry has no interest in them, or Regan and Ellis for that matter. We'll keep heading in opposite directions, and in a few weeks, they can all go back to the ranch house. It's safer there than anywhere else."

I hoped Oliver was right. At least I could take solace in the fact that if I could trust anyone with my sister's life, it was Lisa.

Kaya leaned against me. "So, here we are, running again," she said, weaving her fingers through mine and sending exquisite jolts of electricity through my entire body. "I don't want to do this for another two and a half years, but there's no way to fight Henry. We've gone over everything."

Marlene looked at us in the rear-view mirror. "The enemy of my enemy is my friend," she said. "Could that apply here?"

"It would if that enemy—mainly John Marchessa—didn't want Kaya dead," Oliver said.

"Then maybe she should be," Thomas said.

Marlene swerved slightly. "What? Thomas, you ass—"

"No! I didn't mean it like that. Good Lord, I didn't mean it like *that.* I'm just saying, maybe we should pretend she's dead. Fake it. Buy some time until all this passes."

Thomas's suggestion was lost to the startling wail of a police siren. A cop car with flashing lights was barreling down on us quickly.

"Crap!" Marlene kept the truck steady, not slowing down. "What do I do?"

"If you pull over and they're cops working for Henry, we're in an entire world of trouble. If they're only regular cops..." Oliver twisted around to glance at me. "It could be really bad for Luke."

Marlene stomped on the gas. At the first road off the highway onto a barely plowed strip of white with a few tire tracks, she turned with enough speed to almost flip the truck. The trees were thick on either side, the road narrowing. A sign reading 'Warning: Yellow Lake Road Closed Ahead' came into view and quickly went out again. We were bounced and jarred over ruts with the cops in full pursuit.

"They're gaining on us, Marlene," I warned her.

At a fork in the road, Marlene gunned it and headed left, causing the three of us in the backseat to slam into each other. Thomas's hand pressed against Kaya's thigh, steadying her, either not caring or not remembering that I was there.

"This old truck won't outrun a cop car," Marlene said.

"Where's your gun?" Oliver asked her.

"Glove box."

"You can't shoot at cops for God's sake!" yelled Thomas.

But no sooner were the words out of his mouth when gunfire ripped through the truck, shattering the back window; they were shooting at us.

We both reached for Kaya. I felt his hand over her head as he pushed her down, and I met his eyes as her body slammed into his when Marlene swerved.

"Over there. Take that road!" Oliver yelled. The truck swerved again and hit a wooden campground sign, not slowing. "Up ahead around that bend, floor it and head into the ditch. Hide us up in the trees and snow."

The truck sped on as Marlene did as she was told, then a whoosh of branches scraped the windows and we all flung forward with a crashing halt.

I had to shake the sense back into my head. "Are you okay?" I asked Kaya, reaching desperately for her, thankful the seat belt held us in. I lifted her chin to inspect her face, heart breaking at the fear in her eyes. "Answer me," I said, maybe a bit harshly.

"I'm okay," she stammered.

Oliver was out and stomping around to the back of the vehicle. He started running toward the road we'd turned off, Marlene's gun in his hand. He was going to try to take out the cops before they got to us.

I turned to Thomas, queasy over what I was about to say. "Get Kaya out of the car and head away from the road. Go up into the trees," I ordered.

He nodded, hand latching on to her wrist before she could follow me. The deep snow along with Kaya pleading with me to stop, made slow going getting to Oliver where he kneeled in the ditch.

"Give me the gun," I said, reaching for it.

Oliver squared his shoulders, keeping aim on the road. "You idiot, Luke. Get back to the truck and hide Kaya somewhere. I'll look after this."

He was wheezing. There was blood on his chin. He was sacrificing himself for us.

"You couldn't shoot your own foot with the state you're in," I said, snatching the gun from his shaking hand as he doubled over with a cough. Shoving him as hard as I could, I sent him backward into the snow where I hoped he'd stay, then I took his position. Getting low, I aimed at the road, not glancing back to see Thomas and Marlene wrestling Kaya into the trees.

The cop car had slowed to a crawl, siren off, windows down. I could see the muck turn on the tires as it approached, and the sloth-like movements of Officers Harris and Gabe. My heart-rate slowed. I embraced that scary part of me that brought time to a standstill. It made judging the distance and seconds easy, and I quickly realized I wasn't at the right angle to take out my targets.

So I ran straight for them.

Once on the road, I squeezed the trigger and shot Officer Gabe through the passenger window.

The car stopped. I kept running toward it. Except when I fired this time, the gun jammed. The piece of crap froze solid in my hands. I tossed it aside and dropped to my stomach, squirming quickly up to the car so it was between me and Officer Harris, who had gotten out and slammed the door so hard my ears rang.

"Dammit, you've made a mess of my car!"

He wasn't at all concerned about his dead partner.

"All I want is the girl," he said, angrily spitting at the ground. "You give me Kaya Lowen, and I'll pretend you didn't just shoot a cop."

"You're outnumbered," Oliver answered.

Somehow, he'd sidled up next to me. I'd hoped the big lug would just play dead in the snow, but now he was on his belly, weaponless and wheezing. He was focused though, reaching for the side mirror and angling it so we could see Officer Harris checking the cartridge of his gun.

"No need for a shootout," Harris said, unaware we had nothing but our wits. "With one press of this little button on my radio I can have a hundred RCMP here in moments."

Something didn't seem right about that threat. "Why don't ya then?" I challenged.

Officer Harris pretended to not hear me. "Just hand over the girl, and I'll let you go."

"Kaya Lowen is Seth's friend. He won't like that very much."

Officer Harris laughed. "Friend? Hilarious. Seth doesn't have friends. What he does have are plans for Miss Lowen, and I have recently discovered that those plans don't involve us. Or, me rather, since you blasted my partner's brains all over my car."

Officer Harris was stalling, crouching lower, readying his gun.

"We were coming over to get wasted and pound the crap out of Seth," he continued. "Who would imagine that we'd find Kaya Lowen hiding in his house. What an unexpected bonus! And you did me a favor, asshole. Now I won't have to split the hefty payout I'm gonna get for handing her over to her daddy."

Harris fired a shot that sent us circling away from him, scrambling around to the other side of the car.

"Where is she?" he demanded.

"Who?" I said, playing dumb as I pulled Oliver along behind me when he started to cough.

Harris's voice cut through the serene winter air. "The billion-dollar skin bag you've been hiding. Bring her to me now."

I felt my body flood with heat and I couldn't stop myself from standing and facing a cop who had a gun pointed at my head. "She is *not* a skin bag. Why don't you put that gun down so we can have a man-to-man conversation about that?"

I marched away from the car and onto the open road. Harris grinned as I approached with my hands up to show him I was weaponless. The sun going down behind him was almost blinding, but not so blinding that I didn't see the outline of someone sneaking up behind him.

"Let's talk, man to man, shall we?" I said, challenging him as a distraction. I knew the spineless prick wouldn't drop his gun.

Harris was drunk with the power the gun gave him. Snickering, he kept his aim. "Nothing to talk about. You can call her what you want, but I'm going to call her 'paycheck'. I'm also going to call you and your pal over there 'dumb and stupider' for not following orders when a man is pointing a gun at your face."

"It's dumb and dumber," the person sneaking up behind him said just before sending a bullet through his chest.

Harris slumped to the road, and there, standing stoically behind him, was Marlene. Her jaw was set in determination, birthmark almost black, amber hair flowing around her shoulders as she lowered the gun to her side.

"Are you okay, big guy?" she asked, chest heaving.

I nodded before realizing the question was directed at Oliver, who open-mouthed stared at her like she'd grown wings and descended from the heavens.

A scream breaking through the trees brought me and Oliver back down to earth.

Marlene smiled. "That's just Kaya. She's kinda agitated with Thomas for following your orders." Marlene cupped her hands to her mouth. "*It's safe, Thomas,*" she yelled up at the trees.

"The gun?" I asked, motioning to the piece of junk safely in Marlene's hand.

Marlene stepped over the cop she'd shot, cool as a cucumber. "Oh. It's just a little sticky, like Ron, the thieving uncle who gave it to me. You just gotta know how to handle it right."

Indeed. But how to handle a raging Kaya, who was running out of the trees and into my arms after losing her mind that I had risked my neck for hers? Kiss her fiercely then nod approvingly at Thomas, who'd taken a bit of a beating from her by the looks of it.

Thankfully the radio in the cop car was off and so was the GPS. I was careful not to touch a thing. With my sleeves pulled down around my fingers, I put the car in drive and took it off the road and into the ditch, getting a few feet into the trees before the snow and a few large stumps stopped the wheels. I decided to check the trunk for guns and ammo or anything we could use before I covered it up, hoping no one would find it until spring, and gagged when I turned off the engine. The bodies in the backseat were already emitting that horrid stink of death.

I got out, slipped the key into the trunk lock, and popped it open.

Then I threw up.

I didn't even make it five feet from the rear of the cop car when my stomach decided to purge every bit of food I had eaten for the past year.

"Luke, what's wrong?" said Oliver, marching toward me from the road.

I put my hand up. "Just stop there. Oliver… this… uh oh—"

I heaved again, unable to warn Oliver to not look at what was in the trunk.

"Holy mother of—" Oliver paused. "What the heck were these cops up to?"

It was a body, slightly decayed, and next to it a few brown packages that were so familiar I could picture the hands that had wrapped them. "That's my old boss," I said.

"Holy moly." Oliver had his hands over his mouth and nose. "And I'm assuming those packages are drugs?"

"Yup. Probably cocaine." My legs were not holding me up so well.

Oliver studied the scene then spun to face Kaya who was heading our way. "Stop right there, Kaya, I mean it," he demanded.

Of course she was defiant. "What's going on? Luke, are you okay?"

"Kaya Lowen, I mean it!" Oliver put one hand out for emphasis and used the other to pull me to my feet.

Thomas was next to Kaya, encouraging her back to the road and out of earshot.

"So, ex-boss, as in the drug dealer?" Oliver said quietly.

I nodded. "Can we keep this between you and me?" This part of my past was so ugly, so brutal and horrific, I just couldn't talk about it with anyone.

"Of course," Oliver said.

I took in a few deep breaths, glad the world had stopped spinning. "I recognize those tattoos on his neck even if the rest of him is completely —" my stomach twisted at the thought of the blood and the mangled body with hands and feet bound and mouth covered in tape. But that wasn't what had sent me dry heaving into the snow again.

"What else, Luke. Tell me." Oliver put his hand on my back.

I could barely say her name. "Angela. The girl in the dungeon. She said she was getting me a part of my past to 'play with' as a gift. I had told her my ex-boss's name at one point—it was impossible not to—and how he'd taken Louisa from me and held her for ransom and… Oh, my God, I told her everything."

"Louisa is fine, Luke. I promise." Oliver had a hand on my shoulder. "She's with two of the toughest bad-asses we know. Lisa and Regan will protect her no matter what. Besides, you have to remember that no one is interested in them. It's Kaya they want."

The world around me became so heavy I thought I might fold under the weight. "We are standing amidst a crime scene, Oliver. The murder of two corrupt cops and a notorious drug lord."

"Yeah. So it kinda removes us from the spotlight, don't it? Your past may have just saved our butts in the long run. Cops will be piecing together connections between the body in the trunk and the dead officers. They won't think twice about the likes of us."

"I hope you're right."

"Well, whether I am or not, it's time to get the heck outta here."

We wiped down every inch of the car to erase our prints, then covered it in branches and as much snow as we could. Hopefully the cover of winter would conceal my past a little longer, until we were far, far away.

STOKING THE FIRES

By the time we got Marlene's truck out of the ditch and back on the road, the sun was starting to go down. We were all soaked and shivering as the heat was sucked out through the broken back window. I pulled Kaya close, aching to make her warm, but my hands were blue. So were Thomas'; he had his between his thighs, trying to rub the circulation back into his fingers after he'd taken off his own jacket to drape over Kaya. I was grateful for that, but I still hated him.

"Where to now?" asked Marlene, cautiously pulling back onto the highway after we'd taken every back road we could to get to it. She cast a worried glance at Oliver next to her in the front seat, then accelerated onto the desolate stretch that would weave us between the mountains.

Oliver coughed, his eyes watering. "We'll freeze to death in this truck when the sun goes down," he said through chattering teeth.

Trees whizzed by. Minutes felt like days. When Marlene slowed to let a family of deer cross the highway, I noticed a sign: Rosewood Lake Cabins, closed for winter.

"There, to the left, Marlene," I said.

She was already on it, taking the truck off the highway and onto a narrow stretch of white.

The road was plowed for the first few miles, but came to an abrupt stop where a long length of chain blocked the continuation of what looked like more of the same road. There weren't any tracks or signs of human activity past it, and no way was the truck getting through the snow.

Thomas was out of the truck and grabbing whatever he could carry, trudging ahead without even a glance back to see if we were following.

Teeth chattering, I dragged Kaya along beside me. She was quickly exhausted from marching through snow up over her knees. At one point, despite her protests, I just scooped her up into my arms. Thankfully, Marlene was strong as an ox and able to help Oliver.

By the time we got to the first of eight cabins, I was glad to see Thomas at the door of one using a credit card to try and slip it between the lock. He was swearing under his breath, hands shaking too hard to break in. Oliver marched up behind him, leaving Marlene doubled over and panting with exhaustion, and kicked the door off its hinges.

"Well, that solves the lock problem," Thomas said.

The cabin was colder inside than it was outside and there was no power, but at least there was a fireplace and a stack of dry wood on the hearth. Collectively, we got a fire going, found every blanket in the place, and huddled together in front of the flames to get warm and dry.

Marlene and Oliver sat on the mattress they'd pulled off the only bed. "I hope we didn't set off an alarm or something," Marlene said, arms around her knees.

"As long as the power is out, we should be okay," Oliver said. "It doesn't look like these cabins are used at all in the winter, anyway."

"Geez. Who would even wanna stay here in the summer?" Marlene said, cringing. "Crammed into the trees with no running water or indoor bathroom. I'd rather stay home and shovel poop."

Oliver laughed, and it wasn't lost on any of us that his eyes lingered too long on Marlene. "Ah, it's not so bad. Heck, I'd rather do anything than shovel poop," he said.

"Yeah? You tell me if you still feel that way after you spend a few minutes out back on this love shack's frosty throne."

Kaya was leaning next to me on the couch, her feet bare and thrust toward the fire. I recalled the vision of her pink-painted toes in the sand... river water clinging to her skin as moonlight shimmered behind her... and had to think of anything else.

"I didn't know there were places without bathrooms," Kaya said with a yawn, and I could feel her body getting warmer. "You mean you really have to *go* outside? I know that's protocol when you're camping and all, but at a place like this?"

"Yup. Lots of places have biffies, Kaya. I'd suggest you just squat in the bushes though," Marlene said. "It's better than holding your nose and burning your lungs from the fumes."

"Fumes?" Kaya said innocently, and her voice sent a wild tingle through me.

Marlene was enjoying educating her friend. "Yeah. Nothing gets flushed away there, princess. It's a hole in the ground where uh, *stuff*, just stays.

Kaya's eyes widened. "Holy shit."

"Exactly," Marlene said.

Thomas remained quiet, and I pulled Kaya closer when his eyes met mine; he was dying to hold her, everything about his posture screamed it. If I let go—

"Did anyone see any food in the kitchen?" Oliver asked.

"Just sugar and salt. Nothing edible," I said, glad Kaya's eyes were closed and she couldn't see the pained look on Thomas' face. I pulled the blanket up over her shoulder when she turned and put her head on my chest. Thomas kept staring.

"What?" I finally said when ignoring him became futile.

"She was sick, ya know. Had strep throat or something," he said flatly.

Kaya didn't budge. Her eyes were closed and her breathing even; she had fallen asleep.

"Why are you telling me this?"

"Just thought you should know. Wouldn't want her to get sick again, and she still looks a little cold. I can fix that if you can't."

Marlene cleared her throat, reminding us we weren't alone, but Thomas carried on anyway, his dark eyes narrowed squarely on mine. Challenging.

"It was me she called out for when she had a fever by the way. Not you. Just thought I'd point that out."

I could have killed him. Right there and then.

"Thomas, you're being an ass," Marlene said.

Kaya was limp against me, so I kept quiet, gritting my teeth instead to not wake her. I knew that Thomas had been waiting to drop this bomb on me, and it was ridiculous how jealous I could become, as was his intention.

Thomas played his hand, his voice low, even. "She could have called anyone's name. Yours, Stephan's, Oliver's… but nope. She called out for *me*."

"Thomas," hissed Marlene.

"Just stating the facts," he said.

Marlene bared her claws. "I'll show you the 'facts' and dip you head first in the honey-pot out back if ya don't quit it."

"And I'll help you," Oliver said from the kitchen.

Thankfully, that shut Thomas up. But my tremble remained. Why did everything he say affect me so deeply?

Because of the truth in it.

Oliver went outside and returned with two pots of snow. One he set next to our shoes on the hearth, the other he dumped in half a bag of sugar, some salt, and what smelled like spices. When the pot boiled, he was pleased with himself, handing us what he called his 'Ollie Tea'.

"Sugar for energy, salt for hydration, cinnamon to regulate our blood sugar, and ginger in case anyone finds it nauseating. Drink up."

I roused Kaya because I knew if I didn't, Thomas would come up with something to say about it. We all sat in silence, sipping the oddly satis-fying brew.

"We need to sleep," Oliver said, re-filling our mugs. "But we can't let the fire go out. I'll take first watch. Luke, you're second, and Thomas, third. In the morning we can find something to cover the back window of the truck with and get back on the road."

Marlene shot Oliver a death glare. "Uh, what shift are me and Kaya taking?" she asked.

"Oh, you ladies can just sleep—" his voice trailed off. "Er, I mean you take the fourth shift, and Kaya wakes up early, so she's last."

Marlene nodded. "On it."

With the couch and loveseat cushions on the floor, the fire raged as we arranged ourselves amongst them and the mattress. The whole cabin had become filled with thick, luxurious heat, and I tucked Kaya in close to me, burying my nose in her hair and inhaling the scent of shampoo and sunshine lingering from the day. We were warm and comfortable with Oliver's tea swimming in our stomachs, and I nodded at him gratefully while Kaya fell asleep. He stared at the flames, then at Marlene whose eyes were closed and back curled up against Thomas. The cabin was dead silent except for the crackling of the fire.

"She's not blue anymore," Oliver said, just barely above a whisper.

Whether he meant Kaya or Marlene, I couldn't tell. So I just smiled at him. "Thank goodness. How about you? Are you okay?"

"Of course I am," he said quickly with a wave of his hand. "Get some sleep now, Luke. You're gonna need it."

Oliver's hacking cough startled me awake. I quickly realized my feet were practically frozen and Kaya was shivering again; the fire was almost out.

"Oliver?" I said, pulling myself upright to see him slumped forward in a kitchen chair.

A cough rattled him again. Even in the low light, I could see splatters of red on his hand.

"Oh crap, I'm sorry," he said through chattering teeth. "I… uh, must have nodded off."

Oliver was sicker than he was letting on. There was no hiding it now.

"Go lay down. It's my shift," I said, wide awake and unable to sleep anyway. "Take my place." I motioned to where Kaya lay and the empty spot behind her.

"You won't rip my limbs off?"

"Promise," I said, although it was hard to suppress the urge when he curled up around her. I had to get up and walk it off. Concentrate on something else for a minute besides my dying friend and his arms around the love of my life. So I stoked the fire and pampered it until it was raging, making the whole cabin hot as a Texas summer. Warm but aching head to toe, I then made a mission of finding some aspirin.

I dug through my old backpack, coming across the bar of soap I treasured and the grey shirt of mine Kaya had kept under her pillow when she'd run away—but no aspirin. Then I remembered I'd handed her the bottle in the truck when she'd said her arm was aching.

Her black bag sat next to mine, casually dumped on the floor and forgotten. It was zipped up, and it didn't feel right opening it, but would she care? I didn't think so. I hesitated just the same.

A few lacy things Lisa had bought for her were at the top, and deeper inside was more girl stuff along with a couple of books, but no aspirin. I checked the outside pockets. Empty. So I shook the bag and heard the rattle of pills. Digging to the bottom, I finally found them—and also the envelope Thomas had given to Kaya on Christmas day.

"No," I caught myself saying out loud.

Oliver stirred. "Huh?"

"Nothing. Go back to sleep," I told him.

My stomach had come up in my throat just a bit. We'd left the ranch house in a mad rush, yet Kaya had taken the time to grab it out of the closet. Had she brought this letter to save it and read over and over? I stared at the paper in my hands for the longest time and realized; it was still sealed.

She hadn't read it.

Should I?

"Luke?"

Her voice startled me. I was caught red-handed. "Just looking for the aspirin," I said sheepishly.

She was before me at the kitchen table where I sat, pulling the blanket tightly around her shoulders. "Did you find it?" she asked softly, eyeing the envelope in my hands.

"Um. Yes."

"I didn't read it," she said, but there was a tinge of guilt on her face even though I was the one invading her privacy.

"Then why do you have it?"

She bit her lip. "I forgot it was in there actually. I meant to either read it or throw it away, but I just didn't do either."

I handed it to her, gaze shifting to where Thomas slept.

"I truly love you, Luke," she said. "Please believe that."

I smiled and pulled her onto my lap. She was so light. So delicate. I swallowed down my jealousy, but it made the hunger pains and the desire for her that much worse.

"Are you going to tell me what was in the trunk of that police car?" she asked.

"Yes," I said, "but not yet, all right? There's just too much going on."

Reaching under the blanket I found the soft skin of her back. She sighed and leaned into my touch. "When you're ready then."

She maneuvered around to straddle me, and as the fire in the hearth raged, so did my own. Her thighs on either side of my hips tightened as her hands wandered over the back of my neck and shoulders, eliciting a zing of electricity that surged madly through my every cell. She wrapped the blanket around both of us, and I found her in the dark. Oh, what this girl did to me. My fiancée. My love. My *Kaya*.

I stood with her legs around my waist as her mouth sought mine, and was barely able to make it to the tiny room at the back of the cabin with my knees growing weaker by the second. It wasn't quite as warm as the rest of the place, but the heat between our bodies made up for it. I felt my way past the bed frame and pushed her up against the wall. She breathed my name, and I became desperate to touch her *everywhere*. The love I felt for her along with such intense desire threatened to consume all rational thought.

"I wish I could see your face," she said, fingers stumbling over the scruff on my chin.

"Mmm." I turned to mush beneath her touch.

"Do you believe me?" she asked.

I had no idea what she was talking about. Her mouth was on my neck, the soft mounds of her chest pressed up against mine as her fingers trailed up and down my spine, making it hard to concentrate. I was consumed completely with her. With *this*.

"Luke, do you believe that I love you?" she asked again.

I was glad she couldn't see me because the goofy smile that spread across my face must have been a mile wide. "I'm not sure," I teased, pulling her tighter, feeling her breathe, her heart beat, inhaling her scent.

"Then I'll spend my whole life showing you," she said.

I had no problem with that.

3 4

TELL IT LIKE IT IS

"Well, that was a fun sleepover," Marlene said, jolting us awake with a cutting tone. "Let's *never* do it again, shall we?"

Kaya rolled toward me and her sleepy eyes met mine, her cheeks instantly blushing—oh dear Lord how I loved that.

Oliver stretched. "I was actually having a blast till ya woke me up," he said wearily.

Marlene, stirring a pot of snow over the fire, had something witty on the tip of her tongue but held it. Instead she bounced up and headed for the kitchen, returning with a cloth.

"You got a little, uh… something on your face," she said, reaching for Oliver.

It wasn't a 'little something,' it was *a lot* of something. Blood. Dried on his cheeks and hands, and the pillow. He blocked Marlene's attempt to clean him up.

"Quit fussing,'" she scolded. "Put your hands down and don't act like a baby."

Amazingly, Oliver let her dab away at him. "There's nothing wrong with me, you know," we all heard him say as we pretended to be busy tying our shoes and inspecting our fingernails.

"Of course there isn't," Marlene replied, the affection in her voice as obvious as the birthmark on her face. "Probably just caught a cold. Eh, big guy?"

295

Oliver nodded numbly, lifting his gaze briefly to meet mine. "Yeah."

Kaya sat up. "Colds don't make you cough up blood, Oliver. How sick are you?"

"I'm fine and you know it, so don't start worrying about me. That just pisses me off," Oliver said, struggling to his feet.

Marlene gulped loudly and stood too, the cloth, once white and now red, dropped to the floor.

"Come on, Kaya," she said, voice breaking with the first display of weakness I'd seen from her yet. "I'll show you how to pee outside without getting it on your shoes."

Kaya was pulled out of my arms.

"Just be quick about it," Thomas said as he took over tending the fire. "Five minutes, and I'm coming out there to find ya."

When the girls were outside, I took the opportunity to talk freely to Oliver. "Scale of one to ten, how bad is it?" I asked.

Thomas raised an eyebrow but kept quiet.

"Six," Oliver said, clearing his throat. "The pain last week was a four, but now it's around a six."

"So, it's getting worse. Not better."

"Yes," he said, finally telling the truth. "But I'll do what I can to be useful. The moment I'm not, just drop me off at a pub somewhere and walk away."

My head and my heart hurt with that thought. "There must be something we could try."

"Nah. You know there isn't, Luke. You heard what Sindra said when we were holed up in that motel room. So, listen, when I'm gone, you better look after Kaya. If you screw up and anything happens to her, I'll come back to haunt you every waking moment of your entire existence."

Thomas glared at me. "I will, too. Haunt you, that is."

I remembered the feeling I had when I fished Kaya out of the rapids and saw the blood spilling from her arm—thinking she was dead—and realized that I felt even more for her now than I did then. "Believe me, if anything happens to her, you won't have a body to haunt."

Silence filled the cabin. Thomas adjusted his watch. Oliver stared at his hands.

"There must be a doctor or some kind of treatment, Oliver," Thomas said after a while, and there was genuine sympathy in his voice. "You don't even know what's wrong with you, right?"

Oliver shrugged his shoulders. "Let's just say I know it's not something I'm walking away from."

"So, does that mean you're just going to give up? Not try and get better? Because that's ridiculous."

Oliver leaned back against the cushions. "There's nothing I can do."

"Bull crap," Thomas said bitterly. "There must be something. I mean heck, I don't like you, *at all*. But what about the people who, uh do?"

"Kaya will be fine," Oliver muttered.

"And Marlene? What about her? The fact that you won't even try to find a way to get better will break her heart."

Oliver jerked like he'd been stung by a bee. "*Marlene?*"

"Don't play dumb, Oliver. C'mon, she's head over heels for you, just like you are for her. Surely you can see that. The only reason she's trying desperately to avoid displaying her feelings—let alone even admit them to herself—is because you appear to have given up the fight to stay alive."

I should have stuck up for Oliver, but Thomas was right.

"I would do anything for Marlene," Oliver said softly, looking at me as if needing backup. "Anything. But I can't fix what's killing me and I've accepted that. Besides, I can't allow myself to—uh, oh heck, never mind."

I knew what he was thinking; his whole life had been about Kaya, and he had never known anything else. Oliver, a man of duty and loyalty, was feeling guilty for falling for Marlene.

"You can let Kaya go, Oliver," I said. "I got this. I promise."

Thomas rolled his shoulders and cracked his neck. "Well, Luke, if you don't, I sure as heck do."

"Oh for… listen, it's over, Thomas," I said, barely able to keep my cool. "And you know it. You saw the ring on her finger. *She's marrying me.*"

Oliver flinched and Thomas snarled at me as I'd confirmed what they suspected. I felt bad to spring it on them this way, but Thomas really needed to know. He needed to back off.

And now he was close to exploding. "How did you force her into that, Luke, huh? Why didn't she tell anyone?" There was venom in his voice. "If she really wanted to marry you, she would have shouted the engagement from the rooftops, but she didn't. Instead, she hid it because she still has a thing *for me*."

That was it. I flew at him, not sure if I was going to shove him out the door or start swinging, and I'll be damned if there wasn't a hint of a smile on his face. Thomas was baiting me. Wanting me to lose my cool and take a few rounds out of him—because Kaya would hate me for it.

This realization stopped my rage in its tracks.

Oliver stepped between us. "Just relax, Luke," he said, his hand flat against my chest, keeping me from Thomas as I cooled down. "Count to ten and if you're still angry, walk away. Then I can beat him senseless for ya and pretend I'm having another one of my detoxing episodes."

Worked for me. "Or we can just gang up on him. For fun."

Oliver laughed, but it was so sinister it even gave me a chill. "Hmm. I'm intrigued."

Thomas backed away, his hands dropping to his sides. "The girls have been gone for too long," he said, wisely directing our attention away from him.

Oliver sighed and gave me a finger-point warning to behave, then marched to the back door and peered out the window. "No sign of them out back. Check the front."

A sudden weight of worry dropped into the pit of my stomach as I peered through the front window curtains; there was nothing but snow and trees. "They're not there either."

Thomas was jamming his feet into his boots and Oliver was tugging on a jacket. I pulled the front door away from the frame and a rush of cold swept through the cabin. "There are footprints out there. Lots of 'em." I slid the door back in place. "In and amongst the trees, and it can't all be from two girls."

"I see them," Thomas said from the back door. "And something isn't right."

Marlene bolted into the cabin first, breathless, and Kaya stumbled in behind her.

"We're surrounded." Marlene gulped for air. "We saw something in the trees, found footsteps and blood in the snow. We saw—"

"*Them,*" Kaya said.

By the way Oliver tensed head to toe I imagined that 'them' wasn't Bambi and Thumper.

"Henry's men. How many?" Oliver asked.

Kaya was in the kitchen, digging through the cutlery drawer. "Weapons. We need weapons."

Oliver marched over and grabbed her by the shoulders, her green eyes were wide and filled with fear.

"Kaya, how many did you see?" he asked.

She had a massive butcher knife in her hand that Oliver gently took and placed on the counter.

"Four and… a gun in the snow, I think, and blood. Oh, I don't know," she said. "But *Henry is here*."

Oliver strode to the living room window and carefully peered between the curtains. "We're sitting ducks. No guns. No nothing. Man, this is not good."

Kaya's eyes met mine from across the room, and my heart broke for her. "I'm sorry," she said, then her hand moved back to the knife. "I can't let you all die because of me." The gleaming silver metal shone in her hands and everyone in the room froze. "If I'm dead, maybe he'll let you all go."

"Put the knife down," I said, panicking as the girl I loved stood there willing to offer her life for mine again.

Tears were rolling down her beautiful cheeks. "It would just be so simple. No more running. No more hiding. This would all be over."

Oliver's hands were rising slowly, and Thomas was begging her to put the knife down, but Kaya just stared at me with that same agonized gaze she had on the beach when she told me she didn't love me.

"Oh, for God's sake!" Marlene yelled. In a huff, she stomped over to Kaya and full-on slapped her across the face before pulling the knife from her hand and tossing it in the sink. "Get your head out of your ass!"

I lunged for Kaya, who was in shock and holding her cheek in her hand.

"And you, back off a second," Marlene hissed, putting her hand up in my face and stopping me in my tracks. "Someone's gotta get it through this girl's head that taking your own life for any reason is complete bull crap. I mean, come on! We're surrounded by armed men in trees ready to ambush us at any moment, and you think—" Marlene shook Kaya by the shoulders for emphasis. "You think that offing your-self is going to solve the situation? First, that would mean your enemies have won, and second, look at blue-eyes over there, really look at him, Kaya."

Kaya's gaze centered on me, and I could barely breathe. There was so much pain and confusion on her face.

"This isn't just about you anymore," Marlene went on. "What do you think will happen to him if you aren't around?" Marlene's anger was as scary as the threat outside. "You might as well stab Luke in the chest and get his misery out of the way. Oh, and me, too. And Thomas and Oliver. I mean honestly, you can't give up, if not for yourself but for those around you. So put on your big girl pants and quit being so ridiculously selfish."

Oliver was about to put in his two cents but was promptly shushed.

"Sorry," Kaya muttered, shoulders sagging. "I just don't know what else to do, even though I know that you're right, Marlene."

Marlene patted her on the shoulder. "Darn straight I am. Now let's get back to business. What are we going to do about the dudes outside? Can we make a run for the truck? Think, Kaya. Use that nifty brain of yours for good instead of nonsense."

Marlene's question was answered with gunfire.

I grabbed Kaya, covering her body with mine as I dove for the kitchen floor. Landing hard, I saw Oliver hovering over Marlene to protect her, and her shoving him off. Thomas was at the back door flat on his stomach.

Kaya lifted her eyes to mine, her face so close we were almost touching noses. "I'm sorry," she said, then buried her face in my neck. I stroked her hair. She was crumbling, falling apart at the seams. Not that I could blame her.

I held her tight as the gunfire resumed, pressing her head against my chest as a bullet shattered the back-door window. Thomas remained on his belly where he was, broken glass surrounding him.

"Thomas," Marlene called. "Get in here. The appliances are our best protection."

The cowboy didn't budge. Was he hit? I didn't see any blood.

"Thomas?" Kaya said with alarm.

The gunfire grew even louder, and another bullet whizzed in through the back door, this time through the thin wood paneling inches over Thomas's head, hitting the fireplace, bricks blowing apart.

Thomas was not in a good place.

"He's too scared to move," Oliver said with a cough.

I pushed Kaya toward Oliver. He had both girls now, one under each arm, their breath making white clouds in the suddenly frigid air.

"Thomas," I said, crawling to the line of fire, avoiding the glass as I made my way. His eyes were wide but vacant. "Are you hurt?"

He didn't answer, just stared ahead at the fireplace and the missing bricks. He didn't resist when I grabbed hold of his wrist and tried to pull him toward me, but he wasn't as light as I'd thought. I was going to have to stand to drag him into the kitchen. Another bullet ripped through the door turning more bricks to dust. I gathered my breath, got on my knees, then bounced to my feet and yanked Thomas across the floor just as more bullets were fired.

"Snap out of it," I said to Thomas, slapping his cheek in the safety of the kitchen.

The window above the sink exploded, and Oliver began laughing madly; great, Oliver had lost his mind, and the cowboy was frozen in shock.

"Come on, Thomas." I gave him another smack to the head, and not all that gently. "Snap out of it."

Kaya was blinking back tears. "Thomas, I need you," she said.

That seemed to bring him around. He shook off the glass, sat up, and leaned against the fridge next to me as the cupboards over our heads blew apart with more gunfire. Oliver was still laughing, protecting Kaya and Marlene by covering their faces with his jacket, their heads pressed to his chest as little drops of blood peppered his face and hands.

"Darn, darn, darn, darn," Thomas said, hands over his head.

"I think you could take your swearing to the next level over this," I said, ducking from the plates slipping off a shelf.

"What are we going to do? There's nowhere to hide, we've got no weapons, and if we make a run for the truck, they'll pick us off. Just doesn't make sense, though. They could storm in here, but they aren't. It's obvious we're unarmed. What's the deal with that?"

At least Thomas had come to his senses. Oliver, however, could have easily gotten the role in a Psycho movie.

"We have to get to them first," I said.

The gunfire stopped. The knife on the counter caught my eye, and I lunged for it. Using the blade to sweep away the glass between me and

Oliver, I handed him the blade; he'd take a few rounds out of somebody before they got to Kaya and Marlene.

"I have to go outside," I said to him. "If I can find the gun that the girls saw and scope things out, maybe we'll have a chance."

Oliver nodded as Kaya started to pull away from him, desperate to come to me. I shook my head.

"Stay with Oliver. Please."

"Don't you dare leave me, Luke," she said.

"Just for a few minutes. I promise." I pulled her against me and let the world disappear for a moment—just a moment. I kissed her forehead and memorized her emerald eyes for the first and thousandth time. "Stay here with Oliver. Do as he says. Please. For me."

She was about to protest, but Oliver pulled her forcefully back. "Don't worry, Luke, while I'm alive, they'll both be fine," he said. The whites of his teeth gleamed like the butcher knife in his hand.

I had to believe him.

CHEAP SUNGLASSES

I waited until the gunfire had ceased for a good five minutes before heading out into the glaring sun. The snow was deep and almost to my knees. Thomas trudged along beside me, ignoring my orders to head back and let me do this on my own. He was as stubborn as he was annoying.

It was slow going making the short distance from the cabin into the thick trees, and once in, we kept to the shadows of their branches. Now that my eyes were adjusted to the light, I realized there were tracks everywhere that weren't ours, trails made by many feet that led right up to the cabin—they'd been outside all this time.

Gunfire rang out. Thomas and I dove under a mammoth pine tree, ducking beneath its low hanging branches.

"They're shooting at each other," Thomas said, blowing on his hands.

I didn't need him to point out the obvious or make a racket. "Just go back to the cabin," I said irritably.

"No."

I scanned the area, seeing nothing, and remembered Kaya had said they were up in the trees. Maybe I needed to climb.

"Why did you risk your neck back there to drag me out of the line of fire?" Thomas asked.

The idiot was making too much noise. I put my fingers to my lips as a sign for him to shut the heck up. Shots were being fired, but they were over our heads. I saw a flash of light, like a mirror reflecting the sun, and then another flash not far from it. There was a pained yelp and then some-thing, or someone, fell with a thud to the ground. Still, all I could see was white.

I pointed up, alerting Thomas, and just as I did another man fell in a heap a hundred yards from our hiding place. The Lowen Security badge on the fallen man's camo outfit was clearly visible. A radio was strapped to his chest and faintly a voice could be heard. "Troy, come in. Hey, are you there? The entire front line is down. Retreat. Retreat."

At the man's waist was a handgun, and next to his body, a rifle outfitted with a silencer—our ticket out of here. If I could just get to it before whoever was shooting at the Lowen Security guys shot me.

I made a move for it, but Thomas latched onto the back of my jacket and stopped me dead in my tracks. Wordlessly, he pointed at a mass moving through the trees toward us. I blinked the shape of a bulky man dressed head-to-toe in white into focus. He was soon joined by four more men. Silently and efficiently, the dead Lowen guard was picked up and carted off, leaving Thomas and I holding our breath until they were out of sight.

Now the small clearing was empty. No body. No blood. And certainly no gun.

"What the heck?" Thomas whispered. "Who are those guys?"

I knew exactly who they were. The very people Henry had been protecting Kaya from her whole life. "Marchessa," I said, shoving my hands into my coat pockets.

"Oh crap. That means this is twice as bad as we thought."

I steadied my nerves, pretending not to agree. "Nah. It's a cake walk. We just need to get a gun and go back and get everyone to the truck. Easy."

Thomas arched an eyebrow as if I was completely nuts, then he shrugged his shoulders in agreement. "All right," he said and began trudging ahead of me through the snow.

The cowboy had guts, no question there.

We were hoping to see one of Henry's men now, but the forest had become eerily quiet. Birds chirped. Forest creatures foraged. Thomas took the lead. Whatever had come over him in the cabin and froze him to the floor in fear was gone. He moved carefully, assuredly, climbing over a fallen tree covered in snow and disappearing from my line of sight.

Then I felt the presence of someone behind me.

I turned. A huge blur of white with about fifty pounds more muscle than me stomped closer, rifle in hand. The only thing visible was squinting eyes, and I was familiar with the determination in them.

"Don't move," he ordered.

I needed his gun.

My hands were up in self-defense. He was trying to determine if I was one of Henry's men. I kept still even when he got close enough to strike— I had to give Thomas a chance to get away.

"Turn around and put your hands behind your back," the man in white ordered, voice muffled from a cap that covered his hair and came up under his chin to cover his mouth.

I moved like a sloth.

"Get on your knees," he ordered.

I did as I was told and felt the world slow to a crawl. The breathing of the man behind me became long, drawn out inhales and exhales. A bird's wings fluttered past my head, lifting and falling in slow motion. And just as the cold plastic of a zip tie was about to circle my wrists, I swung back an elbow and connected it with the man's jaw. He was fast to recover, swinging the barrel of the gun toward my face, but I ducked in time, throwing a hit to his kidneys and watching the gun fall from his hands. I sensed someone else behind me, their shadow wide on the snow, and spun around in time to connect my boot with a nose before throwing a quick succession of punches to a firm solar plexus.

Now the men in their white suits blended with the snow, sprinkling it red.

I made for the discarded gun, but a heavy boot stomped down on the barrel of it, flattening it to the ground. There were many sets of eyes on me now. Five to be exact. More men in white—John Marchessa's men— closing in, forming a circle. When they didn't fire, and it became clear that I was to be taken alive, I fought my best fight.

I embraced that crazy thing that happened in my brain, barely registering my hands and feet as they connected with bones and skin. It was easy calculating their moves, countering them, and hitting hard enough to throw their thin white head coverings off and lay them out at my feet. I had a few guns to choose from now, and the closest one was almost in my hands.

"If you don't settle down, I'll take my annoyance out on this one," an authoritative voice said.

I spun around to face a leather clad man with thick, black hair pulled into a ponytail. Tattoos covered his neck, and his hands were gloved. He had a pistol pointed at Thomas's head.

"Well that's just great," I said with a sigh to myself.

"Yes, it's your lucky day," the leather-clad man said. "Now stand down or I'll do away with your buddy."

Thomas stared at me with rage swirling madly in his eyes. He'd obviously put up a fight too, judging by the way his nose was bleeding.

I put my hands up in surrender.

"Good. Now step back. Get on your knees."

Within seconds my hands were tied. More armed men came out of the trees.

"Good." Leather man holstered his gun at his back, releasing his grip on Thomas' shoulder. "We can all act like civilized gentlemen now." He took off his sunglasses and rubbed at a smudge with his gloved fingers. There was the distinct sound of plastic snapping. "Really?" He stared at the broken glasses. "Two hundred bucks and they break the first day? What is this world coming to?"

The glasses were tossed into the trees. Leather man snatched another pair off the face of a bloke standing next to him. After frowning at the label, he slipped them on and shoved Thomas toward me.

"All I ask for is cooperation, all right?" he said, every gun in every hand but his was aimed at us. "That way I won't have to stuff more bodies into the back of the van. It's already crowded and stinking to high hell in there."

"Who are you?" I asked as Thomas and I were being forced to trudge ahead.

No reply.

I asked again, but was cuffed in the back of the head and told to shut up. My only comfort was that at least we were heading away from the cabin.

My feet were numb from the cold by the time we made it to what must have been a service road for the campsite and cabins. There were three parked vans, and Thomas and I were ordered to kneel before one of them.

"It will be all right," I said to Thomas, noticing him shaking.

His dark eyes met mine. They were red rimmed. "That's twice now, dickhead," he said.

The wind howled through my jacket. The blurs of white moved around us, packing up guns, putting the bodies of uniformed Lowen men in the back of a van.

"What are you talking about?" I said under my breath. Someone was binding together my ankles now, and I had half a mind to break their arms.

Thomas scowled. "In the cabin you pulled me out of the range of bullets when you could have been shot yourself, and just now—you had them. You could have made a run for it. But you didn't because of me."

"Uh huh," I muttered, wondering if the keys to the van in front of me were in the ignition. It was so close. Empty...

"That would have been the perfect opportunity to erase me from the big picture, just saying," Thomas said. "Why did you help me?"

"I did it for Kaya." More guns. More vehicles... Good Lord, how I was going to get us out of this one?

"Huh," Thomas said, his voice hinting at the fear now starting to show on him. "Maybe you're not so bad after all."

"It was purely selfish, Thomas. I can't stand you."

"Ya. I don't like you much either."

At least we agreed on something.

"So, how much damage can you do?" Thomas asked after a moment, eyeing my bound hands.

I met his stare. "A lot if I can get free."

"We need to give Oliver more time. Hopefully he's thinking of making a run for it. Marlene's truck is in the opposite direction of us and if he can get them there, maybe—"

Thomas didn't finish. He was horrified by the same thing I was; the last van being loaded up with more bodies.

I spoke quietly. "I'd hoped that Henry might have gotten to her first, you know, the lesser of two evils. But judging by the amount of his men being piled into that van, I'd say that yes, we gotta do something." I gathered my wits about me. Leather man was talking into his phone, eyes never leaving us. "I can at least keep them busy for a while."

Thomas paled slightly. "Me, too."

Leather jacket guy began barking orders. "Watch the blue-eyed one," he said loudly, a gloved hand motioning in my direction. "Put him and the other one in van three." He signaled to a waiting group of men to head in the direction of the cabin. "Go retrieve Kaya Lowen now. The area has been secured."

Thomas and I both breathed a sigh of relief that she was at least alive.

We had to keep it that way.

I stood. Thomas took that as his signal to make a distraction too, and as he bolted for the trees, I struggled against the zip ties, unable to free myself as two blurs of white zeroed in. I head butted one and threw a shoulder into the stomach of another. I didn't know what I could do except fight, which wasn't very effective with my hands and ankles tied, but I stayed on my feet as long as I could. Until Thomas was caught and sent face first into the snow and dragged back onto the road. Until the bones in the faces of a few Marchessa men met the top of my head. Until leather man put down his coffee and delivered a well-placed kick to my abs, leaving me breathless.

"Good grief," he said, annoyed. "I mean, I admire your tenacity, but they don't pay me enough to deal with this nonsense." He motioned to a man next to him. "Just shoot him and get it over with."

I saw Thomas mouth the word *no* as a sharp pain pierced my chest.

Then the lights went out.

KAYA

BURGER AND FRIES

Being deprived of my sight brought forth a near uncontrollable panic. Blindfolded with my hands bound together on my lap, I could hear Marlene, but I couldn't hear Oliver. He'd stopped making any noise what seemed like hours ago. Saying his name did nothing but entice a muffled sob from Marlene. He'd fought for us, holding back the group of men that stormed the cabin, and valiantly gave everything he had until he couldn't breathe. His lungs failed him. This turned Marlene into a vicious wild cat instilling the fear of females in our attackers' hearts before she was eventually overtaken, too.

Now we were held captive in a moving vehicle.

I asked about Luke and Thomas, begged to see Oliver, and gave up after being ignored for the millionth time. When the vehicle came to a stop, we were transferred to a plane. I had lost all sense of time when I was ordered to get out and stand. My legs buckled beneath me.

Hands were under my armpits, pulling me upright. "Almost there," a male said with what might have been a hint of sympathy.

Feet dragged over a flat surface, I was weary right to my bones. Wherever we were now, the air was just as cold and there was no breeze. It smelled earthy and dank, and I could hear the breathing of many men around us. Some were panting; were they carrying Oliver? Keys jangled, and a door opened. I bumped into something with my shoulder and lost my balance only to be grabbed before hitting the ground.

"You can rest soon," the same male voice said.

I could tell by the change of gravity that we were in an elevator going down. When the doors opened, a whoosh of air—sweet with the scent of something floral and—deep fried?—rushed my senses. Ordered to sit, I was glad to find a chair beneath me and not the floor. Hands were working at my wrists, loosening the bonds, and then the blindfold was removed.

I rubbed my aching hands as my surroundings snapped into focus; cement walls, no windows. In a room the size of a prison cell, a lone light bulb cast an eerie glow. Marlene was seated across from me, between us a small table and a mammoth size platter of French fries with little bowls of ketchup. Roses and lavender bundles were plunked into a pop bottle and wilting at the edges.

"What the—" Marlene blinked madly, taking it all in, then flew around the table to me, almost knocking it over. "Are you okay?" she asked as we both crumpled to the floor in each other's arms. The door shut. A lock clicked in place. We were alone.

"I'm fine. You?"

We were both trembling and scrambling away from the table as if it were crawling with snakes. With our backs up against a cold wall, we buried our faces into each other's shoulders and let the utter terror of the day release in tears.

"Oliver…?" Marlene said after a while.

His name caught the breath in my chest and my stomach lurched. "I-I don't know." I didn't know about Luke either, or Thomas, and the worry was almost smothering.

"You're going to owe me big time for riding along on this family reunion of yours," she said, rubbing her wrists where the rope had chafed her skin.

This family reunion was going to result in our deaths.

"Stay positive. We're going to be okay," she added, clutching my hand.

"What makes you think that?" I noted the sink and toilet in the corner of the room, grateful as my stomach twisted in agony.

"They haven't killed us yet."

Hours went by. The scent of the flowers disappeared and the smell of stale fries took over. Marlene had fallen asleep on my shoulder, and I nudged her awake when the lock on the door clicked. We braced ourselves, expecting to see one of the many men we heard pacing outside the door. But the tiniest, most unassuming woman entered instead. She was so small and petite it was confusing. Grey, grandma-hair, a purple sweater with an embroidered Rudolph on the front, glasses, horrible perfume…

"Stay right where you are, girls," she said, voice scratchy with age. She was holding a metal bar in her hand. "This handy device will send your asses into next year if you so much as even pass gas. So behave, or I'll smack ya with it, and let in one of those lard-brained wing nuts outside the door who is eager to do much worse."

When we didn't reply she yelled. "Got it? Or are your ears filled with cotton? Need a demonstration?"

Marlene flinched when the tiny woman made a motion toward her with the bar. "No, ma'am," she said quickly.

"Ah. I can tell you're familiar with this little device, aren't ya?"

Marlene was shaking. "Yes, ma'am," she muttered.

"Good. Now put out your hands."

We did as we were told. The old lady eyed the ring on Marlene's finger, then the scar on my hand. She sneered when her sharp eyes met mine. "You look nothing like your mother," she said, then yelled to whoever was outside the door. "It's all clear. Bring it in."

A tray smelling of cinnamon was placed on the table and the fries were removed. All the while, Marlene stared in terror at the bar in the old lady's hand. Even when she left and shut the door, Marlene was still trembling.

"What was that thing?" I asked.

"That was a cattle prod," Marlene squeaked out. "It delivers a jolt of electricity, and it's the most painful thing I've ever felt."

"What? Why have you felt that?" I asked, realizing exactly what that device was and shivering myself.

Marlene took in deep breaths, trying to calm herself down. "Well, since we're going to die, I guess I might as well tell you."

"Yes. Please do. Anything is better than thinking about what might happen next in here. It can't be as bad as *this*."

She balked. "Twice, Kaya... Ben used it on me twice. The first time on my arm, and the second time, right on my cheek." She rubbed at her birth mark. "He'd been rounding up cattle and had it in his hand when he came into the shack while I was warming up after skating."

My hand flew to my mouth in stunned silence.

"He used it first as a warning, showing me what it could do so I wouldn't move while he, while he—"

I knew where this was going. I was one of Ben's victims, and if it weren't for Thomas, it could have been much worse. I patted Marlene on the leg to encourage her to continue.

She gathered her breath. "One of his hands roamed all over me while the other held the cattle prod. I'll never forget the look in his eyes. I hoped he'd stop, and at one point it seemed the fog lifted and he realized what he was doing. He even said my name like he was just realizing who I was, but when I used that opportunity to push him away, he snapped back into attack mode. He brought that cattle prod to my face. It knocked me out, and I woke up to him trying to remove my pants."

I felt sick. "Did he—get them off?"

Marlene straightened up and rolled her shoulders. Wiping at her eyes, she took in a deep breath. "No. I booted him between the legs with one of my skates and got out of there. Too bad the skate guard was on." She paused and cracked her neck. "You know, the bastard carried on the next morning at breakfast like nothing happened. Offered to clear the lake for me to skate on because it had snowed overnight. I thought I was going crazy. He pretended like nothing ever happened. But the burns on my arm and face that showed up twelve hours later made me certain it did. I spent ages trying to figure out what caused him to attack me like that. Was I dressed provocatively? Did I say something to lead him on?"

"You didn't do anything. It wasn't your fault. Ben was sick."

Marlene nodded. "Oh, I know that now. It wouldn't have mattered if I was wearing a G-string and stripper heals or a head-to-toe burlap sack… no means *no*. But it sure messed with my head for a long time."

"Why didn't you tell anyone?" I asked.

"He was drunk, and he's my dad's best friend."

"Neither is an excuse."

"Yes. I know. It's just that, he did so much good for our family. Saved our farm from bankruptcy. Helped whenever we needed it. He was an angel with a devil on his shoulder."

I sighed in agreement.

"I almost lost myself over it though," Marlene said, her voice bouncing off the concrete walls. "What he did was wrong. He had no right to touch me. No right to take advantage of me in any way, drunk or not. And because I let him get away with it, he tried to do it to you. If I would have just told somebody, maybe it could have been prevented. Maybe he could have gotten some help."

"Yes. Maybe," I agreed.

She turned and traced the raised scar on my arm, running her fingers over the puncture wound, then boldly touched my neck and the other scar there.

"I hate to admit it, Kaya, but you inspire me."

This came as more of a shock than anything. "What?"

"I noticed your scars right away. No one has injuries like that and isn't 'changed' by them. I could tell you were fierce under that delicate exterior even though you couldn't see it yourself."

"I don't feel fierce now," I said, staring at the oddly massive cinnamon buns we stubbornly avoided. Earlier today Marlene had to slap some sense into me, and the words she hurled at that cabin wouldn't soon be forgotten. I felt like such a fool for holding a knife to my chest.

"We all stumble," she said intuitively. "I just had to make sure you picked yourself back up."

The room grew colder. We sat for a long while, stomachs sucked up against our spines, thirst threatening to make us mad but too tired and scared to move.

"How are we going to get out of here?" Marlene said softly.

I'd dozed off after running a million scenarios through my mind, none of which had a positive outcome. "I don't know."

"Ben's dead, isn't he?" she asked.

I wasn't going to lie to her. "Yes."

"By these people?"

"No. My birth mother. He was caught in the crossfire."

"Who are they?" She motioned at the door and the noise of many from behind it.

"My grandfather. He wants me dead. You know—money, power, and blah blah blah."

Marlene had on her brave face again. "Man, your family is super fucked up," she said. "Pardon my French."

Marlene wasn't one to swear, but her description was correct. "Your French is perfect."

There was a commotion outside the door. The lock clicked, then clicked again, and I thought I detected the voice of the old lady tearing a strip out of someone. Marlene and I kept talking, focusing on anything other than the predicament we were in.

"Maybe you fell for Thomas 'cause he saved you from Ben," she said.

There was a loud crash. We both pretended not to hear it.

"He was like a knight in shining armor."

Marlene smiled. "Yeah, and his hair is as glossy as it gets."

This made me smile, too. "I love you, Marlene," I blurted out.

She laughed. "Oh, for crying out loud, I know that. You love *everybody;* the guy at the store, your hairdresser, heck, you probably even loved Ben at one point. That's just who you are. A naïve girl with a heart as big as my aunt Frieda's donut-lovin' butt."

"I don't love *everybody*," I said, sounding childish and whiny.

"Okay, well, very strong like then. I mean, besides your parents and grandfather—because, hello, if you didn't hate them you'd be certifiably loony—who do you hate? Who do you really not like?"

"Lots. There are lots of people," I said, racking my brain. "Ellis. There. I don't think he's very nice. Although, I wonder if it's because he's the baby of the family and gets ignored. There's probably a decent side to him I just haven't seen yet."

"Ha!" Marlene said triumphantly. "There isn't. He's a total dick."

There was more commotion. Thudding, rustling, male voices giving orders, and I was sure I heard Oliver. Marlene and I clutched our hands together, both wanting to call out to him, but knowing there was nothing he could do.

"For what it's worth," Marlene said softly, toying with the wedding ring on her finger. "I kinda sorta love you, too, but I'm only admitting that 'cause we're gonna die."

I suspected her words were also meant for the man she'd married.

"What the heck? You don't like my cooking?"

We woke to the old lady looming over us, thankfully without the cattle prod.

"I'm a weapons expert," she said angrily. "You think I felt like behaving all motherly and fixing you spoiled brats something to eat? No. I don't. Are ya too good for cinnamon buns? Huh?"

Marlene and I collectively muttered, "No, ma'am."

"Well," she went on, "they're all hard as a rock now. I can practice my pitching arm with 'em."

She turned for the tray, and at the back of her pants was a regular hand-gun. I was completely awake now and sitting upright. If I could get to it, I'd have some leverage. I mean, she was old. Probably as slow as molasses.

My body instinctively began to lurch forward. But I didn't even make it half an inch before she swung around and had that gun in Marlene's face.

"I won't shoot you, Miss Lowen," she said, eyes narrowing on me, hand steady as the day. "But I will put a million bullets in this one's head if you even think of jumping me. Got it?"

I nodded in complete understanding.

"Stupid girl," she said, cussing me under her breath, then turned to leave.

"Wait," I called after her. "Can you tell me about my friends?" I used my most respectful voice hoping to win her over just a bit. "Oliver and two other men... I heard someone say they had them. Can you tell me where they are? Are they okay?"

The old lady swung around with fury in her eyes. "Do I look like I work at the hostage information desk? Do I have 'ask me whatever you want' written on my forehead? Did I give you any impression that I care about what's happening here at all? And never mind the food, I'm paid to do that, but I'm sure not paid to dish out info to a spoiled brat. If that bothers you, feel free to take it up with management and slip a note in the suggestion box." With that, a snicker of laughter erupted from her. "Suggestion box. Ha. I crack me up."

We waited until she contained herself. Which seemed to take a while.

"Anyway, we're going to be moving you both to a different facility. Could be in hours. Could be in days. So I'll be bringing by some burgers and cokes. Whatever you don't eat, I will shove down your throats with my bare hands. We clear?"

Mutual nodding ensued.

She left, taking the stale buns with her.

"I don't eat meat," I said, of all the things to be worried about.

"I don't eat buns with sesame seeds," Marlene said as the door lock clicked. "So it's a good thing we have each other or we'd be screwed. That old broad is horrifying."

"Yes," I agreed. "Although, she's kind of interesting. I think there's probably a real softie underneath that gruff exterior. Under different circumstances, I'd probably like her."

Marlene leaped to her feet and pointed at me. "Ha!" she said triumphantly.

"What?" I asked in confusion.

"I'm right!"

She strolled over to the sink, washing up and gloating as I pretended I didn't know what she was talking about.

LUKE

THEY SAY THAT GOOD INTENTIONS…

Thomas was haunting me so, apparently, I had gone to hell.

"Luke… wake up…"

Even in the thick cocoon of darkness encasing me, I could not shut out his voice.

"Luke. Come on, man, wake up."

I opened my eyes—tentatively—and there he was. And by the surge of pain that shot through my arms and shoulders I fully realized I wasn't dead.

My wrists were in chains and up over my head. Throat dry, environment slowly starting to come into focus, I realized Thomas was next to me in the back of a windowless van. Six men, armed and silent on benches, minded us while we sat on the metal floor.

"You've been out for hours," Thomas muttered.

I glanced down at my chest, remembering the pain before I blacked out. I was surprised I was still in one piece, and my confusion was noted.

"We're not savages," the only man not wearing sunglasses said, and I suspected that was because his eye was swollen shut and nose painfully cocked a little too far to the side. I was pretty sure I was the cause of that. "Unlike that sadistic sicko Henry Lowen, we use tranquilizer guns whenever possible." He tapped what looked like a rifle against the side of the van as a warning. "But I can still do some pretty severe damage with it. So don't make me angry or I'll aim for a body part you won't recover from."

"He means your eye, Luke," Thomas said.

"Yeah, I figured that." My muscles screamed in agony. "Where are you taking us?" I asked, assessing the man with the broken nose and the others; three were alert and big enough to put up a fight, and two at the back appeared tired and could be an easy take. "Who are you working for?"

Silence.

I tried another approach. "Did you get what you wanted?"

Broken Nose nodded with an antagonizing smile. "Yes. We have Kaya Lowen. She's pretty. Could be a lot of fun."

My resolve snapped, and the chains clanked as I tried to yank free of them. *"Don't touch her. Leave her alone."*

The man closest to me shrunk back, and even Thomas tried to inch away, but Broken Nose didn't bat an eye. "If we would have 'left her alone' she'd be with Henry right now and the rest of you would be dead. You should be thanking us for saving your butts."

I was—and wasn't—listening. My exhausted body and emotions were getting the best of me. I caught my breath and tried to assess my restraints, which were most certainly intact. I had to try and break free though. If I could take a hostage…

"She's just my type," Broken Nose said, clearly enjoying my torment. "We're taking the long way home, but we'll meet up with her in a few hours. I just hope by then there will be a piece of that sweet ass left for me."

Control—*gone*. Motive—*kill*.

I yanked my fists forward, putting my body weight into the force and ignoring the ooze of warmth as the cuffs cut into my wrists. Rage mixed with fear and desperation kept the pain at bay as I slammed manically against my restraints. After what had happened to me by the hands of the girl in the dungeon, I barely felt the pain now, just the heat of anger and the groaning metal siding of the van heaving around the hooks securing my chains. A rivet snapped, and I imagined that whip against my back as I thrashed forward. I imagined my hands around the neck of every one of the men in this van when the hook pulled free…

And then, the world went black again.

I had new handcuffs on when I woke, now shackled to the wall of a grey cement room. Thomas was free to wander and stuff stale French fries in his mouth, forcing some into mine even though I warned I'd bite him. I didn't know if it was day or night. Nor did I care. And when we were both blindfolded and forced onto a plane, I passed out again. When I came to, dizzy and shaking with hunger from dehydration and the lingering effects of the tranquilizer, Thomas reminded me to be grateful it had been shot into my neck and not my eye, but I was mostly grateful I wasn't alone in this.

When it came time to stand and get off the plane, I was too weak to shrug off the hands keeping me from falling over. There was no heat. No wind. Our footsteps echoed in a cavernous space. I thought I heard Oliver. I thought I heard Kaya. And when I called out to both, all I got back was a sharp slap to the head.

"I'll put more tranquilizers in ya," warned Broken Nose, his nasally voice unmistakable. "That'll stop your heart for good just so ya know."

"Just keep your mouth shut," Thomas recommended.

I pretended to take heed, but really, I was fading fast. I could barely hold my head up when I was slammed into a chair, hands secured behind my back again. Voices came in and out of the fog that was settling over my mind, but one stuck.

"Why is this man chained and the other one not?" asked a male I hadn't heard till now.

"He's a fighter. Took out six of our best men, two while handcuffed." I recognized the voice of the man in leather. "If he could be controlled, he'd be a good one for the team."

"I'll take that under advisement, Troy."

Heavy footsteps came my way. The blindfold was untied, but I could barely get my eyes to stay open. If I weren't bound to the chair, I would have fallen over.

"Luke, is it?" said a man with unruly red hair and a greying beard. The rest of his features swam before my eyes. I tried to bring his sharp nose and close-set eyes into focus. "Kaya is still alive," he said, expressionless. "Let's keep it that way for now. All right?"

Gasoline and oil fumes permeated the air. Crates were piled in a corner. Towering ceilings and dim lights soared overhead. We were in an airplane hangar, but there were flowers. Lots of them. Daisies wilting in boxes and dumped on the floor before us. It was so weird I couldn't decide if I was dreaming or awake.

Then I heard her scream. Bone chilling and terrifying, Kaya let out a bloodcurdling wail that urged every part of me to explode out of the chair. But the bearded man staring at me was expecting that.

"Are you going to behave?" he asked.

Another scream.

I nodded enthusiastically and with a snap of his fingers, Kaya became silent.

Thomas, in a chair next to me, bent over and threw up.

The bearded man snapped orders to Troy, who was rubbing at the tattoos on his neck. "Get this mess cleaned up and address their wounds. Make sure they are fed and watered. Once Miss Lowen is prepared, we will get started."

Get started?

Fog crept in and out of my vision as my hands were untied, wrists bandaged, and water put to my lips. I held myself upright in the chair as best I could. I wouldn't dare move in case it caused them to make Kaya scream again. When the floor was cleaned, the bearded man stopped to stand in front of Thomas.

"I'm John Marchessa," he said. "Who are you?"

"My name is Thomas."

"Does Henry know your face?"

Thomas nodded. "Yes. He shot me once."

John Marchessa's eyes lit up. "So, you're not pals then I take it."

Thomas shook his head.

"And you?" he asked standing before me. His fingernails were dirty, and hands calloused. I found that strange. "Does Henry know *your* face?"

"Yes."

"Name?"

I had no energy or reason to lie. "Luke."

"Ah good. That's very good," he said, toying with his beard. Then he kneeled before me, not afraid in the least. "Can you keep your eyes open for another ten minutes, Luke?" he asked, clutching my chin so my gaze met his.

A cold terror clutched my heart. "Yes," I said, sounding feeble. "Please, though, don't hurt her. I beg of you. I'll do anything."

He laughed, an outright cackle with a bone-chilling timbre that split my spine in two. "Believe me, in a few minutes *someone* is going to be hurt."

I bolted upright and was shoved back down. At some point, cameras had been set up. Lights aimed. Daisies scattered about what could have been a small stage before me and Thomas. I realized then that Kaya's death was going to be filmed, and I couldn't contain the roar that came from within me.

My hands were tied to the chair. Ankles, too.

"Let's not take any chances with these two," Troy said to John Marchessa.

Thomas was restrained as well, and once we were alone, a muffled sob escaped him.

"For what it's worth, Luke, you are the better man," Thomas said, shaking so violently I could hear his teeth rattle.

"Not better.*"* I was fighting hard to not scream. "Just the one she chose."

The cameras were being turned on.

I heard Kaya's voice.

She said one word—*no*.

And that one word sent my mind into overdrive. Every part of me thrashed in agony to go to her, but it was completely futile.

Troy put his gun to my head.

"He's going to kill her," I said to him, to the cold barrel pushed against my temple. "John Marchessa… he is, isn't he?"

Troy sounded completely unconcerned. "Uh, yeah I guess."

The world fell away in a wave and crashed back in agony. "Then kill me first," I said, unable to process any way of getting her out of here. Or saving myself. Or Thomas. "Shoot me now and get it over with. *Please.*"

Troy wasn't expecting that. He silently turned away and marched off, leaving Thomas and I alone to stare at each other.

"You'll have to do it," I said to him. "If she dies, at your first opportunity, just do it. I can't go on if she—oh God. Thomas, promise me… if you have the chance, you will end my life. *Promise me.*"

There were tears in his eyes. "I hate you, but I can't kill you."

"You owe me," I said, desperate to disappear from this nightmare.

Thomas took a moment to process this. "All right," he said sullenly.

I closed my eyes. Kaya appeared to me in the green dress she was wearing the day we met. It swirled around her, emerald eyes flashing…and I would hold onto that memory forever. When she floated to the edges of my vision, fading into the darkness, I followed.

AND SO IT BEGINS

I woke to the sound of Oliver's voice, neck screaming in agony when I twisted to see him. On the other side of Thomas, he too was tied to a chair. One eye was swollen shut, his lips were caked with blood, and his nose was certainly broken.

"You're alive," I said, relieved and terrified for him all at the same time.

"Darn straight," he choked, then wordlessly hung his head forward.

"The old boy doesn't look so good," Thomas needlessly pointed out. "Neither do you, Luke. Ya gotta quit nodding off. I think you're dead when you do that."

"Not sure why you care, Thomas."

"I don't," he replied rather quickly.

There was just the three of us sitting before the small stage in the airplane hanger, amid dimmed lights and most-likely rolling cameras. Oliver was barely conscious. He didn't budge when I asked him about Marlene, until the sound of her raging voice jolted us all to life. Her threats pierced the quiet hanger with the grating force of a chain saw. Through the doors, swinging and swearing while blindfolded, two men struggled to get her onto a chair. Only when Oliver muttered her name did she become perfectly still. Blindfold off and blinking him into focus, she gasped in horror when she saw his face, then tried desperately to be brave as tears rolled down her cheeks.

"It's okay, big guy," she said, "I'll get you out of here."

Oliver forced a smile. "You better."

Then it was dead silent again. A spotlight was turned on and aimed at the floor and the daisies scattered everywhere. It was clear that now we were just waiting for the star of the show.

John Marchessa strode onto the stage. "Well, I must say, I'm glad you're all here." He gave Marlene an inquisitive stare. "Tell me, my dear," he said, shielding his eyes from the light. "What part do you play in this? Who are you to Kaya Lowen?"

Marlene's voice was strong, but I detected panic just below the surface. "I'm her best friend."

"And you pretended to be Kaya at the Masquerade ball, marrying Oliver. Why?"

There was no need to lie. Marlene could see that. "So she could get away from Henry."

"Right. Right." John Marchessa stepped back and regarded each of us again. "So, let me get this straight." He pointed at Marlene. "Best friend." His finger hovered in Oliver's direction. "Bodyguard." Then at Thomas he hesitated and said, "boyfriend. And you…?" He was pointing at me now. "Oh right, betrothed." He clasped his hands together, pleased as if he'd put together a difficult puzzle. "Isn't that convenient. Well, not so much for you, eh, boyfriend? You won't last long in the picture. She whimpered a bit when I threatened to put a bullet in your head if she didn't obey, and she outright went into convulsing hysterics when I threatened her with Luke's life. So you probably should set your sights on another girl."

Thomas seemed to be the only clear thinking one of all of us. I was still seeing spots in my vision, Oliver could not keep his head up, and Marlene had gone into a glassy-eyed frozen stare once she'd realized what the cameras were for.

"You can't help who you love," Thomas replied.

"Love?" said John, wincing at the word. "For a hundred bucks you can find 'love' anywhere you want. A thousand gets you the best kind of love for a whole night."

"Pathetic," Thomas spat. "And weak."

John Marchessa cringed ever so slightly. "I am not weak, young man. You are. *And you know why.*"

And that reason why was dragged across the room and deposited center stage before us. They had put her in a long, flowing white dress, and it trailed out behind her. Her hair was pinned up with daisies and her lips painted a horrible deep berry red. Kaya blinked and shielded her eyes from the light when John untied the blindfold, and my heart broke over and over and over. I couldn't watch. I couldn't...

"Oliver? Marlene?" she said, noticing them first and taking a small step closer. She stopped, and her gaze fell to Thomas. The way she said his name, putting her hand to her chest and heading toward him, hurt my heart. Until her eyes found mine.

Tears started streaming down her cheeks. "Luke," she said with a gasp.

She tripped over the trail of her dress to get to me, picked herself up, then threw her arms around my aching body. I blissfully returned her embrace by burying my face in her hair. I let my senses explode with everything about her, the warmth of her mouth as it carefully grazed mine, and the feel of her hands on my cheeks searching my face for wounds.

"I'm okay," I said, knowing that's what was on her mind. "I'll get us out of this."

She became frantic, moving behind me to work at the handcuffs, and I didn't bother to tell her to stop even though I could see Troy pulling off his gloves from the corner of my vision.

"All right. That's enough of that," John Marchessa said, coming out of the shadows to grab her by the arm and drag her back to where the spotlight was centered. "See there, *boyfriend*? You should be thankful this little experiment put things into perspective for you."

Thomas was panting, his chest rising and falling rapidly, seething with anger while John positioned Kaya where he wanted her. He pushed back a lock of her hair that had come loose, his mouth close to her ear, but I could still hear him. "If you move from this spot, I'll kill him first," he said, motioning in my direction.

She froze.

"So, this is what's going to happen." John Marchessa backed up and straightened the dress fanning out behind Kaya, doing up a button at the back, pulling down the neckline while she stood like a mannequin. "We're going to make a nice little video for your daddy. I am going to count down from five. When I am done, you are going to state your name and who your father is. Then, Thomas is going to muster up all his anger over you dumping him for the blue-eyed guy over there, as well as get back at Henry for shooting him, and do the deed."

"The deed?" Thomas stuttered.

"Yes. You get to play the role of jilted ex-boyfriend so you can shoot Miss Lowen. I was going to do it, but this way I won't have to worry about any pesky legal implications."

"No. You can't make me."

John lifted the hem of Kaya's dress, the white satin draping down around his hands as he exposed her thigh. Pushing the barrel of a gun against her skin, I had the briefest hope that it was a tranquilizer gun. But no, this was a regular Smith and Wesson, and John wasn't joking around.

"If you're sure you don't want to do it, I guess I can," he said, and Kaya tried stoically not to wince at the metal pushing against her leg. "But I'll do it over the course of a day or so. Put bullets in her, or knives, or whatever I have lying around this hanger while you all watch her die in the most horrific way imaginable. So here's your choice, *boyfriend*, you either end it quick, or I make her suffer."

Thomas was stunned into silence. Troy untied him from the chair, forced him to stand before Kaya, and then placed the gun in his hand.

"Make sure you shoot her in the chest and nowhere else," John said. "And if you aim that gun anywhere other than at that exact place, or get any stupid ideas, I'll use your pals for bait when I go hunting tomorrow."

Thomas swayed, then blinked hard as if trying to wake from a bad dream.

"I don't want to suffer," Kaya said softly.

And the sound of her voice drained the last of my resolve. I couldn't help but pull against the restraints or help the word *no* from escaping when Thomas reached out and touched her cheek; he was saying goodbye.

With a glassy stare, he backed away and raised the gun.

My heartbeat rushed into my ears and the room darkened and blurred so the only thing in my line of sight was Kaya. Her eyes locked onto mine and a brave smile crossed her face, meant to comfort me. Marlene was screaming, and Oliver was issuing death threats at Thomas, but my ears were filled with nothing but the roar of my shattering heart.

From behind me, a gun was fired and a bullet grazed Kaya's bare shoulder. It was a warning that if Thomas didn't end her soon, the torture would begin.

My beauty stumbled slightly, but still held my gaze and I held hers. It was the only comfort I could give as she mouthed the words 'I'm sorry'.

She sunk to her knees among the daisies, and for a second I thought Thomas would drop the gun—his arm was shaking violently—but then something overtook him. He became still as stone. His eyes vacant as silent tears poured down his cheeks. He was going to do it... *he was going to do it...*

My body went numb as I pulled from the pit of me the most important thing I would ever say—*Kaya, I love you... I love you... I love you...*

Her gazed remained fixed on mine. "*I love you too*," she mouthed.

I repeated it, as if maybe it could change the world, change this thing happening to us. I said it over and over until it became a guttural scream when Thomas pulled the trigger and her chest exploded in red.

Then, for a moment the world stood still.

Then sobbing. My own. Uncontrollable.

Rage and grief propelled my body toward hers, while the inside of me died in an imploding and violently crushing sort of the most unbearable pain. I held on to the light fading in her eyes, even when Thomas turned his attention to me, and thankfully, kept his promise.

Love dares You...

KAYA

September leaves remind me of you. I can still feel their heat...

A song?

It pulled me from the void. My first thought as the lyrics tumbled in was that I didn't think death would hurt. I mean, I wasn't sure what would happen when the lights went out forever, but I thought I at least wouldn't *feel* anything anymore. Amongst my every ache, there was the sensation of Luke's body next to mine, radiating warmth like the afternoon autumn sun.

I wished it were real.

LUKE

I dared to feel the most…

Words and music blocked the way to the dark. I was willing to give myself over to it and be released from the anguish clawing at every one of my cells, but the exit greyed and faded with the melody. I couldn't escape the pain. I couldn't escape the hurt in her eyes as she died, the agony of losing her an unyielding nightmare I was desperate to break free of. Softly playing, the song brought back memories; her promising me she wouldn't run, her caring for my wounds and the sparkle in her eyes when she agreed to marry me. What I wouldn't give for one more moment…

KAYA

Will I ever know your mind again…?

The tempo of the song matched the beat of my heart, which I was now certain was still pumping blood to my hands as pins and needles jabbed my fingertips. The void in my chest was filling, and the volume of the song and blood in my veins increasing. A tingle up my spine erased all doubt that what I was hearing was a symphony of pianos and violins—and his deep and very real inhales and exhales.

LUKE

Are you gone with the ghost...?

The dark gave way to vivid reality striking over and over like lightening. Music. Memories. I saw her die. *I saw her die.* But I could feel her. Her presence was everywhere. Yet I knew if I opened my eyes, *she* wouldn't be. It was just death playing tricks.

KAYA

Love dares you...

I was back in the tent again. On that mountain. Waking to see him in the depth of sleep with eyelids fluttering against a dream. The scar on his cheek was impossible to resist touching... *Luke?* I traced a fingertip over it. *Luke... please... if you're real, open your eyes.*

With my thumb on his lips, they parted with a sigh.

And the music stopped.

KAYA

KILL HER WITH A CONSCIENCE

"Espresso?"

I jerked awake at the question, completely confused.

"Well, do you want some or not?" A scratchy voice asked. "It's getting cold."

I bolted upright and came face to face with the old lady who'd threatened me and Marlene with the cattle prod, and she was holding out two tiny cups. Questions slammed my head with the force of an atom bomb, but above all was—why *two* cup*s?*

There was a body next to mine…

My heart beat so erratically, I saw stars. Afraid that what I wanted so badly might only be the product of my imagination, I could barely breathe.

But he moved.

I heard the air come in and out of him. The music start up again. And a heavy sigh escape from someone else in the room…

Heat. No mistaking the feel of it coming off his body. He was alive. Wide eyed. Lips parted in shock. Staring up at me with disbelief. I was barely aware of the old lady talking again.

"…sometimes coffee helps with the after-effects of the tranquilizer," she said.

I looked down at my blood-covered chest, but a hand over my heart confirmed I was still whole and the extremely tender feeling there was the start of a very large bruise. Luke sat up slowly, watching me, then patted his own chest where a splotch of what I now realized was fake-blood colored his shirt.

"We're not dead," I said to him with a smile.

Hand shaking, he tentatively reached out to touch my cheek with disbelief clouding his eyes. When his skin met mine, his wariness fell away, and he pulled me into his arms. "I thought I'd lost you."

I had no words. I clung to him. Fell over and under waves of relief and awe, burying my face in his neck and taking in my first full lungful of air in what felt like forever.

We held each other like we could never let go.

"I love you," he whispered.

He did. I could feel it. I said it back, meaning it with every fiber of my being, and for one small and blissfully perfect moment there was no one else in the entire world besides us.

"No coffee then, eh?" the old broad croaked.

We pulled apart just enough to see beyond each other. Beneath us was a pink coverlet on a bed in what seemed like a girl's bedroom. Next to the old lady and a ghastly floral wallpaper of yellow daisies, were two reclining chairs. Thomas was in one, and Oliver and Marlene were in the other. They sat before a crackling fireplace and a coffee table covered in plates of donuts. Everything about the decor was an attempt to instill warmth and comfort, but I knew this kind of room. I knew that behind the velvet drapes the windows would be barred. That in the bathroom not one thing could be made into a weapon. That the door locked from the outside and was manned by at least two guards. Heck, I knew a cage when I was in one.

The old lady was back, hovering now with bottles of water.

"Drink something," she ordered.

Her hand got a little too close to Luke for my liking, and I instinctively slapped it away.

"Touch him and I'll rip your arms off," I warned.

She laughed and put the bottles on a side table. "Ha. Tougher than I thought. That's good. Very good." She ambled off, shutting the door on her way out, many locks clicking into place from the outside.

It was then that I noticed how beat up Luke was. A bruise had dark-ened his jaw, his lip was bloody, and his eyes were not quite stable in his head. It pained him to move, and around his wrists were bandages. He winced as he edged his legs over the side of the bed.

"Oliver, you all right, buddy?" he asked, his voice slow with the sound of exhaustion.

Marlene was curled up next to Oliver, and he pulled her closer. "Alive and well," he replied. "Same with Marlene and…" Oliver's eyes cooled into a glare when he motioned to where Thomas was hunched over, head in his hands. "Unfortunately, *him*."

"Where are we?" I asked.

"I don't know. They jacked me up with the same tranquilizer you two got hit with. Woke up in here with Marlene about fifteen minutes ago." He stroked her hair away from her cheek while she remained motionless.

"Marlene, are you okay?" I asked.

"Of course," she hissed, then pressed her eyes tight against Oliver's chest to block out the world—like I'd done so many times.

"She's just working things out," Oliver said. "Give her a minute. This is a lot to take in."

"What happened?"

"You mean after Thomas shot you and then turned the gun on Luke?"

Thomas—who had yet to make eye contact—cringed. "I'm sorry," he said, head on his knees.

"Because after that, thankfully, it's a bit of a blur," Oliver added.

Noticing I was still in the white gown they'd dressed me in, I tugged at the low-cut part barely covering my chest. The fake blood made the fabric stick to my skin.

"Thomas. You—you shot me," I said, fully understanding all at once what had happened.

Dark eyes full of remorse and guilt met mine. Thomas nodded and bit his lip, drawing a bead of red. He appeared broken. Completely and totally broken. I felt a tug of sympathy for him along with the sudden urge to flee. My breath caught again—with fear this time.

"I was forced to," Thomas said, and there was an extreme shake to his hand when he rubbed at his bruised and puffy eyes.

I wanted to get as far away from him as I could, and the bedroom became way too small. I knew the reasoning behind what he did. I knew the logistics. But… but… Thomas had meant to kill me. He pointed a gun at my chest and pulled the trigger with the sole purpose of ending my life.

"I'm so sorry, Kaya. Please believe me. I didn't know what else to do." He raked his hands through his mussed-up hair.

"How could you?" I breathed, not sure what else to say. "And then you meant to kill Luke."

"I made him do it," Luke interrupted. "I made Thomas promise to not leave me alive if you died. He was just keeping his word."

A snarling sound came from Oliver. "Good thing the cowboy keeps his promises, ain't it?"

Thomas paled. "I would never willingly hurt you, Kaya. He—John Marchessa—he warned me. He *shot* you." Thomas pointed to the bandage I was now acutely aware of on my shoulder, and the wound began to sting. "He threatened to torture you. I couldn't let that happen. I didn't see any other way."

"He really had no other choice," Luke said to my surprise.

"I didn't, Kaya. I'm so deeply sorry—"

Oliver angrily cut Thomas off. "That's enough talking," he warned, muscles tensing. "I have half a mind to get out of this chair and snap every part of you in half."

Luke shook his head. "Oliver, what choice did he have?"

Thomas remained determined to defend himself. "I love her," he said to both men, then stared hard at me. "I do. I love you." He was so nervous he seemed about to snap. "I would never want to hurt you. Please, you have to know that."

I did know that. I really did. All reasonable thought verified he was doing the right thing. But he looked different to me now.

Thomas stood, eager to make me understand. He took a few steps forward, hands out and pleading for forgiveness, and I felt my body instinctively inch away.

"Stop. Don't come anywhere near me," I warned, feeling my throat go dry.

But Thomas didn't stop. The only thing I could picture was his hand raised in my direction and the steely determination in his eyes just before he pulled the trigger.

"Kaya, please—"

"Stop," I said again, my voice pathetically weak.

But Thomas reached for my hand anyway, and my body froze in sheer terror.

Before any of us could even blink, Oliver was out of the recliner and in one swift motion had thrown Thomas clear across the room. "Better just stay where you are," he warned, chest heaving.

I was shaking. This was ridiculous! All that I'd been through with Rayna and my father, and I was terrified of Thomas, *my friend,* who was only trying to do what he thought was best for me.

"Oh my God," Thomas stuttered, not bothering to pick himself up off the floor. "Please don't be scared of me, Kaya, please."

"Maybe just stay away from me for now, all right?"

A stunned silence fell over the room that was brought short by Oliver coughing. His lips turned blue and were horrifyingly tinged with blood after. He was so weak his eyes rolled back in his head. This snapped Marlene out of her fog, and she got him back into the recliner, pillow under his neck, blanket over his legs. Eyes blazing with the ferocity of a mama bear, she stood next to him, ready to face whatever or whoever to protect him. With a nod at me and a glance in Luke's direction, she wordlessly told me to do the same; Luke was weak as well.

Now wasn't the time to let fear take hold.

When the door lock clicked, I stood in front of Luke while John Marchessa waltzed into the room trailed by a guard and too much cologne. His suit was polished and pressed, and a freshly lit cigar dangled between his fingers. There was a nervous twitch tugging at the corner of his eye as he scanned the room before focusing on me.

"This was supposed to be Lenore's room," he said, not bothering with hello. "I always imagined one day she would come back here and enjoy it. Too bad your father killed her."

He was blunt, but I was not surprised. The man I'd hid from for years had no warm fuzzies for the Lowen family. I didn't have any for him either.

"Yup," I said, more casually than I felt. "Henry filled her full of experimental drugs, watched her lose her mind, and when she didn't give him a child, he shoved her off a balcony. I heard she didn't die right away. Sixteen broken bones. Yeesh. It must have been excruciatingly painful."

A nervous tick. Flaring of the nostrils—had I gotten to him a bit?

"Be very careful, young lady," he said.

"Why?" I challenged, and I felt Luke tense behind me. "Are you going to *kill* me?"

Another flinch. A barely imperceptible sign that John Marchessa had a conscience—I would roll with it.

"You don't have the guts to kill me anyway," I continued, ruffling feathers. "You're a coward."

"You don't know me well enough to make that assumption, Miss Lowen."

Oliver pushed the blanket off, his breathing ragged as he sat up and curled his hands into fists. "How 'bout you and me get to know each other, *right now*?"

Luke and Thomas both snarled their agreement. Marlene crouched like a cat about to pounce.

"Just to be clear," John said straightening his shoulders, "I am well protected. There are six men outside this door, and the grounds are surrounded by guards and electric fences. You'll all be dead *for real* if you lay a hand on me. In fact, I would welcome one of you to make a move, and then I could claim self-defense and not lose sleep over all this."

Marlene put a hand on Oliver's shoulder, easing him back into the chair.

John took a puff of his cigar and exhaled my way. The disgusting smoke curled around my cheeks and I held back a gag.

"Anyway," he continued with a heavy sigh, "I came to talk to you, Miss Lowen. I think I owe you an explanation since you are the child of my child."

I contained my desire to dispute that. My real mother, Rayna, was dead. The redheaded woman, Lenore, who had bitten me as a baby, wasn't blood related to me in anyway. And the necklace I was to use to dispute that was gone, so I had no proof. Still, I felt like this little nugget of unshared information might keep me—keep us—alive.

"I'm sorry it came to this." John Marchessa paused to scratch his beard. "I intervened back at that cabin so Henry wouldn't gain the upper hand. Opportunity presented itself, and I took it. As for the dramatic death? I think it was rather brilliant if I do say so myself. How I would love to be a fly on the wall when Henry pushes play on that video. It will kill him. *Kill* him. Maybe he'll feel some of the same pain I did when he realizes he's lost his one and only daughter."

"He won't," I said flatly. "He doesn't love me."

John's eyes flickered with a fleeting emotion I couldn't decipher. "Yes. Anyway, you should be grateful that I rescued you from your father."

"Uh, thanks?" My anger was simmering, and I had to keep it controlled. "But your idea of rescuing is pretty messed up. You shot me." I motioned to my bandaged shoulder.

"Shot you?" He laughed. "I have exceptional aim. That was a little flesh wound necessary so Thomas would believe I would actually torture my own granddaughter."

"You mean you *wouldn't* have?" Thomas asked, voice breaking.

John shook his head. "Good Lord no. I mean really. What kind of sicko would torture someone? Especially his own flesh and blood? Oh wait. I have the answer to that." John's eyes narrowed. "Henry. And torture is what would have happened to you, Kaya, if I hadn't stepped in.*"*

When none of us said a thing, he went on.

"Anyway, I thought the staged death would look realistic if the 'jealous ex-boyfriend' was caught on tape going on a murderous rampage. It will keep the Feds off my door. Don't worry, though, I left clues so Henry will know who really did it."

"Oh good. I was worried about that," I said with as much sarcasm as I could. "The daisies were a nice touch." I tugged at the fabric clinging to my waist. "And what I assume is Lenore's wedding dress? Classy."

John glanced at everyone in the room now. "Henry isn't stupid. He would see through acting. All of your friends' reactions to your 'death' is what's going to really sell it to him."

"You don't have a body," Marlene said, her voice sharp as a knife. "That's sort of a crucial factor."

John clucked his teeth. "It won't be hard to get one."

I felt the world tip as Luke protectively stood and pushed me behind him. The guard flanking John Marchessa readied his gun.

"All right, everybody relax. I'm trying to do this diplomatically," John said, waving his hands for emphasis.

"I don't understand." I came out from behind Luke, needing to face my grandfather on my own. "If you want me dead, what are you waiting for?"

There was a sadness in his eyes, the same kind of sadness Lenore had in her expression in the painting that hung in the estate. The resemblance was striking. "I'm not a savage. For me, your death will not be easy."

I had to laugh. "Ah. A killer with a conscience. Which is hilarious because what you did to us was sick and cold-hearted and just as savage as anything Henry has ever done."

John sighed heavily. "I guess it might appear that way. But you must understand, all this is necessary. I can't let Henry continue. I know what he is researching. I know the effect it will have on this earth. And if you all have to die to stop him, I'm sorry."

My anger shot to the surface. "Sorry? You're going to kill me and my friends, and you're *sorry*? I've lived in fear my entire life because of you," I said, holding back tears of rage. "Locked up in a cage. Bodyguards. Never going to school, never being normal. Maybe if you would have backed off in the first place and not put so many conditions on Lenore's inheritance, Henry wouldn't have had to resort to this! Maybe she would still be alive. You poisoned the earth with your chemicals, and Henry's mind with your greed, and you go on about needing to *stop him*? I call bullshit. Complete and total one-hundred-percent bullshit. You just want your money back and revenge for your daughter's death. If you really gave a damn about this planet and its people, you wouldn't have knowingly sold cancer-causing pesticides to every farmer on this continent. You are a lying, sadistic, narcissist who thinks money can buy forgiveness. You are vile and disgusting and *no different than Henry.*"

My rant caused John's jaw to drop. Chest rising and falling, more words balanced precariously on the tip of my tongue, but I held them back.

Our eyes locked, John blinked first.

"You might have a point," he said after a while. He tipped his head side to side to stretch his neck, then toyed with his beard. "But this is bigger than you and me, Kaya. The only way to stop a man from setting fire to the world is to take away his ability to make a flame."

"Yeah. And thanks to you, I'm a damn torch."

He nodded. "I'm not a murderer. I won't kill you in cold blood. I'll give you time for goodbyes and let nature take its course."

"Dehydration and starvation," Oliver said intuitively. "Is still murder, just the same."

John showed no reaction.

"You only need me anyway," I said. "You can just let them go."

He shook his head. "What I need is Henry's daughter, her jilted ex-boyfriend, and her bodyguard and lover to make this plan work."

I challenged him. "No, what you need is a better plan."

His head tipped to the side as if he found me suddenly amusing. "And what might that be?"

The room turned ice cold. "We can all hide'" I said, trying not to sound as desperate as I felt. "Henry will never find us, I promise. If you want to send the video to stall him and keep him busy, go ahead. That will buy us time to get far away. I'll stay out of sight until I'm twenty-one. On my birthday, I will sign everything over to you and walk away. Think of it. If you rely on that video, Henry will tie everything up in so much red tape that by the time the smoke clears, the playing field will be scorched. You know how the legal system works, and Henry has more law on his side than you can imagine. Six, seven years? That's probably about how long it will take for everything to come back to you in case of my death, *if* it all goes in your favor. But if I can sign it all over to you in a couple years, well… isn't that sort of a no-brainer?"

John laughed. "Not stupid, are you?"

Feeling hopeful, I put out my hand to shake his. "It's a win-win situation. Do we have a deal?"

He didn't respond as his gaze had fallen to the scar on my hand. "Lenore did that to you, didn't she?" he asked, pointing to the bite mark.

Hope. Gone.

"You're smart," he said, backing up, "*and* a Lowen. If I let you walk away, who's to say that in two years' time, you won't want control? The world would be at your feet and yours for the taking. You might even decide your father's vision for the future of mankind is something to get behind. Who's to say you won't continue to fund him?"

I pulled my last card and laid it on the table. "Because I hate him as much as you do."

John sucked in a breath. I held mine.

"My granddaughter," he said, and there was a fleeting glimmer of compassion in his eyes. "I wish there was another way."

And with that he turned and strode out the door, locking it behind him.

40

BEASTS WITH DAISIES

I picked at the wallpaper.

Mauling the little daisies was my only form of retaliation, so I peeled them off in one-inch segments and layered them on a satin pillow. Luke paced the floor. His steps away from me were slow and tentative, and the steps on his return, hurried. He was so wound up I thought he might snap in half. Marlene threw herself into prison style push-ups and sit-ups, working herself to exhaustion, resting, then doing it again, and Oliver settled into watching her after giving up trying to open a barred, bullet-proof, and blacked-out window. Thomas just stared vacantly into the fire, as far from me as possible.

A brief respite of food, and then taking turns showering and putting on clean clothes, didn't eat up enough time. The hours crawled by.

I kept picking at the wallpaper.

My fingertips were bloody and raw when four guards came into the room. I was asked to go with them. After Luke and Oliver were sent writhing to the floor from immobilizing taser guns, I politely obliged, taking a handful of the wallpaper daisies with me.

In a blinding white room that reeked of antiseptic, I was seated in a chair. A metal table was perched in a corner and shiny instruments on a tray next to it made my heart pound madly. I tried not to show any fear when John Marchessa stomped into the room wearing what appeared to be his pajamas.

"I don't believe in letting people suffer," he said clinically, pulling up a chair to sit before me. "How is your health?"

It was a confession and a loaded question; if I was the horse that was lame, would I be put down? "My health is absolutely perfect."

He eyed the scar on my neck. "Uh huh," he muttered, then motioned for a guard to pass him the tray of instruments. I tensed when he picked up a pair of scissors.

"Oh, relax," he said, stifling a yawn. "I just have to check your shoulder and make sure its healing and not infected."

I sat still as he cut away the bandages, wondering if I could get the scissors from his hand and stab him in the neck.

"Good Lord," he said, moving in closer. "What happened here?" He was examining the burn and puncture wound decorating my bicep.

In a bored tone, I relayed the events. "Fell into some rapids. Got impaled by a tree. Luke had to cauterize the wound after he got me out or I would have bled to death."

John looked me square in the eye, no doubt to see if I was lying. "Is Luke the one that kidnapped you?"

I gulped so hard it hurt. "Yes."

"Henry tried to keep your disappearance a secret. My informant told me you'd been lost in the wilderness for weeks."

"Yes," I said again, eyeing the scissors.

"And you and Luke managed to survive in that hellish place without any outside help, for that long?"

Honesty was probably my best defense. "You might call it hell, but it was freedom for me. We found a cave heated by an underground spring. We had shelter, warmth, and water. Just no food."

"A cave…" John repeated, lost in thought as he dabbed at the wound that someone had stitched up while I was unconscious. "And your neck?" he asked, referring to the jagged scar there.

"Restaurant. Sixteenth birthday. Attempted kidnapping. Henry said you set it up."

"Nope. Wasn't me. The day you turned sixteen I was halfway across the world. Boy, Henry sure did an excellent job of making you fear me, didn't he?"

"Seems like he had a good reason to."

John grew quiet, taking more time than necessary taping down the bandage on my shoulder. When he was finished, he sat back and pretended to admire his handiwork. A silence grew between us that spoke volumes of my desire to live and his uncertainty over what to do about that.

I had to stay calm. "If you stoop to Henry's level, you won't be able to live with yourself." His eyes, murky blue and red rimmed, met mine. He rubbed his chest as if it pained him, and a button on his pinstripe pajamas came undone. On impulse, I opened my palm to expose the wallpaper daisies. "Maybe it's time to let her go."

He took the scraps of paper from his beloved daughter's bedroom. At first, anger flashed across his face—I mean, I defiled the room—but it soon gave way to just plain old sadness.

"She never got a chance to come back," he said.

I felt a tug of sympathy for him. I knew what it was like to lose someone you loved.

John took in a deep breath and exhaled, as if the answer to a long drawn-out question finally became clear. "Lenore would be proud of you," he said, then got to his feet and dropped the daisies into the trash. "And just so she doesn't rise out of her grave to haunt me, I'm going to let you go."

My face went numb. It couldn't be that easy.

"But," he started.

But...

I knew there was a catch. He leaned in close enough for me to feel his breath on my cheek. "There will be terms and conditions that cannot be broken. Understood?"

It took a second to find my voice. "Yes."

"I will keep Marlene as insurance. If you waver from your promise or come out of hiding, I will hand her over to your father, who is chomping at the bit to find the girl who posed as his daughter on her wedding day. And to keep Marlene in line, it just so happens that I know where your other friends are… Lisa is it? And the child she tends to, Louisa, Luke's little sister? I won't expose their location to Henry if Marlene cooperates."

"Why Marlene?" was all I managed to get out. I didn't bother asking how he knew so much.

"Because she's unrecognizable without makeup, and I can keep her here under the guise of one of the household help. Oliver is useless to me because whatever is going on in his lungs will kill him in a month,

Thomas would self-destruct without you, and Luke would be an absolute nightmare to contain."

Made sense. "All right. I need you to do something for me then, so Lisa and Luke's little sister are cared for. Then we have a deal."

"What?"

"Lisa needs custody of Louisa and ownership of the home she's in. Make it happen."

John pursed his lips. "Fine."

"And Marlene must receive an education of some sort. She's very bright."

"Agreed."

I felt numb but practically vibrated out of my seat. "And Luke, Oliver and Thomas. They go free."

"Nope. Too much of a liability. They will go with you. Besides, it's best you're not alone. Luke will die before he lets anything happen to you, and Thomas… Thomas will be your best chance of survival because he thinks with his head *and* his heart. You know, he was saving you from what he thought was a fate worse than death. He is the man I would pick for my daughter."

All I could do was blink the stars out of my eyes, vision threatening to turn black with the pounding of my heart.

"I'm giving you a fighting chance, Kaya. If you survive where I'm sending you, in two and a half years you can have your life back. If you don't, then I'll have your body to send to your father. Either way, I'll get what I want."

"And where will I be going?" I asked, barely getting air into my lungs.

John stood. He clucked his tongue. "Someplace close enough for me to drop in monthly supplies, and far enough away from civilization that you will never be seen. Some would call it hell, but you said you survived it once."

Abruptly snapping for the guards to come, John spun on his heels. "If you make it out alive, it will be interesting to see who is with you in the end. Luke or Thomas? I'm a betting man, but I wouldn't touch that one with a ten-foot pole."

SPRING

LISA

41

KNOWING ME, KNOWING YOU

I wasn't surprised when I got an anonymous phone call warning me to leave the ranch house. It was time to move on anyway; Regan and Ellis had, and the loneliness in their wake increased every day. A year and a half had gone by and there was no sign of Luke, just legal documents showing up at the door signed by him, giving me custody of Louisa with a note in his handwriting that said to trust him and not ask any questions. That meant he was alive, and I could legally parent Louisa, and that's all that mattered.

"Where are we going again, Momma?" Louisa asked.

Her beautiful blue eyes captured my heart every single time I looked at her, and when she called me Momma, I felt like it would burst. This love, more real, pure, and true than any I'd ever had in my life, was as strong as if I'd given birth to her myself. She was my child.

Opening her suitcase in which she'd put Brutus's toys, sweaters, and leashes—none of which he ever used—she shoved in a bag of dog treats.

"We're going to see Regan," I told her.

"Oh, I miss him so much," she said, wrestling with the zipper.

I did, too. Painfully so. Over the months we'd spent together I'd grown to like him. Too much.

"Where does he live?"

"Just outside of Vancouver," I told her. "It's a big city."

"Van-coooo-ver," she repeated, testing the word. "I know I'll like it there."

"I'm sure you will," I said with a laugh. "We will be with friends again, and the ocean will accept you like you're one of its long-lost mermaids."

"My bathing suit!" she shrieked before running off to her room.

Her room. My house. Still unbelievable. The deed arrived the day after the custody papers did, with the same sort of note warning to not ask any questions. So I kept my mouth shut and coated every wall with fresh coats of paint, bought a new sofa, and sold the animals and the helicopter. I removed or altered just about everything that reminded me of Seth and did what I could to make the place home. But it never felt like one. Something was missing.

So, paying all the bills a year in advance—even the strange one from the numbered company that arrived monthly in Seth's name—I packed my life into the back of the truck, ready to start over. Again.

Louisa was settled into her car seat. Brutus panted and drooled from his position in the front. They patiently waited as I double checked the appliances, locked every door, and took one last look around. Blowing a kiss into the air, I stopped in the kitchen before the breadbox. Behind it was the scrap of paper I had found on Seth's body the day he died. The address in his handwriting was smeared because I'd held it so often. No matter, I had it memorized. Repeatedly I'd Google mapped the location and wondered over many glasses of wine what was in a storage locker there, then I'd stash the paper back behind the bread box and try to go back to sleep.

Only, the dreams wouldn't let up. They replayed the day he died over and over. They swirled and hovered and danced in the darkness of my mind until I jolted awake in a pool of sweat asking myself whether or not I killed him in cold blood.

"I'm gonna miss it here," Louisa said when I got in the truck and belted up. "And by the way, I'm too old to be in a car seat. It's for babies."

"No it's not."

"Is so."

"Look at the hawk in the sky," I said, pointing up into the wide expanse of blue.

"Do you think we'll ever come back?" Louisa asked, her gaze following the bird's wings.

"I don't know." I put the truck in reverse and grinned at her in the rear-view mirror. "This is an adventure for us, Louisa. As long as we're together, does it matter where we end up?"

She flashed her slightly crooked teeth. Cheeks dimpling. "Not really. And I like how you are trying to change the subject from the car-seat issue."

Issue? Wow. She was growing up fast. And she was smart like Luke.

"But no, Momma Lisa. If I am with you—and there are no mosquitoes because they suck, literally—then I'll be happy."

"Thank you," I said, pursing my lips together to keep my eyes from watering. "Onward and upward then. To new beginnings."

"And maybe no car seat?"

"I'll think about it," I said and headed onto the highway.

We left the valley and the mountains behind, and six hours later were at the west coast.

Just outside of Vancouver in an old, wealthy area, Regan's house stood gleaming white in the sunshine with masses of windows reflecting the blue of the ocean. It appeared so bright and cheery, and nothing at all like Regan. Although, when he came out the front door, something was different about him besides the extra weight he'd put on—all muscle—and the shorter hair. He seemed… at ease. His leg was fully healed but badly scarred, and as he sauntered down the front steps in floral shorts with a bit of a limp, there was a smile on his face. Louisa shrieked and ran to him, throwing herself into his arms. I wished I could do the same.

"Heard anything?" he asked after a brief hug for me, as usual not bothering with hello. It was his default question; every ritual Saturday phone call he opened with it, to which I would say 'no,' or in this case shake my head discreetly so Louisa wouldn't catch on that we were discussing her brother's whereabouts.

"Nice place," I said, following him into the house where enough presents to buckle a six-foot dining room table were wrapped and waiting. The only other thing in the cavernous room was a mammoth sectional couch. Besides the kitchen counter overflowing with pink cupcakes and every kind of treat imaginable, you'd think no one lived here.

"Those presents are for you, Lisa. Practical things like designer hand bags and jeans that aren't second hand. I missed your birthday, so I figured I'd make up for it."

I was speechless. He must have shopped for days…*for me.*

Regan kneeled before Louisa. "I decorated your bedroom myself. There are princess dresses in every color. And…" he pointed down a long, window-lined hallway, "when you find your room, you'll find all your presents, too. Look carefully and you might see a furry one that will hop if you let it out of its cage."

Louisa's eyes widened in excitement. "A bunny? You got me a bunny, Uncle Regan?"

He kissed her on the cheek, his affection for her as clear as the day. "You bet I did."

She squealed and ran off, then a few seconds later, squealed again.

"After what happened to Susan, I thought I better—"

I put my hand up to stop him. Susan the bunny—the one Louisa had gotten at Christmas—lost a fight with a coyote, and it wasn't pretty. The thought still turned my stomach.

"I really hope that Louisa and I staying here is okay," I said, staring in awe at the view of the beach and rolling waves outside the towering living room windows. Marble floors were cool beneath my feet and stretched to a fireplace that soared up into a vaulted ceiling. I imagined hot cocoa, Christmas trees, and a baby in my arms—and quickly shook that vision out of my head. "I don't want to be an inconvenience."

Regan put his hands in his pockets, appearing slightly uncomfortable. "It's not an inconvenience. At all. I'm happy to have you and Louisa. In fact, I missed—"

"Don't you dare say it, Regan."

He cleared his throat and looked at his feet a moment, then gave Brutus a scratch behind the ears. "There's a good school down the street, and I've got a few ideas for jobs for you if you're interested. You'll be happy here, Lisa. I promise. I'll do everything I can to make that happen."

"We still have to lay low and stay out of sight a bit longer, but yes. Thank you," I said, wanting so badly to reach for him but keeping my arms to myself.

With that unwavering gaze of his that made my head dizzy he said, "You look good, Lees. A manicure might help those garden-ravaged fingernails of yours, but other than that, not too shabby."

"Thanks?" I couldn't help but smile. Regan usually said things like that, then fell into whatever scheme his brain was dreaming up and drifted off. This time though, he didn't turn away. I let my guard slip, admiring him, forgetting for a moment that this was *Regan*. Cold, single minded, revenge seeking Regan.

He levelled his eyes on mine. "I'm sorry, I have to say it. I missed you."

Whoa. Maybe there really was something different about him. I felt my heart do a little leap in my chest.

"I know this isn't what you wanted," he continued, motioning to the beautiful house then placing his hand over his heart. "But I kind of thought I'd let you do the decorating."

"It's great," I said, throat constricting. "Really, it is. And I-I missed you, too."

Regan took a long stride toward me. As he towered above me, I had to tip back my head to see him.

"I've finally let go," he said softly, and I knew by the sadness in his eyes that he was talking about his sister. "I still want Henry six feet under for his part in her death, but I—I am free of everything else."

That's what it was. Guilt, revenge, hatred, longing for a long-lost love —all those things weren't pulling at the lines around his eyes anymore.

"It looks good on you," I said, smiling.

"And you?" he asked.

I nodded and tried to swallow.

Regan pulled me in for a hug, and I settled against his chest. "You know, you can't always get what you want," he said, quoting his favorite band, The Rolling Stones. "But if you try sometimes, you just might find—"

"You get what you need," I said, finishing for him.

Regan sighed, holding me tighter, resting his chin on the top of my head. "I was gonna say you get *who* you need."

"So, shopping, eh?" Regan had just finished his workout, and I couldn't ignore the shirt clinging to his damp skin. "Are you sure you don't want me to come along? There are great shops only five minutes from here. You don't have to go all the way into that stinking city."

I tried to remain casual as the slip of paper I'd taken from behind the bread box burned a hole in my pocket and made me a liar. "I like that stinkin' city. Besides, Louisa needs new clothes for school in the fall, and there are a few lingerie shops I want to check out. You know, girl stuff. And I kind of want to have a day to myself."

Regan wasn't buying it. He knew me too well.

"You're not the lingerie type, Lees. I've seen that excuse of a bra you insist on wearing. Unless you're going there because there's someone—"

I cut him off quickly. "Ha. Nope."

I scooped my keys off the counter and headed for the door, not giving him time to interrogate me further. "When she wakes up from her nap, don't give her any more candy, okay?"

He nodded and raked his hands through his hair. I turned to shut the door, but my eyes caught his, and I saw in them genuine worry. So, before I gave myself time to think, my feet were tripping over the marble floor toward him, and completely on impulse, I laced my hands behind his head and got on my tiptoes to press my lips to his. It was a quick kiss. One that left me dropping my arms to my sides and backing away from his shocked expression and stiff posture.

Feeling like an idiot, I turned for the door. "Sorry, I don't know what came over me."

He latched onto my arm and yanked me back to him, then kissed me fiercely. The heat that had been building between us for years burst into a raging inferno. Weird and wonderful, ravenous and unexpected, and in a perfectly imperfect way, it was so right.

"It's about time we came to our senses," he said, scooping me up in his arms and heading for the bedroom.

Indeed, it was.

4 2

A DROP IN THE BUCKET

The warehouse came into view at the end of a crumbling road. There were no cars, no busses, and apparently no garbage pickup either in this mid-city industrial area. Some buildings were vacant and forgotten, others crumbling and dark. The biggest population was the tenacious weeds taking over every crack in the pavement. Fences and barbed wire were meant to keep out the homeless and drug addicts, but by the number of needles and drug paraphernalia next to abandoned shopping carts, the system wasn't working so well.

I was glad I had a gun in my jacket pocket, a crowbar in one hand and metal cutters in the other.

The lock holding closed a chain-link gate broke easier than I thought, and in the waning sunlight, I made my way across a deserted parking lot to one of the many holding units that made up the warehouse. Rows of tall, garage-like doors were numbered, and a few had some tattered signs, but I was only interested in one; unit number twenty-one. My pulse raced with curiosity and dread when I found the place Seth had been desperate to get to the day he died.

Hearing a car on the road, I flattened up against the door, my black outfit blending in with the peeling paint. I held my breath as a convertible full of baseball-capped heads cruised by, car stereo blasting rap music so loud I felt the bass in my chest. When the car rolled out of sight, I jammed the crow bar into the lock, twisted as hard as I could, and snapped every piece holding it together.

373

I wrestled with the heavy door, pushing it up and over my head, then closed it behind me when I inched into the dark space. I had my phone ready, turning on the flashlight so I could find a wall switch.

There was power. And the overhead lights came on. And even though I wasn't sure what I was expecting to find, this wasn't it.

The space was large enough for four cars but empty save for two large crates and a metal kitchen chair. The dust was thick on the floor and the walls were bare except for a few cobwebs and streaks of black. At the far end was a door that led into the bay next to it, which was completely empty, too. After inspecting everything and finding nothing, I turned my attention to the crates and was glad I had brought the crowbar. My intrigue was amped up when I noticed the shipping address stapled to the side of one, made out to the numbered company I'd been paying all this time.

The first crate was filled with boxes. One by one, I took them out and found a very confusing assortment of handcuffs and chains, pillows and blankets, and camera equipment. Was Seth into some weird bondage crap? I kept digging and found packets of freeze-dried food and then a big box of buckets. *Buckets.* Ten of them. My blood turned cold.

Disturbing as this was, underneath a bag of brand-new clothes—all Kaya's size—was something that had me clutching my chest in disbelief; a box containing syringes, needles, and Cecalitrin. Buttloads of it.

My pulse was racing as I tugged on the wood of the second crate, now with an urgency that made tears swell behind my eyes. There were metal rods. Bars. It didn't make sense. Until I pried off the other end of the crate and realized I was looking at a cage.

An actual *cage.*

Every word Seth ever spoke to me came crashing back with lighting speed. When he'd said he didn't love Rayna, there'd been a nervous twitch in his eye. When he'd talked about being glad she was dead, there'd been a tickle in his throat. When he'd promised me he was on Kaya's side and would never harm her, his lip would curl into a slight snarl. They had been signs that he was lying, and I had pretended not to notice them. Now, with this evidence, his motives had become clear. He was going to satisfy his desire for the woman he'd lost with her look-alike daughter, then when he was done, pump her full of Cecalitrin to continue his plan of revenge and blackmailing Henry. Seth had never quit being Rayna's love-sick puppet.

In a nutshell, I had been used. Not loved.

So, I did not pull the trigger in haste.

Tears poured down my face like they never had before. Dust and grime made rivers of mud on my face when I rubbed my eyes. The man I had loved, who had claimed to love me back, was far worse than I imagined. The only solace in this venture was the guilt and confusion lifting from my heart.

The crates were easy to ignite. Flames danced on the wood, then crawled through the bay to reach under the overhead door, it's spiny fingers seeking me, needing more to burn, but I was untouchable now. The past was nothing but a forgettable, dead thing—just like Seth.

Now I could honestly tell Regan I'd let go of it all, too. I was free to love him back.

FALL

43
FREE SPIRIT

"I thought I might have actually sweated my balls off," Luke said, grin as wide as the river he was wading in. "But nope. They're still there."

I laughed and a breeze carried it across the lush grasses and red and orange leaves lining the riverbank. Birds chirped happily, wild flowers bloomed, and the sparkling water gently flowed. This place beneath the blue sky was beautiful... but I was more enthralled by the man in the water. His hair was down past his shoulders, streaked and golden from the sun, skin taut and tanned and every muscle defined from hard work and healthy living. The extra calluses on his hands, the slight sunburn on his back and the new lines around his eyes just added to his allure. Sometimes when I watched him, I forgot where I was—which, I had to admit, for the first few months after we'd been dropped off here really did feel like hell —but not anymore. The mountains, this valley, this river... *him*... was home.

I leaned back to absorb the sun that was throwing more heat than it had all summer.

"Do you want to come in and cool down too?" Luke asked, rubbing his hair with soap and sending little rivulets of white across the scars on his chest.

I gulped and just shook my head.

"Ya sure?" he said. "I'll wash your back. And whatever other parts you can't reach."

He'd lit the fire on our sandy little beach because the nights were getting longer and colder. I felt so peaceful sitting on the shore, listening to the crackle of the burning wood, happy and content. But, how could I turn down Luke's hands armed with a bar of soap?

I stood, and then I felt something entirely and completely new—

Pressure.

And it rapidly increased.

Then it tightened around my stomach so forcefully it brought me right back to my knees.

No… this can't be happening… not yet… not yet…

Then it was gone.

Thankfully, Luke didn't notice. He was drying off, wrestling on a shirt and pants, then sitting on a boulder lacing up his hiking boots.

"So… fish for dinner? Or do you want potatoes. There's enough left we could make a stew out of them or just mash them up. After dinner I thought we could drive to the store. I kinda have a craving for chips and chocolate bars. Oh wait. I don't have a car. And there are no roads. Or stores. Or anything but trees and caves… ha. I guess I'll have to settle for whooping your butt at a game of cards over a cup of rosehip tea."

I gathered my breath and forced a smile, then struggled to my feet again. "Fish is fine."

Luke, always beyond intuitive, stopped stoking the fire. "Everything all right?"

I was free. I was healthy. And I was with the man of my dreams in the most beautiful place on earth. "Yes. Everything is all right," I said, but there was an odd sense of fear settling over me.

"Are you sure?" he asked, standing too, face flooding with concern.

I nodded, and a rush of warmth travelled down my inner thighs.

His eyes were wide as plates when his gaze fell to a large wet stain that hadn't been there a second ago. Luke and I knew everything about each other. Intimately. But peeing my pants would still be hella embarrassing. "I don't know what—"

The words were ripped from my tongue when that gripping pain clutched my stomach again.

"Is it time?" Luke said, easing me to the ground, hand on my swollen belly.

I knew this day would come. But I wasn't ready. "No. No it can't be."

"But your water broke," he said, trying to contain his panic. He stood and stared off down the beach. "Oh my God….where is he? Where's Thomas?"

I breathed deep, keeping calm, focusing on the birds gathered on the other side of the river. "I don't know. He said something about getting us… duck for dinner."

"Duck?" Luke was frantically wiping his now-sweating forehead. "I hate duck. I told him not to go far." Marching to the water's edge, he cupped his hands around his mouth and yelled. *"Thomas… Tho-ma-sss… I need you."*

The pain came again, this time harder and longer, and Luke was kneeling next to me on the ground, holding my hand, telling me to breathe. I listened to his voice, latched onto it as the pressure in my abdomen increased. And increased again. And again.

I screamed when it felt like it would never stop.

But it did. And I finally caught my breath.

"Thomas!" Luke yelled again, the concern and worry in his voice elevating my heart rate.

"Luke… it's… uh-oh—" I managed to say before a scream tore through me. The pain was worse than anything I'd ever felt, and the contractions were coming too fast. I thought they would be spread out, giving me time to prepare. I was completely out of control of my body, and its defiance was bringing the world in and out of focus.

"What's the commotion about?"

Thomas had been in a full-out run, which was obvious by the sweat pouring down his cheeks. He wore an easy smile that had a calming effect, and as he kneeled before me, he pulled his hair back into a ponytail. I focused on it and the new scratch on his cheek.

"Luke and I hate duck," I said, close to freaking out because that pain was getting ready to come back.

"Fine. I'll trap some bunnies instead," Thomas said, exchanging volumes of unspoken communication with Luke. Pouring water over his hands, he shook the blanket and draped it over his shoulder.

"Knife?" he said to Luke.

"You sure you know what you're doing?" Luke asked.

It came again. The pressure, then the pain, now pulling at my lower back too… unbearable…

"Breathe," Luke reminded.

I did. I breathed. I let the tears slide, and the pressure stopped for a moment.

"I've never delivered a human baby." Thomas was cleaning the knife. "But as I said, I've helped the cows on the ranch. Can't be much different."

"I am not a cow, Thomas!" I sputtered.

He laughed. And everything about that laugh brought my heart rate down and eased my mind; Thomas had a way of doing that.

Luke, however, was unraveling. "Do you think we can get her to camp? Everything we need is in the cave…"

Thomas was focused, centered, easing my pants down and pulling them off, then sliding the blanket under my butt. "We are going to have a new human enter this world any minute, Luke. She's not going anywhere. Now get behind her like we practiced, okay? Support her and chill the heck out."

Luke did as he was told.

Thomas's hands were hot on my knees, encouraging them apart. "I have to check the baby's position now, okay? Don't push yet, even if you feel like you have to."

I nodded and braced myself while Thomas probed around inside me. "I can feel him. Or her. The top of the head and not feet. Thank you, Lord above."

The pain came again. I dug my nails into Luke's hand, buried my head against his chest as if what I couldn't see wouldn't hurt. But that didn't work. So I pulled my knees together, deciding right there and then that I would get up and leave. Walk it off. Maybe then it would go away because I wasn't ready. *I wasn't ready.*

Another contraction. This time lasting longer than the others. "Make it stop, Thomas." I begged. "Please, make it stop…"

His hand was on my swollen belly, it brushed against Luke's that had been gently massaging the stretched skin. "You have to do this, Kaya." Tears were in his eyes. Luke's, too. "We're going to help you. You are going to be all right. I promise, okay?"

I didn't know if I believed him. "Okay."

He moved my knees apart.

"Holy… Okay, it's time. You need to push. No fooling around now," he said.

Luke put a stick between my teeth. I bit down as the pain became absolutely blinding.

"I can't do this," I tried to say.

"Yes, you can." Thomas was rubbing my leg. "This is the most important thing you will ever do in your entire life. When that next contraction comes, you give it all you've got. Don't hold back."

There was worry in his voice. I knew the baby would suffocate if it stayed too long in the birth canal, and Thomas knew this, too. This child's existence was entirely up to me.

So I pushed. I felt like I was being ripped apart, but I kept pushing. Luke rubbed my arms, reminding me to breathe. Thomas braced my knees, talked gently about everything he was seeing, and reminded me to embrace the miracle of what my body was doing.

But exhaustion took hold. I could barely keep my head up. I had no strength as the universe robbed me of it in some dark twisted joke. I thought every part of me might break apart as I turned my head away from the pain to see something down the beach. I blinked into focus a majestic, gentle, towering symbol of strength and perseverance—a beautiful buck with creamy golden and ivory fur. Its antlers twisted upward like old branches that were nearly as big as he was. His black eyes pierced mine and when Thomas yelled at me to push, I held its gaze. Head bobbing as if encouraging me, it pawed the ground. It was telling me that I should bring my child into the world with grace and love, not with fear. Not with torment or trepidation. Because it was time. And I was ready.

My body surged with newfound strength, and in one last blinding push, the sky disappeared as I told the life making its way into Thomas's hands that it was loved. Loved madly and deeply.

Then, suddenly, the pain stopped. The sky came back. The buck swayed its antlers and disappeared into the trees. And when I heard the shrill cry of my newborn child, I knew I was going to be all right.

Heck. I was going to be better than all right.

TWO AND A HALF YEARS LATER...

MARLENE

HOLD A FLAME

Twenty-one candles rattled around in a box next to a chocolate cake. It was the only thing in the helicopter, because this time I wasn't dropping off supplies, I was picking up people—or so I hoped.

I alerted home base that I was at my destination and landed on the only clear ridge for miles. I'd left instructions in the last drop off for Kaya and the others to meet me here on this day, but I didn't know if any of them were even alive. So I settled in to wait and find out.

Mountain peaks tipped white with snow jutted into the clouds. The wind was light and rustled my hair. Spring was in the air with the scent of flowers blooming and evergreens stretching their limbs. It was breathtaking. Leaning back against the helicopter—the one John had trained me in—I took in the view. As beautiful as it was, I still wondered how anyone could survive alone in it for so long. Even with the medicines, clothes, canned food, knives, fishing rods, traps, pots and pans and anything and everything I could think of packing into the crates—pancake mix included—it would have been grueling. There were storms so bad I couldn't fly in, and months where the snow was so deep the supplies were swallowed up by it at the drop site.

While time crawled by, I'd thought of Oliver. More than I'd cared to. The nights alone in my room and the days jammed full of flying lessons—and anything else John could do for me that he couldn't for his long-lost daughter—Oliver was always in the back of my mind. I wished I could have told him how I was weaseling my way into the old man's heart and gaining his trust. I wished I could have told him that I loved him, and I missed him. That I hadn't taken off the wedding ring since the day he placed it on my finger. But as Daddy always said, wishes were like fishes; you either caught one or ya didn't.

When the clouds drifted off revealing nothing but blue sky, that's when I saw her. Climbing up to where I was waiting, tanned skin, hair braided and hanging down her back, with green eyes big as saucers, was Kaya Lowen. She scanned the area before noticing me, and I had a hard time picking my awestruck jaw off the ground. *She had survived.*

We ran to each other, and I squeezed her so tight I thought I might break her.

"You're too skinny," I said, holding her at arm's length a moment.

"And you're... a pilot?" She smiled, holding my hands, then stepped back to assess that I was completely in one piece. "Apparently you weren't locked up in that room for long."

"Nope. And I acquired some handy new skills."

"Oh, I missed you, Marlene."

We held each other for a long time until I finally had to pull away. I didn't know how to ask her about Luke and Thomas, and I knew there was no way Oliver survived. But before I could find the words, Kaya cupped her hands around her mouth and yelled into the wind, *"All clear."*

Thomas popped his head up and came over the ridge first, then reached down to help Luke. When they were both on their feet, Thomas reached for Luke's arm and pulled it over his shoulder, helping his obviously injured friend stand.

"Well, that's weird," I said, completely dumfounded at the turn of events between the two men. I figured for sure one would have buried the other. "Has it been that long or am I in an alternate universe?"

"Marlene!" Thomas couldn't get to me fast enough, leaving Luke to lean on Kaya. I realized then just how much I missed him when I was pulled into a familiar bear hug. Smoke and earth and sunshine clung to his skin. His hair was long. His eyes more lined. It suited him.

"Are you okay?" he asked, his filthy hands rubbing my cheeks as if making sure I was real.

I nodded.

"I bet you missed my pretty face," he said.

I nodded again, filled with too much emotion to speak.

He broke into a huge smile, and gross as it was, kissed me on the mouth before backing up and pumping a fist in the air. "Freedom," he howled.

Luke gently put forward a badly scratched hand for a polite shake. "Good to see you too, Marlene."

He seemed happy despite the obvious pain he was in.

"What happened?" I asked, noticing his bandaged leg.

"Wolf," was all Luke said.

Thomas shook his head and laughed.

"He means wolf *spider*," Kaya clarified with a teasing grin. "One tried to attack him, and he fell and twisted his ankle. He won a fight with a bear the week before, but lost to a spider. Go figure."

"The rocks were slippery," Luke said defending his wounded pride.

I watched my friends in awe. I'd been expecting dreadfully greasy hair, vacant eyes, missing teeth, and limbs even… but they all seemed like they had not only been surviving, but thriving.

Except, there was one person missing. Kaya caught my longing stare at the ridge.

"Did he die in pain?" I asked, bracing myself for the worst.

Kaya and Luke gave each other odd looks that I couldn't decipher, and Thomas's mouth turned up at the corners. Without answering me, they both turned to the place they'd just climbed up, and there, looking like he could have leapt from the bottom to the top without breaking a sweat, was Oliver.

My breath caught in my throat. He looked incredible. When he saw me, he took determined strides in my direction while I remained planted to the earth, doubting if my knees would hold me up much longer. My chest tightened. Was this real? He'd been so sick…

Not bothering with hello, he reached for my hands.

"How—?" I faltered.

"Takes more than a little cough to kill me," he said with a wink.

To confirm he was actually real, I placed my palms against his chest, feeling the strong, clear intake of air going into his lungs. I had so many questions, but when he inched closer, I forgot them all.

"Thanks for the pancake mix," he said, still holding my hands, noticing the ring.

Sweat was beading uncomfortably on my forehead, and my stupid lip was quivering—which was fine—but if any tears fell, I'd throw myself over the edge. "I wasn't sure what kind of syrup you liked," I said softly.

He smiled. "I missed you, too."

Then he leaned in and kissed me. Full on mouth-to-mouth contact. I was shocked by his audacity, but even more shocked that I didn't want to punch him in the throat. Instead, I wound my hands up behind his neck and pulled him tight, kissing him back and hoping my actions would tell him everything I could never say before.

I was embarrassed when I realized everyone was watching. Pulling away, he held my cheeks in his hands, breathing deeply, as a heavy sigh came from his throat. "I'm going to marry you for real," he stated.

"You better."

His smile was accompanied by a whimper.

A *whimper*?

Confused, I heard it again. A small voice came from behind him. When I realized Kaya, Luke and Thomas were all staring at me with smiles wider than the Grand Canyon, I beheld Oliver's pride-filled expression and slowly stepped around him.

And there, strapped to his back, just waking from sleep, was a—

"Oh my God!" I was unable to stop the tears now. They poured because staring back at me with eyes as blue as the summer sky and a mop of thick black hair, was the most beautiful baby girl I'd ever seen.

"Marlene, meet Stephanie Faith," Kaya said. "Nine months old today."

A little hand reached out to grab my finger, and my heart almost blew clean out of my chest. She was the most perfect little person, chubby and healthy and obviously incredibly loved by the way Thomas unstrapped her carefully from Oliver's back and handed her to Luke, who promptly cradled her against his chest. I couldn't do a thing but stare in awe as he patted his child's back and got down on his knees next to Kaya.

"She's going to have to be fed before we take off," he said to her.

Kaya nodded and plunked down next to him, reaching for the baby now cooing and grinning madly at her.

This was incredible.

"Since we have a moment," I said after a while, still not trusting my eyes. "We certainly have a few things to celebrate today, and I brought something just for the occasion."

Oliver lit the candles I'd poked into the cake, and while we all sat cross legged in a circle on the edge of a mountain, we sang 'happy birthday' to Kaya, and happy nine months to baby Stephanie.

"Make a wish," Oliver said afterward, lighting a candle just for me.

I guess I could cast in a line and see what I pulled out, so I did. And I wished that we could all stay together as family. I wanted that more than anything in the entire world. I repeated it as I cut the cake, placing massive slabs of it in dirty hands.

"Wait," I said as Oliver was about to stuff his mouth. "I have something to say."

I stood, receiving their full attention. "First, congratulations, Kaya. Under the circumstances, it's incredible that you made it to twenty-one. John has the papers waiting for you at his home, and an hour from now you can officially keep your promise and sign everything over to him. You can have your life back." I felt the threat of tears again but held them at bay. "So, cheers. Here's to freedom."

I lifted a piece of cake as if it were a glass of wine and everyone followed suit. Except Kaya.

"I'm not signing anything," she said.

It was clear by everyone's shocked expression that this wasn't expected.

Kaya stood, the baby in her arms toying with a long strand of her hair. The wind picked up briefly, then stopped. The birds stopped, too. The mountain, it seemed, also wanted to hear what she had to say.

"After I take back what's mine, I'm going to get to work. The earth has been good to me, and I am going to do everything in my power to look after it. I have enough money to do some good in the world, so I'm going to invest in our environment and keep the money out of the hands of people who could use it to mess it up—like Henry and John Marchessa."

A light radiating wisdom and strength shone in her eyes. She was captivating, and the smile she cast in Luke's direction affected him deeply.

"This is my life," she said to him, to me, to Thomas, to Oliver hanging on her every word, and to the baby in her arms. "I'm in control of it now for the first time, and I know for certain that what I love and cherish most in the world, is right here—" She acknowledged each one of us. "I will protect you, my family, and fight for the future of our children on this earth. I'm not handing anything over. I'm not signing my life away. *I am taking control.*"

Luke beamed with so much pride for her my heart hurt. Thomas beamed, too. But Oliver was watching me, waiting for my reaction; he was wondering where my loyalties were. None of them had any way of knowing that I'd been playing the old man for two years so that when this day came, I would be prepared.

"Good," I said, and Oliver broke into a wide grin. "Because while you losers were all playing house, I was busy coming up with a game plan because I knew—don't ask me how—but I knew Kaya wasn't going to walk away. So, the men who were supposed to go with me and make sure I brought you back, are having very long drug-induced naps, and I have their guns and ammo if we need it. John wouldn't dream of me doing anything behind his back, because I've weaseled my way into his brain so deeply he wants me to change my last name to Marchessa. He's busy making sure the catering and decorations are exactly right for your return, so we have lots of time to get away safely. Also, I made sure Lisa and Louisa are safe. They are with Regan, who has room for us and is anxiously awaiting our arrival. So in other words, we are good to go."

Oliver eyed me longingly, holding up the cake in his hand. "Can we eat now?" he said, grinning. "It's chocolate for heaven's sake."

Apparently, I caught a wish. Or two. "Cheers. To family."

Beautiful faces, all beaming, replied in unison. "To family."

EPILOGUE

KAYA

I assumed that the time spent living in the forest would have prepared me for this, but no. The mud was still infuriating and difficult. It formed into cement-like blocks and fused to my feet. Struggling to lift them one agonizing step at a time, I refused the outstretched hands and offers of help. I even blocked out the encouraging words. Because even though this was hard, I *knew* I could do it. If there was anything the years on the mountain had taught me, it was to trust in myself.

And I was right.

Finally getting through the bog and collapsing on the grass in a muddy heap, I didn't dare cry over my exhaustion or my stinging muscles. I got up, wiped myself off, and got back to running. Tenacity; another thing the mountain had taught me.

As the path narrowed and night came, the number of runners in the Death Race dwindled. My feet throbbed, my chest ached, and my partner looked a little worse for wear. I slowed for him. He slowed for me. And never once did we leave each other's side—not this time.

As I ran, I reflected on the past that had disappeared in the blink of an eye. Would I change any of it? No. I never would have met Luke or become part of a new family that genuinely cared about me. What was born of my trials and tribulations had become my strength and harmony. Every second had been worth it.

As the sun started poking through the trees, I thought of the future. The plans I'd made for tomorrow were something I never imagined I'd be writing down in a day timer; talk to Regan about his breakthrough in the new Eronel lab, take Marlene wedding dress shopping, be at the pool no later than seven for an after-dinner swim with Luke while Lisa babysat Stephanie… My life was the stuff dreams were made of. Every day, the tiniest moments were pure bliss, and never would I have thought that a pencil in my hand would have written that.

I could see my loved ones now at the finish line. Thomas was jumping up and down madly, and Marlene was holding up a sign that said 'Go Kaya!'. Luke and our baby girl were beaming ear to ear and waving, and I kept them in focus as my body seemed close to collapsing. Vision blurry with tears of victory, I realized this was it—I was finishing what I started. And as I reached for Oliver, who was beside me sweating bullets, I realized there was no one else I'd rather cross the finish line with.

"I knew you could do it, Kaya," he said, breathless.

I squeezed his hand tight, and not because I *needed* a hand to hold, but because wanted to, and…I loved him. "I never doubted you either."

We stumbled over the yellow line into open arms, Luke smothering me with kisses and worried looks as I collapsed against him, Oliver tackling Marlene to the ground in an exhausted and elated tumble, and my baby girl clapping excitedly.

"Momma did it," I said, kissing her chubby cheeks.

"Good running, Momma!" she beamed.

Regan dove in and swept her out of my arms. "All right, off to the playground," he said enthusiastically. "Your momma needs to rest. And have a shower. Or two."

With a quick kiss on the cheek, he was off with Louisa, Brutus close behind.

"Good job, Kaya," Lisa said with a warm hug. "You rocked it. Now, don't worry about Stephanie. Regan and I have it all taken care of. You just chillax for the rest of the night, okay?"

"Heck no," Oliver said, pumping a fist in the air. "Now, we barbecue!"

The thought of moving an inch, even for food, was too much. I made it a few steps toward the parking lot, then bent over at the waist to catch my breath. When I finally had the energy to stand, there was a bouquet of flowers thrust in my face.

"I knew you could do it too," Thomas grinned.

Perfect red roses. A dozen. Admiration shone in his eyes as he placed them in my hand. "You never cease to amaze me," he added, staring a little too long with that cocky grin on his face. I braced myself for what I knew was coming.

"Good job." He pressed a sweet kiss on my cheek, then with a wink, turned and walked off. "Stop admiring me from behind," he yelled back over his shoulder.

Luke just shook his head and gently plucked the flowers from my hand. "Do you want a lift?" he asked, motioning to pick me up. "It will be like the old days."

This man had captured my heart. Fully and completely. And I could tell by everything he said, and everything he did, that I had his as well.

"I got through twenty-four hours, I can get through another ten minutes," I said stubbornly.

He pulled me close, blue eyes beaming with pride. "Those were the longest twenty-four hours of my entire life," he said. "I don't want to be away from you for that long again. Ever."

I could have stayed in his arms, right where we were, until the world ran out of time.

"Hey. Could you spare her for a second?" asked Marlene. "We need to talk. Besides if I have to watch any more mushy stuff, I might throw up."

Luke sighed, then kissed me fiercely—in that way he did that always took all the breath from my lungs—and it seemed he needed all his strength to let go. "I'll go pull up the car so you don't have so far to walk. Meet you in the parking lot, my love."

Marlene put an arm around my waist as we watched him jog ahead. "You are one crazy chick," she said with a smile.

I limped along beside her. "I feel like garbage," I admitted.

"Smell like it too," she said with a laugh, then grew serious. "Listen, Kaya, while you were in the race last night, something happened."

She didn't have to say it. At one point when the moon was full in the sky, I had felt a shift in the universe.

"Henry died," she continued.

I kept walking, one agonizing step after the other.

"Everyone wanted to wait until later to tell you, but I knew you would want to know right away."

She was right. "How?" I asked.

"They're saying it was a heart attack. But we both know better."

Georgia and Dan had taken Henry in when he had nowhere to go. I'd ripped the carpet out from underneath his feet, obliterated his research and taken back the estate, and the mighty Henry had fallen. Hard. His health had begun to deteriorate, slowly, agonizingly, and I suspected that through poisoning, Georgia had gotten the revenge that so many wanted.

"I guess I better start making funeral plans."

Marlene tightened her arm around me. "It's done. I organized everything this morning."

We made it to the parking lot. There were people everywhere, some crying, some laughing with joy and exhaustion, some sound asleep on the hoods of their cars. I felt a slight sadness for the death of the man who for a long while had made my life a living nightmare. Without him, none of this would have happened. My life wouldn't have been blessed with Luke, who was swearing at the fact he'd misplaced his keys again, or Thomas, who was good-naturedly mocking him in fits of laughter, or the baby that we were raising together.

"It's weird that Luke never gets jealous," Marlene said when Thomas blew me a kiss.

Luke's dazzling eyes caught mine; we had been through too much for that. He knew that for eternity and beyond, I was his. And, that I was Thomas's too.

"Hey, uh…" Marlene's voice grew quiet. "I went through some stuff the other day—things we had when John Marchessa took us from that cabin—and I found that letter Thomas wrote you. The one you and Luke fought over."

I stopped. "Did you read it?" I asked.

"No. But it's on your desk if you want to."

It took a moment to get moving again. "I'm pretty sure I know what it says."

Marlene cast me a sideways glance. "You know, you spent two and half years stuck on a mountain in the middle of nowhere, sometimes snowed in for months, living in a cave with a hot spring that healed Oliver…you survived animal attacks, insane weather, broken bones, star-vation—you know, the stuff novels are made of. Heck, girlfriend, you even delivered a baby on a riverbed under what you call 'the watchful eye of a spirit in the form of an elk'…You told me about all that stuff. But what about Thomas and Luke? What about *them*?"

The car pulled up to the curb, doors opened, and their beaming faces smiled expectantly. I let go of Marlene, able to stand completely on my own.

"That my friend, is a whole other story."

THE END

The Letter Thomas Wrote to Kaya on Christmas Morning

Dearest Kaya,

I've tried to leave. So many times I've opened your door to tell you goodbye, but instead have just stood and watched you sleep. I wonder what you dream of.

I dream of you. And when I wake and you're here, when I can touch you and talk to you and get lost in your glorious green eyes, I wonder if I'm still dreaming. This is why I can't leave. I can't force myself to walk out that door and turn away and never see you again. There is nothing I want more in the world than you, and believe me, I won't go down without a fight. But—as much as it kills me—I genuinely want for you the most blissful existence, the most powerful love, the most soul-fulfilling partner…and if that's him, so be it.

Being friends with you is my most cherished gift. I will not return it. My heart could never shrink back to the empty shell it was before you dropped that bag of flour in Ben's kitchen. I'm willing to do whatever it takes to remain a part of your life, no matter how small, so please, above and beyond everything, allow me that.

Just know that whatever happens, whatever the future brings, I love you, and I always will.

Yours forever,
Thomas

Dear Reader,

Ah. The end. I am overwhelmed, excited, and a little sad to close this chapter of my life. I sincerely hope that you enjoyed reading this story as much as loved writing it.

I cannot express my gratitude enough for coming along on this journey with me and Kaya. Thank you for your encouraging words, for rooting for the love you wanted to win, and for standing up against everything that got in the way. Without you, this trilogy would not have been the same.

We will meet again in the next book! Until then, I wish you the most blissful existence.

♡ Heather

Listen to the song Luke and Kaya wake up to in chapter 39;

'Love Dares You', written and performed by Heather McKenzie, can be heard at:

www.HeatherMcKenzie.com/music

THANK YOU...

This book wouldn't have been possible without the support of my husband, Byran Bueckert, who kept reality in check and looked after life while I wandered about in my dream world–you are my everything.

A massive thanks from the bottom of my heart to everyone at CTP. I am so grateful for all you have done for me and this series. Rebecca Gober, Courtney Spencer, Marya Heiman, Courtney Whittamore and Wendy Martinez — your patience and guidance throughout the whole process was amazing. I am forever honored you welcomed me into your world. And the spectacular Melanie Newton — you breathed new life into this book and I am so inspired by you. Your positivity and determination are forces to be reckoned with. Thank you for everything you do!

Emily Bueckert — your support meant more to me than you will ever know. Thank you for putting so much love and effort into this series. Haley Bueckert — dreaming along with me gave my mind wings. Josh Bueckert — you rocked the honest criticism and encouragement.

All my friends and family who have been positive influences on this journey — I am eternally grateful.

Last but not least, to all my readers — writing would mean nothing without you. Thank you for joining me on this journey. May there be many more.

About the Author

Heather McKenzie is the bestselling author of the darkly-romantic thriller novels Serenade, Nocturne and Rhapsody. A full-time writer, Heather lives in Alberta with a house full of kids, cats, and one very doting husband. In rare moments of spare time she peruses bookstores, paints abstract art and writes music. Fueled by a consistent need to create, she is inspired by the small towns in Alberta she's grown to love, the ever awe-inspiring Rocky Mountains, and the many incredible people she's met while traveling.

Find Heather online at: www.HeatherMcKenzie.com